Two for Roughing

A BROTHER'S BEST FRIEND COLLEGE HOCKEY ROMANCE

LASAIRIONA MCMASTER

DRAMA LLAMA PUBLISHING

Dedication

*For Amy, my darling, enneagram 7, free-spirited, Jell-O shot
making queen bestie who is up for giving anything a try once.
Thank you for reminding me of the beauty in all things, not just
the things we're told to think are beautiful.
And for any woman who has ever been shamed by someone for
their porn collection.
F*ck Chad. Read all the freakin' smut.*

Prologue

Molly
(16 years old - Five Years Earlier)

"To surviving another year of high school." Molly raised the can of Fanta in her favorite 'Zero Shits Given' koozie she'd stolen from her mom, and crashed it against her best friend, Savannah's, hand.

"We survived? I feel like an extra on the Walking Dead right now." Savannah smothered a yawn with her free hand. "But don't ask me to do any walking. 'Cause, no."

The two girls were sprawled out on sun loungers in Molly's backyard next to the pool. It was the first day of summer, and their plans consisted of doing the bare minimum, working on their tans, and consuming candy faster than their parents could provide it.

Savannah slurped from her can, burped, giggled, and leaned back against the semi-reclined chair. Her waist-long blonde hair was twisted into a messy bun on top of her head. Reaching into the picnic-sized cooler next to her, Molly grabbed a handful of ice and ran it over her bare chest and neck. A sigh escaped her at the cool relief from the fierce, overhead sun.

"You kids have sun screen on?" Molly's mom peeked around the back door of the house, always the mother hen.

"Yes, Mrs. Morrison."

"Good. I'd rather not start summer vacation with sun blisters and sunstroke. Will's on his way home, Mol. We'll start lunch when he gets back."

"Sounds good, Mom."

"Wanna swim before lunch?" Savannah was already shucking her Daisy Dukes to the ground and pulling off her tank top to reveal a bright yellow bikini.

"Go ahead, I'll wait till after lunch." Molly pulled her shades from on top of her head and slipped them over her eyes before raking her long, frizzy brown hair off her sweaty neck and into a high ponytail. The unusual humidity wasn't doing much for her cascading waves. She peeled her short shorts off and dropped them over her phone on the hot ground next to her chair.

"Wake up sleepy head." Savannah sprayed her with a welcome dose of cool water from the pool as she climbed out and made her way back to her chair. "Girl, you were out cold. Snoring. Drool, the lot. Pretty sure you farted in your sleep, too."

"Savvyanna we both know my farts smell like gummy bears, so that stink must be coming from you."

The gate to the back yard opened and Molly's big brother – by only ten months, but he never let her forget it – made his way into the backyard, sweat-drenched shirt clinging to his body. "Mom, do we have time for a dip before we eat?" He was already kicking off his flip flops and unbuttoning his shorts before their mom answered "ten minutes" through the open window.

Molly was only vaguely paying attention to her brother

because he'd brought a friend, a guy she'd never seen before. His red hair shone in the sunlight. It was shaved on the sides, but longer and styled with gel on top. His faded, gray Minnesota Snow Pirates shirt stretched across broad shoulders and had dark rings of sweat around his neck and underarms.

Will had wanted to be a Snow Pirate since he learned what hockey was. If she was a betting woman, she'd put money on him striking up a conversation with the stranger over his shirt.

Something cold against her thigh caused her to gasp and jump. "You're staring." Savannah's voice was quiet and close. She pulled her can away, tucking it back into its foam sleeve.

"You can't see where my eyes are behind these shades," Molly hissed, throwing the comment back to Savannah, but she didn't divert her gaze.

Savannah leaned closer. "Yes but your chest stopped moving so I needed to check you were still alive."

A braying laugh escaped Molly's mouth before she could clamp it shut. Whoever he was, was now standing in nothing but a pair of swim shorts, poised to jump in the pool. He hesitated and his eyes tracked to the sound of her ridiculous laugh. He was staring right at her. Her body temperature seemed to have shot up ten degrees. His stare was piercing, intense, and had her wishing she was already in the pool so she had an excuse to be closer to him.

"You getting in?" Will splashed his friend from below. The new guy leaped into the air, folded his body, tucked his legs against his chest, spun and landed in the pool with the precision of an Olympic diver.

Idly dragging a thumb against her bottom lip, she willed herself to look away from the boys play-wrestling in the pool. She'd never been attracted to any of her brother's friends before. From an early age, they'd set up ground rules: she wouldn't mess around with any of his friends, and he would afford her the same courtesy.

With any luck this guy was only in town for the summer, maybe he could be her summer fling and Will wouldn't mind. Something about him pulled her towards him. He was still staring, throwing heated looks her way when Will's attention was elsewhere. He somehow managed to suck the oxygen from the space, despite the fact they were outside.

"Lunch is ready!"

Molly didn't move at her mom's call. She was struck by an unusual barb of self-consciousness and didn't want whoever he was to see her body as she stood to put her shorts on. The boys got out of the pool, grabbed towels from the towel box, and dried off. New guy followed Will towards the house, pausing before he entered.

He cast her a wicked grin that had her girl parts reacting in ways they'd never reacted before. Body tingling from top to toe, she stood on shaking legs and pulled her shorts on. Her chest was tight, her mouth dry, and her head, light. Had she breathed at all in the last ten minutes?

She'd always been the one to ridicule all the lip biting, sighing, and furtive gazes she'd seen on TV or read about in books. That shit never happened in real life. Except her brother had just brought home the most delicious man she'd ever seen and she'd swooned so hard she'd stopped breathing.

Please let him be here just for summer.

Will's voice permeated the air as Molly and Savannah walked towards the house. "Mom, this is Finn. He moved in down the street about a month ago, we're going to be Pirates together in college."

Finnegan

"This watermelon salad is delicious, Mrs. Morrison. I don't even know what half of these ingredients are, but..." Finn shoveled another heaped forkful of what he'd hoped was watermelon salad into his mouth to stop his babbling and made a satisfied 'mmm' sound. With a little luck, a localized earthquake would strike right under his feet and suck him into the depths of the earth.

"It's watermelon, cucumber, feta, red onion, mint, with olive oil and some balsamic vinegar." Will's sister was the one who answered. Although she hadn't met his eyes since she'd come into the house, her gaze had scorched him from the moment he'd arrived in the yard.

Worse still, he'd been drawn to her, too. Her long, dark hair was tied high on her head, allowing the sharp edges of her high cheekbones, jaw, and nose to stand out on her pale skin. He couldn't see her eyes behind the shades, probably a blessing, if he had, he'd likely have come in Will's pool.

Finn had moved to town just over a month ago. Will had found him playing street hockey in the cul-de-sac at the end of their street and asked to join in, making small talk over Finn's

Snow Pirates shirt. Their brolationship had started almost right away. Turned out they were in the same class at school, and when they weren't in class together, they were playing hockey together.

One of the first things Will had said to Finn was that his little sister was off limits. At the time Finn had nodded his agreement. Younger sisters weren't cool, they were often clingy, needy and desperate to hang out with the cool kids. Finn had no plans to date his new bestie's little sister.

But what Will had neglected to mention, however, was she wasn't so 'little', and as Finn stood fighting every urge to reach out and stroke her collarbone, he realized he'd gotten it all wrong. She was most definitely the cool kid, he was desperate to hang out with her, and he'd already screwed himself over by giving his word he'd never touch her.

Mercifully, the girls didn't linger. They piled their plates high with food and went back outside. When the door swung closed behind her a sadness settled in his stomach. The excitement and electricity thrumming through the room left with her. He wanted to know everything there was to know about her. He wanted to make her laugh again, just so he could hear the obnoxious noise that delighted him the first time. She gave off an air of not giving a shit and he was here for it.

"The brunette was Molly." Will scooped a mouthful of pasta salad into his mouth, chewed, and swallowed. "In case you couldn't tell."

Finn's mouth dried up, and the watermelon salad suddenly felt like grains of sand against his tongue. He swallowed hard. "She's your only sister, right?"

Will snorted. "Yeah. I couldn't handle another Molly. Let's take our plates outside."

He'd barely met the woman and her orbit was already dragging him into torment and temptation. Could he sit across the yard from her and eat lunch as though he didn't want to lose himself kissing her? "I..." Food lodged in his throat and he coughed. "I should probably go home."

Confusion tugged Will's brows together. "After we eat?"

Had Finn eaten something he was allergic to? His tongue was thick and heavy, and words seemed to evade him so he settled for a nod. Was this what love at first sight felt like? He shook his head. That was the thing of fairytales and Disney movies. Maybe he'd eaten too much watermelon salad and it was a case of indigestion.

"Which is it?"

"Huh?"

"You nodded, then shook your head. Going, or staying? I figured we could hang out in the pool for a while, maybe play some video games before practice."

"Sure." His traitorous legs dragged him out of the house behind Will, passing Molly and her friend on their way. He stumbled over his own feet – perhaps that was wishful think-ing. Perhaps he'd tripped over the not-so-thin air that hung between them, charged with secretive glances and an inability to stop staring at his friend's sister.

It was going to be a long summer.

Finnegan

The unmistakable crunch of bone on bone rang out in the field as Finn's curled up fist connected with his opponent's jaw. No one made Molly Morrison cry on his watch. Her mascara-smudged cheeks, red-rimmed, sad eyes, and quiet demeanor would be etched in his soul for as long as he lived.

Her new boyfriend had cheated on her after only a month of dating, with someone she knew from school. She'd walked into Chili's with her family for dinner and witnessed the two of them canoodling in a booth in the middle of the restaurant, not even attempting to hide their infidelity from public view.

She hadn't stayed around. Breaking up with him at full volume, spine straight, shoulders squared, she'd looked like a fierce goddess, shooting daggers from her ferocious, green eyes and spitting fire from her lips. Mrs. Morrison had sent Finn and Will after her while she placed a to-go order for dinner, and the striking gladiator deflated in front of his eyes when they caught up to her.

He wanted to swoop her into his arms and dry her tears, to tell her that asshole ex of hers didn't deserve her time. He wanted to press her against his chest, and tell her his heart beat only for her and his very being burned with need to keep her safe forever. But he couldn't. So instead, he was laying into one of his teammates under the guise of being like a big brother to her.

Pretending he didn't want Will to sully his squeaky clean reputation, or get dragged into a fight he might not win, he'd thrown the first punch. With each swing he tried to convince himself it was the truth, but under it all, he was a goner for Molly Morrison and had no idea how the fuck he was going to handle it when she found herself a new man.

CHAPTER 1

Molly

"Get him!"

"Hit him with the stick!"

"Kill him!"

Molly groaned into the fist she had crammed into her mouth. "Fucking newbies."

"What was that? I couldn't make it out around those white knuckles you're gnawing on." Cleo's face contorted, probably in an attempt to school her face into a serious expression, but her body shook with silent giggles.

"Why doesn't he just clock him with the stick?" A group of male college students sat in the row in front of Molly and Cleo in the Snow Pirates home arena. Either the guys had taken a wrong turn on the way to the football field, or this was their first ever hockey game. From the looks of things, it might have even been their first time in public.

"Because that's aggravated assault." Molly didn't take her eyes off the play while she answered, but her voice sounded every bit as unamused as she felt.

Two of the men twisted in their seats to look at her, eyebrows raised.

"Hitting someone with a potentially dangerous weapon? You ever been hit by a hockey stick? Those suckers can do some serious damage. Sure there's fighting in hockey, but they don't abandon the rule of law at the edge of the ice."

It was rarely so severe as hockey players lacked the intent to harm, but that didn't mean she couldn't mess with the newbies just a little.

One of the guys nodded as if that made perfect sense. The Snow Pirates were only ten minutes into the first period, and Molly was already done with the inane chatter and commentary coming from the guys in front.

The newbies had shown up to the game without so much as a trace of Snow Pirates colors between them. One of them even dared to wear green – the color of the other team, the Cedar Rapids Raccoons. He either didn't know or flat out didn't care. If she didn't think it could be construed as wanting to get the man naked, she'd have demanded he remove the offending color until the game was over.

Sure, she was overreacting – every hockey fan had to start somewhere. Not everyone was born with her innate desire to watch a group of peak-performance athletes chase a three inch disk of rubber around a rink on ice skates. She should probably be kinder to those who got there eventually, even if they didn't know anything about anything and didn't give a shit who heard.

If she was being honest with herself, her irritation was less to do with the guys in front of her not knowing which was way up when it came to hockey, and more to do with Finn O'Brien.

The 6ft 2 left winger crouched low in the face-off circle, yet still towered over his opponent. His delicious bubble butt pointed right at her. Desire coated her throat like thick honey on a spoon. She shook her head to clear the shameless thoughts.

She had no business lusting over her brother's best friend. There were lines that couldn't be crossed, and unfortunately for her, the man who held every ounce of her heart was so very, very offside. He was also the dumbass who had promised her brother that he'd never lay a finger on her. Ever.

A finger wasn't all she wanted him to lay on her. She licked her lips.

What the hell was wrong with her? Okay, fine, it had been a couple days since she'd last gotten laid, but she'd sure as shit gotten off before she left for the game.

No matter how tired or busy she was, she needed her game day O every bit as much as Finn needed to tape his stick with military precision... or Will needed his game day nap, or Austin and Seb needed to kick their soccer ball around the hall. It was her game day routine and game day routines weren't to be fucked with.

Maybe if she focused on Finn's opponent's ass instead, the flickering embers of need pulsing low in her belly would stop dragging her attention to Finn's butt, his thighs, and his delicious broad shoulders. Slater Goodwin's smaller frame was less impressive, his backside, too. No matter how much she willed her eyes to stay focused on Slater's ass, it was as though Finn had magnets stuck to his butt cheeks, and the corresponding magnets in her pupils couldn't fight the pull.

So what if his thighs were so thick he could probably crush a watermelon without breaking a sweat? Those thighs were not destined to nestle between her own.

Fuck. She clenched her legs together, smacking her pen off her notebook with increasing aggression as the buzzer sounded noting an infraction on the ice.

What the hell had happened? She'd been so distracted by the idea of her legs curled around Finn's waist that she'd missed a call. She never missed calls. Shit.

"Tyler Lawson, two minutes for crosschecking."

Thank you, Mr. Announcer Man. Molly scribbled on her notebook as she watched the replay on the big screen. The Raccoon in question did indeed crosscheck her brother against the boards.

One of the guys in the row in front elbowed the dude wearing Cedar Rapids green. "What the fuck is crosschecking?"

Green Dude shrugged. "Fuck if I know. Google it."

With an eye roll that almost sprained her retinas, Molly sighed. There was zero hope for this bunch. Crosschecking was the easiest of all the penalties to spot due to the distinctive shoving-with-the-stick action. She needed to speak up and help the poor beings before it all got too much for them.

She cleared her throat. "It's when a player uses the shaft of his stick to hit an opponent."

One of them smothered a snigger behind his hand as the others turned to face her.

"Shaft?" It turned out that Green Dude not only had no clue about team colors, but he also had the sense of humor of a prepubescent boy.

Ignoring his bait, she nodded and jammed her pen into her ponytail. "The player holds his stick like this. One hand at the top, the other about halfway down, and does a pushing motion with it into the opposing player."

Five mouths hung open as the boys stared at her. She shook her head. "The dude in the penalty box hit the other dude with his stick. And that's no bueno, so he got sent to timeout to think about what he's done."

Cleo's body vibrated next to her. "I think they get it."

Molly wasn't so sure. Her eyes followed the puck. Being nice to new people was one thing, missing a potential power play goal was an entirely different matter. Hockey was a turn-on-a-dime kind of sport. If you took your eye off the play for even a fraction of a second – or caught yourself daydreaming about a certain red-headed player's thighs wrapped around your body – you could come back to a different game altogether. The crowd went wild when the commentator announced the Minnesota power play.

"What's a power play?"

"Did we score?"

One of the men produced his phone from his pocket and pulled up Google. After a few clicks, he read aloud. "A power play is a situation in which a team has an advantage on the ice while one or more players of the opposing team is serving a penalty."

"So they're all cheering 'cause we have one more dude on the ice than the other team for two minutes?"

Points for Green Dude. In his defense, he seemed as though he was genuinely interested in the game and trying to understand how it worked.

On the ice, defenseman Lincoln Scott sailed the puck to Finn who grinned and passed it forward to Will. Her stomach flipped. This particular combination of players were proving to be unstoppable. Finn and Will had played together since they'd met as teenagers. They knew each other's strengths, weaknesses, and habits. Molly had always wanted to blindfold the pair to see if it made an impact on their game – she doubted it would. If Will was on the ice, Finn had a way of finding him.

She got it. She and Cleo were ride-or-die close as well. But something about the boys had clicked from day one, and it was a bond she'd never dare mess with.

From the moment they'd met, they'd all but imprinted on each other like some kind of fated bromance. She often joked they were like *parabatai* – Nephilim warriors who fought together as lifelong partners, bound together by oath. Being hockey players and having roughed each other up playing street hockey as much as the two men had, they were probably bound together by blood as well.

She had no doubt they'd willingly lay down their lives for one another. While they didn't have matching rune tattoos like Jace and Alec from her favorite guilty pleasure TV series *Shadowhunters*, the guys were tight AF. "Bros before hos" was a common phrase tossed about by guys, but bros before sisters was an even stricter moral code.

Will passed the puck to Finn who sailed it back to Will. Molly leaned forward in her seat, a chill of anticipation running up her spine. She'd seen this play a thousand times before, and while Cedar Rapids had a solid wall of a goaltender, the combined speed, agility, and sheer determination of Minnesota's top line was impressive.

"Glove side." Her announcement came a split second before Will shot the puck at the goalie's glove side, and the netminder grabbed at it just a fraction too late. She grinned and wrote the goal in her notebook, taking great care not to write something about how delectable Finn's ass looked as he assisted.

"How'd you know?" Cleo shivered, rubbing her biceps with her palms.

While Cleo was dating one of the players, Greek God extraordinaire, Lincoln Scott, she was still learning the subtleties of the game and the nuances of the players on the team. Molly couldn't help but smile. "It ain't my first rodeo." The novelty of Cleo attending hockey games of her own free will, now that she was dating Lincoln, hadn't worn off for Molly. She didn't care how many questions her best friend asked, as long as she didn't grumble and moan every time Molly wanted to go to a game.

Three heads turned to face her from the row in front. "Do you play?" Green Dude pursed his lips.

She snorted. "No. I write for the school paper so I watch a

lot of hockey. And number 82 is my brother. I know his playbook."

Green Dude's eyebrow arched and he nodded. "Wanna come down here" – he patted his thigh – "and help me learn the rules?" His eyes sparkled with mischief.

"Nice try, Green Dude. But you couldn't handle me." She picked up her soda, took a big slurp, and put it back on the floor next to her feet.

He flicked his gaze to his shirt and smirked. "Max. And don't be so quick to judge, Pretty Girl. We might be a match made in heaven."

"Oooh, Max. I judged you the second you wore Cedar Rapids green in my barn."

One of the other guys snickered.

"Also, you're not my type."

"What is your type?"

Finn O'Brien.

Max's friend eyed her as though he was thinking about throwing his hat in the ring.

"Nope." Her head shake was emphatic.

"Ouch. Want some ice for that burn, Hardy?" Random man #3 gave his friend a noogie.

"You realize there's a game happening down there, right?" Molly pointed to the ice with a cursory glance at the five amigos. "We're actually a pretty good team."

"It's too fast. I can't keep up." Random man #4's grumble was almost inaudible over the wave of boos rippling around the arena.

Molly was on her feet, flailing a hand at the ice. "Hey Ref! Maybe if you sucked a little less on the whistle, you'd blow it right!" She plopped onto her seat. "Fucking Iowa."

"Okay, Iowa's like the least offensive state in the United States. That doesn't work. Fucking Florida? That works. Fucking Alabama? Also acceptable. But Iowa? What has Iowa ever done to you other than give you beans and corn?" Max was quickly falling out of favor. Not that he was ever really in favor.

Molly narrowed her eyes. Cleo grabbed her hand and squeezed. "Murder is bad, Mol."

Another ripple of boos erupted around the rink as the Raccoons bagged a power play goal of their own. "Mother fuck."

"She knows it's only the first quarter, right?" Max spoke to Cleo but jerked a thumb in Molly's direction.

Molly rolled her lips between her teeth but still managed to speak before Cleo opened her mouth. "It's a period, not a quarter. And yes, I'm aware we're still in the first *period*, but this is dumb as shit."

One of the guys brayed out a laugh. Was he seriously laughing at the word *period*? She couldn't fathom a grown-ass man still snickering, but so many people cringed at the word *moist*, she supposed anything was possible.

Moist. Her absolute favorite word in the entire dictionary.

Used to describe that feeling between your thighs when you think about fucking Finn O'Brien.

She shook her head. But it did little to dislodge the thought as Finn threw his leg over the bench to take to the ice.

What I wouldn't give to have him throw his leg over—

"C'mon, Obi!" A fan screaming Finn's nickname jolted her out of her lady boner stupor. It wasn't the most creative of nicknames, Obi for O'Brien, but it worked.

Finn hurtled toward the net on a breakaway. Molly scooted forward in her chair, holding her breath. For such a big dude, he moved on the ice with the elegance and grace of a dancer – and when he'd had a few beers, he shook his money maker off the ice as well. She'd seen him dancing on the bar with his shirt off more times than she could count.

Except the memories were burned into her mind. Finn.

Shirtless. Her mouth dried up. Probably because every ounce of moisture in her body was rushing to pool between her thighs.

Fucking pay attention.

Finn lined up the shot, swung, and... clink. The bright chime of a puck hitting the crossbar sent a collective groan around the arena and her stomach to the floor.

It was going to be a long game.

"Where's the goalie going?" The panic in Max's voice at the absence of a goaltender tugged Molly's lips into a grin despite the nail-biting status of the game.

"Why's he leaving the court?" The guy next to Max let out a gush of air as he elbowed his ribs.

"It's not a court." His arrogant, "are you a fucking dumbass?" tone made her giggle.

"I don't give a shit what it is. Where's he going?"

Four out of the five guys turned to face her. With a sigh, she tracked the extra skater leaving the bench and making his way onto the ice. "Coach pulled the goalie so we can have an extra attacker on the ice. With only a couple minutes to go and the game tied, some coaches remove the goaltender from play to try to get the W."

"What's the W?"

She wasn't sure which one of them asked the question, but she rolled her eyes at all of them. "The Win."

"But... surely..." Max's head turned between the action on the ice and Molly. "If one of the Raccoons gets the puck, a goal is a dead cert, right?"

She nodded. "Almost always. Especially at this level. Even

from the opposite end of the ice. These guys could basically score from anywhere."

Max snickered. She ignored it.

"So why risk it?" Throughout the game, Max's questions had gotten progressively more intuitive. She'd even go so far as to say he was becoming a fan.

"There's no rule that says one of your six players must be a goalie. And when you want the win badly enough... sometimes it's worth the risk. Especially if your D-line is solid."

"And..." He squinted. "Stewart and..." He squinted again. "Morgan? They're both... solid?"

She nodded, gnawing on her lip. "Austin has already been drafted by the Wild. They're just waiting for him to finish out his senior year before he joins the team."

"Is that good?"

"Drafted by a major league team before you leave college is a pretty good thing, yeah." Her spidey sense tingled as a defender from the opposing team nipped at Finn's heels. Her stomach tightened. He was headed for a collision with the plexi, and he probably had no idea it was coming.

She held her breath as Finn took a hit against the boards and crumpled onto the ice like an empty potato chip packet.

"Fuck!" Molly was on her feet. Cleo, too. Molly's stomach flipped. "Get up, Finnegan. Get the fuck on your feet."

With a shake of his head, Finn lumbered to his feet, dusted himself off, and got back to the play.

"No, no, no! Don't let him have it." Max yelled at Will with some serious aggression. "I can't watch." He turned his head so his chin rested against his friend's shoulder, peering over the fabric back to the ice. "And yet I can't not watch. Shit. Pretty Girl, you're clearly a masochist. How do your nerves cope with this insanity?"

Despite the knots in her shoulders, Molly smiled. Her jaw ached from clenching as she urged Russell to pass the puck forward to Finn, or Will… hell, anyone in an ice-blue shirt would be great as long as it wasn't in their own defensive zone. "Get. It. The. Fuck. Out!"

Cleo's fingers dug into Molly's forearm as the entire arena watched with bated breath. Russell collected the puck from just behind their blue line and passed to Austin, who cruised forward, sending it back to Russ. Molly's notebook was forgotten as she clutched Cleo's hand like it was game seven of the Stanley Cup playoff finals.

Russ passed to Will. Then Will to Finn. They advanced on the opposition like soldiers riding into battle. The Pirates nearly lost control of the puck in a skirmish at center ice, but Finn threw a last minute open ice hip check that made her knees weak and her eyes roll back in her head.

Nothing stoked her fire more than a well-executed, open ice hip check. If they weren't seconds from the end of the game and trying to send the Raccoons home with their tails between their legs, and she wasn't reporting on the game, she'd have swooned right there in the stands… or hauled ass to the bathrooms to release a little pressure building up between her legs. As it was, she tossed the memory in her spank-bank for a post-game O when she got home.

Finn sailed the puck to Will who passed it to Johnny. She cringed as though she'd bitten into a lemon. Why did that asshole glory hunter have to be so damn good at hockey?

He circled behind the net, pausing as though he wasn't racing against the clock. Faking out the defender, he passed right instead of left, straight to the blade of Finn's stick. Finn one-timed it into the bottom corner of the net, the lamp lit, and a roar engulfed the arena.

The five guys in front of her double hi-fived and hugged each other. Max hopped over his seat, picked Molly up off her feet and spun her around. "You're the least patient teacher I've ever had, Pretty Girl. But I'm buying tickets and coming back next week." He put her back down.

She patted his chest. "Stalking's illegal in Minnesota, Max."

"It's for the protection of potential newbies. If I'm sitting here, I'm saving someone else from your ire. Not everyone could stomach your caustic wit and muttered threats of bodily harm and murder. Yeah, I heard 'em." He winked.

"See you next week, Pretty Girl, maybe I can convince you to come sit on Maximillian's lap while we watch the game together."

"Did you just talk about your lap in the third person?" Was this guy for real?

With a smirk and a wave, he jumped back over his seat and filtered out of the row behind his friends.

"That was... wow." Cleo remained in her seat, staring at the ice. "Does it ever go away?"

"The adrenaline? Nope. It's a doozy. Feels pretty good, right? Know what's good for post-game adrenaline?"

Her friend narrowed her eyes and pursed her lips. "What's that?"

Molly grinned. "Sex."

CHAPTER 2

Finnegan

S tepping into the bar after a home ice win was always pretty sick. Adoring fans high-fiving and patting you on the back like you'd won the Stanley Cup finals, people buying you drinks, and so many beautiful women on the prowl.

"Great game tonight, Obi." Will, his best friend and team captain, slapped him on the back and handed him a frosty bottle of Sam Adams.

"Thanks, man." Finn clinked the neck of his bottle against Will's. "Not too bad yourself. I mean, not as good as me, obvs. But still decent."

Will snorted. "Decent. Sure."

Finn and his geeky best friend were like oil and water, but somehow, they worked. Will studied computer science; Finn studied psychology. Will liked gaming and movies; Finn played sports and loved the great outdoors. Will was a health food nut, and Finn ate like every meal was his last.

Despite their differences, they had been BFFs since they were teens, and considering Finn had little-to-no relationship with his own family, well, the term bromance didn't quite cover what Will and his family meant to him.

Will's family. A well-known stir niggled his insides. As though summoned by his thoughts, Will's younger sister Molly stepped up to the bar and grinned at the bartender. Her dark chestnut waves cascaded over her right shoulder, falling forward to cover her face. Her delicate features were burned into his memory: expressive gray-green eyes, porcelain skin, and signature blood red painted lips.

He'd been there when she'd discovered her obsession with red lipstick. He'd even asked her about it once. She'd told him she was part of some badass, global tribe of rebel women founded online by a burlesque teacher in Iowa. Kick Ass Red Lipstick club – KARL.

Was he staring? Hoping for a glimpse of those pouty red lips? Sure. Did he care that someone might catch him? Like hell. He'd gotten to be a master at staring at Molly Morrison over the years. He'd worked hard to hide his feelings for her under the guise of being a protective big brother figure.

"Finn?" Will elbowed him.

"Mm?" Finn sipped his drink as though he'd just been zoned out, not fixated on his best friend's sister.

Fixated. That was a great word for it. From the second he'd walked into their backyard as a gangly, red-headed teen, he'd been besotted by her.

"I asked how your knee is. It didn't seem to bother you on the ice tonight. Or if it did, you hid it well."

He hid a lot of things well. He'd hurt his knee horsing around on the ice with Austin. That frustratingly strong asshole had gotten the upper hand, and Finn had fallen at an awkward angle, twisting his knee. "I've been working with the new physio, Kenzie. She's got magic hands."

He chanced another glance at Molly. She'd bought two drinks and leaned over the bar toward a curvy blonde chick. It wasn't her roommate Cleo, and from behind, he couldn't tell much more. But from the sparkle in Molly's eye, and the way she twisted her silky brown hair between her index and middle fingers, he knew all he needed to. She was on a date.

"You're just going to leave that hanging?" Will took a long pull from his beer.

"What?"

"Kenzie and her magic hands. Dude, are you banging the physio?" He covered his eyes and shook his head.

Wait, what? Finn started, bolting upright. "Banging Kenzie? Fuck no. I mean, don't get me wrong, she's hot in a sassy-southern-belle kinda way. But she's not my type."

His type leaned even further forward toward her date, oozing confidence, and owning every ounce of her sexuality. Her slim fingers skimmed up the side of her date's face, tucking blonde locks behind her ear and trailing her fingers down the woman's neck. Goosebumps sprung up over his skin, sending shivers along the curve of his ear and down the column of his throat.

Did he care that the woman he'd loved for years was bisexual? Hell no. But the unhappy rock-solid dick pressing along the seam of his jeans was epically pissed that Molly wasn't sandwiched between him and the blonde.

He shifted on his stool. He hated wearing underwear unless it was absolutely necessary – like the playoffs when he wore his lucky Calvin Kleins. He preferred not to be contained, to let his junk hang free, but in moments like this, it would have been great to have another layer between his raging hardon and the unforgiving denim.

"I thought every beautiful woman was your type."

"What?"

Will shook his head. "Where the hell is your head at tonight, man? I said I thought every beautiful woman was your type."

"Usually. But I don't fuck where I eat. I need Kenzie's magic hands to keep me in the game. I don't want to ruin that by giving her a taste of the big D. Y'know?"

"Right." Will nodded. "Because if you did that, she'd want more, and you're just not that kinda guy."

"You know it."

"Cocky bastard."

"Confident." Finn raised his bottle in an exaggerated gesture before taking a sip. The cold liquid soothed his irritation as it trickled down his throat. He needed a distraction. Something... someone... to take his mind off the fact Mini Mo had her tongue down the blonde's throat, and all he wanted to do was fuck her from behind while she did so.

He cleared his throat and took another drink. Sure, he'd be beating one off in the shower as soon as he got back to the hockey house. Maybe two. And maybe if he tried hard enough, he could convince himself that all he wanted from Molly Morrison was her body – but his dick and his heart would both call bullshit.

Molly's fingers curled into the blonde's hair, tugging her head back to deepen the kiss. Okay, fine. Maybe three.

"You noticed them too, huh?" Will slammed his bottle onto the bar with a little too much force. "Can't they just leave it alone?"

To be fair, if Molly was his girl, Finn wouldn't leave her alone, either. His heart quickened. If anyone else in the world saw him lusting after Mini Mo, he wouldn't care. But if Will ever found out... it didn't bear thinking about. "Uh, noticed who?"

"Those assholes leering over my sister."

Considering Finn was one of the assholes leering over Will's sister, he had no room to judge. "Oh yeah. I'm keeping an eye on them so they don't overstep." Thank you, alibi.

"Why does she have to be so... so...?"

"Molly?"

"Ugh." Will face-palmed.

"She's in college, man. It's what we do. Step out from under our parents' shadows, figure out who we are, what we like, and go at it like rabbits." He winked at Will, but his still-aching dick reminded him that he wanted to go at Molly-fucking-Morrison like a goddamn rabbit. "We aren't all born fully grown with a newspaper in our hand, mister stick-in-the-mud."

"I'm heading back to the dorms." Will stood and picked up his coat from the stool.

Finn sighed. He'd struck a nerve. "Want me to keep an eye on her?" His stomach clenched. The watchful eye he wanted to keep on her and the eye Will would want him to keep on her weren't the same kind of watchful eye at all. He should feel guiltier, right? But he'd already given his loyalty to his best friend. He'd taken one for the brotherhood and hung his heart on a hook at the back of the closet. Just 'cause he couldn't pursue Ms. Morrison, didn't mean he couldn't think about her.

He'd never get to enjoy Molly's porcelain skin or the curves of her tits or her self-proclaimed flat ass. What he wouldn't give to chow down on that ass like he was in a motherfuckin' hotdog eating contest. Finn had chosen his side. He was Team Will all the way. But that didn't mean he didn't want to be Team Molly, too.

And from the assholes she had a tendency to bang, one might think Will would even relish a decent guy like Finn taking care of his sister.

If only wishing made it so.

"Nah, like you said, she's a big girl, she can take care of herself. She probably loves having an audience."

A growl threatened to break free from Finn's mouth at the derision coating Will's words. Instead, he held up a hand. "We don't kink shame in this family, William." Whatever the hell kinda kinks Molly Morrison had, Finnegan Aiden O'Brien volunteered as tribute.

"We absolutely kink shame when it involves my little sister."

"She's only ten months younger, man."

Will made it sound like she was sixteen or something. Her eyes flickered open as though she felt Finn's stare, but she didn't stop kissing her date. Then, without missing a beat, she paused to throw a wicked grin and wink at him, closed her eyes again, and kept kissing.

Molly Morrison was definitely not a baby anymore.

Finn unlocked the door to the eerily quiet hockey house, stepped inside, and toed off his shoes – taking care not to step in any of the fresh snow that fell from the soles as he put them on the rack. The silence and darkness meant only one thing – the team were off engaged in drunken debauchery on someone else's front lawn. There was zero chance they were all tucked up safe and sound in bed.

Men's college hockey teams were limited to eighteen scholarships. Linc and Russ lived together in the dorms – well, lived together was a stretch. Russ split his time between the campus housing and his mom's so he could see his little girl, Jude.

Will was an RA in one of the dorms because he claimed he needed the "peace and quiet." How a dorm room was any quieter than the hockey house was yet to be seen, but the straight A, 4.0 GPA team captain and computer science whizz got whatever the hell he wanted.

If it was anyone else on the team, Finn might have wondered if he wanted space from his brothers to hide a girlfriend or something more salacious, but since Will's spare time was consumed by school, hockey, and gaming... Finn knew better.

Austin lived in an apartment off campus, thanks to his rich parent benefactors and a healthy bank account. Finn lived in the eight bedroom hockey house with a bunch of his teammates. Best thing about the hockey house was that even if he hadn't been a senior, he was well liked so he got the biggest room and dibs on what chores he wanted – or more importantly, didn't.

A shiver passed through him as he made his way into the kitchen and yanked open the fridge. February in Minnesota was frigid AF. It had snowed every day for almost two weeks, and a not-so-small part of him wished he'd picked up a delicious warm body from the bar to keep him company.

While the darkness in his chest urged him to grab another beer or something stronger from the top shelf, he reached for the quarter-full gallon of milk and chugged it down. He hated February. His brother's birthday and the anniversary of his death fell within a few days of each other.

How could so much grief be crammed into such a short month? It didn't help that he couldn't escape the icy grief coating his life by stepping out into the warm sunshine.

Liam's absence was felt year-round, but it hurt all the more in February. He raked his palms over his face and through his hair. *Shake it off, Obi.*

A vibration in the front pocket of his jeans jarred him from getting in too deep. A selfie he'd taken with Will when they were younger lit up Finn's screen announcing his call. Their faces on the screen were smushed together, tongues sticking out, noses crinkled, and crazy wide eyes. They were at the state fair, hyped up on sugar and, as always, trying to one-up each other – even when it came to something as simple as making faces in a photograph.

"S'up?" Finn padded through the house and up to his room.

"Home safe?"

"Yes, Mom."

Will didn't laugh, or even reply, but the heavy silence hanging over the line between them said it all. For as long as they'd been friends, throughout the month of February, Will called Finn every night before he went to bed. Neither of them had ever talked about why, but the gesture warmed Finn's heart. He stripped off in the darkness and climbed into bed.

Will cleared his throat. "It's okay to talk about him, you know?"

Some nights the calls were lip-service, a "Hey man, I tried this new flavor protein bar I think you'd like," while others were a little deeper. The former he could handle, the other took a cosmic effort to keep himself together. It looked like tonight was gonna be the latter. His muscles thrummed.

"I know."

"It's okay to miss him, too."

Another sigh. "I know that too."

"You don't have to be strong all the time, either."

Finn couldn't reply, his throat clogged by years of self-blame and never having the right words.

"Have you heard from them?"

"No." He wouldn't, either. Finn's relationship with his parents had gone from bad to worse after Liam's death, and while a tiny part of him wished they'd reach out, it was better for everyone that they didn't.

"Mom called." Will took a drink of something. "She's worried about you. She wants you home for dinner some night this week."

Home. From the minute Finn had first stepped into the Morrison's house, Mrs. Mo stepped into the role of being his mom. Without question.

"I'll try."

Will's laugh was strained. "I told her you'd say that."

"What else did you tell her?"

"I said I'd drag your ass to dinner as long as she made your favorite meal."

His mouth watered. He groaned. "That's not playing fair. You know she makes the best ribs in the Continental United States, man."

"Whatever it takes. I'm not above playing dirty."

Finn snorted. "From the most vanilla guy on the team. Says a lot when you get down and dirty, Will. I appreciate it." And he did. Despite the urge to retreat further into his shell, to hide under the covers and sleep until March, the warm tug of his chosen family, their insistence to not let him suffer alone... it was everything.

Finn woke up with a start, his legs tangled in sheets, and firm hands clutching his shoulders. In the darkness, his chest heaved, beads of sweat slid down his face, and his hot skin meeting the crisp night air made goosebumps prickle up his arms.

After a beat, Sébastien, the Snow Pirates goaltender, spoke, his hushed whisper piercing the silence. "Ça va?"

Finn patted his hand. "Yeah, man. I'm good."

Séb released his hold on Finn's shoulders. "Are you sure? It sounded like a bad one."

They were all bad. And while he didn't have nightmares often, they were always worse in fucking February. "I'm fine, Séb, thanks. Don't sweat it."

"I think you are sweating enough for the both of us, Finn."

Séb wasn't wrong. Finn's bare back stuck to the sheet.

"I think I'm also glad the light is off."

Finn chuckled. "You wanna be me but you can't be me. Thanks for coming to wake me up. Was I...? Uh. Did it last long?"

"About ten minutes. It wasn't bad at first, but when you got worse, well... I had to come in."

A new wave of heat scorched Finn's skin. "Sorry, Séb."

"It's okay. Try to get some sleep, eh?"

Finn smirked. The French Canadian had picked up some Minnesotan intonation. It was the weirdest accent he'd ever heard.

"See you at early skate." Sébastien left, pulling the door closed behind him with a soft click.

The green digits on Finn's clock read 04:02. He'd never get back to sleep, and despite the bone-deep ache in his back and the heaviness weighing his muscles down, he sat up and rubbed his temples. Austin wouldn't be awake yet to kick Finn's ass in the gym which meant Finn's options were either hit the ice early and take his frustrations out on a few slap shots or go for a run.

If experience had taught him anything, it was that no matter how fast or how far he ran, he could never outrun his past, so he got dressed, grabbed his kit bag, and hit the rink.

CHAPTER 3

Molly

"Alex? Alex! Can you check the TV please?" Mom's voice carried through the house, despite Dad only being in the next room.

It was Wednesday night, three days after Finn had watched her make out with her date at the bar. A shiver rattled up her spine, hardening her nipples. If she hadn't known better, she'd have said he was turned on by the sight, but she did know better. Unfortunately for her, there was no way Finn O'Brien felt anything other than annoying-little-sister vibes from her and over-protective-big-brother vibes for her. Shame.

Finn's brother Liam's birthday was coming up, Friday? Saturday? She'd have to check her calendar, and maybe drop by the hockey house with a pizza and some beers to distract him from the deep ache living in his chest. He didn't like to make a big deal out of it, but, understandably, it knocked him on his ass every year.

"What the hell are you yelling about, woman?" Dad crossed the room and stepped up behind Mom at the sink. He slid his arms around her waist and dropped a kiss on her cheek. "I'm right here. There's no need for all the hollering."

Molly laughed. She'd rather drag her bare clit across broken glass before she caught feelings like those shared between her parents, but it warmed her cold, dead heart all the same.

Maybe if she kept repeating it to herself, some day she'd believe it.

She'd had exactly one serious boyfriend in her life, Justin Ashe, in high school. She should have known that a guy with two first names was going to be trouble, but she went along with it. At least until she'd walked into Chili's with her family and found him on a date with one of her friends.

The pain she'd felt was so bone-deep, so visceral, that it brought her to her knees and in the moment, she'd vowed: never again.

Never again would she put herself in a position where someone had so much power over her that they could break her.

Never again would she allow herself to feel so deeply, expose so much of herself to someone, when the only likely outcome would be heartbreak.

Project Cold and Dead took a while. She'd cried over Justin for far longer than she'd cared to admit, and while she tried to harden her heart, it was only cold and dead until it came to the charming hockey player sitting across the breakfast bar from her.

Then she only wished it was cold and dead.

Mom turned to nuzzle against Dad's beard. "All three of our kids are home at the same time, and we didn't even have to threaten them. There has to be a hurricane... tornado... derecho, or *something* going on. Maybe hell has frozen over."

Dad's deep chuckle must have tickled because Mom scrunched up her shoulder, and Dad backed away. "To what do we owe this rare pleasure, kids?"

"Rumor has it that Mrs. Mo was makin' ribs tonight."

Finn grinned, but the mischievous sparkle from his eyes was missing. His shoulders were rigid, his pale skin somehow paler, and dark circles underlined his heavy, bloodshot eyes. "I was in the area." He grabbed a chunk of cucumber from the top of a bowl of salad in front of him. "And ribs means my favorite watermelon salad."

Molly wasn't generally a fan of rabbit food, but she could change her ways if it meant she got to watch Finn wrap his lips around a chunk of cucumber again. "Same. You know I'd never pass up a free meal."

Will sat at the dining table a few feet away. "Need any help, Mom?"

"Sure. You could move the salads from the breakfast bar to the dinner table before Finnegan ensures there's none left for the rest of us."

Finn O'Brien blushing was an uncommon treat, and Molly savored his darkening cheeks. "I got it, Will." He swept the potato salad and the pasta salad bowls up and carried them to the table.

"What about the watermelon salad?" Molly pointed an accusing finger at the bowl still in front of where Finn stood.

"But you know it's my favorite, MoMo."

She wanted to bite that pouty bottom lip until he cried uncle. Sparks ignited low in her belly. "Don't call me that." She loved when he called her that.

"Okay, Mini Mo. But I'm still not sharing my salad."

"Finnegan." She gritted the word out between clenched teeth, flames kissing her cheeks.

He popped a piece of feta in his mouth and chewed. "Yes, Molly?"

The oven dinged. Mom stepped back from the sink and wiped her hands on her apron. "Can you grab the cornbread and mac and cheese from the oven, Molster? I'm going outside to bring the ribs in from the grill."

"Saved by the oven cornbread bell." While Finn smirked and took a sip of his beer, his shoulders were rigid and his eyes dull.

"You're lucky I don't have any pucks on hand right now."

Finn rubbed his face as though recalling the memory. "That was a lucky shot."

Will snorted. "Children, children. Less chit chatting, more food bringing." He rubbed his stomach. "I have been waiting all week for this."

"Great game last weekend." Dad already had a rack of ribs on his plate and was tearing into a cornbread muffin.

Will had too much food in his mouth to answer. Finn squeezed past Molly and took his seat at the table. "Yes, sir. Not to jinx it or anything, but we're a game away from... well, y'know."

Dad nodded, waving a rib between Finn and Will. "It's your year. I can feel it." He felt it every year.

"Molly?" Mom's quiet voice still made her jump enough to almost drop the bowl she was cradling. "You okay?"

"What? Of course. I just spaced out for a minute." She hadn't spaced out. She'd been too busy wrestling the concern welling in her chest. Finn's eyes stayed pinned to his plate, his fun banter and broad smile nowhere to be seen.

Finn hadn't been in her life when Liam was alive. It was partly why his parents moved to the Morrison's neighborhood a few years after he'd died – to get away from the memories. But Molly had been present for the aftermath.

If he was going to pretend he was fine at the table, she'd let him, and she'd pretend she was fine, too. She took her seat and tore a rib off the rack on her plate. Sinking her teeth into the juicy meat, she hummed in appreciation. "So good, Mom."

A comfortable silence descended over the table as everyone tucked into their meal. Molly searched Finn's face, looking for something, anything to suggest she was overreacting, that he was fine.

As though he felt her eyes on him, his gaze flicked from his plate to meet hers. The raw pain in their depths hit her like a slapshot to the chest.

It had been almost five years since Finn had turned up in their backyard in the middle of the night, distressed and trembling.

Finn had thrown tiny pebbles at her window until she'd woken up and hurried downstairs. She'd met him at the back door, his tears mixing with rainwater as they coursed down his cheeks. Split lip, bloodied nose, and marks darkening his beautiful face under red-rimmed eyes.

It was the first time she'd wanted to reach into another human being's chest and cradle their heart to stop it hurting.

The cornbread in her mouth turned to dust at the recollection. Without a word spoken between them, she had ushered him inside out of the rain, grabbed a towel and some of Will's clean clothes from the laundry room, and sat quietly while he got changed.

The bruises on his back had been so dark she'd seen them with only the dim moonlight filtering through the living room windows as he'd peeled off his shirt. She'd stifled her gasp, but stood and reached out to touch him, unable to resist. In the darkness, her fingers glided along his still-damp skin, rising and falling over angry, raw welts that made him hiss. She'd whispered his name with more emotion than she'd known was possible, and he'd answered with only one word: don't.

Even now, the sound of his voice in the moment chilled the blood in her veins. Under the shirt pulled tightly across his body lay scars. He'd gotten a tattoo of a phoenix on his back during his second year of college. When people asked about it, he told them it was a rad bird and he liked the picture, but Molly knew better.

The symbolism of the phoenix rising from the ashes like Finn rising from the ashes of his broken family was part of it, but the other... he was desperate to cover the scars left from years of abuse at the hands of his father.

The first night he'd shown up, Molly had grabbed the med kit from under the bathroom sink, applied antibiotic ointment to the cuts on his back, and put a thin-cut BandAid over the still-bleeding wound just above his lip. She'd sat with him on the couch in silence for over an hour, holding his hand and watching the muscles twitch in his jaw, tears coursing down his face.

She'd ached to take his pain away, to hurt the monster that dared mark the boy who held her heart. "Does he do this a lot?" She'd asked the darkness.

Even once was too often. She had known the answer before she'd asked the question. His father had drowned his grief in scotch and taken his rage out on the boy that lived, on Finn. Her Finn.

She'd brushed his wet, floppy hair from his eyes and made him look at her when he didn't answer. "It's okay. You don't need to talk about it if you don't want to, but I will always be here to sit with you. And I'll always patch you up."

Even at sixteen, she'd meant it with the fierceness of a grown woman, and as she'd matured, so too had her desire to protect him from his pain.

The men still chatted over ribs, tearing into the meat like cavemen while Mom watched her with worried eyes.

Another memory assaulted Molly as she struggled to breathe. Mom had found her and Finn the next morning: Finn laid out on the sofa, his head in Molly's lap as she'd stroked the side of his face. Mom had carried on like it was totally normal to find her teenager alone in the dark with an older boy, but her sorrowful eyes conveyed all they needed to: Mom knew, too.

When she'd gotten home from school that night, Mom sat her and Will down at the table. As a teacher in their high school, she'd heard rumors about Finn's father in the staff room. Finn's behavior in school, picking fights, detention every day, and joining any and all after school or weekend activities suggested a disruptive home. It was hardly surprising, all things considered.

Finn's mom had sunk into a dark depression after Liam's death. She'd received treatment, but spent most of her days in an almost fugue state at a local medical facility. It had been just Finn and his dad at home. Molly shivered.

Mom's brow creased. "You okay?" She mouthed, glancing around the table.

With a barely noticeable shake of her head, Molly pointed at Finn. Mom's mouth pulled into a grim line, and she nodded. It was the same every February. As a family, they mourned: the loss of Liam who none of them had ever met, the loss of Finn's own family, who he never spoke to anymore, and the loss of Finn's childhood.

The food on her plate had lost its appeal, and the food already in her stomach churned, curdling with each breath she forced into her body. She pushed back from the table, her chair squeaking against the tiles. "I'm not feeling great. I'm going to the bathroom."

Mom nodded, Will and Dad kept eating, Finn met her stare and canted his head, but she waved him off.

She was used to Finn's February Funk, it happened every year without fail. It shouldn't impact her as badly as it was. There'd been no trigger, nothing new or out of the ordinary to send her into such a spiral. Yet she sat on the edge of the bed in her old room, clawing at her scalp as she held her head in her hands reliving fragments of her past with Finn, unable to stop the surge of anguish over what he had to endure.

She locked her feelings down for a reason – she never

knew what to do with them when they hit, and when it came to Finn... they always hit that much harder.

Recalling the morning after she'd patched him up for the first time, she pressed the heels of her hands, against her eyes to stop the prickling of tears behind her eyelids. He'd bounded off the couch, pleading with her not to tell anyone and apologizing for dumping his shit on her lap.

She'd wanted to go to him, to wrap her arms around him, but Will burst in, ruining the moment and asking why Finn was there, looking like crap.

"That must have been some shit, MoMo. You've been up here for a while." Finn's unexpected voice was smooth, like bourbon pouring over perfect ice cubes.

She rubbed her tummy and gave him a small smile. "Period shits. They're the worst."

He pointed a finger, tossing a grin at her. "Your period was last week."

She shook her head. He couldn't possibly know she'd had her period last week. But he was right. Was it a lucky guess? Or did he really know? She dreaded to think how he knew the inner workings of her cycle. She shook her head, he couldn't. He had to be deflecting. Her heart twitched. "Stop pretending you're okay. I know you're not."

"Don't be sad for me, Molly." He didn't deny it, but wouldn't meet her eyes, either.

A sob caught in her throat as she stepped toward him. "I'm sad because you're sad. What can I do?" She reached out to touch his chest but stopped short. If she touched him, he might feel how much she... liked him, which would only be embarrassing for the both of them. She curled her fingers, lowering her hand to her side.

A heavy smile tugged the corners of his mouth. "What you always do, Mini Mo." He ruffled her hair.

"Pizza and beer?"

He nodded. "And patch me up when Austin kicks my ass in the ring."

She hugged herself. "I hate when you go fighting."

"But you'll still patch me up?"

"I'll always patch you up."

His cornflower blue eyes were sad as they held her gaze. They flicked to her lips, and her skin caught fire as he took a step toward her. She bit the inside of her cheek. Was he going to kiss her? She had to have read the signs wrong, right? He was sad, emotional, looking for comfort and she was a warm body who knew his darkest moments, standing in front of him in an empty room.

Her heart stuttered as he reached for her jaw. A throat cleared behind Finn and he dropped his hand. Dad hovered a few feet back. "Mom's boxing up your dinner, Molly. Will's heading back to the dorms. Are you staying?"

She took a very deliberate and long step back from Finn. "Nah, I'll head back to ChoCho." She needed to be alone, to distract herself from the crappy feelings toying with that traitorous heart of hers. Maybe she'd find a party to hit up, or call the hot blonde from the bar, maybe she'd booty call one of the Murphy brothers, and if he said no, maybe she'd try the other one.

She had options. She always had options. Except the option she wanted most.

Dad nodded. "Great game the other night, Finn." He patted Finn on the shoulder. Finn just smiled and nodded, outwardly ignoring the fact Dad had said the exact same phrase to him at the table.

"Thank you, Sir. It was a fun one."

"Yeah for you, perhaps." Molly threw an eye roll. "I had these godawful newbies in front of me. Didn't know a thing about the game. Kept asking me dumb questions."

Dad chuckled. "It's all practice for when you're a hot shot expert commentator for ESPN, Bug."

She shrugged off Dad's resolute belief in her with a dismissive wave. As much as she wanted it, it wasn't likely to happen. The world of sports commentating was pretty male dominated. A lot of those women who did manage to get their foot in the door were the supporting acts to male stars. If they got lucky enough to headline, it was temporary – until they were too old or too saggy and needed to be replaced by a younger, hotter model.

She followed the men downstairs, rode in silence back to her quiet apartment, stripped off, climbed into bed and grabbed her trusty vibe from the bedside table. The best way to forget about feeling bad was to make yourself feel good.

CHAPTER 4

Molly

(17 YEARS OLD - FOUR YEARS EARLIER)

How the hell had Finn been in college for only a month and had not one, but two leggy, bottle-blonde, scantily clad women dripping from his arms?

Molly took a slug of the beer she'd commandeered from the cooler next to the back door in a bid to wash the bitter taste from her mouth. With a heavy sigh, she dropped onto the very same sun lounger she'd been sitting on when Finn had walked into her life the previous year.

Molly and Will's parents were gone for the weekend, which – to a bunch of freshmen hockey players – meant only one thing: pool party. Did it matter that it was October in Minnesota? From the ripped, bare chests parading about her parents' yard, she was gonna go with no.

Despite the chill in the cool fall air, the beautiful women strutted around in bikinis and heels next to the pool. Most of them weren't her type, but she could still appreciate an attractive woman. Especially when they were scantily clad and didn't care who saw them. To be fair, she didn't mind the view.

It wasn't their coldest fall, but at 70 degrees above the water, Molly didn't care that their pool was heated. She was snuggling all-the-way up in her well-worn Snow Pirate's hoodie and jeans, with zero intention of stripping off. She shivered.

There was no way any of the half-naked bunnies draped over hockey players in her backyard were warm. Idiots. She took another drink, knowing she was being unkind to her gender but completely unable to stop herself. Green was an ugly color on her, and she should go apologize to the women whose nipples were almost cutting holes in their bikinis.

Idiots. It wasn't that Molly didn't like women or didn't think women should celebrate their bodies. She did, and she did. It was more the fact they were celebrating quite so loudly near her brother's best friend. Finn-fucking-O'Brien

Did it help that Molly's guts were in a tangled knot over the boy? Probably not.

Did it help that said boy had developed into a glorious example of a man and stood less than twenty feet from her, shirtless? Definitely not.

Did it help that upon arrival to the party Will stood at the door glaring at his teammates and snarling, "Stay away from my sister" at each of them? Not in the slightest.

She was a goner for Finn O'Brien, though. It didn't matter which of Will's teammates might have wanted to make a move, she only had eyes for one of them. She attempted to convince her eyes to look at something, anything that wasn't licking every ridged ab on Finn Aiden O'Brien's body and trailing a line with her tongue along that V leading into his—

"How the hell does Obi do it?"

Molly couldn't see who had spoken but she held her breath and picked at the label on her beer.

"Do what?"

That voice she recognized. Will wouldn't mind her having

a beer – he was almost as underage as she was – but she tucked the bottle between her thighs all the same.

"He's got three of the prettiest chicks at the party hanging off him."

The blondes were multiplying. Finn looked like a young Hugh-fucking-Hefner.

"Yeah. He certainly has a type." Will's words coated her like molasses. Sticky, goopy, slow-pouring, and impossible to move through. She swallowed, but his words clogged every pore.

Their voices faded to the buzzing in her ears as she repeated the words over and over in her mind. Finn had a type, and it wasn't Molly.

Tall, leggy, big-busted, bottle blondes, who probably didn't know how to spell hockey, let alone follow what happened on the ice.

She winced. She was being cruel and she hated it. But at least if she was cruel about someone else, she wouldn't have to face the fact her heart was cracking wide open in her goddamn chest.

She swallowed again. Finn's type was not Molly. Tears pricked her eyes, but she gulped down her beer to fight the urge to cry. Belching in front of forty people and-or choking to death chugging a bottle of beer was preferable to crying.

While Molly wasn't short, she wasn't tall, either. Her hair was anything but blonde, bottle or any other kind – hers was long, wavy – aka fuzzy AF, and a brown that didn't know if it was brown or red. She trailed her eyes from the red painted toenails of one of the girls, all the way up her never ending legs to her red bikini.

Molly did not have hot legs like that, and her arms were too scrawny. Her ass was too flat, she had average tits, and her green eyes always just seemed a liiiiittle too close together.

She slid a fingernail under her already chipped eggplant

colored polish, shearing the paint from her nail. Her skin was too pale, her lips were too thin, her eyebrows too thick, and if she didn't wax every few weeks, she looked like Cousin-fucking-Itt.

Sure, Will would never stand for Molly dating his best friend, but she'd always thought... she'd always thought what? That a guy with a fondness for beautiful, camera ready blondes would ever look twice at her?

She cringed. Confidence oozed around the garden, tangling in the lapping flames of the fire pit and wafting into the atmosphere on tufts of smoke. Of course, skimpy clothes were what men wanted, but why did women feel a need to give it to them? Was it a power thing? Did they feel every bit as gorgeous as they looked? Or were they trembling inside like newborn kittens, just trying to fit in?

The only boyfriend Molly had ever had, had broken her heart in two. He'd cheated on her with someone she knew from school – earning himself a beat down from her brother. She almost laughed at the memory. How Will had managed to kick anyone's ass when he couldn't have beaten his way out of a wet paper bag was anyone's guess. But he'd done it. For her.

The clip-clopping of heels on the tiled floor drew her attention to another bikini in astronomically high heels, hurrying toward Finn, brandishing a guitar. "Play for us, Finny. Pleeeeeeease?"

Finny? That was a keeper. Molly tucked it away in her memory banks to use at an appropriately embarrassing moment in the future.

Wide, doe-eyes pleaded with Finn, and even in the dim light, Molly could tell his cheeks were pinking. If she batted those eyes at him much more, her falsies would fly away.

Fuck, Molly, you're being an asshole. Get it together and stop being a dick. You like ogling them as much as the guys do.

Finn held up his hands, but didn't claim his guitar. He

shook his head and spoke quietly to the girl who – if she leaned over much more – would be on full frontal display to Finn.

Molly expected to find a bulge in his swim shorts, but she couldn't make one out. Either he had a tiny dick, was too cold to get hard, or he wasn't interested. She mulled on the options while other girls joined in the whiny pleading, and Finn finally relented.

In the far corner of the yard, two curvier women wearing booty shorts and tied up t-shirts performed a dance routine. Two of the hockey players had pulled out dining room chairs, and music played softly from one of their phones. The women gyrated to the beat as though no one was watching. They didn't touch the guys they were dancing for, but Molly's mouth dried up at just how beautiful they were.

"Wow." Her whisper escaped on a gasp. How did they move like that? And better yet, where could she learn? She wanted to love her body the way those women seemed to love theirs. Maybe if she was confident and could move like they did, it wouldn't matter how she looked. It wouldn't matter that she was broken, rejected by the only boy she'd ever been with, or in love with someone she could never have, because she'd love herself, damnit. And maybe that would be enough.

A soft tap on the door pulled her from light sleep. "Molly? You home?"

Molly grunted. "S'up?"

"You had a couple of visitors while you were out."

"Oh?" Playing dumb never worked with her astute best friend. From the fourteen unread texts and a bunch of missed calls from the Murphy brothers, Cathal and Ciaron, and their best friend Jayden, not only did she know exactly who'd come to call, she knew why, too.

"Yeah." Cleo somehow made the short answer into a dozen syllables. "Mol... What's going on with you?"

Molly inched the duvet over her head. "Sweet summer prude. Haven't you heard? Cum guzzling is the new fountain of youth." She cringed and peeked over the edge of the blanket. She was being a dick, but couldn't seem to stop herself.

Cleo wasn't going to let her get away with deflecting from the fact she banged a dude and his best friend – not at the same time – with crass humor.

Cleo wrinkled her nose. "Gross. And be shitty all you

want, Molzilla. I'm not letting you avoid this discussion. Are you really dating a guy and his best friend?"

Molly groaned. She was kind of doing that, yes. "I'm sorry for being snappy."

Cleo nodded but didn't speak.

"Ugh. Fine. It's not serious with either of them, and they're both seeing other people, too. It's not technically cheating." The argument sounded weak even to herself.

"Do said guy and said best friend know you're dating the other one?"

Molly's stomach clenched. No, ma'am, they did not. But she didn't say it out loud. Would either of them care? The sex was decent, she wasn't looking for strings... isn't that what every college guy wanted?

"You know I love you."

Here it comes. Buuuuuut?

"And I'm not slut-shaming you either, so don't even go there. But I'm worried about you." Cleo crossed the room and sat on the edge of Molly's bed, tugging the quilt back from her face. "You're a free spirit and love sex, sure. But this... eh... extreme? This isn't like you."

She wanted to defend herself, to deny that it was out of the norm for her, but Cleo was right, it wasn't like Molly. Her feelings for Finn had gotten so scary big in her chest that she hadn't known what to do with them. So instead of facing them, or God forbid, actually dealing with them, she'd decided to ignore them and instead fuck damn near anything with a pulse.

Was she proud of herself? Hell no. But she'd had some pretty good orgasms lately which almost made it worth the reputation – though it did little to sate the desire to ride Finn O'Brien until his dick didn't work anymore.

She sighed. It didn't matter what she did or didn't do, women who loved their bodies, who owned their sexuality, often got branded as hos and sluts. She'd been labeled when she started burlesque dancing, and it hadn't gone away. She leaned into it as she grew older, owning it, shrouding herself in it like it could somehow protect her.

"You know I'm here for you, right?" Cleo's persistence warmed her heart.

Molly nodded.

"And you know this is a judgment free zone?"

Another nod.

"When you're ready to talk about him, I'll be here, okay?"

Another nod. Molly hadn't yet come out and admitted her Finn-Feels to Cleo, but Cleo knew, and Molly knew Cleo knew that Molly knew. There was a lot of knowing, but not a lot of speaking.

If Molly spoke, there was a chance the wind would carry her words right to her big brother's door, and she could lose them both. Taking a chance that Finn might want to kiss her the way she ached to kiss him, wasn't worth it. She couldn't lose either of them, never mind both.

CHAPTER 5
Finnegan

On any normal day, there was something Finn loved about being up before the sun and just getting shit done. It was freeing. But he'd had nightmares every night for the week since he'd been at dinner at Casa Morrison. His body was heavy, and his muscles ached from the overworking he'd been giving them. If nothing else, at least his liver was fine.

Though the lure of drowning out his pain with liquor was strong, having a piece of shit, alcoholic father made him question every drop that passed his lips. The fear of becoming anything like the man who beat him for years was enough of a deterrent to finding peace at the bottom of a bottle.

It was 6.30 on the morning of Liam's anniversary. Finn had barely slept. Lying in bed with a hand tucked under his head, he stared at the ceiling. He wasn't sure when he'd last consumed a meal that wasn't cereal, and that "something has died" smell permeating the room was probably him. He hadn't showered for two days. His phone chimed from the nightstand.

> MoMo: You doing okay?

Molly was anything but a morning person, which meant she'd been out with someone the night before and wanted company on her walk of shame. Something bitter stirred in his stomach.

> Finn: Is the apocalypse coming? Have the zombies arrived? WTF are you doing awake?

> MoMo: I get up early sometimes.

> Finn: Good night?

> MoMo: Totes. ChoCho and I devoured a few pints in front of some chick flicks after a very healthy dinner of bacon cheese fries.

Huh. So it wasn't a hot date with steamy, wild sex all night.

> Finn: With ranch?

> MoMo: Always ranch.

> MoMo: You didn't answer my question, Finnegan.

Few people used his Sunday name, he didn't let them. But Molly... she could call him whatever the fuck she wanted and he'd answer.

He started typing. Stopped. And started typing again. His stomach tightened. He didn't have the words to describe the vortex of agony that sucked his chest every year. The irony of all ironies was that if he could rewind to a happier time, to a time before Liam died, a time before his parents needed mood altering substances to get through the day, things would have been completely different.

If Liam had lived, Mom and Dad would never have moved to the Morrison's neighborhood, and Finn would never have met Will or Molly. His phone sounded in his hand.

MoMo: Finny?

Finn: Don't call me that, Mini Mo.

He grinned. She'd called him Finny like she called Will Willy – they both hated it, and it was a button she pressed on-the-regular to wind them both up.

MoMo: Want me to come over?

His heart warmed. She was the only person who'd seen him in all his broken glory, and she hadn't run, she hadn't paled or winced, she'd simply fixed him up and sat with him until dawn chased away the demons. It was why he loved mornings so much, light always conquered the darkness.

Finn: You know it's weird when you get nice like this.

MoMo: It comes but once a year, Finny. Make the most of it before it's gone.

Finn: It's like Emotional Christmas. Do I get gifts?

He wanted to ask her to dress up like a sexy elf and come jingle her bells to cheer him up. He wanted to bury himself in her soft flesh until they didn't know where she ended and he began. He wanted to hold her, lying together in silence, until he found words to explain to her the things he was feeling, the things he lived through, what he'd seen. A shiver rattled through his bones.

> MoMo: I am a fucking gift. Also it's too early for pizza and beer so no extra gifts.

> MoMo: I wouldn't wanna bump into your flavor of the week.

Was she fishing? Did she think he had a revolving door of fuck buddies? He had a few regular friends-with-benefits, but she knew he hadn't been in a single, long-term relationship since he'd started college. She also didn't know she was the reason why.

He rubbed at his chest. Some days he considered telling her, getting everything out in the open and dealing with the fallout. But then he and Will played Mario Kart, or went bowling together and his better judgement kicked in.

> MoMo: Come downstairs. I don't want to wake everyone and have the whole team pissed at me 'cause they're sleep deprived.

Why the hell was she at the hockey house at ass-crack-of-dawn time?

> Finn: Plus you want to interview them.

> MoMo: That too.

He bounded out of bed and pulled on a pair of boxers before taking the stairs two at a time to the ground floor. He pulled open the door and a grinning Molly stood with her hands behind her back.

Her gaze flicked to his chest. She didn't bother to hide her appreciation of his half naked body. He had a good body, he took care of it, and knew people found him attractive, but she looked at him like he was a tray of tacos on a Tuesday.

Her eyes trailed lazily from his shoulders down to his boxers, rolling over his abs as though they were steps down to the Promised Land. She raised an eyebrow. "Morning Sunshine."

"My eyes are up here."

"Seems' like they're not the only thing that's up."

He snorted, but his cheeks heated. Her razor sharp tongue was one of his favorite things about her. She rocked back on her heels. Was she nervous? He couldn't really blame her, like it had no understanding that she was off limits, his dick was most definitely getting hard under her stare.

"What can I say? Little Finn likes mornings." He shifted his feet, and tried to think of something to make it soften.

"Little Finn is also not so little."

She wasn't helping. Was she enjoying tormenting him? Damn straight he wasn't so little.

Despite the crisp weather, Molly wasn't wearing a coat. Her oversized, navy cable knit sweater slipped off her shoulder, revealing the straps of her underlying tank top and ornate, red lace bra. He pointed at the fabric. "Well I can see your bra."

She pursed her lips. Right, like her seeing the bulge of his morning wood, and him seeing one half-covered strap from a bra he wanted to tear from her body, was totally the same thing.

"Good. It was fucking expensive." She flicked her loose hair over her shoulder.

He stepped back from the doorway. "You coming in?"

She shook her head, the pompom on top of her hat bobbing with the movement.

"Something wrong?"

Another shake. A nostril flare. A lip bite.

What the fuck was wrong with her?

From behind her back she pulled a long, black cylinder. A loud pop echoed around the foyer before brightly colored shards of paper exploded into the air above his head. What the hell? Had she just set off a confetti cannon?

She tossed the empty cannon into the air and it landed at his feet with a dull thud against the tiles. He'd never seen a hotter mic drop in his life.

"Did you just declare confetti cannon war, MoMo?"

A smirk tugged at the corner of her mouth. "And what if I did, Finny?"

While the gesture was small – and messy – her attempt to distract him, to pull him out of the darkness, to cheer him up... it meant the world to him. So he was going to hit up Party City, buy a dozen confetti cannons, and win the freakin' war, *that's* what he was going to do.

"That's it? That's what you came for? To pop a confetti cannon at me?"

She threw a casual shrug, opening her arms as if to say "What are you gonna do about it?" and left.

After a five mile run and a cold shower, Finn arrived at the rink for skills practice. It hadn't originally been on the schedule, but Coach Swift wasn't content enough that it *looked like* the team were winning the finals of the NCAA college hockey tournament – the Frozen Four – he was determined to make damn sure it happened. Even if it killed them all to get there.

Laced up, Finn stepped out of the locker room and headed toward the ice. Molly stood, notebook in hand, chatting to Fowler – the backup netminder for the team – taking notes as he spoke. Her brows knitted together in a frown and her tongue poked out from the side of her mouth as she scribbled.

"Why are you interviewing Fowler, MoMo? Don't you think I'd make a better subject for your story?"

If eye rolling was an Olympic sport, Molly Morrison would be a gold medal winner. Every. Damn. Time.

"What can you do, Obi? I am loved by the people of Minnesota." Fowler shrugged.

"He's also hot."

Finn's brows shot up. She thought he was hot? Huh. He wasn't quite sure what to do with that information, but he didn't like the sour feeling that sat heavy in his stomach. Fowler grinned. "She... she says I'm hot."

Molly laughed, the sound echoing around the corridor. "I meant that you're on a winning streak right now, Cameron. You're on a hot streak."

"Ah. You mean je suis au top de ma forme... comme gardien." Fowler's shoulders sank and his face fell. Of course he wanted Molly to think he was hot. Every guy on the team who had eyes in their head and hot blood in their veins wanted Molly to think they were hot. But perhaps Fowler had forgotten his "talking to" from Will. Everyone got it at some point. Those who didn't listen the first time, got a more severe second warning, but Finn hadn't known anyone to get to three. Will had the overprotective big brother thing down pat.

He folded his arms. "Watch it, Fowler. Cap's sister is off limits to the team. Remember?"

The French Canadian's entire face turned a dark shade of red, all the way to the tips of his ears. "Oh, I, uh, I'm... I didn't mean... I wasn't..."

Molly waved it off with a sympathetic smile. "Will can bite me. I date who I want. In case you've forgotten, Finny, I never signed my name to any of his bullshit patriarchal demands." She examined her nails. "I just haven't found anyone on the team worth my time yet." Her smirk almost undid him.

Date? What the hell? She wanted to date Fowler? Over his

dead body was that smug prick taking Molly on a date. Fine, he wasn't a prick, he was actually one of the good ones. The Snow Pirates had two French Canadian goaltenders, and as far as Finn was concerned, one was more than enough when one of them wanted in Molly's pants.

Fowler's eyes lit up at her declaration of independence, and he turned a hopeful stare back to Finn who shook his head and forced his best "don't fuck with her" glare. Fowler had better get the friggin' message.

The goalie nodded. Finn couldn't blame him for trying. The woman was stunning. And as long as he had Will's mandate about players dating his sister to hide behind, it all looked as though Finn simply had his best friend's back. If only it was as straightforward as that.

If looks could kill, the frosty glare Molly tossed at Finn might have sent him six feet under, but her stare didn't scare him. As far as she was concerned, he was simply doing his duty to make sure Will's wishes were upheld among the team.

Her being screwed over by one of the players on the team and having Will try to hand their ass to them scared him. Or worse still, Finn having to dole out a beating because someone touched his girl. He'd done it once before and while satisfying, he'd almost been busted by Will for having feelings for Molly.

His girl. He almost laughed. Molly Morrison didn't belong to anyone but Molly Morrison. If she ever settled down – regardless of whether she settled with a man or a woman – her partner would need to recognize that the only way Molly would commit to being tied down was on her own terms.

Fowler's face still sizzled. Molly would eat him alive if he went on a date with her. But Finn couldn't take the risk that she'd develop feelings and he'd somehow hurt her – then he'd have to bury the body of a hockey brother. Ain't nobody got time for that kind of complication when they were set for victory at the Frozen Four.

Finn hovered as Molly asked Fowler what his favorite pizza topping was – she liked to include a question or two from the fans in each of her interviews. It added a little personality to her reporting and gave the fans something to engage with.

Finn choked back a snort when he answered Hawaiian. If there had previously been a shot for Fowler to get into Molly's pants, it was snuffed out by the proud declaration that he loved pineapple on pizza. He didn't even have the decency to be ashamed by his admission. Molly's face contorted, but she remained quiet.

Finn hadn't needed to intervene after all. Molly would never get serious with someone who committed crimes against pizza. Fowler hauled ass onto the ice, followed by Seb and a few of the other players making their way from the locker room.

"Thought about what you're doing for the summer yet, Mol?"

Her eyes narrowed. "Who have you been talking to?"

"No one." He held his hands up. "I just saw something I thought would be perfect for you. A summer internship. Eight weeks – okay, so it's unpaid, but it's with—"

"ESPN, I know. I saw the ad." She turned her attention back to the notepad in her hand, adding something to the end of her notes. That was it? Just "I know?" He'd thought she'd be at least a little more excited at the idea of getting one step closer to her dream job.

When Finn and Will had played street hockey as teens, Molly grabbed the nearest cylindrical object, pretended it was a microphone and gave a play-by-play the whole time. She was pretty damn good at it, too.

"What gives, Mol? Don't wanna be a color commentator anymore?"

"Uh, only since forever."

"Then why aren't you more excited about the internship?"

"Maybe I'm excited in here." She pointed at her chest, but his eyes strayed just a little. Was she distracting him with her perfect tits? If so, it was totally working.

"You don't look excited. You look like you ate something that made your stomach hurt and you're about to get a bad dose of the shits."

"Wow. Thanks, Finny. Nothing quite says ethereal goddess like 'you look like you have the shits.'"

"Wait... hold up..."

"On the ice, O'Brien." Will hollered from the end of the hall. "Less talking, more working."

"This isn't over, MoMo. That internship is perfect for you. I demand an explanation."

She flipped him off over her shoulder before walking back toward the locker rooms. If he didn't know better, he'd say she was afraid. But Molly freakin' Morrison was fearless. What was so big, so scary or bad that it was holding her back from pursuing her lifelong dream?

CHAPTER 6

Finnegan

(FOUR YEARS EARLIER)

Finn flung open the door to Puck's with gusto. He'd finished his first year in college, they'd missed out on getting to the final four by one measly point, but tonight was about celebrating. He'd survived.

"We're going to need some volunteers." A long-legged brunette wearing six inch heels, fishnets, and very little else spoke into a microphone in the middle of the bar next to a row of empty chairs.

"I volunteer as tribute!" Determined to have a good night, Finn threw his hand into the air.

The sign on the door on their way in said there was a burlesque show that evening, and there was nothing he loved more than women who loved their bodies and celebrated them with fervor. And food. He loved food. Some days it was a toss-up between the two.

Will shook his head and groaned. "Of course you volunteer as tribute."

Finn slapped his open palm on Will's chest twice. "We're celebrating, Mo. We survived our first year in college. We didn't burn the house down, get food poisoning, or get kicked out of school."

"We also passed all our exams."

"Well, you did. I need to wait for my official results."

Will chuckled.

The asshole was already going to graduate top of his class with a slew of interesting job offers from all around the country. The CIA and FBI would probably be kissing his feet any day now, schmoozing him to work for them. Not only was his IQ off the charts, but he was killing it on the ice, and he had also begun development on his first computer game. Guy had it all.

"Excuse me." A short redhead pushed past in a blur and Finn lurched to grab the door for her before she ran into it face-first. Short was a generous descriptor. She was dinky.

"You could have opened the door for her, man."

Will shrugged.

Okay, so he almost had it all. His social skills left a little to be desired. Especially when it came to the opposite sex. The technical term was flummoxed. Will Morrison lost all power of speech and capacity for human interaction when a beautiful woman opened her mouth and spoke in his direction.

"Come on up, sir." The woman in the fire-red heels in front of the bar beckoned Finn forward.

He nudged Will's elbow. "She called me sir."

"Yeah, because she doesn't know you." Will deadpanned and Finn laughed, making his way forward to the empty seats. Three guys had already taken their places on his row, Finn made four, which left two empty seats in the front row. The back row of another six chairs had already filled up.

Once each seat was taken, Beyonce's *Naughty Girl* started playing through the speakers, and every person in the bar cheered. The cheering escalated when – Finn assumed – the dancers appeared behind the two rows of chairs.

Instead of looking decidedly gleeful, Will's brows hung low over his eyes and his arms banded across his chest. How could any hot-blooded human being not enjoy a burlesque show?

Delicate fingers trailed across his shoulders, sending a shiver down his spine. He should have worn looser pants. Mercifully, he hadn't worn jeans, so his bare dick wasn't chaffing against a denim seam.

From fingers on his neck, to a perfectly jiggling peach shaped ass all up in his face, Finn had died and gone to heaven. He gripped the underneath of his seat with both hands to save himself from the embarrassing urge to touch the gold sequins molded to the lush butt cheeks. He clenched his jaw. It was going to be a long few minutes and it really wasn't cool to touch dancers.

The ass then moved to his crotch, gyrating and brushing against the stirring bulge in his pants. He pinned his gaze to the back of her red, jaw-length bob, maybe that would tell his dick it wasn't okay to caress a strange woman's ass through the fabric of his pants. Was she wearing a wig?

Like Finn's grin, Will's scowl only grew. What the hell was his deal?

Another brush against his groin, the dancer straightened up, threw her hands over her head, and dragged the fingers of one hand down the length of her other arm. Shimmying her chest forward and ass back, the sequins on her costume tinkled against each other. She was clearly intent on killing Finn and sending him to hell for sitting in a chair in front of a room full of people and letting a beautiful woman with curves in all the right places shake her ass in his face for three minutes. Was it only three minutes?

He resisted the urge to pull his shirt away from his neck. The last thing he needed was Will – or any of the other team-mates that were making their way across the bar to stand next to him – making fun of him for not being able to handle the heat. Finn grinned at Linc and Russell, pulling his brows up and pursing his lips.

Riiiiight? Look how fucking cool this is.

Except neither of them seemed to agree with Finn's assessment that it was in any way cool, or hot, and neither of them was in any way jelly that they weren't in Finn's shoes. What in an alternate dimension was going on? Were the dancers wearing masks? Was she underage? He cringed. She still hadn't turned around but from behind she was a ten. Was it legal for him to think she was a ten? His chest tightened.

She took a step forward and Finn's shoulders unclenched. She turned side-on and the curve of her breast hung in front of his eyes. She had a delicious rack – also clad in gold sequins. Surely she wasn't underage. She couldn't be. While he couldn't see her face, he also couldn't see a Chucky mask, so maybe his teammates were just feeling a bit of the green-eyed monster. He didn't give a flying fuck what they thought, the woman standing in front of him was a perfect fucking ten.

He dragged his gaze up her collarbone, up the column of her neck, and to the profile of her face. Sharp, angular bones, protruding from behind the curtain of flame-red hair. As the music grew, she spun to face him and his perusal of the beautiful dancer lifting her leg, with any luck to throw it over his thigh and mount him, continued.

Wide, green, familiar eyes met his.

Shit.

Fuck.

Mother fucking fuckety fuck.

Molly. It was Molly.

Behind her, Russell smashed his fist into his mouth. Linc shifted so he stood a step in front of Will. Finn made a mental note to thank Linc for his protective instincts later. He flicked his gaze back to Molly, who'd stuttered to a halt and was staring, even wider eyed and open mouthed.

"Keep going!" The woman who'd picked Finn as a sacrificial lamb encouraged from the sideline with a wide smile and two thumbs up.

Finn nodded. "It's fine. Don't stop."

"Will." She gritted the word out from between clenched teeth.

"Don't worry about Will, keep dancing."

Molly's throat bobbed as she swallowed. Her eyes never left his as she hooked her legs around his waist, settled onto his lap, and caught up to the music. She ground her hips against his as she leaned all the way back until she was perpendicular to his body. He groaned.

Will's glare burned into him from only a matter of feet away. Finn was a dead man. He was officially going to be murdered and no one would ever find his body. The still-giggling Russell would probably even help bury Finn's body, too. Asshole.

Molly's weight shifted deeper into his crotch as she leaned even further backward, arms outstretched. Using what had to be unbreakable core muscles, she pulled herself upright and rolled her head from left to right, flicking her hair. Her red wig brushed against his face, but her cleavage was *right there* and if he took even so much as a deep inhale, he was going to drag his stubble across the bare skin of the top of her breasts.

Molly closed her eyes and kept dancing. She unhooked her legs and pushed herself up to standing. Her feet were planted either side of his thighs and he was pretty sure if Will didn't kill him, the mounting pressure in his pants would.

He'd always tried not to notice changes in Molly Morrison's body, she wasn't a little girl when they'd met by any means, but his little MoMo had certainly grown all-the-way up. She'd filled out in all the right places and his body responded to it in kind. He wanted to trail his tongue along the edge of her sparkly gold bra. He wanted her to jostle that sequined ass in his face again so he could take a bite out of it.

Fuck.

She dismounted his lap and he heaved a breath of relief as a bead of sweat trickled down his temple. It was hot, the bright lights and number of bodies had driven the temperature of the bar up to surface-of-the-sun level hot. But Molly's scantily clad, whirling body and long limbs... he swallowed hard. Double fuck. She wasn't just scorching hot, she was a good dancer, too. *Really good.*

His chest swelled, counterbalancing the prickling heat stabbing at his entire body. She dragged her fingertips across the front of his shoulders before stepping behind him.

Good. If he couldn't see her, he couldn't react to her, and Will might let him off with a severe beating rather than complete loss of life.

He hissed out a breath, attempting to school his features into a casual "Meh, it's no big deal Molly's hot pussy was just grinding against his rock hard cock" face. But it didn't work. He could feel her heat, her closeness behind him. Her face lingered close to his ear as she gripped his shoulders from behind. He'd kill to see what she was doing back there. The ogling crowd was going crazy, applauding and coaxing the dancers to continue. As much as he hated any other man in the room having their eyes on his Molly, he hoped their enjoyment of her performance fed her confidence. He hoped she absorbed every ounce of applause, every catcall, holler, and whistle and let it feed her inner badass.

The end of the dance came much too fast and not fast enough. Thankfully he hadn't jizzed his pants like a horny pubescent teen, but his balls ached. The damp fabric of his shirt clung to his back. He needed a cold shower. If Will let him live that long.

The dancers disappeared back from whence they'd come. The hostess asked the audience to give the dozen volunteers a hand, then the dancers. Before she'd finished speaking, Finn had pushed his way through the crowd, slammed the door of a bathroom stall behind him, and pumped his pulsing hard cock to the memory of Molly Morrison's hips grinding against it.

A few minutes later, he was less drunk on Molly's – eh – assets being all up in his space, his balls were still blue, but they didn't hurt with every step, and his mind was clearer. He spied Will and the guys, and he made his way toward them, stopping when Molly approached from the other direction with a shy smile on her face.

Finn swallowed, but his mouth was still dryer than an Arizona summer. It would be better to get it over with. He stood next to Molly, parted his lips to congratulate her, but Will's arm shot out to clutch her elbow.

"What the fuck do you think you're doing?" He jerked her toward him. "Cover yourself up." He threw his jacket around her shoulders.

Her jaw dropped open. Finn's jaw dropped open. Every muscle in Linc's body visibly hardened and his hand snapped out to grab Will's arm. "That's enough, Will. We get that she's your sister and you're a protective older brother. But if Molly wants to dance a kick-ass burlesque number and shake her shit – you don't get a say in that."

Finn blinked. Will's face softened and his shoulders relaxed. Linc tugged Will's arm from Molly's. "And I love you man, God knows I do, but if you ever grab any woman like that again, I'll lay you out." Without a second of hesitation, Linc grabbed Molly into a bear hug. "You were fucking awesome, Mol."

The lion in Finn's chest rattled the bars of its cage at Linc's arms closing around Molly's back. Linc barely knew Molly. He'd met her maybe a handful of times – at most. Sure, he was probably trying to not only diffuse the situation but to drown out any feelings of shame Molly might be experiencing, but Finn still didn't like the fact Linc's hands were on her body. Anywhere. At all.

Will grumbled something about how at least it was Finn who experienced her dance and not some horny asshole he'd have to kill. Finn's dick twitched. Finn was definitely some horny asshole, he wanted to bang Molly Morrison every day for the rest of her damn life. But the knots in his muscles unfurled as Will's lack of rage in his direction made him feel better about the whole situation, until Molly curled her shoulders, rocked back on her heels, and bit down on her lip.

Had Will made her feel ashamed of dancing? Why had he given *her* shit, but not Finn? For that matter, why had Will given anyone shit at all? If she wanted to dance, it was none of his goddamn business.

He nodded at her. "Linc's right, MoMo. You were amazing."

Her face lit up in the most heartwarming, genuine smile he'd ever seen, and her sunlight split his heart into a million pieces. He wanted to make her smile like that every day for the rest of her life as well.

"Wait till you see the next dance."

Finn's nostrils flared and his stomach tightened. "There's another one?"

She nodded. "I've got pasties."

CHAPTER 7

Molly

Molly waited until practice was well underway to come out from her hiding place and stand behind the boards. She couldn't exactly report on the state of the Snow Pirate's pre-playoff game if she was hiding in the locker room and not actually watching their pre-playoff game.

She wasn't sure standing closer to the ice would help, considering her head was in the clouds, but it couldn't hurt. She'd found a lump in her breast while showering a few days before. After a Google search, she'd learned that no matter what age you were, a lump of any kind needed to be checked out. Despite wanting to ignore it and pretend she hadn't found it, she'd pulled on her Big Girl Pants and made the call.

Her phone buzzed in her pocket as Will ran puck control drills up and down the length of the ice. The little orange cones appeared haphazard, but by this stage, even Molly could have run the drills blindfolded – and she couldn't skate for shit.

Everyone said Coach was a hard ass, relentlessly pushing the team to greatness, but Will was every bit as bad. His hunger for the cup drove everyone forward, not least of all himself.

Molly pulled her phone out of the pocket of her jeans to find a text from Mom.

Mom: I have a problem I'm not sure how to handle.

Molly's stomach clenched. Was Mom sick? Was Gram sick? Had she finally snapped and killed Dad because of his shitty dad jokes and needed help burying the body? Why was her instinct to jump to worse case scenarios? She probably needed to unpack that with a therapist, but she wasn't blind to the internal shift from zero-to-freak-out.

Molly: You still have a week to pick something up for Dad's birthday. Just take him to that shitty place he loves to eat, buy him new socks, and call it good.

Mom: Finn's mom just called.

Hell no. The woman had abandoned her grieving son. They had no space for someone like that in their lives. Sure, she'd gone to a mental health facility to get treatment, but once she'd come out the other side, recovered, she'd moved on with her life, and Finn hadn't been in it.

Mrs. O'Brien had divorced Finn's asshole dad, remarried, and had another child with the new man – but she hadn't made an effort to reconnect with Finn.

Molly: What did she want?

Molly needed to run interference on whatever shitstorm was brewing for Finn. Or at the very least head the woman off at the pass until March. March was a new month, a better month, a month where Finn wasn't beaten to shit by grief, or something else, something heavier.

Molly had always suspected Finn blamed himself for Liam's death but they'd never talked about the details. She'd never wanted to press him for information that clearly pained him to think about.

Molly: Reconciliation?

Mom: I think so. I got the impression she might need something from him too, though. She asked for his cell number.

Molly groaned. Mom wasn't an idiot, she knew Finn's wishes and wouldn't just hand out his digits like they were candy at Halloween. But by the same token, she was also a mother, and perhaps Finn's mom had tugged at her bleeding mom-heart.

Molly was halfway through typing "Please don't tell me you gave it to her," when another message came through.

Mom: Didn't give it to her. I took her number though, just in case he wants to call her.

Mom: You know Finn better than I do. Do you think he'd be open to hearing from her? She seemed insistent that it was important.

Would he? For all his anger and resentment toward his past, deep inside, Finn was still just a little boy aching for the love of his parents. He probably would be open to talking to her, especially since it sounded urgent.

Molly: I'll handle it.

Mom: I don't mind approaching him about it
if you don't want to break the news, but it's
so sensitive and I don't want to upset him.
(We both know it'll upset him anyway.)

Molly smiled. Finn was like the youngest of the family. The one who got away with just about everything because his older siblings had already put their parents through their paces. Mom made a point of nurturing Finn in a way she didn't with Molly or Will. It was as though she made a concerted effort to ensure Finn always knew *someone* loved him, even if he didn't think his own family did anymore.

"You're still here?" Will's voice made her jump. Sweat dripped into his eyes from his floppy hair.

She tucked her phone in her pocket. "Yeah, I wanted to talk to you about Dad's birthday." She hoped she was convincing. That wasn't why she'd stayed, but if he bought it, it didn't matter.

Will nodded. "I was thinking we'd take him for dinner at that place he likes."

Molly laughed. "That's what I told Mom to do."

Finn appeared over Will's shoulder and her cheeks flared. "What about sending him for a racing experience? One of those track things?"

Her heart swelled. Her dad was a motorsport fan and loved anything with an engine and wheels. It was a great idea, though Mom would probably object to letting him behind the wheel of something so speedy.

"Mom will hate it, but Dad will love it." Will narrowed his eyes. "I'm in. There's probably even a Groupon for it." Always Mr. Pragmatic.

"What about a cake?" Always Mr. Leads-with-his-stomach. Finn rubbed his tummy.

"I already asked Sabrina's roommate, Quinn, to take care of that. Have you tried any of her treats?"

Both men shook their heads. "Oh shit, you're in for a treat. She makes the best cake."

"Ah, but does she make good carrot cake? You know it's his favorite." Will pointed at her like he might have one-upped her.

"As a matter of fact, she does, smart ass."

Molly's phone chimed in her pocket. She pulled it out and a message from her primary care provider waited for her on the screen reminding her of her upcoming appointment. Finn arched an eyebrow, but didn't say anything. Had he read her message upside down? Was that something people did, or was she simply being overly sensitive?

She ignored Finn's burning stare and turned to leave. "Later, gators."

She hadn't made it more than two feet from the men before Will spoke again. "I found someone for you, man. Her name is Charlotte. She's hot, funny, knows the game... she's perfect for you."

Finn cleared his throat behind her. "I... uh..."

She slowed her steps, intent on hearing the conversation play out. The idea of facing cancer, or something else sinister in her body didn't make her feel nearly as queasy as the idea that Finn might find someone to love that wasn't her.

"I told you I'm not looking for anything serious right now, Cap."

Thank the fucking stars.

"I know, I know. But you've totally lost your mojo lately. It seems like you're not looking for anything at all right now, never mind anything serious."

Finn's chuckle sounded strained. "I'm just not in the 'meeting new people' frame of mind right now, I guess."

"I understand. I didn't mean to push you. I just think you might need to get back on the horse."

Or the hussy.

Ah! Ah! Ah! Don't be mean, Molly. She's probably a perfectly nice woman. It's not her fault your brother is a traitorous asshole who keeps trying to set your man up with other women.

A growl rumbled in her chest and she coughed to hide it as she kept walking. He wasn't hers. He would never, nor could ever, be hers either, no matter how badly her heart – or her vajayjay – might want him.

"Molly, I'm Dr. Klein. It's nice to meet you."

Hi, I'm Molly and I'm pretty terrified you're going to tell me I'm going to die. I deflect serious emotions with cutting wit, and salacious sarcasm, and I'm a fucking idiot for coming here today all by myself.

Her hands trembled as she wrung them in her lap. In hindsight, she probably should have called Mom, or ChoCho – someone, *anyone*, to go with her to the medical center for her appointment. At least if she'd brought a friend with her she would have someone to keep her distracted from the twisted mess in her stomach while she waited. Her insides felt like a can of silly string had exploded, covering all her organs in a goopy, sticky mess.

She wasn't even sure why she'd gone alone. While there was something to be said for not unnecessarily freaking people out without cause, and while she wanted to face her life all by her big girl self, she had quickly realized – the moment she stepped off the elevator outside Dr. Klein's office – that she was out of her depth.

"Molly?"

She started. "Sorry. I guess I'm nervous."

"Perfectly understandable. You want to tell me a little bit about what brought you in today?"

She didn't. She'd given the woman on the phone her entire medical history while making the appointment. She didn't want to say it out loud. The more she said it the scarier it became.

Her mouth felt small, like her tongue had doubled in size, and an acrid taste tickled the back of her throat. Was she going to puke? She pressed on her stomach in a bid to make it sit the hell down and stop messing around. "I found a lump, right here." She pointed to the side of her left breast, close to her armpit.

Dr. Klein made a note. "How long ago was this?"

"Three days."

Dr. K made another note. "Do you do self-exams often? When was your last one? Did you feel anything unusual then?"

Molly sat with the questions for a moment before answering. Dr. Klein had a full skeleton in the corner of the room. Molly would call him Bones. She wondered if Dr. K would leave her alone for long enough to take a selfie with her new BFF.

"My dad's mom died of breast cancer, so my mom has been hyper vigilant about checking herself – and getting me to check myself for years. Just in case."

The older man with salt and pepper hair around his temples nodded, his glasses slipping down his long nose. And despite having her extensive medical history on the forms in front of him, he wrote something else down.

"I check myself every month. I haven't found anything until a few days ago. It's not huge by any means, but it was still there the next day, and the next."

"And today?"

She nodded. That's why she was there. Dr. K pursed his lips and the lines on his forehead deepened. He examined her, making the almost required and universally expected doctor noises of "hmmm" a couple of times. He scribbled more notes – probably his grocery list since there was only really so much a person could write about another person's boob. Though it was her left one – her favorite – so it was pretty special.

She was being unkind, he was a good doctor, who was just being thorough taking notes. But the more he wrote, the more she fixated on the unknown, and the more tension crept into her already stiff muscles.

The physical exam didn't hurt, but it still irked her. The more he pressed against her flesh the more acrimonious she grew toward her own body. She took care of it. She ran three times a week, drank water – okay, fine, ice cubes melting in her drinks didn't exactly count as water, but she *always* got lettuce on her tacos. That had to count for something, right?

He'd asked her something, hadn't he? He stared at her with warm eyes, waiting for her to answer a question she hadn't heard. This was it, this was when he'd tell her to lose a few pounds, cut back on drinking, and eat fewer tacos and more kale. It was what every doctor did, right? The professional answer to most problems was shifting some weight and eating healthier.

She shuddered. Over her dead body. Life was too short to deprive yourself of all the fun things it had to offer.

"I want to send you for some tests. We'll draw some blood and start with a mammogram, then an ultrasound of your breasts to see what's what. Then we'll do a biopsy and figure out where to go from there. Do you have any questions?"

Am I going to die?

She shook her head.

"I know it's easier said than done, but try not to panic

until we have more information. There's every chance it might not be something sinister."

But there's also every chance it is.

Molly had just gotten back to campus after her trip to the doctors. She pulled up outside her apartment and stared out the windshield, her hands still on the steering wheel. Dr. Klein had said don't panic, but that was easier to say than to wrangle the warring feelings coursing through her veins. Maybe if she gave the lump a pithy nickname she'd feel less intimidated by it.

A knock on the window startled her and she clutched her chest. Finn gave a small wave before opening the driver door of her car letting all the toasty warm air out into the bitter cold. "Spill."

"Spill what?" She didn't meet his gaze because she already knew he didn't buy it. If he looked into her eyes he'd be like a dog with a bone until she told him what was bothering her. He somehow always saw things in her that no one else seemed to. And when he did, he didn't let up until she caved and told him what was up.

He crouched down next to her. "Don't bullshit me. It's too cold for your stubbornness. Either I'm coming inside for a sandwich, we're going to the Sugar Bean, or I'm getting in the passenger seat and not moving until I get answers, but I *will* find out what's going on with you."

She sucked in a shaky breath and got out of the car, slamming the door too hard behind her. With a wince, she locked the car and followed Finn up to her apartment in silence. "Cleo? You home?"

Silence greeted her question and her shoulders loosened. They had a lot to talk about, and talking to Finn was going to be difficult enough without having to worry about whatever Cleo overheard. Not to mention, Molly didn't want to talk about her own problems, especially when he had his own shit to deal with.

It would be easier for her to talk to him about his mom... Molly's stomach churned. A cowardly move indeed considering Finn was already going through so much. Would bringing up his mom be the thing to push him over whatever breaking point he was edging closer to?

They couldn't both avoid their problems. She gestured for him to sit at the table. She grabbed a bowl of pasta salad from the fridge, two forks, and two cans of Fresca. Her stomach lurched at the smell of the pasta, but she had to at least pretend to eat something.

"What's going on, Molly?"

Had she ever seen him so concerned? His usually bright eyes were heavy, his eyebrows were drawn together, and the muscles in his jaw rippled as he clenched his teeth and flexed his jaw. Her heart squeezed. He was worried about her.

Despite the fact he was her brother's best friend, he'd always made a point of letting her know he was there for her, too, no matter what. She didn't often take him up on his offer, but whatever he'd seen on her face at the rink that morning was bothering him, and that made her whole body warm.

She swallowed twice, but whatever coated her throat making it hard to get words out wouldn't budge. "I'm scared to talk to you about it."

"And you're scaring me by not talking about it. What is it? Whatever it is, we'll figure it out. You know I've got your back, Will too."

Her ovaries squeezed. She'd never be able to settle down with a man. Her daddy, Will, and Finn, had ruined all other men for her. They were all the things Cleo's book boyfriends were made of. Molly couldn't have Finn, but she wouldn't ever settle for less than Finn either.

"It's not me." It was, but she wasn't going to tell him that. At least not yet. She couldn't bring herself to say it aloud. Being confronted with her mortality in the doctor's office was one thing, speaking it out loud, sharing it with someone who cared for you... she wasn't there yet.

His nostrils flared. "Who? Mom?"

Her breath caught like the thorn of a rose stem pricked her lungs. "Kind of. Your birth mom, not your bonus mom."

She let him sit with the information for a moment in silence. His hand clenched on his thigh and he cast his eyes toward the ground. After a few audibly deep breaths, his chest and shoulders heaving with visible effort, he nodded. "What about her?"

"She called to see Mom." Her fingers were cold, her hands shook harder than when she was in the doctor's office.

His handsome face hardened. "What did she want? And why didn't Mom tell me?"

Molly's hand twitched. The urge to reach out and squeeze his hand was almost too overwhelming to think of anything else. But if she touched him, if she allowed herself to slide her hand over his, if she took a step over that line, she wasn't sure she'd ever have the strength to drag herself back.

She caught a droplet of condensation from the side of the can and wiped it along the aluminum. "Mom texted me this morning at the rink. She said your mom came to visit, she wanted your cell number so she could call you to talk. Mom said she didn't give your mom your number, she took hers instead, but she wasn't sure how you'd react or if you'd even want to know. She was asking what I thought and I told her I'd talk to you."

She twisted her hands in her lap. "I dunno. I guess I

figured it would land better coming from me... Stupid..." She barely whispered the last word, but he heard her.

"Not stupid. Kind. I appreciate it."

Her heart stuttered along in her chest as she scanned his face for any sign of reaction. "I feel like I need to remind you that she doesn't have the right to come back into your life if you don't want her to. You wouldn't be a terrible person if you wanted to maintain your distance and boundaries. She might have made the first move, but if you're not ready to talk to her, you don't have to. Even if you're never ready to talk to her. You need to protect yourself and your own mental health."

He nodded, but stayed silent.

"And you don't have to talk to me, either." She gave a small smile.

"I know I don't." He heaved out a long sigh. "I don't mind talking to you."

She snorted. "High praise, Sparky."

His mouth twitched but she still wasn't rewarded with a smile. "I..." He raked his hands through his auburn hair and when he met her stare again, his cornflower blue eyes shone. "I don't know if I can see her after all this time." His voice was thick.

"Then you don't have to."

Seeing him so broken, so fragile, unlocked the box of anger in her chest. She hated his parents for doing this to him. She understood that they'd lost a child, but that didn't mean they could abandon their surviving son to fend for himself. Did his mother know that his dad beat him? Did she turn a blind eye? Waves crashed in her stomach like a raging storm against the side of a jagged cliff.

"And if I want to?"

She ached to reach out and wrap her arms around him, to protect him from any more pain. But she couldn't. "If you want to..." She paused, digging her fingernails into her thighs so she wouldn't touch him. "I'll go with you." Her breathing quickened. "Or Will. If you'd rather he go with you, I know he would. As much as you both have my back, we have yours, too. You know that."

Finn nodded. "You'd really come to see her with me?"

"Or sit with you while you call her. Of course I would. You're family, Finny. We love you."

I love you.

"And if I fall apart?"

"I'll always patch you up." Her voice broke as her back-stabbing heart flexed in her chest. She'd walk through fire for the man sitting in front of her and he had no idea.

He gave a watery smile and sniffed. "I'm going to think on it. I don't want to make a snap decision."

She nodded, staring at the untouched pasta and soda cans sitting between them on the table. He would call her, she knew it. He wasn't the kind of guy to abandon people when they needed him – and his mom might need him. And if she broke him again, Molly would be there to pick up the pieces, even if it ripped her up inside.

"What else?"

"What do you mean, what else?"

"That's not all that's bugging you, MoMo."

She folded her arms. How did he always know? "What makes you think that?"

"I've known you for a long time, Mol. Just give it up, it'll be easier for both of us that way."

She watched his face for a long moment. He arched his brow and leaned back in his seat, his muscles relaxing. He'd taken his own drama, tucked it away, and was ready to help her deal with whatever she was facing. That was just who he was. Reliable, dependable, and Will's freakin' best friend.

She sighed. "It's probably nothing."

He pointed at her. "But it might be something?"

She nodded, gripping her lip between her teeth, blinking back the dumb tears burning at her eyelids. He scooted forward, dragging his chair across the kitchen tiles with a screech and picked up her hand.

Her heart stopped. All the air in the room disappeared and the only thing keeping her alive was the warmth radiating through her skin from his. He was touching her. Finn O'Brien was holding her hand between his.

His Adam's apple bobbed. Did he feel it too? Surely holding her hand wasn't affecting him the same way.

"Molly? What's going on?"

She heaved another sigh, urging the dirty thoughts tugging at the edges of her mind to shut up. She needed to just come out and say it, to let it hang in the air between them, to voice it out loud to someone who cared about her. He'd give her the sad, sympathetic eyes, he'd smother her with compassion, but at least it would be out there. It would no longer be a heavy secret vibrating in her chest. A problem shared, and all that.

"I found a lump in my breast."

He didn't answer right away, but he dragged his thumbs along the back of her hand. "Have they taken a look yet?"

She didn't want to look at him. Once the words left her mouth, she wasn't sure she could handle the sadness she'd find in his eyes. "Not yet. I have scans in a few days. They took blood. He said I'll probably need a biopsy..." That was all the information she had. It wasn't enough.

"Does anyone else know?"

She shook her head. Finn sat quietly, but his hands never left hers. She couldn't tear her eyes away from where their bodies connected. Sparks licked up her arm. She'd felt pleasure before. She'd had a lot of sex, a lot of orgasms, but she'd never felt such inner warmth from human contact. It somehow seemed even more intimate than sex.

When she finally met his gaze, she didn't find a trace of sympathy in his eyes, only resolve. "I'm coming with you."

"Where?"

"To your appointments."

An almost hysterical laugh bubbled up inside her. "You don't have to do that."

"And you don't have to sit with me when I talk to my birth mom. You didn't have to sit with me any number of times when Dad..." His voice cracked. "You said it yourself, MoMo, we're family, it's what we do. I'm not letting you face this alone."

CHAPTER 8

Finnegan

She'd found a lump. While Finn had hoped she'd seen strength and determination when she'd finally lifted her head, inside he was a fucking mess. They'd argued for twenty minutes about telling the family. In the end, she'd relented and said she would tell them after the biopsy results.

He'd eventually peeled his hands from hers and left. On his way out, on impulse he sent his mother, Meabh, a message asking if she wanted to meet for a coffee before he changed his mind, then hit the streets. He'd gotten her cell number from Mrs. Mo, and after he'd sent the text, he ran like he was being chased until his legs and lungs burned and sweat streamed down his face. Molly had found a lump. He was meeting his birth mom – Meabh – for the first time in years. His chest tightened, squeezing the air from his lungs, and he doubled over trying to catch his breath.

By the time he got back to the hockey house, his mind raced and he had three messages waiting for him. Meabh could meet him for coffee later that afternoon – he wanted to get it over and done with before he could talk himself out of it again. A quick shower and some stretching later, he messaged Molly.

> Finn: Whatcha doin'?

> Molly: I don't need a babysitter you know. I found a lump, I'm not dying.

> Finn: Down, girl. I was just asking. Meeting bio mom in 90 if you're around.

> Molly: Well, now I feel like an asshole.

> Finn: Good. You should. I'm over here crying into my protein shake.

> Finn: Have you named it yet?

> Molly: My lump? I'm thinking Gizmo.

> Finn: Like the Gremlin? Here for it.

> Molly: Sugar Bean in 90?

His muscles unclenched. Having Molly there would help. Even if she sat a few tables away, her presence would still be reassuring, a reminder that he didn't *need* to let Meabh back into his life if he wasn't feeling it. He'd at least hear her out. Then he'd make a decision.

Ninety minutes later, Finn held the door to the Sugar Bean open for Molly and followed her into the coffee shop. Meabh sat at a table in the corner, gnawing on her thumbnail. Finn froze. She looked good, better. Rosy cheeks, bright eyes, and shiny, combed hair. The last time he'd seen her, she'd been in a medication haze, her eyes were cloudy and her hair matted to her head.

She didn't seem to have noticed him yet. A cool hand slid into his and gave a squeeze. Molly. She'd just been told she needed to have medical testing for an ominous lump in her breast and there she was, being strong and stoic for him. She was fearless. She squeezed again and he turned to face her. "I'll be right over there, okay?"

He nodded, afraid if he opened his mouth he might cry at her. He clutched her hand for just a beat more before letting her go and making his way through the tables to the woman with red-rimmed eyes waiting for him. When she spied him, she stood, smoothing out her dress pants and blouse as she did.

"Finnegan." Her quivery voice was barely a whisper, her lip trembled, and she wrung her hands. They twitched, as though she wanted to reach out and touch him.

"Hi. Can I get you a coffee?" His voice sounded like it belonged to someone else.

She cast a wary glance at Molly a few tables away before nodding.

"MoMo, you want a coffee?" Finn raised his voice to be heard over the din, drawing a few strange looks and wary glances from people at other tables, but he didn't care. He was low on spoons and patience.

"Do bears shit in the woods?" Her arched eyebrow made him chuckle, easing the tension holding his muscles hostage. He ordered, waited, and carried the coffees to their owners before taking the seat facing his mom.

"Long time." He ran a finger around the lip of the mug. Understatement of the year, but if he didn't break the awkwardness, or fill the silence somehow, he would scream at the top of his voice, and he wasn't sure he'd be able to stop.

She didn't look up from her drink. "I'm sorry it's taken so

long. I really am. I needed to get better, to work on myself. Then I figured you needed space, and space stretched into years. I thought if you wanted to talk you'd reach out, and the silence grew louder and it was easier to just—"

"Make a new family with someone else and forget the old one?"

She recoiled as if he'd thrown acid over her. "I know we have a lot of ground to cover and things to talk about, but I am sorry. You look so much like your brother it was just so hard, Finnegan. I don't mean to in any way blame you, or put any responsibility on you. You were just a child and you needed your parents. This is completely on me, and I know that. I know you might never forgive me. I'd deserve it. I know that too. I just... I had to try."

He sipped his drink, his nerves thrumming like a fallen electrical cable bouncing on a road, sending sparks throughout his body. "Did you know he hit me?" He forced himself to watch her face, to study her for any reaction to his words.

Her cheek muscles twitched and she lowered her stare. She knew. "Not at first." She glanced again at Molly over his shoulder. He'd deliberately sat with his back to her so he couldn't see her. Strength radiated from her in waves, but he couldn't handle looking at her while he talked to Meabh.

"She cares about you a great deal, doesn't she?"

He nodded. She didn't deserve details of his personal life, not yet, maybe not ever.

"Her mom came to see me in the hospital a few years back. She told me about your fath—him."

It took everything he had to focus on his breathing and keep his limbs steady. He wanted nothing more than to punch the wall next to him, but he loved the Sugar Bean and didn't want to get banned for life because of the asshole who whipped him with a belt. He'd stolen enough of Finn's enjoyment.

He hadn't known Mrs. Mo had gone to see her at the facility, but he hoped his face didn't betray his ignorance.

"She told me he hurt you while I was gone." Her voice broke, and tears trickled down her face. "I know it's not an excuse, but I was drowning. I needed help and I didn't know how to help anyone else when I was under water myself. I had no concept of just how broken I was until I got treatment."

His breath caught. "I was just a child."

"I know. I'm so sorry, Finnegan." She picked up his hand in hers and stroked it with her thumb. "I know you're angry, and you have every right to be."

He wouldn't last much longer before breaking down. His skin burned from where his father had taken out his anger and grief on him. His chest ached. His head throbbed. His mind swam with memories and flashbacks.

"What do you want from me?"

"I'm not naïve enough to think I can just walk back into your life and it will fix everything."

"Then, what? What do you need?"

"I want us to catch up, to talk about your life, to get to know who you are now. I want to try to mend what I broke, Finn."

"Bullshit." The simmering in his chest threatened to boil over. "Why now? Why right this minute?"

Her shoulders sagged and her eyes dropped to the mug on the table in front of her. "Your brother is sick."

His stomach lurched. "My brother is dead."

She winced again and shook her head. "Your half-brother."

A bitter laugh escaped him before he could stop it. "You show up after years of not talking to me, to ask for my help for a kid I've never met? Wow." He raked his hands through his hair. "That's... something."

"No, Finnegan." Her face softened. "That's not it. If

you don't want to help Noah, that's fine. It's your choice and I won't hold it against you. He needs a kidney transplant and the doctor said there's a higher chance of finding a match if we ask family to get tested. But I still wanted to talk to you, to ask if you would consider letting me back in your life in any way." She dropped her shoulders. "I miss you Finnegan."

He didn't reply. His muscles ached from holding themselves poised. Would he want to help a brother he'd never met, from a family she abandoned him for? His replacement.

She cleared her throat. "I... I'm going to go... give you time to think it over. You have my number and I'd love nothing more than to hear from you again. Truly. I know showing up here doesn't do anything to fix the past, but I'm hoping over time we could maybe move forward together."

She stood, leaving her untouched coffee, and hesitated. He didn't stop her. She'd shown up, asked for a favor, and told him what she thought he needed to hear. He wasn't going to ease her guilty conscience.

She took two steps toward the door before laying her hand on his shoulder and patting twice. "I have no expectations, Finnegan. Just hope. We've both been through enough pain to last us a lifetime, and while I don't want to forget about what happened, I'd rather not lose another son if I can help it. I'm ready to try to rebuild our relationship, and I hope someday you will be too. Let me know."

He didn't turn around to watch her walk away, and he still didn't stop her. He wasn't sure how long he sat staring at the wall before Molly slipped onto the chair where his mom had been sitting. She didn't say anything, she simply picked up his hand and cradled it in hers. Her eyes burned into his face but he couldn't bring himself to lift his head to meet her piercing stare.

After a couple of minutes, Molly brushed her hand over

his damp cheeks and stood, not letting go of his hand. "Let's get you out of here."

He nodded and followed her out of the café. They didn't speak again until they were back at Molly's apartment. She guided him to the armchair in the living room and waited for him to sit before crouching down to his level. She plopped onto the floor at his feet and crossed her legs before picking up both his hands and holding them on his knees.

Her touch was comforting… warm… safe, the only thing penetrating the tingling numbness spreading from his heart into his chest and the assault on his mind by his childhood memories. Tears plopped from his face onto their joined hands. He still couldn't look at her. She sat in silence for a minute before standing, sitting next to him, and pulling his head onto her shoulder.

He should have been stronger, he shouldn't have needed her consolation, and he certainly shouldn't have allowed himself to touch her. Once he'd held her hand – had that first taste of how soft her skin felt in his palms – he'd wanted more. With his head on her shoulder the embers in his chest burned brighter.

She smelled like the beach, wild and free, strong waves crashing against the sand, and with just a hint of oranges and vanilla. He shuffled his face closer to her neck so it could envelop him entirely.

He could get lost in her and for just a moment forget about his dead brother, his half-brother, transplants, his manic depressive mother, and his abusive alcoholic father. She was his lighthouse in a raging sea, his rock, the north point on a compass when he was lost in an unknown land – and she had no idea how much she really meant to him.

Her strength was a force of nature, her soul was pure, and she had the heart of a lion. Her delicate fingers stroked his hair as she held him, gliding along the curve of his head and down his neck. When another wave of tears hit, she shushed him like she had so many times over the years. "I've got you."

And she did. She owned him body and soul, and she was clueless that all she had to do was ask, and he'd walk through the fires of hell for her.

He loved Will, with everything he had, but Will didn't feel emotion the same way he did, Will didn't understand the extent of the trauma he had been through, and Will wasn't always the best at providing comfort.

The more Finn cried, the tighter Molly held him against her. "It's okay," she whispered. "Everything's going to be okay."

He could have sworn her lips brushed against his head more than once which only drove his heart to hammer harder. He drew back enough to look up at her face. Her profile was striking. High cheekbones, pale skin, perfectly shaped eyebrows over green eyes with tiny flecks of gray around her pupils.

When she met his gaze, his breath caught. What did she see when she looked at him?

"You gonna make it?"

He nodded. "We've had a lot of feely things in the past twenty-four hours. You must need an exorcism."

A laugh shook her body under the side of his face. "Feelings aren't my favorite. But I'd never let you suffer alone, Finny. You know that."

Her lips taunted him, called to him, a few inches were all that separated him from kissing her until she was breathless.

Her warm breath tickled his face. Closing his eyes, he forced himself to breathe. He lifted his head from her shoulder and moved his lips toward hers. When she didn't move, his eyes fluttered open, and he dared to inch closer still. Her breath hitched. Her pulse hammered at the base of her neck and her cheeks grew red.

Their eyes locked, and the slight knot pulling her brows together gave him pause. She reached out and trailed her fingers along his jaw sending a shiver down his spine.

The Imperial March from *Star Wars* boomed from his back pocket in the otherwise silent room. Will's ringtone. Will. Her brother. His best friend. The one person who had brought them together was also what kept them apart.

The heat in her eyes only a split second before, had been replaced by sadness. Neither of them moved. Will had broken the spell between them and reality crashed into the room on Darth Vader's coat tails.

"I should go."

Her nod was slight, but she didn't speak. Her teeth held her blood red lip pinched tight. Her eyes swam with emotions he couldn't decipher. And Will wasn't relenting. The phone vibrated and rang and rang in his pocket. Did she want to kiss him too? Would their near miss make things awkward between them?

Or worse, would she think he was only intent on kissing her because his mother appeared back in his life and upended his insides? While he had wanted to kiss her from the moment they met, he didn't want her to think it was simply a moment of emotional weakness that drove him toward her lips.

He peeled himself off the couch and stood. "Thank you." It didn't feel like enough but it was all he had.

"Always." How could she make one word sound so powerful, so packed full of emotion, of meaning?

He backed away from her before he did something stupid, like grab her and kiss her until neither of them could think rational thoughts and all there was, was each other.

On his way back to the house he emailed his therapist. It had been almost a year since he'd seen Dr. Hermannsen. Finn had missed an appointment because he was sick and never got around to making another one. But with his mom back in his life and two near misses with one Miss Molly Morrison, things were escalating, and he needed an adultier adult in his life to help him adult.

His email said he'd like to chat, and asked Dr. Hermannsen's secretary to give him a few options for available appointments. He'd never admit it out loud, but Finn was in way over his head. He needed help.

CHAPTER 9

Finnegan

(TWO YEARS EARLIER)

Finn's throat closed over as Molly Morrison paraded past him toward the closet with Johnny-fucking-White. The closet. At the first frat party of the year. Molly Morrison. In college. Finn's brain short circuited.

Wait. Johnny White?

That asshole wasn't getting seven seconds of heaven with Finn's Molly, let alone seven minutes. Clenching and unclenching his fists he gritted his teeth. What the hell was she playing at? Correction – what the hell was *he* playing at? He'd been given the same briefing the rest of the team had received. Don't touch Molly Morrison. Or Will would lose his shit.

JW sidled up to Molly, slipped his hand down the curve of her ass, and squeezed. Lava sloshed in Finn's gut as Molly pulled open the closet and ducked inside tossing a coy smile over her shoulder. Johnny was right behind her, but Finn intercepted, grabbing him by the shoulder, he jerked him back, and shoved him at Russell who stood a few feet away.

"Can you remind him of the rules regarding Will's sister please?" He jerked a head to the closet. "I'll remind Mini Mo."

Russell's jaw twitched, his eyes dark, and he nodded.

When Finn stepped into the dark closet, Molly fisted his shirt and yanked him toward her. Their noses were touching. He could smell her berry lip balm and her breath sent goosebumps scurrying across his skin.

She dragged her thumb across his bottom lip, down to his chin and held his jaw between her thumb and forefinger. He'd wanted her for so long. No one would know he wasn't reading her the riot act for being stupid with Johnny. Maybe it was time to give into the push-pull they'd been fighting since the moment they met and kiss the woman at long last.

He stepped toward her. She stepped back. Another step and she'd be flush against the wall. He closed the distance, she bumped against the wall and caressed his jaw once more. Her knuckle found the scar under his chin and she tensed, switching out her digit for the pad of her thumb. Running along the scar once, twice, a third time, his name escaped her on a gasp.

He nodded, but didn't trust himself to speak. He lowered his face to hers, she tilted her head back, sliding her hand around his neck. His chest heaved, and his heart pounded so loudly he was convinced it was telegraphing his location to Will in the other room.

Just as her lips brushed against his, something smashed outside the door. He jumped back, smacking his head on something sharp and burst out of the closet on a string of profanity. He didn't have time to address the throbbing in his skull.

Outside the closet, a clump of people were squeezed around the door to the hallway outside. Sounds of a scuffle were almost drowned out by the cheering of the crowd. Fuck. He pushed his way through the sweaty, intoxicated group. In the hall outside, to his right, Johnny White clutched his mouth, drops of blood oozing from between his fingers and a bruise already darkening under his eye.

To his left, Will jabbed his finger around Linc's frame –
who was body blocking Will from getting anywhere near JW.
What the hell?

"You knew the fucking rules, Johnny. No one goes near
her."

Johnny grinned, blood smearing across his teeth. "She's a
fucking grown-ass woman, Mo."

"And she can do whomever the hell she wants to – as long
as he's not a brother on my own goddamn team."

JW shrugged. The fucker really shrugged, raising an
eyebrow as he did. "I didn't agree to any such patriarchal bullshit, Mo. If she wants to ride me like I'm a fucking bull at the
rodeo..." He shrugged again. "Who the fuck am I to stop her?"

Will surged forward, crashing into a wall of solid Linc.
"Hey, hey. Easy, Will. Don't let him wind you up." Linc
braced both hands against Will's chest, pushing him back.
Russell and Jeremy Lewis – from Alabama – had each grabbed
one of Will's arms. What the hell was Jeremy doing at a
Minnesota frat party?

Finn didn't have time to ask. Will had a cut over his eye
dripping onto the white carpet underfoot and bruising
spreading from his jaw into his cheek. Jeremy was exactly
where Finn should have been, not trying to mack on Molly in
a dark closet, but having Will's back against an asshole. Guilt
smacked into him like a tsunami.

Yet another brother he wasn't there for when he was
needed. It should have been Finn's face split open by Johnny's
fist, not Will's.

Speaking of, JW examined his fingernails and smirked.
"Anyone would think you want your sister's pussy for yourself,
Mo."

Gasps, quiet rumbles of 'ooooh', hissing, and 'oh my
God's rippled around the spectators. Will renewed his effort to
surge forward from Russ and Jeremy's grasp as Finn launched

himself at Johnny, raining his fists down onto his face. Who the fuck said that shit?

Strong arms banded across his chest and dragged him off Johnny's body. He was still awake, and somehow he was still grinning. He'd lost a tooth in the melee – Finn didn't know if it was a real one or a fake and he didn't care, the asshole deserved what he got.

Whoever had him by the shoulders lost their footing and hit the deck, ass first with a thud, but they didn't let go. In fact, they scooted closer to Finn's ass and wrapped their legs around his waist. "Don't be stupid." Linc growled in his ear. "He's not worth getting a record for, Obi."

Fuck Johnny White, and fuck Lincoln 'Captain America' Scott too. Who the hell did he think he was? Swooping in and getting involved in something that was clearly between Will and Finn and Johnny.

Finn beat Linc's arms like some kind of deranged caveman. "Let me go."

"Sorry, brother. I'm not letting you get your ass thrown in jail because of that waste of space. We need you."

Movement in the corner of his eye tore his glaring, rage-twisted face away from Johnny White. Molly stood leaning against a doorframe, hugging her body, eyes shining in the light. She kept glancing between Finn and Will, not sparing a single look in Johnny's direction. There was no trace of fear on her face, only heat. Finn's stomach fluttered. She hadn't resisted him after she'd discovered his identity in the closet. In fact, she'd leaned into him, tilted her head back, and sighed when he'd brushed his lips against hers.

Was she drunk? Teasing him? Punishing him for switching out with Johnny? Or was there something more?

The fluttering in his stomach bolted to his chest. She dragged her thumb across her bottom lip and hot damn he could have sworn he felt a tingling on his own lip as well.

Not breaking their connection, he tapped on Linc's arm to let him know he'd calmed down, at least outwardly. Something had shifted between him and Molly Morrison in that closet, something profound, something dangerous, something exciting. While he'd always been attracted to her, he'd never once let himself think or believe she might return the attraction.

Until now.

The corners of her mouth twitched like she could read his mind and he fought to keep a smile from breaking out on his face.

"I'm going to fucking kill him!"

Will. Right. He needed to get his ass off the ground, stop thinking about the girl, and help keep his best friend out of prison for murder.

Linc sprung to his feet and tackled Will onto his back, the two men landing in a heap. Will huffed out a gasp of air before he burst into a fit of laughter. "Shit, Linc." He sat up, rubbing the back of his head. "If it doesn't work out for you in the NHL, I think the Vikings might have something for you."

Linc stood, reaching a hand out to help Will off the ground. His red haze had seemingly cleared. Finn risked a glance at Molly, but she wasn't leaning against the doorframe anymore. A quick scan of the lingering mass revealed she was gone.

He turned back to Will, but he wasn't there anymore either. The knife twisted in Finn's stomach. Will was his ride or die. It didn't matter that his younger sister might have wanted to make out with Finn in the closet. What mattered was the unbreakable bond between the two men. Nothing could come between them.

Nothing.

Not even his love for his best friend's sister.

He couldn't put himself in a position where he might

need to choose. He needed to lock up his feels for Molly, file the near miss under "small mercies." He needed to go back to being the best friend Will needed him to be, the man Will deserved to have watching his six, the man who was head over heels in love with his best friend's sister.

CHAPTER 10

Molly

"Come on, ChoChooooooooo."

Cleo snorted. "You sound like a whiny train."

Molly hurled a throw cushion from the couch at Cleo's head as she dangled her legs over the arm of the recliner. "If you did what I wanted I wouldn't need to whine."

"I don't feel like going out partying tonight. You can go, I won't stop you."

Molly didn't want to go out partying, but the weight of the past few days was bringing her down. She needed to do *something*. "You're such a drag now that you're all lovey dovey with Luscious Lincoln."

Cleo groaned. "Ew."

"Okay, fine. What about a quiet dinner? A compromise. We can go to that new Italian place you like and feed our feelings pasta and parmesan."

Cleo hugged the pillow against her chest. "You know I'm a sucker for alliteration. So. Hot. But I have a counter offer."

"I'm listening."

"The Rusty Taco."

"Don't tease me with a good time, Cleo Martinez, that's just plain mean."

Cleo laughed and stood up. "I'll get my coat."

Few things got Molly's blood pumping more than delicious tacos, great drinks, and a casual atmosphere with her favorite people. The Rusty Taco covered all bases – oversized mango-ritas that were never watered down, framed pictures of patrons' pets lining one wall, while old license plates covered another, and reasonably priced tacos that had her mouth watering.

But when she stepped inside and practically walked straight into the broad shoulders of Finn-freakin'-O'Brien on a goddamn date with the most beautiful woman Molly had ever seen, her stomach soured.

She hadn't seen him in the three days since she'd almost stuck her tongue down his throat. Her body heated at the memory. She'd almost taken advantage of him when he was vulnerable and exposed, and she hated herself for it.

She didn't want him to kiss her because he felt sad. She wanted him to kiss her because every cell in his body drove him to cover her mouth with his, because he couldn't breathe, or live another second if he didn't.

"Oh, hey, there's Finn. Who's that he's with?" Cleo's face fell as she reached the same realization Molly had. "It's a date, isn't it? Shit, Mol. You wanna go get Italian instead?"

In truth, the idea of any food made her queasy, but she nodded, taking a step back toward the door. She was met by a hard body.

"Oof."

"Fuck. Shit. Sorry." She spun to face the guy she'd bumped into and back to Finn to make sure he hadn't heard the kerfuffle. He stared straight at her. She threw him a cursory wave. It was fine. Totally fine. So he was on a date in the same place she was having dinner with Cleo. What could possibly go wrong?

If the night was a meme, it would have been the dog sitting at a table, surrounded by flames, with wide eyes saying. "This is fine." Except *she* was the dog and she wasn't surrounded by fire, she was all-the-way *on* fire. And she certainly wasn't fucking fine.

Her pulsing clit warned her to leave, to run fast and far, not to stay in the same building as him for a moment longer than she needed to. But he'd seen her, he knew she hadn't eaten and if she ran, he'd know that, too. She was trapped watching him on his date with the tall, beautiful curvy model standing six feet away. Fuck it all to hell.

Her pulse quickened as she glanced between Finn and the gorgeous woman. Threesome. Visions of Finn fucking her while she ate out his date spread heat across her whole body.

Finn wore a black button-down dress shirt tucked into a pair of black dress pants. And not that she was looking, but if she had been, his ass was delightful in those pants. She wanted to take a bite out of that perfect hockey butt. He was sinfully handsome. His unruly hair was styled and he smelled delicious. His pheromones had a direct line to her pussy and were stuck on redial. He nodded a greeting at her before guiding his date to a table.

"Molly?"

"Hm?" Molly tore her gaze from Finn's date's perfect ass. "Yeah?"

"I asked if you wanted the usual."

The guy she'd bumped into behind her sighed. "Hurry up, already."

Dang, dude. Don't be an asshole. Her inclination was to take even longer, but she didn't want to make any more of a scene. Or get sent to prison for a smackdown with some impatient jerk she'd accidentally body checked while in line for tacos. She could totally take him. With a nod at Cleo, she ventured into the busy restaurant to find seats. The only available table was – of course – the one a few feet away from Finnegan and the Future Mrs. Finnegan Aiden O'Brien.

She pulled her phone from her pocket and scrolled TikTok with the volume low as she waited for Cleo. In her periphery, Mrs. O'Brien-to-be plucked the tortilla out from under her tacos and picked at the filling with dainty fingers. Finn's frown made Molly hide her snicker behind her hand.

His wide-eyes met Molly's and he scrunched his face up. Strike one – eating like a bird. Finn O'Brien *loved* his food. He could never settle down with someone who didn't eat every meal like it was their last one on earth.

Why hadn't she ordered something else? Like a salad. Or suggested another restaurant? Who the hell got tacos but didn't eat the glue that held it all together? Was she some kind of sociopath?

Strike two – she smacked her food and talked with her mouth open. Molly couldn't help but laugh, forcing it into a cough when Finn gave her the look – the one that said "if you crack up, I'll crack up, so don't crack up." The date set up must have been her brother's doing. His heart was in the right place, but his success rate for setting up his friends was less than great.

Cleo returned to the table, tray of tacos in hand. Molly made a deliberate show of taking a huge bite from her bbq beef brisket and making audible yummy noises. Finn rolled his eyes.

Cleo canted her head. "Why are we overdramatizing our meal?" She leaned forward and hissed out a whisper.

Molly smirked. "I'll tell you later." She took another bite. The date had two tacos on her plate, Molly had four, though since the nausea at seeing Finn with another woman had passed, she could have made a good faith effort on six. Maybe she'd get some to take home.

She finished her first brisket taco and moved on to the roasted pork. Another groan. This time it wasn't fake though. Some days she wondered if she could be brought to orgasm just from really mind-blowing tacos.

Cleo chewed in silence, her eyes narrowed as though she was evaluating the situation. Molly opened her mouth to speak, but snapped it shut when The Date started talking.

"Do you know her? You keep staring."

Molly fought a smile and willed her cheeks not to go pink. She'd have to deal with the fact she loved the idea of him staring at her, later.

"She's my best friend's sister."

Her eye twitched. She was Will's sister. But she'd hoped she'd become a friend in her own right. They'd been through a lot together. Cleo's eyes widened, but Molly shook her head. Cleo had already finished her three tacos, and Molly was beyond done witnessing the date from hell. "I'm going to take the rest of these to go."

Cleo nodded, a grim-set line in place of her usual bright smile. As Molly pushed back from the table, The Date continued. "So why are you staring at her so much? Do you have a thing for her? Is that what it is? Why are you on a date with me if you like her?"

Strike three for The Date – Finn O'Brien *hated* jealous girlfriends. He was too easy going and laid back, and at least until recently he enjoyed the company of too many people – sometimes at the same time – for a jealous partner to work for him. Too bad, so sad, she'd never be Mrs. Finnegan Aiden O'Brien. Though if Finn kept referring to Molly as Will's sister neither would she.

Molly had attributed his recent dry spell in the revolving

door of Finn O'Brien's booty calls to his stress levels being above average, to keeping his head in the game and not wanting distractions. But what if it was more? What if he'd been secretly dating the blonde committing crimes against tacos? What if it was serious?

Molly's face burned as she carried her plate of tacos to the counter and asked the server to put them into a box and to make her three more. She hadn't heard what Finn's answer had been, but Cleo was a good best friend, she'd be taking notes.

Molly paid the check and beckoned Cleo who – by all appearances was casually scrolling her phone. Molly knew better. Cleo's face had *eavesdropping* written all over it.

"Let's go." Molly picked up the bag from the counter and turned to the door without a glance back at *her brother's best friend*. Sigh. Would it kill him to acknowledge she was more than Will's sister?

Let it go, Molly. Bless and release. "We're going to Target." She stepped into the darkness with a shudder.

"What do we need in Target?"

Molly snorted like Cleo was new and had never before experienced the Target Phenomenon. "It doesn't matter, no matter what we need it won't be what we come out with."

Cleo laughed. "True story. No more ceramic animals though, we're running out of space."

"There's always room for ceramic animals."

With a shake of her head, Cleo walked toward the car. "We're walking. It's just across the parking lot. That way, if we can't carry it back to the car, we won't buy it."

Molly loved her bestie's optimism. Clearly history had taught her nothing. She balanced along the curb as they walked across the parking lot. Every few steps, her balance wavered and her foot brushed against the grassy bank next to the concrete, the wet blades of grass tickled her ankle and sent shivers through her cold legs.

"Molly? Have you fallen in love with him?"

"I'd rather fall down the stairs." She grinned. Deflecting with funnies was an easy way to ignore the pangs in her chest. She was ass-over-tits in love with him, but she couldn't say the words out loud. Molly Morrison didn't do love. She did no strings, fun, do 'em and ditch 'em.

Her foot slipped off the edge of the concrete and she fell with a shriek they probably heard three states over. As she landed on the cold, wet grass she swore and let out a grunt. A stabbing pain shot through her foot and into her calf. Her ankle throbbed. Who the fuck sprained their ankle getting tacos? There was an irony in spraining her ankle while running from the man she wanted to eat her taco.

If she ever needed a sign she should have stayed home and eaten ice cream for dinner, a burning ankle and a wet ass was probably it. "Mother fucking fuck." She slapped the hard soil on either side of her butt.

Cleo stood two feet away, she'd somehow managed to rescue the tacos from being squashed under Molly in the fall. She was the real MVP. "You okay?"

"Twisted my ankle."

"I can't help but feel like this is a sign."

Molly held a hand up in the darkness. "Don't. Just, don't."

"C'mon. You can't deny it. You say you'd rather fall down the stairs than fall in love with... *him* and the next second you're on your ass. I think the universe is telling you to stop pretending you're not in love with..." She checked over both shoulders. "*Him* – and just go with it."

Molly laughed. "Right. My rational, reasonable, level-headed best friend is telling me to listen to messages from the universe." She shifted her weight and a new stab of fresh pain radiated through her ankle making her hiss. "Shit. Fuck. Fuckety mother fucking fuck."

"Tell me how you really feel, Mol."

"Wet. And not the fun kind."

Cleo snorted. "Need help?"

"I think so." She rolled onto her knees and pressed her hands into the dirt to stand, ensuring her right foot didn't take any weight. "It burns worse than Chlamydia."

"Dare I ask how you know?"

"It was years ago. Let's just say I became much more choosy about who I let near my cooch after *that* experience."

Cleo slipped her arm around Molly's waist and took some of her weight, then let go. "Know what? I'm going to bring the car to you." As she turned to leave, Molly wobbled on one foot.

"You okay, MoMo?" Finn and his shivering date stood next to his car across the parking lot.

"I'm fine. It's fine," she yelled back.

Cleo shook her head. "She fell. I'm getting the car."

Finn jogged across the lot and swept her into his arms.

"Are you fucking crazy? Put me down!" *Don't put me down*. She inhaled. He smelled of *Acqua Di Gio* – his signature scent since he was a teen. She'd been obsessed with it from the first time she'd smelled it. She'd saved up and bought a bottle which she sprayed over her pillow every night for the first six months after they'd met.

A wave of nostalgia had her holding him tighter. "Where's your date?" She hated herself for how jealous three words managed to sound.

"Let's get you sitting in the car and we'll take a look at your foot."

Cleo opened the door and Finn eased Molly onto the passenger seat. He crouched in front of her and slipped off her shoe.

"I'm cold. Can you hurry up?" The Date appeared over Finn's shoulder and clearly wasn't used to not being the center of her date's world. She shifted her weight from foot to foot and rubbed her arms.

"You brought your car, go warm up in there."

He hadn't picked her up? Interesting. Finn was traditional to the letter. If he hadn't picked her up it meant he didn't want to drive her home or get naked with her. Finn naked. Fuck. She swallowed.

The woman's jaw dropped and her perfectly coiffed blonde hair fell into her eyes. "You're staying here?"

"I'm checking her out."

"I'm aware." The scowl on The Date's face deepened.

"I've had my fair share of injuries on the ice. She might need to hit the hospital to get checked out. If I leave it to her, she'll go home, pop some Tylenol and call it good."

She would totally do that.

The woman shook her head. "So if she needs the hospital are you going to take her?"

Finn rolled his eyes and turned over his shoulder to address the still shuffling woman whose teeth chattered so loudly Molly could hear from a few feet away. "You're pissed at me for being a good person?"

Molly started to tell Finn he should go and finish his date, but said date talked over her.

"I'm pissed at you for taking care of her and not me."

An honest-to-God growl broke out of his body. Sorry, lady. Strike four. Kindness above all else was Finn's motto – helping those who couldn't help themselves, loyalty to your friends, and not leaving a man behind. He pinched the bridge of his nose, probably torn between kicking her to the curb and taking her home himself. "Just go."

Kicking her to the curb it was.

"Nothing going on between you, my ass," The Date muttered as she turned on her heel and strode toward her car.

Molly couldn't make out Cleo's expression in the darkness, but she could almost hear her "another sign from the universe" thoughts. Damnit. She'd have to tell her opinionated bestie to stop thinking so loudly.

Finn rotated Molly's foot in a circle and back again. He flexed it up and down. While it ached, it was tolerable. "I think you got lucky."

"Sure I did."

"I don't think it's broken – that's a good thing, right?"

Molly groaned into her palm. "It's just not my day. It could be raining titties and I'd still get hit in the head by a dick." She glowered at him, still not ready to forgive him for relegating her so far into the brother's friend zone.

He chuckled. "But you like dick. I'd offer to take you home but..." He jerked his chin at Cleo.

"It's fine. I don't want to burden my brother's best friend."

He winced like she'd slapped him hard across the face. His nostrils flared and he dropped his voice. "I didn't mean—"

"It's fine." It was never fine when a woman said it was fine, but she swiveled in her seat and tucked her legs into the car before grabbing her shoe from his hand. "Thanks for checking out... my foot." Her cool voice was laced with the acid bubbling low in her stomach, but she couldn't stop herself.

"Molly..."

"Don't. Like I said, it's fine." *Fight for me.*

He hesitated, pained eyes and creased forehead, he nodded and stood. "Catch you 'round, MoMo. Get some ice on that foot, 'kay?" He closed the door and walked away.

Cleo slid into the driver's seat and took the steering wheel but didn't move or speak. Finn's car didn't move either.

"I know." Molly sighed.

"I didn't say anything."

"You're thinking it." Her foot throbbed, but it didn't come close to the ache in her chest. She should have kissed him. She should have grabbed him and macked on him until he forgot her brother even existed.

Instead she'd hurt him.

He cared, that much was obvious, but until she made a move, until she opened the door and took a peek through the crack, she'd never know if he felt the same way she did. But did she have what it took to open the door? What if he didn't feel the same? What if those near misses were simply that – nothing more? She definitely felt more.

Those eyes said feels, right?

"Is there a small chance you overreacted just now?"

Molly spread her finger and thumb so there was a tiny space between them. "I don't know why I got so mad when he called me Will's sister. I *am* Will's sister."

"But you want to be more."

She still couldn't say it out loud. "I think I need to get my foot looked at. It really hurts."

An hour, an x-ray, and some Vicodin later, she curled up in bed, and cried. When she was done crying, she scrolled her inbox. Dick pic after dick pic after dick pic harassed her from the screen.

The door creaked as Cleo entered the room and sat on the edge of Molly's bed. "Wanna talk about it?"

"Did you wait for my meds to kick in and lower my defenses?"

Cleo giggled. "Maybe? I was going to come in under the guise of bringing an ice pack, but you already have one. Molly?"

"Mhmm?"

"Why is there a purple, veiny penis on your screen?"

"Why do guys think dick pics will work on girls? I mean, I

know I have fuckboy tendencies, but I still have standards... dreams... and goals and shit."

"And emotions."

Molly groaned and covered her face. "I don't like those."

"That doesn't mean you don't have them. You should talk to him."

"And say what, ChoCho? Real life isn't like that cliterature stuff you write. Sometimes a woman just wants to be bent over and banged like a screen door in a hurricane."

Cleo patted Molly's shoulder. "Except that's not what you want from Finn."

It was absolutely what she wanted from Finn. Though it wasn't *all* she wanted from him.

"I'm worried about you, Molly. Like, really worried. I see what you're doing to yourself. You're pushing down your feelings for him more and more. I see how it tears you apart when you watch him with someone else. I see you fight the urge to comfort him when he's sad. I get that Will made him promise. I get that you're afraid of losing him, even losing both of them, but I'm afraid you're losing yourself."

Molly hissed out a long breath.

"I know. We don't talk feelings. Especially not Finn O'Brien feelings. And I know you'll say it's different for me because Linc and I are together now and I'm projecting, or trying to pair you off... or whatever the hell else you're going to say about it being different."

She stood up and paced a few steps back and forward. "But ultimately, it's not different. And what you're currently doing isn't working. Trying to fuck Finn O'Brien out of your brain by getting tangled up with best friends, or making your way through a list of fuck buddies... By the way, you were lucky there were no consequences to that. Okay, so they were pissed, but they're both players, so I guess it didn't matter. But none of this is helping fix the root of the problem. You need to talk to Finn."

"Ha." Molly smacked a hand over her mouth.

"Don't 'ha' me. I'm serious. You need to lay it out on the table and tell him how you feel."

"What if I lose him?"

"What if you don't?"

"What if I lose Will?"

"What if you don't? He's your brother, Molly. He's never going to just walk away."

"Stop coming at me with logic, ChoCho."

Cleo giggled in the darkness. "Never. You need to talk to him."

"You keep saying that."

"And I'll keep saying it until you do it."

CHAPTER 11
Finnegan

Finn had been staring at the ceiling of his therapist's office in silence for fifteen minutes. He had so much to say that when he opened his mouth the words all rushed into his throat leaving him unable to say anything at all.

"It's been a while, Finn." Dr. Hermannsen didn't ask Finn to lie on the couch. Did anyone ever expect an invitation to lie down in the shrink's office? Was that something you only ever saw in movies?

The office had a straight backed chair facing the doctor across the oak desk, a plush blue recliner to one side, and a paisley patterned chaise longue to the other. Patients could choose how they wanted to unburden their souls. Finn chose staring at the ceiling.

"Your email said your mother is back in your life. She wants to talk? To reconnect?"

"Molly came with me to meet her. I still haven't decided what to do."

"She's a good friend."

Finn's non-committal hum triggered the Dr. to write something on his notebook. "What are you writing?"

"I wrote 'Does he love her?'"

Finn sat upright. "Why?"

"It's been a year since you last came to see me. And the first person you mention is Molly. I read through my notes from our previous sessions and her name came up in every one. It doesn't matter what we start out talking about, Molly gets brought into the conversation."

Finn's fingers twitched to spin the globe on the edge of the desk. "And you think I love her?" His stomach flipped.

"Do you love her?"

He leaned forward planting his elbows on his thighs. "Her brother is my best friend."

"That's not an answer."

Finn stood. "Her family is the only family I've known since Liam died."

Dr. Hermannsen remained quiet. It was a commonly used technique by therapists – and cops. Fall silent, let the person you're talking to fill it with whatever was making them feel guilty, or sad, or whatever else brought them through the door.

Finn started to pace. Four feet toward the window, four feet back toward the door. He raked his hands through his hair. He'd never admitted to anyone but himself how he felt about Molly. Once he said it aloud, there was no putting it back inside.

"Do you love her, Finn?"

Finn plopped back down onto the edge of the sofa and leaned his head back. "Only since forever." The heavy weight that crushed his chest for years on end eased. "Yes. I love her. I tried not to. I tried to stop. I tried to pretend I didn't, but I do. And I'm so fucking scared it's going to ruin everything."

"I can understand your reluctance. You don't want to upset Will, you don't want to upend the family dynamic and make waves... but what about what you *do* want? What about the chance that things between you and Molly could work out?" Placing his pen on his notebook, he leaned back in his chair.

"What if she's The One and you're wasting all of this time and energy fighting your attraction to her?"

"Isn't it selfish?" A flutter in Finn's chest made him scratch at his shirt like he could chase it away.

"Being selfish isn't always a bad thing. In fact, sometimes it's necessary."

After pushing food around his plate for an hour, mulling over what Dr. Hermannsen had said, Finn had left the hockey house with snacks and headed to Molly's apartment. Cleo was leaving as he arrived.

"She home?" He scratched a hand over the back of his neck.

Cleo gave a knowing smile. "She is. She's in her room." She pushed the door open.

Finn took a step forward, then hesitated. Was he ready to potentially change everything? Was he ready to find out if she felt the same as he did? Blood pounded in his ears and there was no way the racing in his chest was normal.

Cleo placed her hand on his bicep. "Finn?"

He jumped. "Yeah?" He chuckled, cheeks burning.

"Go talk to her."

He nodded. Maybe he shouldn't talk at all. Maybe he should just grab her and kiss her until she thought it was a good idea, too.

The apartment was quiet as he dropped the snacks onto the dining table and made his way through to Molly's room. He knocked quietly, but a sound from beyond the door gave him pause. Was that moaning?

Her breathy voice spoke straight to his dick. It twitched in his pants and Finn shifted in a bid to prevent it from growing hard. More moaning.

Should he stop? Absolutely. Was he going to?

He knocked again, harder, before pushing the door open. He popped his head around and cleared his throat. "Molly?"

Molly's foot was propped up on cushions, ice pack draped over her ankle. She had a laptop and a vibrator sitting next to her, and her hand was up her shirt. Her hair was loose around her face, her cheeks were flushed, and her signature red lips were au naturale. She looked incredible. So. Fucking. Hot. His dick twitched again.

"Finny!" She jerked her hand from under her shirt and stopped the video on the laptop. Her already pink cheeks darkened.

"Are you watching porn right now?"

She shrugged but wouldn't meet his gaze.

So. Fucking. Hot.

Don't shrink. Let your freak flag fly, Miss Molly...

"Too medicated to do much else."

"Mustn't be all that good. You don't even have your hand in your pants." *I wanna be in your pants.*

She sighed and snapped the laptop shut, placing the vibrator on top of it. "What can I say? Porn has gotta touch me before I touch myself."

He snorted. He loved how comfortable she was with her sexuality.

"What's up?" She patted the bed next to her, but her body was rigid.

He hesitated, but eased himself onto the edge of the bed so they faced each other but didn't touch. He reached into his pocket, pulled out a stick of lip balm, and handed it to her.

"Huckleberry lip balm? What's this for?"

He shrugged. What seemed like a good idea on the way over, was suddenly feeling dumb as rocks. "I brought snacks. Figured you might wanna watch a movie, or play a game or something."

Her brows knitted together in a deep frown. "Why?"

Hooking a thumb over his shoulder he chuckled. "Figured you'd be laid up and bored out of your mind. Thought you might want some company. But if you'd rather get back to your..." He cleared his throat. "Recreational viewing... I can go."

She shook her head, twisting open the tube of lip balm and applying it to her lips with a loud pop. Giving her lip balm was a terrible idea. He couldn't look away.

"Have you heard from Ms. Deconstructed Tacos?"

Something about her tone was different. Was she jealous? Her eyes were glued to the small tube in her hand as she put the lid back on.

"I haven't." He sighed. "We're oil and water. It wasn't a good fit. And my griefcase is way too big for someone like her."

"Surely you could make up for that with other things that are big." The woman was shameless, staring straight at his crotch – and the traitorous thing fucking responded. She bit the inside of her cheek, clearly fighting a smile.

"I never got around to wowing her with my attributes."

She met his gaze. "No?"

He shook his head. "Wasn't feeling it." *She wasn't you.*

"You've been off your game lately." Ms. Morrison was fishing. His heart picked up speed.

He wasn't ready to go there. "Have you applied for the ESPN internship yet?"

She folded her arms.

Wrong question. Abort. Shit. Rewind.

"Sadie Summers is applying."

"So?" He scooted closer to her on the bed, the red silk sheets making it hard to stay in one place.

"So she's a better candidate for the job." A shrug. A down-turned gaze.

"And that means you don't even try?"

Another shrug. She traced the edge of her laptop.

"Who the fuck is this woman and what have you done with my Molly Morrison?"

Mine. If only.

Her eyebrow arched and something flickered in her eyes. "You think you know me."

He reached out to tuck her hair behind her ear, but stopped and dropped his hand to his thigh. "I do know you. I know you're smart and talented... and ESPN would be lucky to have you as an intern. Fuck Summer whats-her-face, she ain't got shit on Molly-Fucking-Morrison. Don't let them get in your head."

Molly smiled. "You make it sound so simple."

"It is simple."

She ran her thumb along her bottom lip and a shiver trickled up his spine. "I need to go."

"Go where?"

"I have a scan at the hospital." She slid her thumbnail between her teeth and chewed on it.

He sprung to his feet. "I wanted to go to that with you."

"Cleo's going to take me."

"So she knows?"

"What? No. She thinks I'm going to see about changing my birth control."

"So why am I not taking you?" He dropped onto the bed again, tucking his left hand under his thigh so he didn't do something dumb like run it across her plump bottom lip like she'd done.

She didn't answer, or look at him.

He slipped his knuckle under her chin and turned her face to his. Stroking her cheek with the pad of his thumb he repeated the question. The stain across the apples of her cheeks darkened.

"I can't." Her chest heaved.

He swallowed. "You can't what, MoMo?"

He held her gaze with all he had. A door slammed. His stomach sank. He needed more time. They needed more time.

"Molly? Are you ready? We need to go or we'll miss your appointment." Cleo's voice was like iced water over Molly. Her soft eyes hardened, walls going up right in front of his face.

"Let me take you to the doctor." He refused to let her face go. Her skin was so soft, so warm, and if he let her go she may not let him get that close again.

"I can't."

"Can't or won't?"

"Please don't make me choose."

She wasn't talking about choosing between can't or won't. She was talking about choosing between Finn and Will. His heart twisted.

He nodded and stood. "Let me know how the scan goes." He didn't wait for her answer before leaving.

Cleo waited by the door, keys in hand. "Everything okay?"

He nodded, not trusting his voice to speak. Her sad eyes watched him leave. Back at the hockey house he sank onto the sofa, bottle of cold beer in hand and turned on the TV for background noise.

"Knock, knock." Russell poked his head around the door.

"You know you're supposed to knock before you come in, right? What if I was naked?"

"Obi, I've seen you naked more times than I've seen you with clothes on. And you're in a communal space – that shit's on you." He dropped onto the couch next to Finn. "Day drinking? Man, why so blue, schmoo?"

Finn shook his head and took a drink. "What brings you to the common folk here at the hockey house, Stewie?"

"Ah. Classic deflection. Maybe I just wanted to hang with you."

Finn clicked off the TV and turned to face Russ. "What gives?"

Russ shrugged and plucked Finn's bottle from his hand to take a drink. "You having girl trouble?"

Finn took his drink back. "I don't have a girl."

Russ picked his feet up and planted his heels on the coffee table. "You sure about that?"

"What are you talking about?" Finn forced calm into his voice, but his pulse ticked up. Had he said something or done something in front of Russ that had given him away?

"At ease, soldier." Russ held up a hand. "It's nothing you've said or done."

Finn's mouth dried up and his stomach soured.

"He doesn't know. Fuck, Finn, breathe. You look green." Russ shook his head.

"Nothing happened." Finn rubbed at the knot in his chest. Was that weird feeling what a heart attack felt like?

"I know. I think that's the problem."

Finn arched an eyebrow and chugged the last half of his beer. He needed way more alcohol if he was going to talk to Russell about anything to do with Molly Morrison. "Bre?"

"She put it together and dumbed it down for me. We met Molly one night a while back, she was drunk and upset so we offered to take her home. We got to the parking lot and you were there with some blonde. Molly made some kind of cryptic comment and I don't speak "Woman" so it went over my head."

Finn chuckled. Sometimes men were pretty fucking dumb.

"Sabrina explained to me that Molly must be upset over something big. Someone big."

"Betchurass I'm big." Finn puffed out his chest, but his bravado was 100% false. His stomach sloshed.

Russ patted Finn's shoulder. "Everyone knows you're a big boy, Obi. But not everyone knows you are in love with Molly Morrison."

Every muscle in Finn's hand twitched to slap itself over Russell's mouth to shove it back in, in case someone heard. Sweat pricked down his neck.

"She loves you too. It's clear as day. Well, it's clear once a smart woman points it out."

Finn didn't answer. His heart took up all his energy racing in his chest like a stampede. She loved him? Like he loved her?

"What are you going to do about it?"

"Move to Mexico and change my name?"

Russ snorted. "What about getting the girl?"

Finn laughed. "Are you fucking insane? Are you high? Are you listening to yourself right now?" After a beat he smacked his forehead. "Wait. I know what it is. You want me murdered. This is your way of getting me killed and my body disposed of without having to lift a finger."

"Hear me out, man."

Finn opened his mouth to protest but Russ smacked a palm over it. "I said hear me out."

Finn nodded and shifted his weight on the couch.

"Will will be fine about it."

"Ha!"

The hand smacked over his mouth again. "Goddamnit I said shut up. He won't be fine about it at first. At first you might die." He shrugged. "But after a while he'll realize you're in it for the long haul, you l-o-v-e her and you aren't just fucking with her like one of your fangirls and he'll calm down."

When Finn still didn't answer, Russ continued. "We just gotta make sure you survive the first part."

Finn licked Russell's palm and when he recoiled with an "ew" Finn cleared his throat. "And just how do you propose *we* do that?"

Russ grinned. "I thought you'd never ask."

"And I feel like you're never going to answer."

"Secret dating."

Finn placed his empty bottle onto the coffee table. "She wouldn't even let me take her to the doctor earlier. She's definitely not going to agree to secret dating."

"Convince her with your magic Light Saber. Wait – Doctor?"

Finn's chest tightened. Shit. "Foot checkup. She fell and busted her ankle."

Russell fell quiet as he tapped his index finger on his chin. "Secret double dating? Bre and I can be your beards."

"What's the world coming to when you're helping me bag a woman?"

Russell laughed. "Everyone needs a little help sometimes. Think about it. Let's make a game plan and get the girl."

He made it sound so easy. Except the girl's brother would skin him alive if he made a move of any kind on her. And Finn wasn't even sure she wanted him to make a move.

Guess I'm gonna find out.

CHAPTER 12

Molly

Molly stepped out of the doctor's office onto the street, the heat and bright sunshine somehow catching her off guard. She squinted. Her boobs ached, her head pounded, and she was hungry.

"How'd it go?" To her left, sitting on the steps outside the office building next door Finn leaned back on his elbows, ankles crossed.

Her heart stuttered. He was gorgeous. "Wh-what are you doing here?"

He stood up and dusted off his butt. "Since you wouldn't tell me when your appointment was, and I couldn't flirt it out of the nice old lady at reception, I figured I needed to take matters into my own hands."

"You followed me?"

He nodded. "I followed you."

"I'm pretty sure that's illegal."

"I mean, I went home first, but I just couldn't settle. I pulled up find my phone and yeah, I followed you. But I wouldn't have had to follow you if you hadn't been so damn stubborn and just let me come with you MoMo. You don't have to face the world alone, you know."

"Cleo came with me."

He gestured up and down the street. "Where is she then?"

"In the car."

"Then she didn't come with you, MoMo. She dropped you off. It's not the same thing." He stepped toward her and she froze. Was he going to touch her in the street? She wouldn't be able to keep her shit together if he took her hand or hugged her.

She'd pressed it all down – her feelings for Finn, bitterness at seeing him with another woman, his mother making her way back into his life and asking him for a huge favor, uncertainty over her own future... both with her career and her health... everything. But it wasn't far below the surface, bubbling and spitting in her gut.

If Finn touched her, if he showed her affection, if he kept being nice to her, if he kept showing up places and being supportive and dependable, it would break the dam inside her she'd spent years building and keeping strong.

His everyday paleness was worse than usual. His shoulders sagged and his eyes and lips were downturned. "Please tell me you're okay. Then I'll leave if that's what you really want." His hands trembled as he jammed them into the front pockets of his jeans.

"I'm okay." She shifted her weight and pain radiated from the side of her boob. She hissed. "Fine. I hurt like hell. But I'm okay."

"You're sure?"

She nodded. He stepped toward her. "The fact that you're in pain is the only thing keeping me from wrapping you in my arms right now. But I need you to know it's taking all I have not to do it anyway."

She nodded again. Her mind buzzed.

"You applied for the internship yet? You know it's closing soon, right?"

"I..."

"Don't BS me, MoMo. I've seen that BS face before and I'm not buying it. Carpe the shit out of that Diem. Shoot your shot."

Uncertainty swelled inside her, creeping through every cell in her body. Did she have a chance of landing the internship? Did it matter as long as she pursued it with all she had? Nobody had to know.

"Coffee?"

"Cleo is in the car."

"Tell her you're having coffee with me. I'll make sure you get home safely."

He wasn't playing fair. He knew she'd need to be cold in the ground before she'd say no to coffee. But she had to. He deserved better than she had to offer and she didn't want to be the reason Finn got murdered by her brother, either. She had no time for coffee and complications with a man she couldn't really have. Her heart screamed in her chest. She'd been scared to face her mortality, scared of dying, she'd been even more afraid of losing Finn.

Her stomach sank. If she couldn't find it inside herself to pursue Finn after the life-changing, terrifying thing she'd just faced, would she ever?

"I need batteries."

Cleo's bedroom door smacked against the wall with a thud as Molly burst into her room, her phone light illuminating the way. Molly pulled open the top drawer of Cleo's bedside chest. "ChoCho, where are your batteries?"

"Molly? What the fuck?"

"Oh, were you sleeping?"

"It's the middle of the night, of course I was sleeping!" Cleo smacked the duvet in the darkness.

Molly paced.

"Are you on drugs? You seem kinda... manic. Are you going to tell me what the hell's going on with you?"

"My vibrator died."

"And you need to fix that right now? Right this very second?"

Molly sank onto the edge of Cleo's bed. "I booty called one of my fuck buddies to distract me. But I couldn't... we didn't... I kicked her out before we even got naked. What the hell is wrong with me?"

Cleo sat up in bed and scooted back against the headboard. "We don't have that kinda time, girlfriend."

Molly smiled in the darkness despite herself, but a lump lodged in her throat. The bedside lamp clicked on and Cleo pulled her knees to her chest under the quilt. "Okay. I'm awake, damn it. Talk to me, Molly. What's going on with you?"

Molly bounced on the balls of her feet. Winced and stopped. If she couldn't trust her best friend with everything that had gone on, who could she trust? The longer Molly kept everything inside, suffering through her feelings alone, the more compounded and tangled everything became. Perhaps a problem shared really was a problem halved.

After a heavy pause, Molly sighed. "I found a lump in my boob."

To her credit, Cleo didn't gasp or clutch her chest, she didn't reach out to touch Molly, and she didn't ask thirteen thousand questions. She simply sat, listening, watching Molly with sad eyes in the dim light.

"The appointment you took me to wasn't for birth control. I had a mammogram. Which, for the record? Not fun. It was the worst kind of boob squishing." She winced at the memory. "I had an ultrasound, too. Because apparently multiple people needed to squish the girls. They say the lump is 16mm, and they found a couple of other spots that are 'mildly suspicious' so I had to have another mammogram and ultrasound."

Cleo picked up Molly's hand and put it on top of her knees, clutching it tightly. Molly fought the emotion welling up in her chest, but she couldn't press it down. Her eyes filled but she blinked back the tears.

"The smaller ones are by my nipple so that mammogram was beyond not fun. The rad tech apologized for smashing my nips. I told her I've had bad dates before."

Cleo gave a pity laugh. "What happens next?"

"I had a biopsy this morning." And her boob was very, very mad at that fact. "Hurt like fuck. I bled a lot, and my boob is super bruised. They put a metal chip in by the mass so they know where it is for future reference. I'm now referring to my left boob as my titanium titty."

Concern pinched Cleo's brows in a deep V. "Surgery?"

"No surgery right now. I'll have another mammogram in six months to check everything. But for now it all seems okay."

As Cleo launched herself at Molly. "Why didn't you tell me?"

A stab of pain rattled through her side. Molly yipped and Cleo eased her hug.

"I don't know why you think you have to go it alone, Mol."

Molly didn't know either. "Finn knows."

Cleo relaxed around her. "I'm glad someone knew." She spoke into Molly's hair.

"I wouldn't let him come with, so he followed me. Things are getting complicated with him, ChoCho."

Cleo nodded against her shoulder. She was probably afraid

to speak in case Molly stopped talking. It was easier to open up when she didn't have to look into her friend's sad eyes.

"I don't know how to do complicated. Life's too fucking short for complicated."

"It doesn't have to be complicated, Molly. You like each other. You should see if there's something there – which, spoiler alert, there totally is. If Will doesn't like it, then I'm sorry, but he's your brother, he's kind of contractually obliged to be a pain in your ass. He's also sticking around no matter what."

She sat back and held Molly by the shoulders. "He's gonna be pissed, sure. But he'll get over it. And there's no guarantee that he and Finn wouldn't fight over something else even if you weren't a factor. You just never know. Stop putting your potential happiness on hold just because your brother might not approve."

"Dang ChoCho. Tell me how you really feel."

Cleo laughed. "Your results today could have been way worse. For someone with such a zest for life, you're being really dumb about denying yourself Finn O'Brien. Life is short, girl. You live like every day is the last in every aspect of your life. Why stop at Finn?"

Molly shrugged. She had no answer. Other than she didn't want to lose either Finn or Will. To her, that was reason enough. A life without her brother – or his best friend – in it wasn't one she ever wanted to consider.

"Fine. Answer this one. Why did you kick your fuck buddy out earlier?"

"I..." Molly swallowed. Shadows danced along the wall as Cleo shifted in bed. "I felt guilty."

"Why?" Cleo wasn't letting it go.

"Because I..." Sweat beaded at her hairline.

"Say it, Molly."

Why was this woman her best friend again? Could she file

for friend-divorce? Sighing, Molly covered her face with both hands.

"Say. It."

"It felt like I was going to cheat on him."

"On who?"

"Finn."

"Why?"

Her heart flickered and she met Cleo's dark and intense stare. "Because."

Cleo didn't speak, she simply raised her eyebrows.

"Because I have feels for him. Happy now?" Molly flopped back on Cleo's bed.

"What kind of feelings?"

Molly was going to hurl in less than ten seconds if she couldn't find a way out of the conversation. "The four letter kind. I have four letter feelings for Finnegan Aiden O'Brien."

"This is like pulling teeth. Be specific."

"Ugh." She threw her arm over her eyes. "Why?"

"Because you need to admit it to yourself if nothing else."

"Maybe I admitted it to myself and I just don't want to admit it to you."

"Stop stalling."

"I love him, okay?" Chest in knots, she swallowed. "I've loved him for almost as long as I've known him." Her body burned, her mind raced, and her heart had taken off out of her body and galloped into the next state. She groaned. "I don't do love, or commitment."

"Everyone loves. And just because one asshole treated you like shit doesn't mean they all will. So that asshole cheated on you in high school, is that really a good reason to keep everyone at arm's length for the rest of your life?"

Her heart still bore the scars of that summer. Mom had sent the boys after Molly while she ordered takeout instead of sitting in like they'd planned. The guy she'd been dating,

Justin Ashe, was one of Finn and Will's teammates, which had just made everything worse.

"If Finn ever hurt me, Will would kill him, Cleo. You didn't see Justin after Will got done with him. His face was so swollen... so messed up with multicolored bruises. If he ever did that to Finn..."

"I think this every time we talk about it, but I honestly can't imagine your brother – that Will beat someone to a bloodied pulp. Not even for you. He's just so... placid."

"Which is why I have to make sure he never Hulks out on Finn. If things went badly between us, and he got hurt because of me... I'd never forgive myself."

"Except you've been friends for years. Some of the best relationships out there grow from friendship. Finn has had your back forever. You just need to let him."

"I don't know that I can."

Cleo leaned over on the bed and flicked Molly's forehead. "Stop being a stubborn wench and try."

Molly stood with another groan.

"Do you still want batteries?"

"No. It's fine. You killed my horn with all that real talk. I'm going to eat my feelings instead." She pulled the door closed behind her as she left the room before limping to the kitchen. She pulled out a pint of ice cream and attacked it with the ferociousness of a pregnant woman in her second trimester.

When her stomach rebelled at the too-quick consumption of an entire pint of dairy, she dug her laptop out from under the couch, plopped onto the sofa, and pulled up the application form for the internship at ESPN.

Before she could talk herself out of it, she filled it in and hit send. Despite the throbbing boob driving her crazy, she went to bed with a smile on her face. She'd done one scary thing. All she had to do next, was figure out how to do the scarier thing, without losing the most important people in her life.

❄

A frantic banging on the door woke Molly up with a start.

"Molly! Open up!"

Shit. Will was pissed.

Cleo's door swung open and she shuffled presumably to let Will in. "What's wrong? What happened? Did someone die?"

"Get her up." His growl wasn't at all friendly. "Please." At least he still remembered his manners while he was being a dick to her best friend.

"What the fuck, Will?"

Cleo's shuffling steps got closer before she knocked on Molly's bedroom door. As soon as she opened it, Will yelled from somewhere deep in the apartment. "Get up, Molly. We're going for coffee."

If he'd said anything other than the magic C-word, she'd have told him to go fuck himself. But she needed coffee. And from the sound of it, he wasn't leaving until she got her ass up.

"I feel like he wants you in a public place so he doesn't kill you. He's big mad." Cleo's face softened. Her sympathetic eyes, and small half-wince half-smile made Molly's skin crawl.

Molly's breaths came in panicked pants. Did he know she wanted Finn? Had Finn said something about her boob? Shit. Had Will killed Finn?

She ground the heels of her hands into her eyes and bounded out of bed. She'd make sure the Sugar Bean was bustling with potential witnesses before she went inside. If Will was going to kill her, she wasn't going down without a fight.

Twenty minutes later, she sat facing her scowling, vibrating brother. He hadn't said a word since his bellowing announcement of his arrival at the apartment. He'd silently pointed at a table when they'd gone into the busy café, bought two coffees, and joined her.

"Cap." Team asshole and resident pain in everyone's ass, Johnny White, gave a salute to Will as he passed. Will nodded. The muscles in his cheeks flexed as he squeezed his teeth together. Shit. Shit. Shit. He was really mad.

"Get out of bed on the wrong side this morning?" Johnny stopped, took a few paces backward, and clapped Will on the back. "Happens to the best of us."

Will glared at Johnny's hand – still resting on his shoulder – then up at Johnny's face. A smirk danced across Johnny's lips. "Does someone need to get laid? I could hook you up if you need to decompress a lil. Littler Mo." Johnny gave Molly a salute, too. He jerked his chin at her. "We should hook up for real this time."

Ew. What the hell? Why would he bring that up?

Will sprung from his chair and turned to face Johnny, squaring his shoulders. He still hadn't said a word. Molly jumped up too, but kept her distance. There was no way she could stop Will and Johnny from throwing down, she'd only get her ass handed to her and she was already hurt. Somehow, Will's glare intensified as he stood staring down a grinning JW.

Johnny lifted his hands in surrender. "She's gonna fuck one of us some day, Cap." He glanced over Will's shoulder at Molly. "At least one of us."

"Fuck you, JW. You wish." Molly flipped him the bird.

A vicious growl rattled through Will and Johnny's grin grew. The guy really didn't know when to stop, did he? What the fuck was his damage?

"That's quite enough from you, asshole." Finn – forever her white knight – stepped between Will and Johnny and placed a splayed palm on Johnny's chest. "It's time for you to leave."

Had he been there the whole time and she hadn't seen him? Or had he arrived after Will and Molly? Was this an intervention?

"But we're just getting to the good part."

Finn's shoulders were taut, a vein strained in his neck, and his pale, Irish skin was blotchy and red. "Today is not the day, JW. Back it up."

The gleam faded from Johnny's eyes. To be fair, if Finn had squared up to Molly like that, she'd have just gone right ahead and pissed her pants. He was an imposing figure, not least of all when he was defending someone he cared about.

A shiver passed through her. What was Will so bent out of shape about? She sat back down and waited. Finn escorted Johnny to the counter, and stood watch over him while he ordered. Eventually Will sat down, too.

"What's going on, Will?"

"You're making a show of yourself, that's what's going on. And as you can see from that display of assholeness, it's impacting my life now, too."

She held up a hand to stop him from speaking before taking a sip of her still hot coffee. She hadn't yet consumed enough caffeine to deal with her brother's bullshit. After a long sip, she smacked her lips and gestured for him to continue. "What are you talking about?"

"I'm talking about you dating brothers."

Her stomach dropped.

"Or best friends, or whatever the hell you're doing with the Murphy brothers."

Then her jaw dropped. "They... tattled to you?"

"Doesn't matter how I know, Molly. That's not what the problem is."

Something twisted in her gut. "You're saying my vagina is

the problem? My sexuality?" Her voice kicked up a notch as she spoke, and Will winced.

"Keep your goddamn voice down." He groaned into his palm.

"If you were afraid of people hearing about what I do with my body, then you should have thought about that before dragging me to a public place to chastise me for enjoying sex."

Johnny walked past again, raising his cup at them both before leaving, but Finn hadn't stepped out yet. He was still there. And while she couldn't see where he was, she felt his presence.

"I have no problem with you enjoying sex, Molly." Will sighed and sipped his drink. "Not that it would make a difference if I did." He snorted. "I want you to be safe. I want you to be careful. I want you to..."

Her face creased as she reacted to his words. Frown deepening, nostrils flaring, eyes growing wide, she stopped him again before she hurled her beloved nectar of the gods at his freakin' face.

"I don't care what you want, Will." She totally did, but she'd had it with the slut-shaming. "My body, my choice – remember? And unfortunately for you, you don't get a say in what I do, or with whom. How about you worry about who you put your own dick in and worry less about who's putting—"

"Don't finish that sentence. Molly." He sighed again. He'd perfected the disappointed dad sigh already. God help his future children. "I don't want you to get hurt. Or worse..." He cast his eyes down to the mug on the table. "What if the Murphy brothers weren't such nice guys and tried to do something to you for playing them?"

"Hurt me how? Like rape me?"

He flinched at the word. Good. She wasn't going to sit

back and take such patriarchal bullshit from someone she thought was raised to know better.

"You think they would hurt me because I gave them a good time, didn't kiss and tell, and didn't want anything more than a one-time deal? That makes total sense. So they were pissed I didn't tell him I was seeing his best friend. You don't see me getting pissed that they didn't tell me who else they slept with. Such fragile male egos. One night stands, Will. That's all they were. I wasn't in a relationship with them and I didn't owe them anything, either. So I fucked a guy and his best friend – it wasn't the first and it won't be the last. Sometimes I even do them at the same damn time. But that's all it was, good fucks."

He cringed every time she dropped the F-bomb, but she wasn't slowing down. Her skin burned. Who the hell did he think he was? And how delusional did he have to be to think he could somehow control her body just because her behavior embarrassed him? She wasn't embarrassed by her own behavior. Was it smart to fool around with a guy and his best friend? Probably not. Was it a crime? No. Did it make her a bad person? Also no.

She took one last drink of her coffee and stood. Something snapped in her chest, clawing at her insides to break free and smack her brother senseless. "I'm going to say this once and once only. Rapists cause rape. Not women who sleep with a guy and his best friend. And if that's what they'd jump to because I banged them both, then the problem is more them than me, don't you think?"

His chocolate brown eyes burned into her. "Have you finished up there on your soapbox, Molly?"

She nodded but didn't sit. A few people turned in their seats or cast glances over their shoulders, but she didn't care.

"I wasn't talking about them..." He dropped his voice to a whisper. "Raping you. They're good guys. I mean, that's not to say other guys out there wouldn't think twice about doing something like that, but that wasn't my point. Your reputation is suffering because of your actions. Have you no shame?" Mr. By-The-Book was Dad up and down. But they both knew he wasn't talking about her reputation.

Her insides trembled. The irony of all ironies was that if he'd just lifted the ban on her being able to get closer to his teammates... one, very specific teammate, she probably wouldn't have slept with anyone other than Finn O'Brien for years. Years. She waited for the familiar clench of her insides at the idea of being committed to one person for so long, but it never came. Interesting. She'd unpack that later, but for the time being, she had some righteous indignation to unload on her brother instead.

"You mean your reputation, William. Not mine, right? That's what this is really about. It's not that I'm enjoying my time at college, it's not that I'm embracing my sexuality and loving my body... It's that it looks bad for you if your sister is deemed a slut by the college proletariat, right?"

His features darkened but he didn't answer and wouldn't meet her gaze. Coward.

"Well, my whore self has better things to do than to sit here and be slut shamed by my own fucking brother." She pulled out her wallet and dropped a five dollar bill on the table next to his hand. "It's been real."

Once she was outside, she didn't stop. She kept walking until she slammed into her Interactive and Data Journalism professor. "Professor Alvarado. I'm so sorry, I didn't see you." She sniffed and wiped her wet cheeks with the back of her hand.

"That's what happens when your vision is blurry, Molly." He cupped her elbow and led her to the side of the path, out of the way of people traffic. "Do you want to talk about it?"

My brother thinks I'm a slut and I have four-letter-feelings for his best friend.

She shook her head. "I'd rather not."

"Okay, then let's pivot. Have you given any further thought to a summer internship?"

When she didn't reply, he kept going. "I've been reading your articles for the school paper, and your blog. You really have something special, Molly. I think any of the big stations would be lucky to have you. You should really think about putting yourself out there. I know the deadline for ESPN has passed, but—"

"I applied for ESPN." She tugged at the hem of her shirt.

"You did?"

She nodded.

His face broke into a grin. "Good, Molly. Very good. I know you weren't sure about it, but I think you'd be a good fit. There are a few others still looking for people too – if you don't want to put all your eggs in the ESPN basket."

"Sure, could you email them to me, please?"

His beaming face warmed something in her. Did he really believe she was capable of kicking ass at ESPN?

"Absolutely."

"Thanks. Well, I better be going." She took a step to the side to get past him but he touched her elbow, giving her pause.

"Molly?"

"Whoever he is that's making you cry like this? He's not worth it."

If only he knew.

CHAPTER 13

Finnegan

Finn had been sound asleep when his phone had rung at midnight, waking him up. The bartender at Pucks had called him when he couldn't reach Cleo.

"Just one more?" Molly's voice in the background had sounded almost pathetic.

Finn had bounded out of bed, pulled on sweats and a shirt, and made his way to take her home. He was prepared to carry her if she objected. He pulled open the door and scanned the room. She sat at the bar, arms crossed, deep scowl on her beautiful face, and a glass of ice water sitting untouched on the bar in front of her.

"You're who he called?"

Finn sighed. Would it kill her to be at least a little grateful? "He coulda called your brother."

She snorted. "Fuck Will. And the high and mighty horse he rode in on."

Despite Molly's volume at the coffee shop, Finn hadn't heard all the details of what she and Will had been talking about. Will hadn't wanted to retell the story either. But Finn had seen her run down the street, tears streaming down her face. He'd chased after her before she'd collided with her professor. Whatever Will had said had clearly cut her to the quick.

"You ready to go home?"

"I don't need a babysitter." Her scowl deepened.

He grunted. Good cop wasn't going to cut it. "Molly, I was asleep. I get that you're going through something right now but I'm tired and I have practice in a few short, precious hours. I need my sleep, so if you don't get your ass outside and into my car, I'm picking you up."

Her eyes narrowed. "You wouldn't dare."

Challenge accepted. In truth she should have known better. Sober Molly would have. Drunk Molly was beyond the capacity for rational thinking. He stooped and threw her over his shoulder before she could utter another word. He swiped her coat from the stool she'd been sitting on and used it to cover her near bare ass as he carried her out the door.

"Put me down." She hammered on his back with clenched fists. It actually felt kinda good.

"Not till I get you to the car. I don't wanna play cat and mouse with you MoMo. I'm tired. I'm taking you home."

He jerked open the car door and dropped her onto the passenger seat. She let out an adorable squeak as she landed. Even furious and drunk, she somehow managed to be beautiful.

"Wanna talk about it?" He slammed the door behind him, started the ignition, and tinkered with the dials until hot air blasted through the vents.

She shook her head and turned away from him. Fine. He was too tired to press for information she didn't want to give.

He drove her home in silence. By the time they pulled up outside her apartment she was making soft snoring sounds and her head hung forward. With a sigh he eased out of the car, careful not to slam the door. He circled, found her key in her coat pocket, and slipped his arms around and under her to carry her inside.

Outside her apartment, he shifted her weight so he could reach the lock and stumbled inside into a dimly lit room. Presumably Cleo had left the lamp on in the living room so Molly wouldn't fall to her doom when she got home. She was still limping from her previous fall, the last thing she needed was for a matching injury to the other foot – or worse.

She stirred in his arms, making cute sleepy noises and muttering to herself as he moved with the grace of a hippo in a china shop. He stumbled, she slipped, he righted himself. Her grip on him tightened as he walked, but after a few moments her hand fell slack around his neck, her chest rising and falling with even breaths.

In her room, he toed off one of his shoes and used his foot to pull back her quilt before laying her flat on her back. She had a chunky necklace around her neck that he removed with minimal under-his-breath swearing. Bras he could work, necklace clasps, not so much. He fought with the straps on her heels, but finally eased them off before tucking her feet under the blanket and covering her.

He sat on the edge of the bed, brushed her wild hair from her face, and stroked her cheek with the back of his hand. "You're going to be the death of me Molly Morrison."

She stirred under his touch. "You're not allowed to die."

He smiled. "You let me carry your lazy ass all the way from the car and you were awake the whole time?"

She didn't answer. The bartender said she'd had way too much to drink, and from the stench of whisky seeping from her pores, she was pretty far gone. He should leave, but his hand kept stroking her soft skin and his heart wouldn't let his feet move.

He sighed, a lump forming in the back of his throat. "I really wish you weren't my best friend's sister, Molly."

She sighed and stilled.

"If you weren't his sister I could tell you how much I love you, how much I think you're a freakin' badass, and how badly I want to be with you." He leaned over, planted a quick kiss on her forehead and made his way back through the house to the kitchen. He grabbed her a glass of water and a banana, a tub of Tylenol from the bathroom and left them by her bed.

The next morning, Finn found Will at the breakfast table of the hockey house, scowling at a bowl of Lucky Charms.

Finn spun a chair around so he could sit on it backwards, hugging the back. "Who are you and what have you done with my best friend? Will Morrison never eats that shit."

Will sighed and dropped his spoon with a clang in response.

"And while we're at it, what are you doing here?" Finn picked up Will's spoon and shoveled a heap of cereal into his mouth. "How can you not like that delicious mallowy goodness?"

Will pushed the bowl across the table to Finn. "Knock yourself out."

"Spill."

Will shook his head. "It's good. I'm good."

Of course he was. Will saying "It's Good" was the equivalent to a woman saying "It's fine" – Finn had learned the hard way, it was never fine. Finn took another bite and pointed the spoon at Will. "Are you trying to convince me, or yourself? To be honest, I'm not sure you're convincing either of us, man. What gives? Girl trouble?"

"Worse." Will leaned back against the chair and folded his arms. "Molly trouble."

Finn knew it was Molly trouble, but half the battle with the Morrisons was getting them both to admit the problems they were facing out loud. Once that had been accomplished, things flowed a little easier and they could work to a solution. Some days they were more stubborn than others.

"Again I say: spill."

Will leaned forward on his hands, fingers spearing into his hair. "I don't know what to do about her."

Something coiled in the pit of Finn's stomach. "Do? About her?"

"She needs to check her behavior."

The serpent in Finn's gut coiled a little tighter, slithering up his chest and wrapping itself around his pounding heart. He loved Will with everything he had, but his sometimes low opinion of his sister made him madder than a hornet in a tin can. He clenched his jaw, hoping gritted teeth would prevent him from lashing out.

"What do you mean?"

"Her promiscuity is getting out of hand, Finn. Surely you have to see it?" Every word dripped with disdain.

Finn snorted, but the snake in his chest rose higher. "Promiscuity? What's this, the 50s? You and her have always been different. You're the quiet book nerd, she's the outgoing wild child. You're oil, she's water."

"I'm not a prude."

"Hey." Finn held his hands up. "I never said you were."

"But?"

"But I think you're being kind of a jerk about her."

Will lurched upright like he'd been punched in the face. Good. He needed a dose of reality.

"What?" Will's eyes widened like it was the first time Finn had ever disagreed with him about something. It probably was, but he wasn't going to let him bash Molly in his presence. Not anymore.

"I'm just like her. For years, I fucked damn near anything in a skirt."

"That's—"

Finn held up a hand, a bubbling in his stomach forcing him to suck in a deep breath. "Don't you dare tell me that's different because I have a dick and she doesn't, Will Morrison."

He had the courtesy to blush and avert his stare. But Finn wasn't letting it drop.

"It's not different. It's the same thing. I'm a 'manwhore.'" He made bunny ears with his fingers. He hated the term. He hated any term that was derogatory about someone's sex life. Some people liked sex, some people didn't, but no one needed to be labeled because of it.

"And it's celebrated as this great thing – by guys and girls alike. So your sister likes sex, big deal. As long as she's safe and she's not asking you to join in, or watch..." He shrugged. "Where's the harm? Just 'cause you don't approve of her life choices doesn't mean you get to slam them. That's dickish."

Finn dropped the spoon onto the table and pushed the bowl of cereal back to Will. "I'm going for a run."

Will opened his mouth to speak, but Finn shook his head. "You need to do some serious soul searching here, man. You should be in her corner, screaming 'Fuck the patriarchy' from atop the highest building. Not this..." He waved an open hand at Will and left him to stew in his mood.

"Finnegan O'Brien."

Finn jolted to his feet at the mention of his name and strode toward the tall, blonde nurse with the clipboard. The clinical, hospital smell somehow permeated every doctor's office he'd ever stepped into. Did they bottle it and sell it as air freshener to every health care provider in the world? Was it a universal cleaning product?

His stomach sloshed like an overfilled mug of coffee. He swallowed twice but it didn't help. He smoothed out his sweatpants.

"Follow me please."

He made his way through the near-empty waiting room, dodging a toddler on wobbly legs as he crossed to where the nurse waited.

"Do you have a good arm?" She spoke with her back to him as she collected whatever equipment she needed to draw blood.

He shrugged when she turned back to him. He had no idea. Other than needing to be stitched up from time to time after a particularly brutal game of hockey, or some deep tissue work from a pulled muscle every now and then, he was healthier than a horse.

He had asked his mother to send him the details about his brother's kidney problems. She'd emailed the information he needed about kidney transplants. He hadn't replied to her when he'd received it, but he'd booked an appointment to start the testing process to see if he was a match.

The phlebotomist skillfully withdrew the blood she needed for the test without hesitation. If he hadn't been watching the needle slide into his skin, he wouldn't have known she'd started.

As his blood trickled into the vial, his stomach clenched. Would he go through with surgery and give his half-brother a kidney if he was a match? He pushed the question aside, when he had an answer on if he could even donate, he'd figure out what to do next.

"You're all done." She smiled at him, the crow's feet at the corners of her eyes deepening as she did. It was over before he could blink.

"Thanks." He nodded and made his way outside into the fresh air. The thrashing in his stomach had calmed down enough for him to breathe easier. He'd taken the first step, either they'd be a match or they wouldn't. Until he knew which it was, it didn't bear worrying about. But that was easier said than done.

He rubbed at his chest. Why didn't he feel better? There was only one place he ever went when he needed guidance, but Mrs. Mo wouldn't be home from teaching at school yet. Maybe he could find a reason to stop by and chat with her. Or maybe he'd call her and leave a voicemail.

His pocket vibrated as he walked to his car. Despite being disgruntled that Finn wasn't "Team Will" for a change, Will had sent a message to check in. Finn paused, leaning against the roof of his car to read his texts.

Will: How'd it go?

Finn: I barely noticed she'd stuck something into me.

Will: That's what she said.

Finn: Ha. We both know they always notice when I stick something in them. It's hard to miss.

Will: I see what you did there.

Finn: I'm here all day.

Will: Wanna grab lunch?

Finn's stomach growled in response.

Finn: I could eat.

Twenty minutes later, Finn slid into a booth across from Will in Applebee's with a sigh.

"Why do we always end up here?" Will sipped on his ice water.

"I've never met an Applebee's I didn't like."

Will shook his head and perused the menu like he wouldn't get something bland and boring like grilled chicken and veggies.

"Hey guys!" Sabrina appeared next to them at the table. "What can I get for you?"

They ordered and Will studied Finn's face like the answer to world hunger might be etched across it somewhere.

"What?"

He shook his head. "I'm worried about you. You're having a tough month."

"I'm good."

Will arched an eyebrow. "Have you told your mo—anyone else about having the test done?"

Finn shook his head. "I didn't want the extra pressure, y'know? She'd be all hopeful and shit. And when I get the results... she says she wouldn't pressure me, but even if she didn't say anything, there'd be pressure. There's always pressure." He pinched the bridge of his nose.

Will played with a sugar packet. The door to the restaurant opened and a group of retirees walked in, laughing and joking as they passed Finn and Will.

"I was thinking of telling Mom." Finn paused and scratched his chin. "Your mom, I mean. Just so I had adult supervision for my decision, or input, guidance, whatever."

"You don't have to correct yourself. Mom's been your mom since the day you came to our house and ate every last bit of her watermelon salad."

Finn chuckled at the memory. "I love that salad."

"That's not changing now that your birth mom might be

coming back into the picture. Not for Mom, not for you. You're family, Finn. You're stuck with us."

Finn nodded and pulled out his phone. "I'm going to text her."

> Finn: Hey Mom, I took the kidney compatibility test today. Haven't decided what to do yet, but I needed all the information before I made a decision.

Something ceramic smashed behind the bar and Finn jumped. Will shoveled chicken and veggies into his face like he'd never been fed, but Finn couldn't eat while waiting for Mom to read his text. Mercifully, she replied right away.

> Mom: I'm proud of you for being so mature about this decision, Finn. I know it's not easy for you. And I hope you know I'm here for you if you need to talk anything through.

> Finn: I was hoping you'd say that. Depending on the results, I might take you up on it.

> Mom: Always here for you. No matter what.

CHAPTER 14
Molly

Molly blinked, head tilted back in her bed, eyes fixed on the white ceiling. Finn had said he'd loved her. What was she supposed to do with that information? Her stomach fluttered. Sure she had been drunk, and half asleep, but she was almost completely, totally, 100% convinced she'd heard him tell her he loved her. Hadn't he?

Fine, she was more like 45% sure, but every time she replayed the trip from the car to her bed she'd heard him say it. A whispered secret.

It had been two days. She'd managed to successfully avoid him, but it wouldn't last long. Her stomach flipped again. Could he really love her? He'd left Tylenol, water, and a banana after he'd put her to bed and left Post-Its saying 'Eat Me' and 'Drink Me' stuck to them.

Sweet was Finnegan's middle name. Crammed right there between Aiden and O'Brien. Heat spread across her chest. It was hardly fair that she knew what he'd said, but she didn't have the lady balls to tell him she felt the same. If he'd known she wasn't asleep, he would never have said it, but once he had, he couldn't take it back. It was her treasure now.

How long had he loved her for? How could she look him in the face ever again? Where did they go next?

She grunted and slammed her clenched fists into the plush quilt draped over her body. Wasn't this what she'd always wanted? Confirmation that Finn not only found her attractive, not just Will's younger sister, but that he also wanted more from her?

Her gut twisted. Did that mean he was done caring about what Will would think? Her mind reading capabilities were failing her. If she wanted answers, she'd have to – gulp – talk to the damn boy and get them.

The night before, she'd fed her confusion whisky. She'd woken up, mouth dry, head thumping, got out of bed and dressed. She needed to escape, to go for a drive and clear her head. Windows down, music up, and wind in her hair. That would help. It had to.

She got in her car and headed west out of the city. After twenty minutes of driving, even her car decided it had had enough of her grousing. The red light taunted her from the dash. Running out of gas was Molly's specialty. That and making jello shots. She eased the car to the shoulder as it juddered to a stop.

Shit.

She couldn't face calling Finn. Her cheeks sizzled at the thought. Her parents were both at work, Will wasn't talking to her, Cleo was in class and there was no way on earth she'd check her phone during lectures. Molly scrolled through the contacts on her phone.

Jared. Fuck buddy extraordinaire. But he'd brought her tacos once, so maybe he would bring her gas in exchange for a blowie? As dicks went, his wasn't half bad and he knew how to use it well enough for a call back.

She hit the call button.

"Yo?"

"Jared, it's Molly." Her stomach clenched and unclenched. Clenched and unclenched. She hated asking anyone for help.

"What's up, pretty girl? I'm busy right now but I could stop by later, at like... eleven?"

"I'm stranded. I ran out of gas and I'm wondering if you could—"

His obnoxious laughter swallowed her words. "I'm not your boyfriend, pretty girl. Go call your mamma." He hung up on her.

She really didn't want to call Finn. If she did, she might do something stupid like launch herself at him vagina first, or say something dumb like she loved him too. But calls to two more fuck buddies later, and she was out of alternatives.

He should have been her first call, like always, but the L-Word was mounted on a neon sign inside her brain, flashing every few seconds to remind her he'd said it. The call connected almost instantly.

"Molly? What's wrong?"

She sighed. How did he always know? She pulled the phone away from her ear and hit the speakerphone button. "Are you busy?"

Finn took a drink of something. "What do you need, Doll?"

Her throat constricted. Was he giving her a new pet name? Did he even know he'd called her it? What did it mean? Her brain ached from all the thinking and feeling.

"I... eh..." She cleared her throat. "I ran out of gas."

"Again?" He chuckled. "You know that red light isn't a challenge, right? I'm coming over."

"I'm not at the apartment."

He groaned. "Where are you?" His muffled voice sounded like he was talking from behind his hand.

She told him where she was and he told her it would take

him twenty-five minutes to get himself organized and out to her.

She had twenty-five minutes to figure out how to hide the fact she'd heard him say he loved her from her easy-to-read face.

"My hero!" Molly pasted a fake smile on her face. While she hated the damsel in distress bit, she genuinely could have kissed his beautiful mouth. But that would have led to misdemeanors – like being naked in public. Somehow his admission of feelings for her had dialed her lust up to an eleven.

He had parked behind her, gotten out of the car, and pulled a gas can from the trunk. When he'd emptied the fuel into her tank, he snapped the cover closed and pointed a finger at her. "We're going to gas up your car."

"You don't have to do that. I got it from here. Thanks though."

He wagged the still outstretched finger. "Ah! Ah! Not so fast. You owe me."

He had her there. She did owe him. He'd rescued her when she had no one else to turn to. "What's it going to cost me?" She'd happily sink to her knees at the side of the road and blow him, but that might have been a little strong for their first more-than-friends encounter. Her vagina didn't seem to think so, however, as a strong pulsing sensation in her pants had her clenching her thighs.

"Llama hugging."

"What the...? You've got to be kidding, right? That's totally not a thing."

With a satisfied grin he pulled his phone out from his back pocket and pulled up a website. Carlson's Loveable Llamas.

Was it really a thing? Surely people didn't just go visit a farm and hug llamas.

Her eyes bugged out of her head as she read that was exactly what people did. It was totally a thing. She pointed at his screen. "You want to go hug a llama?"

He nodded, still grinning. "It's about twenty minutes from here and I haven't been out there in a while."

"You've been before?" Was she being punked? She looked over her shoulder half expecting someone to be filming the exchange.

"I adopted a llama a few months ago. Freakin' love them. They're cute and fluffy and they give great hugs."

She covered her face and shook her head. "You... adopted a llama?"

He shrugged. "We went out to Carlson's when we were kids." He kicked at an invisible pebble at his feet. "Liam..." His voice broke over the word. "He loved the llamas and cried when we had to leave. Every time. He begged Santa for a pet llama, but he never got one. I went a few times since. Decided to adopt one a while back."

Her arms ached to hold him. "You just go... visit your llama?"

He nodded, jamming his hands into the front pockets of his jeans. "You can walk them, train them, groom and feed them. You in?"

Hell yeah she was in. Her veins thrummed with adventure. "I could take a llama for a walk."

"Let's get gas for your car and move it somewhere safer than at the side of a busy road. Then I'll take you to meet Liam the llama."

Her heart squeezed. The man would be the death of her. With trembling hands she climbed into Finn's car and waited for him to return. He'd insisted on taking her car across the freeway to gas it up, and bring it back. While she waited, she opened Venmo and sent him the cash. His car smelled of him. She wanted to wrap herself in his scent and never leave.

The door swung open and she squawked.

"Jumpy today?"

She nodded, mute.

"Ready?"

Another nod.

She hadn't thought it through. Twenty minutes in a confined space with the man she wanted to mount and do dirty things to, was a bad plan. She risked a glance at his face and almost fainted when he licked his lips. It was a very bad plan. She swallowed and wiped her damp palms on her thighs.

"You okay?"

She nodded a third time. She was starting to feel like a freakin' bobble head doll. "I'm fine, just embarrassed about the gas thing."

"Molly Morrison running out of gas is hardly front page news, Mol. Still not back on good terms with Will though? I mean, he'd usually be your first call."

She shrugged. "Not really. I mean, he'd have come if I called him. I just..."

"You didn't want to?"

A whooshing sigh escaped her. "I didn't want to."

"I get it." He turned his head to her before flicking his gaze back to the road. "He was out of line for whatever it was he said to you."

She opened her mouth to speak, but words didn't come out.

"He didn't tell me, and I'm not asking. But he's wrong."

She snorted. "How do you know he's wrong if you don't even know what he said?"

He looked at her again, his bright blue eyes hypnotizing her with their depths. "I know enough. Your body, your choice, right?"

She nodded. "Right." Apparently nodding was the only thing her body had oxygen left to do. That and fuel the fierce ache between her legs. His finger brushed her thigh as she shifted in her seat.

He was cradling the gear shift. If she moved again he'd touch her again. How many times could she brush against his pinky before he noticed? How many brushes against him would it take to make her come?

Her whole face burned. If it was really her body, her choice she'd have already had her way with Finnegan O'Brien. She opened the window, staring at the blurring scenery as they passed and willing the breeze to cool her flaming cheeks.

"You're not allowed to hurl in my car, MoMo."

She shook her head, afraid that if she spoke she'd tell him she didn't have an upset stomach, rather an aching clit that needed his atten-tongue. Maybe he'd even oblige her desires, but as soon as they came down from the post-coital bliss, they'd both regret it.

Wouldn't they?

She studied the profile of his face. A nose broken and reset more times than she could count. A firm jaw, flame-colored hair licking at his ear, and a tiny, almost imperceptible scar on his cheekbone from having caught a stray puck to the face. Another scar on his upper lip, and a third just under his chin.

A muscle twitched in his cheek. "You're staring."

The burning from her face flashed over her entire body like she was a donut being dunked into a pan of hot oil. She gasped and turned back to face out the window. She'd stared at him more often than was considered socially acceptable and had never once cared about being caught. Now she cared.

Her pulse thundered, rattling through her veins, making her body thrum. She tugged at the collar of her shirt as the unrelenting heat scorched her, consuming her from the inside.

What had to be nothing less than a million years later, they arrived at the farm. Her heart hadn't stopped racing, her panties were damp, and if Molly and Finn hadn't already gotten to their destination, she was about three minutes away from having him stop the car so she could take a full breath. And possibly get herself off by the side of the road.

Finn O'Brien had a habit of sucking all the air from any room they were in, and she had a sneaking suspicion he'd only give it back if she sucked it from his—

"You getting out? You gonna come hug my llama or are you just gonna sit and ogle it from the car?"

Her eyes widened as she met his cheeky gaze. It was as though he could tell the dirty thoughts that had been running through her head for the entire car ride. His left hand hung loosely by his side, clutching his keys. His right, however, she could grab it, shove it between her thighs and sink onto it, showing him the effect he had on her.

"Molly?"

Her breath caught. She needed to get the hell out of dodge, go the fuck home, and use every vibrator she had until her batteries ran dry and her clit no longer ached for his touch.

He reached out an open palm. Was he reading her mind? Those long fingers... Shit. Fuck. Nope. There was no amount of batteries that could convince her that the man in front of her wasn't everything. His mouth curved into a slow smile.

Yeah. He was everything and then some.

She slid her trembling hand into his, and he tugged, guiding her from the car. The farm stretched as far as the eye could see, and to his credit, Finn really was an adoptive parent to a llama named Liam. He wasn't messing with her. But it didn't track. Finn wouldn't even adopt a cactus in case he somehow killed the damn thing. He wouldn't even house sit someone *else's* cactus in case he killed it. He shirked all long term commitment, and responsibility, yet he'd adopted a... llama? Who was this man?

Liam was a glorious specimen of llama – not that she had much to compare him to. His shaggy cream mane was spliced by a chunk of chestnut brown hair down his neck and back. As llamas went, the farm couldn't have picked a better one for Finn to adopt. The juxtaposition of light and dark... well... it was the perfect blend for him. Liam was the only two-tone llama, too, the others were all seemingly perfect and flawless, but something about Finn's bucktoothed buddy was a little 'off,' a little quirky, just like him.

Liam's hair tickled her nose as she snuggled into his neck. She sneezed, the llama jumped, head butting her full-force in the face. Hobbling back, she hit something hard that quickly gave way. She stumbled, turning to see what she'd hit, but her foot caught on something, she tripped, and was freefalling – almost in slow motion, and she couldn't stop herself.

She was falling right onto an already horizontal Finn-fucking-O'Brien. He stretched his arms out, as though he thought he could somehow stop her from splatting right on top of him. She wasn't graceful. She wasn't going to land on him with a dainty huff of air, she was gonna starfish him with a smack.

Heat consumed her body as time slowed to a crawl. She barely contained herself in the car on the ride to the farm, if her body landed against his... she'd spontaneously combust. Or orgasm on contact. While she didn't mind a little exhibitionism, it wasn't the time or place, so she found herself quietly hoping for the combustion option.

Finn huffed when her body landed on his. Torn between scrambling to her feet and snuggling her face into the space between his head and neck to take an intoxicating sniff, she froze.

Liam head-butted her ass, rocking her crotch against Finn's. Jesus Christ on a Crumpet was he getting hard?

"Are you okay?" His voice was husky, she wasn't sure if it

was from the fall, her landing on top of him, or if the lust seeping through her veins was leaking out through her clothes and onto him.

She pressed her palms against his firm chest and groaned. Hot damn, he was ripped. She nodded. Her mouth drier than an Arizona summer – probably because all the liquid in her body had made its way elsewhere. "Did I hurt you?" She stood, holding out a hand to help him up.

He shook his head as he clasped his palm against hers and bounded to his feet. "It's all good." Dusting off his butt, he chuckled. "Let's go." He led Liam back to his pen and took Molly's hand.

"Where are we going?"

He didn't answer, but fifteen minutes later, despite numerous protests, she was the proud new owner of her own stuffed llama named Liam. He even had the same hair. No one had ever bought her such a sweet gift. She'd never tell Finn, but she'd treasure Liam the second forever.

"I can't believe you didn't want to take him home." Finn shook his head as they headed back toward where they'd left her car parked.

"That's not... I didn't... I wanted the stuffy. I just didn't think you should have bought him for me."

"Something to mark the occasion. It *was* my llama that knocked you on your ass after all."

She shifted in her seat. Being knocked on her ass didn't even make the top five things she wanted to do with Finn O'Brien's *llama*. Rolling her lips between her teeth, she gave a slow nod. "True. But I scared the shit out of him by sneezing. Will you please let me pay for him?"

Please say no.

"Absolutely not."

Her heart swelled. "Thank you."

They rode in silence for the rest of the way. Her heart and

mind thrashing wildly as Finn drove, singing to the local pop music station. While he was a reasonably skilled guitar player, he wasn't the best singer. She smiled as he battled his way through Kings of Leon's *Sex on Fire*. He was definitely a better accompaniment than front man, but he didn't care. He sang loud and proud – like no one was listening, and even if they were, he had zero fucks to give about it. And she was there for it.

He pulled up next to her car in the parking lot, but instead of keeping the engine running and letting her hop out to flee the mounting tension in his vehicle, he stopped and got out. What the hell was he doing?

She opened the door, swiveled in her seat, and dangled her feet. She didn't want to leave. Stroking her thumb along the soft fur of the stuffed toy in her lap, she sighed.

"You must really like my car, MoMo. You seem to be quite happy in there."

She laughed it off and hopped out before she had to touch his hand again. A shiver trickled up her spine. He shoved his hands in his pockets and rocked back on his heels, bending a little at the waist. "Catch you later?"

Her phone rang in her pocket. When she pulled it out, the number on the screen made her heart quicken. She'd memorized the number from ESPN's HR department so she didn't get blindsided by a call from them. "Oh God. It's ESPN."

He nudged her elbow. "Answer it!"

Answer it. Right. She nodded and pressed the button. "H-hello?"

Finn leaned in toward her, placing his ear closer to the phone. Gooseflesh rippled along her arm as she inhaled his scent. How was it possible for one man to have such an impact on her?

"Hi, this is Bella from the HR department of ESPN. Is that Molly Morrison?"

Molly cleared her throat. "Yes, this is Molly. Hi Bella."

Please don't say I didn't get it.

Please don't say I didn't get it.

Please don't say I didn't get it.

"We really liked your application, and we want to offer you the opportunity to come in for an interview. Would tomorrow at three work?"

Did the Tin Man have a metal cock? Hell yes three would work.

Finn's elbow jabbing at her suggested she hadn't actually answered the woman waiting patiently at the other end of the phone.

"I'd love to. Thanks so much."

"We'll email you the address."

"Yes ma'am. Have a good day."

"You too."

Molly stared at the screen as Bella hung up. Had it really happened? Was she a step closer to becoming a play-by-play commentator for ESPN?

"Wow." She met Finn's eyes, they were warm and rich with pride.

He pursed his lips and jerked his chin. "Is this where I say I told you so?"

"I got an interview." Her voice was a whisper.

His grin grew. "You got an interview."

"I got an interview!" With Liam the llama clasped in one hand, she flung her arms around Finn's neck with a squeal.

Finn's arms banded around her back before he picked her up and swung her around, making her squeal even louder. When he stopped spinning her, she slid down his body, landing on unsteady feet. Chest heaving, adrenaline pumping, and all sense of rational thought leaving her body with every weighted breath she licked her lips.

His hands flattened against her back and he lowered his head to hers.

Her pulse kicked up.

His heated stare flickered between her lips and her eyes.

Need pooled low in her belly.

His breath tickled her face as she rolled onto her toes to meet his lips, but instead of the mind-blowing, life-altering kiss she expected, her ankle smarted and she swayed. She fisted his shirt before she knocked her elbow against the wing mirror of her car with a thud.

"Shit." Ignoring the throbbing in her funny bone, she stared into Finn's soul. His nod was so slight, so small, she was almost convinced she'd imagined it until his hand pressed against the small of her back. She righted herself and glided her hand from his chest up over the curve of his shoulder, slipping her fingers into his hair.

He inched his face closer to hers, their lips so close the wing of a butterfly couldn't fit between them. There was no going back once they crossed the line but the need to have her lips on his drove her forward. She sucked in a steading breath. Every inch of her skin tingled. Her hard nipples brushed against his firm chest with every rise and fall of their synched breaths.

A deafening wail pierced their blissful bubble. She jumped back from Finn like he was on fire and she was lighter fluid. A car alarm screeched somewhere close by. As heat rose in her cheeks, she smacked at her pockets. Producing the keys from her jeans pocket, she pressed on the unlock button, again and again but it didn't silence the squalling alarm.

"It's not your car, Molly." He touched her arm and she gasped, snapping it away like his touch burned her. In many ways it did.

She tried to say "I should go," but nothing came out. She might have grunted, but by the time words filtered back into her mouth, she had already slammed and locked her car door behind her.

She needed to flee the scene of the crime. Almost crime. Distance from Hottie O'Brien would bring her brain back online, and with any luck hit the kill switch for the throbbing mess in her panties.

She tossed Liam onto the seat next to her, taking a moment to right him before she started the car, put it in drive, and pulled out of the space. In the rearview, Finn leaned against the side of his car, cheeks flushed, eyes dark, and arms folded. Was his heart thundering as violently as hers was? Did his stomach feel heavy while his chest soared? She hadn't even kissed him and her body was a freakin' light show of contradictions and sensations and emotions. How the hell could she ever look him in the eye again?

Later that night, unable to settle and intent on hedging her bets, Molly submitted two more applications for other local summer internships.

With shaky fingers she sent a screenshot of the "Thank you for your application" screens to Finn with a message that said, *Hey friend. Adulting is hard. Now we wait. Thanks for the kick in the butt to shoot my shot.*

She cringed at the triteness in her words, but the suffocating need to fix what she might have broken by almost kissing him engulfed her with every breath. She needed them to be okay. She couldn't lose him just because she led with her clit... and her heart, instead of her brain. *Fuck it all to hell.* It wasn't her fault he was so freakin' hot.

She stared at the screen like her eyes might pierce through the phone and show her his face. The three dots taunted her for a few seconds before words appeared.

Finn: I'm proud of you. You deserve it. You
needed to give yourself the chance.

The knot in her chest eased a little. It was nice, sure. But where was his grand declaration of his love for her? Her phone vibrated again.

Finn: I want to make one thing crystal clear,
though, because it seems you're not getting
my subtle hints and it's time to be not
subtle.

Her chest tightened and her stomach lurched like she was cresting the top of a rollercoaster, preparing for the freefall.

Molly: What's that?

Finn: Well, if you'd give me a freakin' minute
to type, you'd know…

Despite the tension, she couldn't help laughing.

Molly: Are you typing the Magna Carta?

Finn: Fuck this.

The phone rang in her hand and a picture of Finn appeared on her screen. His helmet was slanted off his head, he was chewing on his mouth guard and beads of sweat dripped from his hair and the tip of his nose. Hot damn he was delicious. When she didn't pick up, he texted her again.

Finn: Pick up, MoMo.

He called again. She scrunched up her face and hit the red button. Was this where everything changed? Was he going to tell her he needed to be responsible and they had to somehow roll back whatever feelings were oozing toward each other? Or was he going to say screw it, 'let's fuck around and find out?'

Which did she want it to be?

Finn: Molly, pick up the goddamn phone.

On the third try she picked up. "Hey." Her voice was croaky and caught on the sharp edges in her throat.

"I don't want to be friends with you, Molly Morrison."

Her heart stopped beating. She didn't blink, or breathe, or even move.

"I want all of you."

He wanted more, too. She blew out a hard breath.

"But how?" Her voice was barely a whisper, as though her brother might somehow hear if they were too loud.

"If you want to try, we'll figure it out."

CHAPTER 15
Finnegan

Droplets of sweat trickled down Finn's forehead and seeped into his eyes. He blinked to clear his vision and squirted cold water into his mouth before dousing his face. His legs burned after his shift, and he was grateful for the reprieve of sitting on the bench for a few minutes before his next shift on the ice.

The ref's shrill whistle blew, stopping play. Alabama Mustang's player Jeremy Lewis had bagged himself a penalty from a skirmish with Snow Pirate Johnny White and was bickering with the referee. From the consternation painted across Jeremy's face, he felt as though he was the one who had been wronged. When it came to JW, he probably was.

While the heated discussion on the ice continued, the Kiss Cam appeared on the jumbotron. Finn gnawed on his mouth guard, popping it off his teeth and hooking it around his cheek as an old dude, no younger than eighty-five macked hard on the giggling, elderly woman beside him.

More power to them. If Finn got anywhere near that age and had a woman who'd let him mack on her like that, he'd have considered himself a very lucky man.

Molly's pale face appeared on the screen next. Cleo sat to her left, but to her right, a dark haired guy Finn had never seen before lit up as bright as the screen itself. With a gleeful grin, Mr. Sleaze slouched back in his chair, hooked his arm over the back of Molly's seat, and wiggled his eyebrows at her.

The crowd cheered. Finn's stomach dropped. Molly and Finn had sat for what felt like an entire twenty four minutes in complete silence on the phone the previous evening before Molly had whispered one word before hanging up. *Okay.*

Whatever had been simmering between them for years on end was approaching boiling point. Finn was caught in the wheels of a steam train, being dragged toward Mollyville. Population: one. Sassy, classy, and badassy as hell. He couldn't fight it even if he wanted to.

While part of him almost wished for the chemistry between them to die off so the tugging in his chest would stop every time he saw, or spoke to Will. Another part – a much bigger part of him – yearned to explore whatever was between them.

His dick twitched in his cup. *All* of whatever was between them. On the screen, Molly's eyebrow arched and the cocky asshole next to her shrugged as if to say "What are you gonna do?"

The camera cut to a younger couple, teens decked out in Snow Pirate's jerseys and holding hands. The young girl's face turned scarlet and her blush only deepened the minute her beau's lips brushed against her cheek.

The crowd booed, relentless in their pursuit for overt PDAs. The camera panned back to Molly, who thumped the screen of her phone like it had done her wrong. Was she texting him? His heart fluttered. He was a goner. Once she'd said okay, his heart was off to the moon on a rocket ship. There was no reigning it in.

The crowd escalated their encouragement, screaming and

applauding. The douche nozzle next to her leaned toward her, pointing to his cheek. Storm clouds gathered in her eyes right there on the big screen. Man, homeboy was about to cop a headbutt from MoMo if he wasn't careful.

The crowd booed harder when Molly covered his face with her palm and pushed. Finn chuckled. She could have just kissed his cheek and been done with it. But that wasn't Molly. She dug her heels in, doubled down on the stubbornness and said not today, asshole.

No one painted Molly Morrison into a corner – unless she wanted to be in the goddamn corner. The camera moved to a father, cradling adorable twin girls on his lap. The girls bounced and pointed at themselves on the screen, tight, ringlet curls bobbing with the movement. The father's lips moved, presumably explaining why they were on the huge TV over the ice pad, and within seconds both little girls planted kisses on their father's cheeks.

A collective 'awwwww' and wave of applause washed over them from the spectators before Molly's face appeared on the screen once again. The prick next to her elbowed her, catching what would have to be a still tender boob from the procedure she'd had done. Molly winced and scooted a couple of inches away from him. Her brows were drawn tight together in a deep frown and the apples of her cheeks were stained red. Her eyes flickered to Finn's on the bench, full of heat and fury.

He'd seen that look in her eyes a thousand times before, but it had never spoken straight to his dick the way it did when blown up on a larger-than-life screen. That was Molly Morrison's action face. The guy puckering his lips and making smacking, kissy kissy faces at her was about to end up with blue balls and a broken nose.

Molly

If that asshole didn't get his puckered lips out of her face she was going to smack him. Or worse, junk punch him. Weren't parents teaching their sons that no meant no? Why did women have to work to dissuade a man's interest, while a whole arena encouraged his advances – despite her very clearly having said no? Multiple times.

Her entire body burned, not with desire for the douchebag sitting next to her. Not even with anger. No. Finn O'Brien's panty-melting smolder burned through her clothes from the bench. He was furious on her behalf and it was hot as fuck.

Her chest tightened. While it was just a kiss, and aside from not being attracted to the jerk at her side, she could have done it without consequence, but images of every time she'd seen Finn kissing another woman accosted her senses.

Tina Morelli behind the bike sheds in high school. The blonde after they'd lost the championship game in their first year of college. The brunette in the bar as Molly made her way to the bathrooms. And countless others.

A bitter taste filled her mouth. If there was even a remote

chance that her kissing someone else would have anywhere near the same effect on him, she couldn't do it. But the cameraman wouldn't relent. It was great entertainment.

The crowd chanted 'kiss him, kiss him,' clapping and whooping like she was on the ice, during a playoff game and on a breakaway. Will stood in front of the box, waving a hand between White and Lewis, obviously pleading his case for his teammate to get away with his infraction. Finn arched an eyebrow that said *What are you gonna do, MoMo?*

So she did the only rational thing she could think of. She swiveled in her seat, arched an eyebrow at Cleo and silently prayed she was down with helping her best friend out. With the smallest of nods, Cleo smirked. Molly grabbed her by the collar of her game worn *Scott #13* shirt, and laid one on her. They'd kissed before, they'd kiss again, it was no biggie.

"What the hell?" The guy next to her snorted as Molly snuck a glance at the big screen. Sure, she was kissing her – very much in a relationship – best friend, but surely Linc would understand given the circumstances... right?

Fuck. She sure as shit hoped he would understand. She didn't miss Finn's small smile as he slipped his mouth guard back over his teeth and took to the ice. She pulled back from Cleo. The corner of Linc's mouth twitched into a smirk. He tilted his head, and Molly shrugged, the camera still on her. She'd smooth things over with him later if she had to, but his grin didn't suggest she was in any major trouble with her bestie's boyfriend.

Molly rolled her lips between her teeth, kept her shoulders square, and eyes hard. The camera finally panned away from the two of them and Molly trailed her thumb under her lip just in case her impromptu kiss had smudged her red lipstick. "I can explain. I'll apologize to Linc."

"No need." Cleo squeezed Molly's thigh. "You didn't wanna kiss another guy in front of Finn. I get it. I've seen your face when he's kissed other girls. And I've seen his when you kiss guys. I can understand wanting to avoid that pain. For both of you. Especially now you're edging out of denial and into acceptance."

"You've seen his face when I've kissed guys?"

Cleo nodded as she tracked the puck on the ice.

"And you never mentioned this before because...?"

"Because. We were in the 'let's pretend we can't see all the signs' phase of your denial, Molly. That's why." She lifted a shoulder and dropped it again. "I wasn't going to push it until you were ready to admit you had a problem."

She jerked her chin at the ice. "A tall, broad-shouldered, red-haired beast of a problem named Finn get-in-my-pants O'Brien. This has been brewing for a while between you guys. You both decided to ignore it, or you're both idiots. Either way, I kept my mouth shut. I wasn't suffering your wrath."

Had Molly been deliberately avoiding the signs between her and Finn for the sake of her relationship with Will? Sure, she'd wanted Finn from the minute he'd walked into her back-yard as a gangly teenager, and she'd grown to love him more as he'd developed into the solid, well-rounded, compassionate man on the ice in front of her.

But willingly ignoring signs of mutual attraction that went beyond surface deep 'hey you're hot'?

As Finn assisted on a goal on the ice and gave back-pats and high-fives to her brother, she raked back over their time together. She'd denied every romantic instinct she'd had about Finn, from day one, and she'd still managed to piss Will off by sleeping with anyone who wasn't Finn. It was time to stop denying her instincts and make a move to get what she'd wanted for years. If Will was going to be mad, did it truly matter what he was gonna be mad about?

She untucked her phone from between her thighs, pulled open the messaging app, and sent Finn a text.

> Molly: Can we talk? The diner. After the game?

He'd probably want to go to the bar after the game, he was a party creature of habit and they hadn't been to Joe's diner in a long time. But she hit send, ignored the shiver that rattled through her bones, and pretended to stare at the ice while tracking every second on the countdown clock as she waited for the game to end.

Molly's knee knocked on the underside of the table in the booth of the diner as she waited. She'd hung around at the rink for long enough to get a reply from Finn before driving like she'd stolen the car to the place they used to go as teens. "10-4" that was all it had said.

Was 10-4 good? Was 10-4 I've changed my mind? Was 10-4 let's get naked and do the pelvic tango?

"You want a shake, Molly?"

"Yes, please, Joe. Thanks."

The white-haired man with wrinkles at the edges of his eyes smiled. "By yourself tonight?"

Her muscles tensed. Was it a mistake to go somewhere so familiar? Joe's diner was on the outskirts of the city. It wasn't somewhere often frequented by their friends, but Joe and Susan – the owners – had known both Molly and Finn for years.

Had she picked the diner so she wouldn't be tempted to make a move on Finn under Joe's watchful eye?

"I said, are you by yourself tonight, Miss Morrison?"

She giggled, but her breath caught and she coughed. "No, sir. He's on his way."

He nodded at the TV. "My son hooked up the TV to his

laptop so we could watch the game." He scrubbed at the counter with a rag. "Obi had a good game."

She couldn't disagree. Finn's skates had been on fire for the whole three periods. He'd bagged three assists and managed to keep his ass off the naughty step – an accomplishment if ever there was one. "Great game." She nodded in agreement, twisting the paper napkin resting on her thighs.

A blender sounded somewhere in the back as the door opened. Finn had ditched his suit jacket, he wore shiny black shoes, perfectly pressed black dress pants, a black belt with a shiny silver buckle, and a dark gray dress shirt. With Finn's wild colored hair, bright eyes, and pale skin... Molly melted into the cheap red pleather booth seats like a popsicle on a hot summer day.

"Great game tonight, Obi!" Joe waved his rag over the counter at Finn. "Coulda been four, but great game."

"Yes, sir." Finn chuckled, throwing a wave in Joe's direction before making a beeline across the black and white checkered floor tiles straight for Molly.

He slid into the booth, dumped a pile of quarters on the table between them, and turned to the mini jukebox mounted on the wall at the end of their table.

"Close your eyes, Molly."

As teenagers, they'd spent a lot of their time scrounging up quarters in preparation for their next shake date. Unfortunately, it was never a fun date, and certainly never a *date* date. Their shake dates coincided with *episodes* of violence from Finn's father. They were therapy dates. Wellness checks. A safe place for Finn to decompress after an evening with his dad's belt, or fist.

Finn would show up at her house, or send her a text simply saying 'shake?' She'd collect her coin purse, ask Dad for a ride to the diner, and go.

Their routine was as predictable as a lighthouse in a storm.

Strawberry shakes, and a few bucks worth of quarters between them on the table in a bid to see who could pick the worst song on the jukebox.

They'd sit in silence until Finn had consumed enough frozen strawberry deliciousness to calm down. Then they'd talk about anything and everything except what had brought them together at the diner: Finn's father.

Joe, Susan, nor Dad had ever asked questions, it just became routine. After a while, Joe even stopped charging them for their shakes. Some nights, he and Susan even gave them a hot meal. It was funny the things grownups picked up on, the things she missed as a naïve teen that, looking back, were clear as day. So many people rallying around a child in a man's body who needed more help than any one person could give.

Plastic clinked against plastic as Finn flicked through the song lists mounted on the wall – despite the fact they both probably had every song memorized. He punched some buttons, flicked a few more pages, and pushed a few more buttons.

"Can I look yet?"

He tugged her hand away from her eyes, and she pointed at the jukebox. "How bad is it?"

He shrugged and gave her a wicked grin. "Wait and see."

The Spice Girls broke into song over the speakers and Molly hung her head. "That kinda night, eh?"

Joe appeared tableside and slid their shakes in front of them. The sweet, thick liquid never fitted up the straws right away, but that didn't stop Molly and Finn trying. Just like old times. "You guys want any food?"

Finn nodded and patted his stomach. "It's game night, Joe. Gimme the works."

"Rings and loaded fries?"

Finn nodded.

"Wings and fully loaded cheeseburger?"

Molly's stomach lurched. She was starving, but the idea of eating when this... thing... hung between them made her queasy.

"What about you Miss Molly?"

She shook her head. "I'll steal some of Finny's. Thanks Joe."

Finn reached out and grabbed Joe's forearm, stopping him from leaving. "She'll have her usual, Joe."

Once Joe had left, Finn lowered his voice. "I love you, Molly Morrison. But not share-my-food-on-game-night love, you hear me?" His stomach growled as if to punctuate his sentence.

Her skin tingled like he'd brushed a feather along her whole body. How could he throw the L-word about so blasé like they'd been together for fifty years and this was their weekly routine of dining out?

She refused to look at him, but felt his eyes on her, burning with the intensity that radiated from him despite his laidback attitude. He nudged her knee with his, forcing her head up.

"Hey." His soft features made her want to cry and jump him all at the same time.

"Hey yourself." She played with the straw in her glass, pushing it through the softened ice cream.

The door opened, the overhead bell rang, but she didn't know the couple who walked in and took up a table at the opposite end of the restaurant.

"Take a breath, MoMo."

She gave a smile, but her fingers trembled around the straw, and her knee knocked on the table again as her foot jumped. She searched his face but found no trace of humor.

"Talk to me. What are you thinking?"

She bent the straw over the rim of the tall glass. What was

she thinking? She was sitting contemplating doing the deed with her brother's best friend.

She shuddered. When her ex had cheated on her all those years ago, she'd resolved to be done with long-term deals.

So why was she sitting across the table from Finn hot-AF O'Brien contemplating carving her heart out of her chest and handing it to him on a plate?

Because Finn wasn't Justin, and she wasn't the Molly from back then, either. Because if she couldn't have Finn, she couldn't have anyone. Except now she had a shot – a real chance – to see if something real was between them. Could she find it inside herself to take it? Could she really have Finn?

He'd already told her he loved her, could she get her shit-for-brains together enough to ever say it back?

"Talk to me, Doll." His forehead crinkled as he frowned. Picking up her hand from her glass, he cupped it between both of his, and her heart spluttered in her chest.

She pulled her eyes from their clasped hands to the counter, Joe and Susan were nowhere to be seen.

Tucking a knuckle under her chin, Finn turned her head so she faced him. "Stop freaking out."

She snorted. "Right. You know what has a 100% failure rate? Telling someone to stop freaking out when they're freaking out. What if he comes here?" The door opened and a family of five ushered in from the cold.

"He won't. Why would he? This was always our place. He hates greasy spoon food." He brushed the pad of his thumb across her cheekbone. "Liam got you good."

She nodded. "It's fading, thankfully. Do you know how awkward it is telling people the bruise on your cheek is from getting headbutted by a freakin' llama? No one believes me."

He chuckled and the sound looped around the knot in her chest, teasing it loose.

"I suspect they all think I got blackout drunk and hit my

face when I fell. But llama headbutt? Hell no. That's too out there."

The strokes of his thumb back and forth across her skin sent little sparks dancing across her face, she leaned into his hand.

"You're touching me."

"You're letting me." He paused, frowning. "I can stop."

She shook her head. "I don't dislike it. I'm just not used to it."

That brought a full on laugh out of him. "We touch all the time, Molly. All the time."

"Sure. Platonically. This..." She pointed a finger back and forth between them. "This isn't platonic."

"Tell me about your interview. It was this afternoon, right? How did it go?"

She nodded and hissed out a slow breath. Her interview was neutral territory, a safe conversation. It made her stomach ache but for way different reasons than the risk of being caught canoodling with her brother's best friend.

"It was fine. Good. I think I did okay. I answered all their questions, I didn't look like a swamp witch, I didn't cuss..."

"Then why do you look like someone kicked your puppy?"

She smiled. "Tough competition. There was a line of people out the door clutching thick binders full of experience. People who know people. Competitive as hell people. I did my best, but I don't think it was good enough this time."

Finn sighed, but didn't stop stroking her cheek. The slow rhythm of the sweeps against her skin was reducing the chances she was going to have a heart attack right there in the diner.

"What's with the sigh?"

"You're your own greatest critic, Molly."

"Aren't we all our own greatest critics?" She reached out to touch his face.

Joe cleared his throat and Molly shot back in her chair, her face flaming. Joe's lips twitched and his nostrils flared like he was fighting a smile, but he said nothing. He placed the food on the table, gave Finn a shoulder pat, and disappeared back behind the counter and into the kitchen. Finn tucked into the food like he hadn't eaten in years.

"You might want to slow down on the shoveling, Finny. If you choke and die before we..." She covered her mouth with a slap.

He wiggled his eyebrows and pointed his fork at her, swallowing hard before speaking. "You've thought about it." His eyes lit up like high beams on a country road in the dead of night.

Were all men so dense? Did he really have no clue about how often she'd thought about having his skin on hers?

She rolled her eyes. "Only every day since we met."

He snorted. "I bet you don't even remember the day we met." He shook his head and shoveled half an onion ring into his mouth. Joe came out of the kitchen, arms laden with plates he delivered to the family of five around a circular table in the far corner.

She picked up a fry, skimmed it across the top of her milkshake, and pointed it at him. "Do too." She lowered her voice. "It's etched in my memory. I prayed so hard that you were just in town for the summer so we could hook up without upsetting Will."

His brows shot up. "You wanted rid of me?"

Her throat tightened. "Never. It just would have been easier than..." She shoved the fry in her mouth, hoping it would be enough to stop the word vomit that had somehow made its way out into the space between them. "You know, I almost died that day. I inhaled soda and almost choked to death. That shit burns."

He laughed. "I remember that but never knew why."

"I pretty much saw you and swallowed my tongue. My brain stopped working."

He chuckled. "It happens."

She threw a fry at him. "Jerk."

"Your friend... what was her name, Savannah? She just about killed herself laughing. Do you still talk to her?"

Molly nodded. "Sometimes. She went to college in Iowa and we drifted apart. I miss her."

Finn had already consumed half of the food on his plate and made a healthy dent in the sides he'd ordered, too. She rubbed her chest. In all the years they'd known each other, his voracious appetite never failed to simultaneously astound and disgust her.

"You're staring."

"I'm wondering how in the hell you're not getting heartburn. I have secondhand heartburn just from watching you."

He gestured at her with a chicken wing. She'd never thought chicken wings were sexy until one was brandished at her by someone with a wicked, bbq-sauce covered grin on his face. "It's a well-honed skill. Took years."

"You've had hollow legs for as long as I've known you. If I ate anywhere near that amount of crap my ass would be huge."

He tore at the chicken wing with his teeth. Hot damn, she'd give a limb to become a chicken wing. "I happen to like your ass. And many other things about you." His magnetic gaze wouldn't let her go. Light danced in his eyes as he chewed and she was sure her mouth hung wide open but she had no control over closing it.

"Where is all this coming from?" She dropped a fry onto her plate and licked her fingers before taking a drink of her milkshake.

"It's always been here, Doll. It's just been locked away in a dark corner of my heart. Forbidden love is the hardest kind, but

I think in many ways it's also the strongest. I've fought it for so fucking long, Molly." He dropped the bones into his bowl. "I just can't do it anymore. I want you. I can't watch you and any more guys when I'm the guy, Mol. I'm the fucking guy."

Her chest ratcheted tighter and tighter with every word, squeezing air from her body. Finn was the cocky, happy-go-lucky, laidback, no strings kinda guy. That she could deal with. But the romantic, soft eyed, warm-hearted man sitting in front of her might break her. "Who knew you were so poetic?"

He shrugged but a faint blush kissed his pale Irish skin. "I almost drowned in the pool the first day we met. I thought if I stayed under the water and held my breath the water would wash away whatever arrow shot me to the heart when I walked into your yard and saw you in all your half naked splendor. Or at least be cold enough to kill my raging boner."

A laugh bubbled up in her chest. "From day one, eh? You did a very good job of adopting an older brother role. I had no idea."

Another shrug, but his eyes darkened. "I needed my friendship with Will, my relationship with your family... if it wasn't for you guys taking me in..." His voice thickened, curdling the milkshake in her stomach.

"I know. I'm not blaming you, I just... I didn't know. I mean, when I got to college I knew you thought I was attractive."

"Molly, any hot blooded person in your presence thinks you're attractive. If they don't they're blind or stupid."

Her heart flared. "It's going to take a while to get used to you saying things like that."

"I'd suggest you adapt quickly, Doll. Now it's out there..." He motioned between them. "I can't seem to cram it back in the box it came out of."

"From day one?"

"From day one."

When they'd finished their meal and Finn had used no less than a dozen wipes to clear down his face and hands he flicked through the playlists again. "Eyes."

She snapped them shut. His music choices for the evening hadn't been awful, though they had resulted in a rather painful rendition of *Barbie Girl* that had Susan and Joe covering their ears behind the counter. The other patrons clearly weren't digging their performance either – one of them even asked for their order to go.

After a few moments, warmth surrounded her hands on the table as Finn cupped her hands with his. From the moment he'd sat down they'd been connected somehow. Either holding hands, him stroking her face, or even just their feet touching under the table.

Every time their bodies touched her raw nerve endings sizzled. He picked up her clasped hands and kissed her knuckles, his breath tickling her skin as he caressed her fingers with his lips.

If she wasn't careful, she could become addicted to the tender side of Finn O'Brien.

The song from *The Little Mermaid* started playing and Finn hummed quietly. "Keep them closed." He dropped her hands. The sound of the fabric squeaking as he moved was followed by the side of her body warming as he slid onto her side of the bench. Keeping her eyes closed she turned to face him.

He cupped her face with both hands and brushed his nose against hers. The tiny trembles in his hands vibrated through her cheeks as he rested his forehead against hers. He pulled back and pressed his lips against hers, but her muscles held tight, unrelenting. Her eyes snapped open and met his pained stare. Brows pulled into a deep frown he didn't give up, instead he tilted her head to the side and kissed again, but it made no difference.

Nothing. She felt nothing.

Her heart and stomach sank as disappointment curled itself around her spine and yanked on her whole body. Kissing Finn wasn't supposed to feel like she was kissing her brother. Kissing Finn was supposed to feel like breathing for the first time after holding your breath, or opening the window to the first day of spring after a long, dark winter.

He stared her down, still cupping her face. "This isn't right."

Tears welled behind her eyelids. Had she placed so much importance, so much pressure on kissing him that she'd neglected to account for the fact they might just not be a good match? She shook her head. It wasn't right. Their chemistry had been off the chart. Every time he touched her, sparks flitted across her skin.

She'd heard women talking in the bathroom about his bedroom prowess, and she sure as shit knew she wasn't a bad kisser. So what the hell was wrong?

Brushing a thumb over her lips he leaned toward her, dotting a kiss on her forehead. "We're gonna call that the warm up, the pre-game."

Her throat tightened. "You're just gonna ignore that disaster?"

He nodded, draping his arm across the back of the bench. "I am. We're both in our heads too much about it. We've built it up to being this vast, life altering moment. Sometimes there's just no choirs of angels, or fireworks when people kiss and that's okay. It doesn't mean they aren't meant to be together."

But what if it meant exactly that, that they weren't supposed to be together?

CHAPTER 16

Finnegan

Maybe they weren't supposed to be together. Molly had threatened bodily harm if Finn didn't let her pay for her half of the bill. As always, she'd written "Math" in the tip line, scrawled a total and her signature, and hopped up off the seat like it had morphed into a cactus and was jabbing at her ass cheeks.

He led her out of the restaurant, but she raced ahead to push the door before he could open it for her. Huh. It was going to be like that, was it? Two could play at that game.

Sure, one single asshole in high school had ruined Molly's outlook on his entire gender when she was sixteen. And yeah, Mrs. Morrison had made sure Finn hadn't grown up into some asshole, sexist mansplainer, but in some ways, he was pretty traditional. And he couldn't wait for Molly to be his girl.

His gut clenched. Would she ever let herself?

"We'll talk tomorrow." She tossed a wave over her shoulder but didn't look back as she strode across the parking lot to her car. He sprinted to catch up – hard to do with a stomach full of grease and milkshake, but he was determined not to let her leave on such a bum note.

If she left with things the way they were, there was no guarantee she'd ever let him kiss her for real, or take her on a proper date. Tiny drops of rain fell on his head and clothes as he reached out to grab her arm.

She spun to him, palms facing him. "This isn't a good idea, Finn."

"Why?" He stepped toward her, but the gap between them was still too wide. "Because we had one average kiss that didn't make you jizz your pants?"

"I just can't. Because of Will, Finn. He's in both our heads." She took a step closer, placing her hand on Finn's chest. "He's in our hearts, too."

The drops of rain grew heavier, weaving their way into her hair and trickling down her face, even still, he could tell she was crying. He'd seen Molly Morrison cry precisely once before – when her cheating, asshole boyfriend broke her heart.

"Maybe he has too much power over us, Molly. Have you considered that? Maybe we need to get him out of our heads for once." Their night wasn't ending with Finn inadvertently making her cry, even if he had to crawl through fire to make her smile again. "I know there's no such thing as a second chance at a first kiss, but I want you to promise you'll let me kiss you again."

She shrugged, pulling her lip between her teeth. "Maybe we just won't work." She hesitated, brushing her soaking hair from her face as rain fell from her nose. "Maybe we waited too long."

The hell they wouldn't work. He grabbed her wrist just as she turned toward her car and pulled her to him. She landed against his chest with a thud, but before she could react, he snaked his hand up the column of her neck and into her wet hair.

"Finn..."

His mouth covered hers before she'd even taken a breath after saying his name. Rain pelted their heads and clothes. She melted against him, her muscles softening. Her fingers curled around the open collar of his shirt and tugged him forward until her back hit the driver's side window of her car.

Hungry growls pierced the sound of the rain pouring around them. Their tongues battled in a fierce, frantic dance, but they still weren't close enough. He cupped her ass and picked her up, bracing her against the car and sliding his hands along her thighs to wrap her legs around his waist.

She leaned back as he ran his hands back along her legs and sank his fingers into her plush ass cheeks drawing a moan from her. He wanted all of her. Wild child, bi-sexual, badass, confident, outspoken, goddess. He wanted it all.

Dragging his teeth along the column of her neck he pressed the bulge in his pants against her. It wasn't awkward anymore. He ached to strip her naked and worship her from head to toe and back again.

She tugged his hair so his head snapped back and he snarled at the distance she'd put between them. "Down boy."

"Not a fucking chance." He pushed his cock against her again and she wiggled her hips with a small growl of her own.

She licked her lips, a feral gleam in her eye under the street lights. Rain streamed down her face as she tugged his head back once again with a grin. His blood ran like lava in his veins, thrumming through him like she was his life source.

He couldn't get enough. He broke free of her grip on his hair and crashed his mouth against hers in a clash of nipping, biting, and thrashing tongues.

He was a moth to her flame, only too happy to beg her to set him on fire if it meant he could spend forever kissing her.

"Take that girl home, Obi."

Molly's legs jerked from Finn's waist at the sound of Joe's

voice. As she pulled her body away the cold air met his wet skin. His stomach dipped. He wasn't ready to let her go.

"You'll both catch your deaths out here in this rain!" Joe tossed a stuffed garbage bag into a dumpster and hurried back inside.

"Yes, Sir." Finn saluted Joe but didn't take his eyes off Molly's face. She gnawed on the edge of her lip and her eyes darted back and forward as though searching for something in his expression.

He waited for the guilt to hit, but it never came. "Molly..."

She smacked a hand over his mouth and shook her head. "Don't. I need space from your..." Gesturing at his crotch she tried to step back but cracked her elbow off the wing mirror. "Fuck."

"You need space from my fuck?" His nostrils flared as he fought a smile. Perhaps if he showed her things could still be relatively normal between them despite the fact he just had his tongue in her mouth and his hands cupping her ass she'd relax about the whole thing.

Her brow crinkled and she gave him a look that loudly proclaimed he was an idiot.

Then again, maybe not.

She stared him down as he raised his hands and brushed them through his hair, shaking off the rain. He was drenched to his skin but he didn't care. Her kiss had fanned the smoldering coals in his chest and turned them into a blazing inferno. The cold couldn't touch him.

Phantom sensations lingered in his palms and on his lips and his fingers twitched to wrap themselves in her hair or curl around her ass cheeks. Fighting every urge to pick her up again, he took a step backwards and nodded. "Okay."

"Okay?"

"You need space, time, to think... whatever. You can have it. But I'm going to be here when you're ready to give in to this…" He pointed between them both. "I'm not done with you, Molly Morrison."

His dick twitched in agreement as he backed away toward his car. She clamped her lips between her teeth and bolted into her car, starting the engine and pulling away from Joe's parking lot faster than he could blink. As he stood in the easing rain, with droplets of water cascading down his back under his shirt and between his ass cheeks, all he could think about was kissing Molly Morrison again.

He rocked out to old school Stereophonics as he drove home drumming on the steering wheel and not caring that the sorority girls in the car next to him at the red light were very clearly laughing at him.

He was walking on air. His shoulders were lighter than they'd been for months, maybe even years. He'd finally made a move on Molly and she hadn't murdered him with her laser stare. Things were looking up.

He parked his car and skipped up the path to the house, whistling the song from the Little Mermaid. So he'd been a little cheesy, so what? He happened to know that Molly loved Disney movies – okay, fine, she preferred the villains – Ursula, Maleficent, the Queen of Hearts, but she'd kissed him back nonetheless. Behind her cool and confident exterior there was a squishy core. Bring on the cheese.

Sure, their first kiss was somewhat of a disaster, but he'd more than made up for it with the second. Hadn't he? He paused at the door and checked his phone. Nothing from Molly, but a slew of messages from the team in group chat about missing an impromptu team meeting.

Shit.

Had he not redeemed their flat first kiss? He closed his eyes as drops of rain fell from his hair onto his nose and a shiver rattled along his back as his cold, wet shirt skimmed his skin. He could still taste her lip balm. Was it the Huckleberry he'd bought her? He didn't care if it was ear wax flavor, he was addicted. That kiss was the best he'd ever had, there was no better, there could be no better, it was everything. She was everything.

Animated voices behind the door gave him pause, his teammates were playing something on the TV in the living room, and there was no sneaking past them. The door squeaked as he pushed it open, and he winced.

"Ah ha! He has returned." Linc raised a bottle of beer in the air in Finn's direction. Russ arched an eyebrow. Austin stood against the waist-high bookshelves in the corner, arms folded. He wasn't big on computer games, it usually took something big to pry his ass off the counter to join in which meant this was a DEFCON three or higher level team meeting, not DEFCON one or two.

Will erupted into cheers as Princess Peach crossed the finish line in Mario Kart. "Victory is mine!" He turned to face Finn, and pursed his lips. "Where you been, Obi? You might wanna get upstairs and get out of those wet clothes before you leave a puddle and someone falls on their ass. That's all we need. Man down due to slipping on the tiles and putting his back out."

Always responsible. Often somewhat exaggerated or worst case, but always thinking of others. That was Will. He was the moon to Finn's tide. Finn had no doubt that if he knew Will when Liam got knocked down, Liam would still be alive. Will would have known what to do. He wouldn't have frozen, clutching to Liam's body, sobbing instead of getting help.

Finn's gut clenched as Will raised his eyebrows and mouthed "You okay?"

Finn nodded and brushed the excess water from his hair onto the doormat. Taking off upstairs, he pulled his phone from his back pocket. Still nothing from Molly. He'd never really been in the position of wanting to message a woman so soon after a non-date-date to talk to her. But nothing about his feelings for Molly was normal as far as his history with the opposite sex.

He toed off his shoes inside his room and leaned on the door to close it behind him. His fingers hovered over her name to call her, but he couldn't bring himself to hit the button. Tossing his phone onto his bed, he sighed before stripping off his suit and grabbing a towel.

By the time he'd dried himself and thrown on a pair of sweats and a Snow Pirates hoodie, she still hadn't messaged. Flailing tendrils in his chest curled around his heart and squeezed. Was this what women felt like when guys didn't text after a date?

He was being ridiculous. She'd asked for space and she'd get it. He left his phone on charge in his room – so he couldn't be tempted to message her, and made his way back downstairs.

In the kitchen, he chugged milk straight from the gallon container in the fridge, maybe it would drown the guilt clawing at his insides.

"Hey, man. You okay?"

Finn jumped, spraying milk over the front of the fridge. "Shit. You scared me."

Will narrowed his eyes. "You wanna talk about it?"

"Talk about what?"

Will handed Finn the roll of paper towels from the counter and pulled out a chair at the dining table. Dropping onto the chair, he gestured at Finn. "Wherever you were, whatever you were doing, whatever's got your panties in a knot?"

"I'm fine Will, I was just—"

Will held his hand up as Finn put the milk on the counter and cleaned his spit off the fridge. Perhaps if he didn't make eye contact, Will's shrewd stare would simply bounce off Finn's back.

"You know I know you better than that, Finn. What gives?"

His stomach twisted as he schooled his face and turned around to lie right to the face of his best friend. "I just miss Liam, that's all. I needed to clear my head after the game."

Will's stern face softened and Finn's heart sank. Could he have been any more of an asshole? Using his grief over his dead brother to sate his friend's suspicion was the lowest of the low. But what was the alternative? *Don't sweat it man, I just got home from playing tonsil tennis with your sister. No biggie... I had her pinned to her car by my rock hard cock?*

Yeah, no. Something about that suggested it might not sit right with Molly's over-protective big brother sitting in front of him with sad eyes.

"And clearing your head didn't involve the comfort of a beautiful woman?"

Yes. "No. I'm not in the mood."

His dick twitched, as though calling him on his bullshit. "What was the team meeting about? Did I miss anything important?"

Will wagged a finger, shaking his head with a smile. "Okay, fine. I see how you want to play it. Deflect all you want." He brushed his index finger along the edge of one nostril. "Don't want anyone to know. I get it."

Heat flashed up the back of Finn's neck and he shook his head. "It's not like that, Will. There is no one."

Will narrowed his eyes for a long moment before nodding and slapping the table with an open hand. "I better get going. Busy day tomorrow."

"What do you have?" Finn scrubbed a palm over his jaw before tugging at the neck of his hoodie.

"Just studying, practice... you know, the usual."

Finn walked Will to the front door and closed it behind him. He dropped his head onto the cool wooden surface and groaned. Clearly if anything further were to happen between Finn and Molly, he'd need to do a better job at covering his tracks – and his traitorous face.

He made his way back upstairs and checked his phone. Still nothing from the woman whose breath he could feel tickling his skin. "Fuck it." He picked it up and typed out a text.

> Finn: I know you said you need space and I really am happy to give it to you. But I just need to know that you're okay.

After a couple minutes, the message status changed to 'read' but the dots didn't appear to tell him she was typing back.

> Finn: I can't breathe around this lump in my chest thinking I've upset you, or that things will somehow shift between us. If you want to go back to being just friends, I can try. It's not what I want, but I'd rather that than lose you forever.

The dots appeared almost the moment he hit the send button and every muscle in his body clenched while waiting for her to reply.

> Molly: I don't want to go back to being just friends.

Finn threw the mother of all fist pumps as he jumped onto his bed, sinking into the soft mattress as he bounced. She didn't want to go backwards. He wasn't going to lose her. In fact, he was going to do everything in his power to make sure she'd be his forever.

"What's wrong with you?" Cleo's eyes narrowed, her stare prickling Molly's already sweat soaked skin.

"What do you mean?" Molly buried her face in a towel to mop up her sweat. She'd just gotten home from burlesque practice, every inch of her ached and was sticky with sweat. As it turned out, you couldn't dance Finn O'Brien out of your system. "There's nothing wrong with me."

Lies. She didn't even believe her own thin, wholly unconvincing voice.

"I mean..." Cleo pointed her open-book at Molly. "What's going on with your face? You can't still be smiling."

"I like dancing."

"That's not it."

"I really like dancing." Molly patted the towel to the back of her neck and shrugged.

"Enough that you're practically frolicking around like a Disney princess? I don't buy it." Cleo slammed her hardback book shut with a loud pop. "What gives? Did you get laid?"

Molly snorted. She should have been prepared. She should

have known that Cleo's spidey sense would tingle the moment she'd given in to every urge she'd ever had and kissed that freakin' boy. Cleo wasn't going to let it go.

"I need a shower." That might buy her fifteen minutes, twenty at most, but Cleo had picked up a scent and she was going to hound Molly until she caved and told her everything. It was just a matter of time.

ChoCho got up from the gray, battered old recliner in their living room and stood over Molly as she sat on the edge of the couch. Cleo crossed her arms and flattened her mouth. Molly almost laughed out loud. Cleo Martinez was intimidating as hell to just about everyone else. But not to Molly.

"Come on, Molly. Gimme the good stuff." Cleo crouched down in front of her and batted her eyelids. "If you don't, I'll shave your eyebrows off during the night."

Molly's mouth dropped open. Bitch wasn't playing around.

"Or I'll go straight for the jugular and cut your hair instead."

"Savage, ChoCho. Utterly savage." Dropping her towel onto her lap, Molly held her hands up in surrender. "Fine." She sighed and Cleo squealed.

"It's Finn, isn't it? Did you..." She dropped her voice despite them being the only two in the apartment. "You know..." She squeezed Molly's knee and winked at her.

"Did I fuck him? No!" A wildfire started in Molly's core and spread to her extremities before she'd finished her sentence. She hadn't fucked him, but she was going to. She wanted to. She *ached* to. And the very thought lit her up like Time Square yet simultaneously crippled her.

"Then what?"

"We just kissed." If Molly's face could get any redder, she'd eat her hat.

Another squeal from Cleo. "And? Was it life altering? Did it melt your panties? Did you *swoon*?"

Molly couldn't help but chuckle at her friend's enthusiasm. "I don't swoon. And no, our first kiss was pretty unimpressive."

It was Cleo's turn to gawp. "But... no... that's not... what? How? Wait... first kiss? So it wasn't so bad that you didn't go back for seconds. Tell me everything. All the details. Don't leave anything out." Cleo still crouched before her, she grabbed a mint-green throw cushion from the sofa that said "Nothing quite says I love you like anal," and cuddled it to her chest.

Molly's heart felt like two llamas had taken up residence inside and were head-butting both each other and the edges of the organ in her chest. "It's usually me wanting all the down and dirty deets."

Cleo waved a dismissive hand. "It's not every day you give in to your core desires to climb your childhood crush like a tree."

Molly's mouth dried up.

"Chingona, Molly! Siiiiiiii! You *did* climb him like a tree!"

"He picked me up..."

Cleo fanned herself. "Keep going."

Molly twisted the towel on her lap. "I tried to leave after the disastrous first kiss..."

"But he followed you, didn't he? He's such a romantic." Cleo clasped her hands to her chest, dropped the cushion onto the floor and plopped onto her butt at Molly's feet. "Go on."

"Now who's getting her Disney on?"

Cleo leaned over to grab another cushion from the couch. It said, "Sorry, the give a fuck you ordered is out of stock," and she thwapped Molly with it. "Quit stalling. Details, woman." She hugged the second cushion.

"Yes, he followed me, and he kissed me in the rain."

Her best friend swooned – honest to God swooned – right there in front of Molly and waved a "keep going" kind of hand.

"He picked me up by my ass and kissed me until it felt like…" Molly touched her hand to her chest.

Cleo leaned further forward. "Felt like what?"

"Like I'd never be able to breathe again if he stopped."

Cleo leapt to her feet. "I told you! I told you! Didn't I tell you?"

Molly laughed, grabbing a "Let that shit go" pillow and clocking her friend. "And not an ounce of smugness to be found, ChoCho."

Another wave of Cleo's hand. "Screw that. I told you. That boy looks at you like he bought a cake and ate the whole thing for breakfast when it wasn't even his birthday."

Molly wanted cake. Preferably licked painfully slowly off Finn's washboard abs. She'd happily coat his dick in buttercream frosting and—

"You're imagining eating cake off of him now, aren't you?"

Molly draped the towel over her head and flopped back onto the couch. "No."

"Liar."

Her still sizzling face practically burned a hole in the towel still covering her. "Lil bit."

A sharp knock at the door bought Molly a reprieve from her mortification. She yanked the towel from her face with a gasp. "Did you order cake?"

Cleo giggled and shook her head.

"I'm going for a shower. I stink." Molly bolted up from the couch, and made her way to her bedroom. She toed off her shoes and fought like a writhing octopus to get her workout gear from her still damp and sweaty limbs.

Why did getting in and out of exercise clothing always feel like additional exercise? She felt duped. Like it wasn't enough she couldn't eat endless tacos without her ass doubling in size, she also had to psyche herself up to run the sports bra gauntlet so she didn't give herself a black eye when she danced. What a crock of bullshit.

A quick shower later, the aching in her arms and legs eased off thanks to some inferno-temp water and a worth every penny shower head. She pulled on a pair of Snow Pirates sleep shorts, and Finn's shirt. Holding it up, she took in the faded letters of his name across the shoulders.

He'd bought it right after his first game as a Snow Pirate. He'd been so proud of the fact he'd made the team and was skating his dream on the ice with her brother, that he walked right up to the merchandise shop and bought one of everything.

Molly had rescued it from a pile of dirty laundry in her parents' house one weekend when she was visiting. Fine, she'd stolen it, but that was such a strong word for liberating a T-shirt that not only smelled like the man she was desperate to lick all over but had been wrapped around his naked torso.

No swooning. Molly Badass Morrison didn't swoon.

She bunched the fabric up and shoved her nose in it, taking a deep breath. If she closed her eyes, she could almost fool herself that he was there.

She'd never admitted to him that she'd taken it. It was her dirty little secret, and while it no longer smelled of him, she'd bought a bottle of his cologne and sprayed it after she washed it, so it kinda, sorta did. She shook her head. Jerk would never let her live it down if he knew.

"ChoCho? Who was at the door?" Molly walked into the living room, twisting her long hair into a bun on top of her head so it didn't drip all over her shirt. "Are you sure you didn't order cake? I could really go for cake."

Yeah. Eaten off Finn's rod-hard dick like a fucking skewer. She cleared her throat. She was spending the evening with

Cleo, she had no time to be a horny wet mess, but her battery operated boyfriends were all fully charged and ready for her Finn-tasies before bed.

"That would be me, Doll." Finn's voice from behind her stopped her in her tracks and she spun to face him.

"Finnegan." His name caught in her throat, or floated to her clit. Either way she sounded like Phoebe in *Friends* when she had the cold and that weird nasally voice.

He tipped his head, a slow soul-melting smile spreading across his face. "Hey."

"Wh-what are you doing here? Where's Cleo?"

"She went out to see Linc."

Molly toyed with the edges of her shirt. "In her pjs?"

Finn's deep chuckle should have been illegal. "She threw on some yoga pants and a sweater before she headed out. She wanted to give us space."

He reached out to drag his knuckles across her cheek and her breath stopped. Her faithless, double-crossing lungs just up and quit processing oxygen. His eyes tracked her face, dropping slowly over her nose, lingering on her mouth before moving lower.

As long as her heart kept scampering in her chest she'd be fine. Who needed oxygen anyway, right??

Something flickered across his eyes before he reached out and stroked the hem of her shirt. "Turn around, Molly."

"Why?" Her chin trembled, her hands shook, her heart was pounding so fast she was sure it was making the room spin.

"Because I'm pretty sure you stole my shirt. And I want to see my name across your shoulders." His grin was wicked, and his eyes filled with heat.

She told her feet to move, but nothing happened. Her entire body was falling under his spell a limb at a time and not a single piece of her was responding to her own brain's commands. She needed to regain some semblance of her dignity, so she folded her arms, narrowed her eyes, and opened her mouth. "If you're going to steal it back, you're going to have to take it from me."

As soon as the words left her mouth, her skin danced with an aching need. Her nipples strained against the soft, worn fabric, like if they just reached out a tiny bit more, he'd touch them and put her out of her misery.

He arched an eyebrow. "What if I don't want it back, but I want you naked?"

Brain. Fried. All available power had been directed to her core. If she checked, she was a bazillion percent sure she'd find a damp patch on her shorts. He took a step back and shook his head.

"Molly." He scrubbed his jaw. "Fuck. This isn't why I came here tonight."

He picked up his hand in slow motion, like it was a montage in an old 80's movie, and glided the pad of his thumb over her left nipple. Her flesh was still tender and bruised close to her armpit but his caress was so gentle, so soft, that all she felt was a deep yearning.

"This isn't why I came." He repeated as though torn between what he needed to do and what he wanted to do.

"Why did you come?" When he didn't reply, she cradled his face. "Why did you come, Finny?"

His lazy once-over of her from head to toe and back again left a trail like he'd touched every piece of her. "I want to do things to you, Molly." His voice was low, heavy with the weight of what he said. "I want to fuck that pretty pink pussy until your eyes roll back in your head and you don't remember your own name."

Her jaw dropped open and her soul left her body. Finn O'Brien was a dirty talker. She was dead. Deceased. Former. No longer present on the mortal plane.

"But I came here to have a more serious discussion with you." He shifted his weight, reaching down to move the crotch of his pants.

Fuck. He was hard. The outline of his cock pressed against his sweats. "Finn..." She reached out, her hand twitched, and she pulled it to her face, biting down on her thumb to keep from tugging the band, freeing his cock, and sucking him all the way to O-Town.

"Make no mistake, I want to do filthy things to you Molly Morrison. I do. But..." He shook his head. "Not to be that guy, but I think we need to talk. I want to lay my cards out on the table."

She wanted him to lay her out on the table.

Finn's head canted and mischief danced in his eyes. Had she said that out loud?

"Yeah, Doll. You said it out loud."

Her entire body was broken. Nothing worked the way it was supposed to. "What did you want to talk about?"

"I know you don't do serious, you don't do commitment, and you avoid feeling feels at all cost. But I need you to know this is real for me. I've had feelings for you for as long as I've known you and this..." He waved a hand between them. "This isn't just some quick fuck, or one and done thing. If we do this, we're all in, both feet."

His words washed over her like tequila over ice cubes and her brain clinked against the sides of her skull. What was he saying? Did he mean... commitment? "What does...?" The words got stuck. She cleared her throat and tried again. "What does that mean?"

His thumb made it back to her left nipple, which was still striving for his touch. "It means exclusive."

Her throat tightened at the idea of committing to one person, even if that person was Finn.

"You want to fuck other women, I'm down with that.

Hell, I'll even join in and fuck you while you do. If they're down for it too – obvs."

Dirty, dirty boy, saying dirty words. She was pretty sure she was dying and this was what heaven felt like. She shifted her weight, hoping for some kind of friction against her pussy, but it didn't work.

"You wanna be spitroasted, gangbanged, and worshipped like the sexual goddess you are, you talk to me. We'll work something out."

Holy. Fucking. Spitroast. While his words vied for her attention, the tiny, featherlight circles he made around her nipple were taking up all her bandwidth. Spitroasted. By Finn and someone else. A shudder passed through her. If he kept putting ideas into her head, she'd come right there in front of him in her living room. Would he notice if her hand slipped into her shorts?

"But at night, you're mine. It's just us. You don't go fucking people without me at least knowing about it. And I'll fuck you as many times as you want."

Her chest heaved. He'd notice. He'd probably even help. But he needed to say his piece and she needed to let him.

Her head bobbed in agreement, but her core was heavy and tugging her to sink to her knees. She'd known Finn was an adventurous man, but something about how he was offering her freedom and commitment at the same time melted her frozen insides. Could it really be true? Was it possible for someone to love her, and be in a relationship with her, yet still accept that sometimes she might want fucked in all holes at the same time? Surely not. Her clit tingled, her heart short circuited.

He sucked in a breath and shook his head, like it was now or never. "I love you Molly Morrison. Always have. And I'm on the edge of what might have been and what's left to lose."

His somber tone, and the words coming out of his delicious mouth snapped her out of her horny stupor.

He said the L-word. Again. Just spat it out onto the growing web of emotions pulling them toward each other. It hadn't been an accident. She couldn't even pretend to herself he'd meant it like a faux-brother. He really meant *love*, love.

Holy.

Fuck.

He was still talking, but she had to strain to hear him over her ragged breathing filling the room. "I can't fucking bear watching you dating other men, Molly. I can't. Each time I see you with someone… someone who isn't me…" His voice cracked. "It rips another layer right off my heart."

She jolted forward, reaching out to rub his chest, to try to ease his pain. She knew what it felt like, watching someone you love be kissed and touched by someone else, watching someone else make him laugh. She nodded. She loved him too. She couldn't bring herself to say it, but maybe he already knew, maybe he could see it in her eyes when she looked at him. Maybe she'd grow to love him so much that she'd be brave enough to say it out loud.

"I know that Will…" His voice broke again and she slammed her eyes shut, trying to block out his words. They didn't need to bring him up, they didn't need to mention her brother, or talk about how he'd flip out and kill them both. Except they did, and Finn was never one to ignore the elephant in the room – unless of course it was his love for her, for five freakin' years.

"Look." He cupped her face and his piercing stare cut through all the white noise, speaking straight to her soul. "Letting go gives us freedom, and freedom is the only condition for happiness. If in our hearts we are still clinging to anything, we cannot be free. You live in my heart, Molly. I can't ever be free."

Dead. Deceased. No longer alive. Shit. Was she crying?

"Who are you and what have you done with my Finny?" She sniffed. "That was... some soppy ass shit right there."

He grinned and nodded. "Nice, right? I can't claim credit. Thich Nhat Hanh."

"Bless you."

He chuckled. "He's a Buddhist monk."

"You converted?"

"Austin's a Buddhist. He leaves these sticky notes with quotes around the locker room sometimes when our juju is off, or when someone's having a bad time. He thinks we don't know it's him but..." He shrugged. "We're kind of getting off message right now, Doll."

Damnit. He noticed her dirty tactic to pivot away from talking about The Feels. Of course he had, it wasn't exactly subtle. "The feelings..."

"I know. But we need to have this one talk, to get us both on the same page so we both know where we stand and how we feel and then I won't make you deal with icky feelings for like at least a week."

"Three."

"Two."

"Deal."

"I know that asshole in high school broke your heart."

She tried to turn away, but he held firm.

"But it's time. Whether you admit it or not I know you feel something for me, Molly. Give in to my sexy charm and be my girl. We'll deal with Will..." He sighed, beautiful features twisted with a visceral pain she felt in every cell throughout her body. "I can't lose you." His shoulders slumped.

"Can you lose Will?"

His tear-filled eyes met hers, and he huffed out a ragged breath. "If that's what it takes."

Her body froze, and her eyes bugged out so wide she was amazed her retinas didn't lose their grip on her eyeballs.

"But we won't."

She searched his face for some sign of uncertainty, some trace that perhaps he was second guessing himself. Surely he couldn't pick her over Will.

All she saw was resolve and it stopped her heart dead in her chest.

CHAPTER 18

Finnegan

"Cap." Finn nodded at Will as he skated out onto the ice. It was the first of two practices of the day ahead of the game. Because what else would the universe do right after Finn confessed his undying love and affection for his Captain – and best friend's – sister, other than put him in uncomfortably close quarters for extended periods of time? Not only did they have to spend hours in each other's company, but Will had any number of creative weapons to hand to sever Finn's head from his body, should he wish to.

Finn shuddered. Will wasn't a violent man, but where Molly was concerned… he could easily envisage him beating Finn to death with a hockey stick, or slicing his carotid artery with a hockey skate.

"Morning Obi. You look green, man. You better not hurl on my ice." Will patted his shoulder. "Everything okay?"

Finn nodded, afraid if he opened his mouth to speak he'd either puke on Will, or confess everything he'd said to Molly the day before. If he told Will he wanted to suck his sister's soul from her clit, it wouldn't end well.

It had taken every ounce of decency, chivalry, and higher brain function to leave her standing in her living room to process their discussion. Standing in those tiny pj shorts, lean legs leading up to the Promised Land, and her perfect, pebbled nipples pressing against her shirt. His shirt. Sneaky temptress.

She wanted him, and his raging boner had almost carved a path through his pants just to get to her. But he didn't want to rush. Molly's heart had wrapped itself in a cocoon of fear and barbed wire years ago, she needed a beat to process everything he'd said, before he went to town on whatever holes she'd let him.

Jesus fucking Christ on a cross.

He'd heard the stories, the whispers among her conquests. Molly loved pleasure, she lived for it. She was shameless in her pursuit of it, and Finn was there for it. Hell, if she wanted to tie him to the bed and make him her sex slave, he was down. His dick twitched.

"Finn?"

Finn jumped, his stick clattered to the ice with a snap that echoed around the rink. All heads turned to him.

"Someone's got butter on their hands today." Sébastien snorted.

"I think you mean butter fingers," Will corrected the goaltender.

"Sorry, I just spaced out."

Will's eyes narrowed. Finn was already sucking hard at playing it cool. Nothing said "I want to fuck your sister," more than damn near shitting your pants for no reason in front of the captain of the team. He needed to pull himself together, and somehow skate with a sword between his thighs.

It was going to be a long practice.

❄

Sitting in the locker room after the practice session from hell, Finn tapped the edge of an official-looking envelope against his palm. His freshly washed hair dripped beads of cold water down his neck. His teammates had all left the rink, but he couldn't bring himself to either leave, or open the envelope.

"Wanna talk about it?" Will jerked his chin at the letter in his hand.

"What are you still doing here?"

"Dude, you played like shit out there. You really think I'd either not notice, or not care? I'm here because you're here. What gives? Talk to me. You know you don't have to carry shit alone."

Some things he most definitely had to carry alone, at least for the time being, but he didn't have to share those with Will. "In this envelope..." His voice stalled out, turning to grains of sand in the wind. He swallowed. "This tells me if I'm a match for my brother's kidney."

The V between Will's eyes deepened.

"If I open this, and I'm a match... I gotta make a decision whether I help save a boy's life." The vise holding his heart tightened and the hand holding the envelope trembled.

Will closed his hand over Finn's. "Even if you're a match, you aren't under any obligation to donate your kidney to a stranger, Finn. That's what he is, a stranger. Just because the same blood runs through your veins doesn't mean you owe him something."

"I..." Finn sniffed. "I just figure maybe if I save him, I can somehow redeem my soul for letting Liam down." There, he'd said it, out loud and for someone other than his own guilt riddled mind to hear.

"Finn..." The agony twisting Will's tone was tangible. His voice was clouded by emotion. "That's not..." He took a breath and squeezed Finn's hand. "You didn't fail Liam. You couldn't save him, so you did the next best thing you could – you sat with him so he wasn't alone. I know the guilt eats you up inside, but I'm telling you, you're carrying a whole ton of shit you shouldn't be. You're not responsible for Liam's death any more than you'd be responsible for your half-brother's death if he didn't get a kidney in time. The world's problems aren't all your fault, man. You can't save everyone."

Finn nodded, but so many years and layers of guilt had caked themselves up the insides of his chest that the walls were almost impenetrable.

"Want me to open it for you?"

Finn sat up straight. "Nah, thanks. I gotta do it. But if you'd sit with me, I'd appreciate it." He hated feeling weak, vulnerable, and out of control. Whatever was in the envelope in his hand could potentially change his entire future and he had absolutely no power over the facts. All he could do was control his reaction to it. Would his mother still want to pursue a relationship with him if he was of no use to her shiny new family? Did he want her to?

"What if she just contacted me to ask for my kidney?"

Will elbowed him. "I want to make some kind of joke here about how she at least asked and didn't just knock you over the head with something and carve out your kidney, but I don't know that we're there yet."

Despite the mounting tension in every muscle in his body, Finn chuckled. "I suppose that's true." He slipped his thumb under the seal of the envelope and tore the paper open. With warring wasps in his stomach, and a team of drummers beating in his head, he pulled out the expensive, headed paper, and swallowed.

Dear Mr. O'Brien,

We are sorry to inform you that you are not a match...

Not a match. Instead of feeling a soaring sense of relief, his stomach sank. He had nothing to offer his mother in exchange for her affections. Would she still want him in her life once she found out he had nothing to give her?

"What's going on in there, Obi?" Will leaned over as though he was looking into Finn's ear and knocked on the side of his head. "What's the verdict?"

"Not a match."

Will patted his shoulder. "That's good news, right? Why do you look like someone taped their stick badly?"

Finn chuckled again. He taped his stick with meticulous precision. It was part of his routine, and the straight lines of tape comforted his soul. Only a monster would throw tape around the blade of his weapon willy nilly. Who didn't want the nice, even lines?

"What if she doesn't want to see me now that I'm not a match for her golden child?"

"Then she's a sorry excuse for a mother and we'll deal with that reality if we get there. I'm guessing from that reaction though, that you *want* her back in your life, which makes it harder, sure. But if she doesn't want to be in your life, she's an idiot."

Finn paused for a moment. The gaping wound in his chest where his happy family used to reside, pulsed. He nodded. "I think so. I miss her. I know our family will never be what it was. But she was sick, y'know? She didn't choose to just up and leave me. She was mentally ill, she got treatment and got better, she got her life back together and when she was ready she came back to me. Assuming it's not just for one of my organs, I think I'd like to get to know her again."

Will nodded. "And if that's not what she wants, it's going to be hard for you. But we've got you if things don't go well. You know that, right? We've always got your back. It's what family does."

Just like that, another thick, heavy layer rippled its way up the inside of his ribcage. How would Finn ever be able to tell the man who would walk to hell and back for him that he was breaking his most cardinal of rules?

Finn paced like a ferocious animal in a cage. His mother was running late, but she'd agreed to meet him. Mom had offered her kitchen as a place of familiar comfort, but Finn had declined. Then she'd offered to go along with him, to sit a few tables away in case he needed her help – as it turned out, Molly Morrison was more like her mother than he'd realized. He'd arrived at the Sugar Bean early, ordered a drink that was sitting cold on the table next to him, and started to pace back and forth.

He was probably muttering to himself, it would explain why the three sorority girls sitting in the corner had moved seats, and why no one else came near his table.

"Finnegan." Meabh's voice quivered, soft and pained. "Finnegan, stop." She touched his arm and he snapped his gaze to meet hers. "Let's sit."

He chewed on the inside of his cheek and nodded.

"Do you need a fresh drink? That one looks like it's been sitting a while." She touched the mug, picked it up, and took it with her to the counter.

A few minutes later she was back with steaming, large mugs of hot chocolate. When he and Liam were kids it was a weekly secret, when Dad worked late. Mom would make three towering mugs of hot chocolate, with lashings of whipped cream, an entire bag of marshmallows, chocolate shavings, and a knob of salted butter – her secret to the best hot chocolate in the world.

His throat tightened at the visual, but he dragged a fingertip through the cream and savored the taste. "I'm not a match. I'm sorry." He pulled the letter out from his back pocket and smoothed it out in front of her. "Here. In case you need proof. I—"

She closed her hand over his. "I don't need proof, Finn. Even if you were a match and you didn't want to donate your kidney, I'd have understood. It's not a small ask." After a beat of silence, she took a sip of her drink. "So..."

Finn searched her face for any clue to her next move. "I guess you'll be going."

"Going?" She almost choked on the marshmallow she'd popped into her mouth. "I just got here. Why would I leave?"

A clawing at his throat stopped him from answering.

"Finn, did you think because you're not a match I wouldn't want to see you anymore?"

He tried to snort his derision at the absurd idea but the noise that escaped him sounded more like a whimper. She took another sip of her drink. "I see. I don't blame you. I show up in your life after years of absence and I ask you for help to save another child I had while we were apart. Pretty classless, eh?"

When he didn't answer, she continued. "I'm sorry. I'm sorry for everything. For... your father... for leaving, for coming back in such a crappy way... but I need you to know." She cupped both her hands around one of his and paused until he met her eyes. "I didn't come back into your life because I wanted your kidney, Finn."

The words seeped into his skin, like lip balm into chapped lips.

"I guess it gave me the courage to reach out. The timing was unfortunate, I'll grant you. But I came back because I love you, I miss you, and while I'd never dare hope we could be a family again, and I know for sure things will never be the same... I just... I hoped maybe we could start over in some way. Maybe I could convince you to give me a second chance. Maybe I could check in with you sometimes, learn about who you are as a man. Maybe someday meet your friends. If that's not what you want..." She shrugged. "It's probably what I deserve after everything you've been through. But I needed to try, before it's too late." She rubbed at the fabric over her heart. "I couldn't take it anymore."

Finn knew that feeling. The feeling of needing to act before the inaction tore your chest wide open. He nodded and took a long, comforting drink of molten chocolate. "Someone needs to tell them about the butter thing."

With a smile, his mother reached across the table and swiped a speck of whipped cream off his nose. After wiping it on a napkin, she clapped her hands together. "Tell me something about yourself. Anything. Something I've missed out on. Something I don't know."

He skimmed his fingertip around the rim of the mug, collecting tiny shards of grated chocolate and whipped cream residue. "Well, there's this girl..."

Mom clutched her hand over her chest. "Again? The three of you here, together... again? The apocalypse is upon us. Quick – to the bunker!" She waved her towel toward the front door. "Can you believe this? They're all back."

Mr. Mo grabbed the end of the towel and tugged her toward him, slipping his arms around her waist. "It's your disarming wit, they can't get enough of your funnies."

She giggled, her cheeks turning pink. "Well obviously. Molly? You wanted to talk to everyone?" Mom gestured at her to go ahead.

Molly's pale face was punctuated by dark circles under her eyes, and she twisted at the hem on her tank top. Dad had the heating turned up to somewhere around "Beelzebub's living room" level of heat. Sweat prickled Finn's forehead and neck, he was a few minutes away from peeling his shirt off. Molly had already ditched her hoodie and tee. Thankfully she wore a bra under her tank, but it did little to steer his thoughts from wanting to bury his head between her delicious titties and blow. He could just imagine the look on her face if he motorboated her boobs – and added it to his to-do list when he eventually got her alone.

It had been days – *days* – since he'd stood in her living room itching to touch her creamy skin and delve into the warm depths of her delectable pussy. But they had both been busy since and their texts had been casual, friendly, platonic. Maybe Molly hadn't been busy, maybe she'd been taking space to process, or maybe she was pulling away. He needed to know which. He needed to find a way for them to get together. His dick semi-hardened in agreement.

"Here Finn, take this to the table for me?"

"Sure thing, Mrs. Mo." Finn accepted the dish of mashed potatoes.

"Holy shit, Molly. What the hell happened to your boob?" Will pointed his fork at the Titanium Titty bruising that peeked over the edge of her tank.

Molly dropped the fork she was placing on the table. "That's... that's kind of what I wanted to talk to everyone about."

With stern faces, and silent movements, everyone took their seats at the table.

"I wanted to wait until after we'd eaten. But I can see from all the probing eyes around the table, that's not going to happen." She steeled herself right in front of Finn. Strength straightening her spine. He ached to reach out and squeeze her hand, or thigh, to offer some form of physical comfort. He had to settle for stroking her calf with his, under the table to let her know he was there for her.

"I found a lump." She barely paused when Mom gasped. "It's fine. I'm fine." She pulled down the side of her tank top and flashed the side of her boob. Dad's face went crimson and he averted his eyes. "They did a biopsy – hence the multicolored boob Will got a glimpse of because it's hotter than hades in this freakin' house."

Dad chuckled, Mom smacked his forearm as though she'd asked him to turn down the heating a million times.

"What can I say, I'm a heat lover. One of these days your mom will get so sick of our heating bill that she'll cave and agree to move to Florida."

Finn's stomach lurched at the idea, Will frowned, and it was Molly's turn to gasp.

"At ease, children. That's not happening any time soon. But I must say, it's reassuring that you don't want rid of us just yet." Mom reached over and patted Molly's quivering hand. "Keep going, Molly."

She nodded, and ran her finger and thumb along the edge of the napkin in front of her. "They put a chip in there to keep an eye on things. They found a couple of smaller lumps..." She sucked in an audible breath and gave an unsure smile. "I go back in a few months to get everything checked over. But for now, I'm okay."

A heavy silence settled over the table. "Mom... I..." It was rare that Molly Morrison ran out of words. Finn wanted to swoop her into his lap and hold her until the sads were gone.

"If you haven't been in a while, you should go and get checked out. They said regular self-exams and early detection are really important."

Mom rubbed her palm along Molly's forearm. "I had my tune up not too long ago. I'm all good. But thank you." Mom must have felt what Finn did too, she got up, rounded the table and pulled Molly into a tight embrace. "Why didn't you tell us?"

"We could have gone with you." Will picked up a green bean from the probably-cold bowls scattered across the table in front of them.

"I didn't want to worry anyone in case it was nothing."

Dad sighed like the weight of the world pressed down on his shoulders. "And so what if it was nothing? We're your family, Molly. We're here for you. You shouldn't have gone through this alone."

Molly nodded against Mom's shoulder. "I just didn't want everyone to get weird over something that ended up being nothing."

"But it might have been something," Dad pushed harder, but Finn knew if she were to do it all over again, she'd make the same choices and do everything the exact same way – it was who she was.

Someone was staring at him, and when he looked up from his plate, Will's eyes were drilling into his face. "You knew?"

How could Will possibly know that Finn knew? Finn opened his mouth, but had no idea what to answer. If he said yes, Will and their parents would be pissed for not telling him, and Molly would be pissed for sharing.

"Finn overheard a phone call with the hospital. He tried to come with me, but I didn't let him." She laughed. "He followed me to the appointment like a stalker and waited for me to come out."

Dad gripped Finn's arm and squeezed, his eyes betraying his every fear for his little girl. "Thank you, son. I'm glad she has you."

Mom stood up and went back to her seat. When seated, she dished out heaped scoops of mash potatoes onto every-one's plates.

"You knew." Will's voice was harder, colder.

"You didn't tell him?" It was as though Molly had just realized Finn hadn't shared her secret.

"Why didn't you tell me?"

"Why didn't you tell him?"

Molly and Will spoke at the same time. Will's question angry and demanding, Molly's laced with surprise.

He turned to Molly first, held her stare. "You asked me not to and I wasn't going to betray that trust. You were ready to share when you were ready to share. God knows you've kept my secrets over the years, and I wasn't going to force you to talk about this when you weren't comfortable."

Next he turned to Will. "She asked me not to. She agreed to tell everyone when she was ready and it was her story to tell, not mine."

If he pushed back again, Finn would remind him that he'd kept his fair share of secrets for Will over the years as well. And as long as someone had Molly's back, it should be all good. Molly's face was unreadable, she gnawed on her lip, but didn't take her eyes off Finn.

Will shoveled a forkful of mashed potatoes into his mouth and swallowed. "You'd be pissed if it was the other way around." He jabbed his fork toward Finn.

Finn sucked in a breath. He didn't want to fight, especially not under the Morrisons' roof. Dad arched an eyebrow and gave the smallest inclination of his head toward Will, like he was somehow giving Finn permission to stand up to him.

"You're right, Will. I would. But I'd be comfortable in the knowledge that you had her back, she wasn't alone, and if it was bad enough she'd have told me herself. I trust her to make her own decisions and speak up when she needs help."

Will's scowl deepened. "You should have told me."

"No, son. He shouldn't." Dad reached across the table and speared slices of meat with his fork.

Having Dad's backup should have made Finn feel better,

but it seemed to only serve to make Will stew harder. Mom patted Finn's hand. "Thank you for watching out for our Molly."

Without taking his eyes from Will, Finn nodded. "It's what family does."

CHAPTER 19

Molly

Molly didn't know whether to laugh, cry, or jump Finn's bones and make him sing her name. Watching him stand up to Will the night before... how he kept her secret, even from his best friend... her lady parts were ready to party.

"You okay? You seem... antsy."

Molly nodded at Cleo as Sabrina, their server for lunch at Applebee's, approached, pen and notebook in hand. "You ladies need a minute?"

Cleo's narrowed gaze burrowing into Molly's face was unnerving.

"Yes please. Can I get a Coke?"

"Just a Coke? No liquor in there?" Cleo shifted her legs as though she expected a swift kick under the table from Molly.

"It's not socially acceptable to drink before 11.30 on a Sunday, ChoCho."

"Says who?" Sabrina shrugged. "People do it all the time."

"And you sure as hell look like you could do with a drink." Cleo arched her perfectly waxed eyebrow and smirked.

"Whisky mule."

Sabrina grinned. "Yes, ma'am. What about you, Cleo?"

Cleo returned the smile. "I'll have a Moscow Mule please – I don't like whisky."

Molly gasped, made a sign of the cross over her body, and tipped her head back to talk to the big guy upstairs. "Forgive her, Father, for she knows not what she says."

Sabrina laughed. "Don't worry, I'll make sure you get her share of whisky, too."

Molly fist-pumped. "Yassss. Not all superheroes wear capes."

"I'll be right back with your drinks."

When Sabrina's back was turned, Cleo continued her assault. "What happened?"

"Nothing."

She dropped her voice and looked from side to side like she was about to talk about some super-secret criminal exploit. "Did you do the nasty nasty with Finny Winny?"

"I'm going to vag-punch you."

"As long as Finn—"

"So help me God, Cleopatra Martinez if you say anything about Finn punching my vag with his dick I'm going to hurt you."

Cleo hooted with laughter.

"Lincoln Scott has changed you, girl. We need to wash your dirty mouth out with soap." Molly fanned herself with her menu. "No. We still haven't slept together. I feel like a horny teenager. It's like now that I've opened that door, every dirty fantasy and wet dream about Finn is assaulting me on the daily." She paused. "He pushed back at Will for the first time ever last night."

"And you're scared it's going to escalate? With Will I mean, not the fire in your panties – we both know that's not going anywhere until Finn fucks you senseless. But are you scared it's going to get worse with Will?"

Molly squeezed her thighs together. "Is it wrong that there's a teeeeeenie tiny part of me that kind of hopes it does? It was so fucking hot ChoCho. I had no idea a man keeping my secret and defending it to his best friend – my own brother no less – could be such a turn on. I think I found a new kink."

Cleo held her ribs as her whole body shook with laughter. "I can't believe you're this bent out of shape over something so small. Can you imagine what you're going to be like when Finn finally vag-punches you with his dick?"

A throat clearing had both their heads snapping toward a sheepish-looking Sabrina. She moved the two drinks from the tray in her hand onto the table and hugged the tray against her chest. "So..."

Molly held up her hand. "It's not what you think." Dizziness crashed into her as dominoes tipped in her head. While Molly was fairly certain Sabrina knew Finn was the object of her affections – from a rather ill-timed, drunken night of hating Finn O'Brien at the top of her lungs – this was bad.

Sabrina telling Russell was probably not life or death. Russ wasn't a gossip queen. She was pretty certain he'd keep his mouth shut. But if Russell said it in passing to Linc – then the lid was off the box and containment was impossible.

Wait, had Cleo already told Lincoln?

He was a smart man, a reasonable man. He had sisters. Maybe he would understand the gravity of everything and know better than to rat her out to her brother. There was probably some hockey-brother-code that meant he should tattle on her, but hopefully he'd see reason.

"She didn't... it's not..." Heat closed around her throat and her vision tunneled.

"Shit, Molly, take a breath. It's okay." Cleo's cold hand slipped into Molly's as she said something to Sabrina. Who knew how long later, Sabrina handed her a glass of iced water.

"He can't find out. You don't understand. This thing

with…" She couldn't even say his name out loud in case the walls heard. "We're barely off the ground, we don't even know if it's going anywhere… There's nothing to tell."

Sabrina placed the drinks tray on the table, slipped into the booth next to Molly, and wrapped an arm around her. Stroking Molly's bicep, Sabrina shushed her. "It's okay. I won't say anything, I promise."

Cleo squeezed Molly's hand. "I haven't told Linc. You're good. He won't find out. Well…" She leaned back and took a sip of her mule. "I mean, he might if you keep reacting like…" She waved an open palm in front of Molly's face. "Like this every time Finn's name comes up."

"I remember the night at the bar." Molly buried her head in Sabrina's shoulder. "I remember telling you I was in love with a hockey player."

Why did Sabrina's rhythmic stroking of Molly's hair feel so good?

Sabrina hummed. "It didn't take long to figure out who you were talking about."

"Russell too?" Molly's voice was barely a whisper. If she was so freaked out and terrified of word getting out that she was even considering a – gag – relationship with Finn, was it the smartest thing in the world to pursue it?

Sabrina's shoulder jiggled with movement. Molly pulled back and found her laughing. "What?"

"Russ didn't exactly catch on right away. It took a little explaining, and a lot of sign posts for him to get from A to B. He hasn't said anything to anyone though. He knows it's a… sensitive situation.

Molly snorted. Sensitive was an understatement. "I don't want them to fight and lose each other because of me."

Cleo and Sabrina both nodded. "But you can't let fear of how your brother will react control whether or not you take a chance on Finn."

Damn. Sabrina was smart.

"What if we break up?"

Sabrina cupped Molly's face and shook her head like Molly was an idiot. "You broke up the day you met."

"I don't understand." Molly wrinkled her nose.

"You're meant for each other, and you fought it from the get-go. While you haven't been together, you've forced yourselves apart – that's way worse than any break up."

Cleo reached a hand over to Sabrina for a hi-five. "She's right, Mol. You said you've had feelings for him from day one. Ignoring them, burying them, watching him be with other women... you've been broken up for as long as you've known him. It's time to see what could be if you just let it."

Ugh. She was surrounded by hopeless dreamers who loved romance novels and Disney movies. "Real life doesn't work like that."

Bre squeezed her arm and slid back off the bench. Molly almost forgot she was working and wasn't eating lunch with Cleo and her. She picked up her mule and took a few deep swallows.

"Molly, I don't know what you've done or haven't done yet with that boy, but you broke the seal. All your repressed ooey-gooey feelings for that man are going to seep out of the cracks in your chest until they consume you. You can't fight fate."

"Dang." Cleo held out a fist for Sabrina to bump. "Girl, you are wicked smart."

Sabrina gave a little curtsey. "You and I both know, the heart wants what it wants. I've seen you fight it, Molly Morrison. Nothing good comes from denying your feels."

Molly chuckled. "You said ooey-gooey." She drank more of her drink.

"No deflecting." Cleo leaned over the table and flicked

Molly's forehead as she was drinking, causing Molly to spray precious alcohol over the table.

Cleo and Bre laughed. An email appeared on Molly's phone next to her on the table.

Dear Miss Morrison,

Thank you for your application to ESPN's summer commentator internship. Unfortunately, we are unable to offer you a position at this time. We will keep your name on file...

"Fuck."

"What?" Cleo swiped Molly's phone across the table before Molly could close her mail.

Cleo frowned. "Assholes. Don't they know who you are? You'll get the next one. No biggie." She pointed at the drinks on the table. "Keep 'em coming, please, Bre. We got some commiserating to do."

Sabrina nodded, her features somber. She paused like she wanted to say something.

"What is it?" Molly turned her head between Cleo and Bre, what was she missing?

"I was just going to say. If you guys need an alibi... Russ and I already know you like each other. I can't imagine it's going to be too easy for the two of you to get alone time together while you're keeping it under wraps. I just..." She picked up the tray from on top of the table. "If you need cover when you're dating, we can help." She nodded, then was gone.

"Romantics." Molly rolled her eyes again, but the idea of going on a real life date with Finn made her stomach swoosh and flip. With a shake of her head, Molly downed the last of her drink. She had no idea what she was going to do, about the internship of her dreams, or her potential relationship with Finn. But every time she thought of him, her stomach, her heart, and any trace of rational thought shot into the atmosphere. She was so... very... fucked.

✳

"Drunken louts."

Finn stood next to the table, hands on his hips and a wide grin on his sexy-as-fuck face. In fact, there were two Finns. How many mules had she had to drink?

"Day drunken louts no less." He cupped his heart. "And without me? I'm wounded, Doll."

Molly gasped and covered her mouth with her palm, then covered his mouth with the other before casting a rueful glance at Cleo.

"What did I say?" Finn looked over his shoulder. "Oh. You don't want your friend to hear me call you Doll, *Doll?* You might want to stop touching me, Mini Mo Your brother is due to arrive here in less than ten minutes and if our skin keeps touching I'm not going to be responsible for my actions."

How did he ignite every cell in her body with one sentence?

"What are we celebrating, Cleo?" He picked up Molly's half-drank mule and took a swig. "Whisky mules. You ladies know it's the afternoon, right? Isn't this like... I dunno... mimosa O'Clock?"

"Commiserating." Molly held up a finger, wanting to rub it along his damp lips. In fact, she wanted to throw her leg over him and grind up on his lap until he jizzed his pants like a fucking teenager. "ESPN said no."

Warmth from his hand seeped through her shirt as he stroked her back. "Oh, Doll. I'm sorry. I know you wanted it."

"Fuck 'em." Cleo raised her drink and Finn clinked Molly's against it.

"Indeed. Fuck 'em. They don't know what they're missing. Don't they know who you are?"

"Thassssssss what I said!" Cleo clinked her drink against

Finn's, or at least tried to. It took three attempts before the glasses actually connected. Girl. Was. *Wasted.*

"What in the day-drinking-party do we have here?" Lincoln slid into the booth next to Cleo, who practically mauled his face with her lips. "And why the hell wasn't I invited? Obi, I do believe these women are intoxicated."

Finn snapped his hand back from Molly's body, leaving a profound chill. Why couldn't he keep touching her? They were consenting freakin' adults. What business was it of anybody's if she wanted every inch of Finn's body stuck to every inch of hers?

The side of Finn's face called to her to attack it with as much enthusiasm as Cleo peppering kisses on Linc's. "Molly..." The pained tone to his voice had her eyes snapping up to his. "If you keep staring at me like I'm a s'more on the fourth of July and you want to drag your fucking tongue around my edges, I'm going to drag you out back and fuck you."

Her jaw dropped. Cleo gasped. Linc spun his head to Finn. "What the actual fuck?"

Ice-cold tendrils curled around Molly's chest.

"You didn't know?" Finn pointed an accusing finger at him.

"Know what? That you want to... with...?" Linc raked a hand over his pale face. "When the fuck did this happen? And how the fuck are you still alive?"

Cleo giggled. "He says fuck a lot when he's stressed."

"You clearly knew!" Linc turned his confusion to Cleo who giggled again.

"I thought she told him." Finn dropped his forehead to the table with a heavy clunk. "I thought he knew."

"Well, I'm not sure what exactly it is I didn't know, but I kinda know it now. I'm guessing Will doesn't—"

Cleo smacked a hand over Linc's still-moving mouth. "I swear to the almighty, Lincoln Scott. If you breathe so much as a word of this to another living being you will never get laid for the rest of your life."

Cocky bastard had the cheek to grin at her. "With you? Or...?"

"I will rip your junk off with my bare hands and feed it to wolves."

Finn winced, and Molly yelped. "That's my girl." She hi-fived Cleo. "Thank you."

"I mean it, Lincoln." Cleo wagged a wavering finger at Linc.

"I get it. I mean... it's about friggin' time... but... damn. He's going to lose his shit."

Sabrina arrived with another round of mules for Molly and Cleo. "You drink it." Molly pushed hers at Finn. "I can't. Wait." She almost pulled a dozen muscles in her neck straining to look at Linc. "What do you mean it's about time?"

Linc shrugged. "I thought you'd take the plunge last year, but nothing came of it. You..." He pointed at Finn. "I fucking knew you weren't going through a fucking dry patch."

Molly's cheeks crackled so loudly that the table next to her probably thought their sizzling fajitas were coming out from the kitchen. "Oh my God." She covered her face with both her hands and groaned.

"Hey guys, what's going on?" Will sauntered up to the table and Molly wanted the floor to grow arms and drag her under the table. Like things couldn't possibly have gotten worse.

Go big or go home, Molly.

"I didn't get the ESPN gig for the summer." She raised her mule and clinked it off Finn's. "My friend is getting day drunk with me in sympathy."

"And how'd you rope two of my best guys into joining you?" He dragged a chair from a neighboring table and placed it at the end of their booth before dropping onto it.

"Like I need roped into supporting my friends." Linc raised his appropriated mule and clinked it against his girlfriend's glass with a grin. "Or my girl."

Gag. Puke. All the vom. But part of Molly wished Finn could be so openly supportive. Sure, she wasn't a die-hard romantic, but the idea of Finn being able to hold her hand, or say the words 'my girl' so casually warmed her chest.

She'd spent so long shoving all her feels in a trunk in her heart that she wasn't sure what to do with them once he'd cracked it open. Especially when Will couldn't see or hear anything that might tip him off.

She needed to see Finn alone. She needed to be able to kiss his face off until her lips tingled.

Will ordered a glass of water and a salad from Sabrina as she passed.

She needed to tell Finn she was ready to take the leap and be his girl. Even if it meant making her brother big mad. Pulling out her phone she checked to make sure no one was watching her as she unlocked it and opened the texting app.

> Molly: Can we talk tomorrow night after your game?

Will was chatting to Lincoln, and Cleo's head rested on Linc's shoulder, her eyes closed and her breathing heavy. There was every chance Molly's best friend was taking a nap right there in Applebee's in the middle of the day. What a badass. Molly chuckled and stirred her drink with her paper straw.

After a couple of minutes, Finn replied.

> Finn: Absolutely. Please tell me we're going to do more than just talk?

Her breathing picked up speed and she bit down on her

lip to ground her, to stop her from reaching under the table and palming his dick.

Molly: We're going to do more than talk.

Someone had lit a fire under Finn O'Brien's skates, and the buzzing in Molly's chest had her hoping it was the prospect of seeing her. Wishful thinking. The stakes of the game were too high for Finn to be distracted by her lady bits.

The Snow Pirates were 3-1 up nearing the end of the second period. They'd lost Johnny White to a potential wrist injury, and two of the rookies had come down with a case of the shits before practice that morning, so the Pirates' bench was definitely light. Despite their shortcomings, the Pirates dominated.

Russ crunched another opponent into the boards as Finn skated toward their net. If they won the game, they were playoff champs. Twenty minutes was all that separated her brother's team from victory.

They'd come close the previous season, and the one before that, but it always just seemed out of reach. She wrung her hands in her lap and sent up some good juju to the hockey gods. Finn looked dashing with a playoff beard.

Dashing? Fuck. She was spending way too much time with the romantics.

Her stomach jumped. Speaking of romantic, she was going to see Finn after the game. She needed to get a few quotes from some of the players on both teams before she could go home. But Cleo was staying at Linc's so Finn could stop by and they could *talk*.

Her lips prickled. She was going to talk alright. With her

tongue. She was going to get on her knees and give Finn O'Brien the best goddamn blowjob of his life.

Clink.

Finn had hit the crossbar.

"Fuck."

"Eeeeeasy, tiger." Cleo patted her thigh. "Have no fear, this is our year. It has to be." She rubbed her hands together.

For someone Molly had to drag to the rink kicking and screaming for her first game, Cleo had not only come around, she was an all-out fan. She'd learned the game, the players, and was invested in the team beyond her adoring boyfriend – number thirteen.

Austin slammed some poor fucker into the boards with a hit that was felt collectively around the rink. She couldn't see who he'd hit, but she imagined he'd deflated like someone letting go of a balloon. Austin had that effect on people.

The final whistle of the period blew and the team skated off the ice. Despite being two periods in, they were light on their skates and an electric energy rippled around the crowd. No one – but Cleo – dared say it out loud, but the hope was tangible. Perhaps it was their year at last.

"You going to get a quote during the break?"

Molly shook her head. "I really want to talk to Seb, but I'm not getting anywhere near his zone while he's killing it. They're so fucking hot right now."

"I'll say." She fanned herself.

Molly shoved Cleo with her elbow. "I mean they're focused. In the zone. And kicking ass out there."

"And *I* mean they're hot as hell." Cleo laughed. She also wasn't wrong. "I'm not wrong."

"I know. I just have a job to do, you know?" Sure, she'd gotten rejections from three internships over the summer. And sure it stung like someone had given her papercuts all over her body then poured vinegar on it, but being a play-by-play commentator was all she'd ever wanted to do. She just needed to be patient, dig deep, and not give up. Someone would give her a break at some point, and she needed to be ready.

"I was thinking of submitting a couple of articles to some of the nationals if we... y'know..." She couldn't even bring herself to say the word out loud.

"That's a great idea. Mom has mentioned your last three articles."

"She has?"

Cleo nodded. "Things still aren't great between us, y'know... what with..." She waved her tattooed arm at the ice. "But she knows she needs to let me live my life and I think she's trying. You're neutral ground, she takes an interest in the team because of Lincoln but uses you, your brother, and your talent with exciting reporting to ask about him in a round-about way. It's kinda funny."

"When faced with the prospect of losing someone, or accepting who they are, the fear of loss can be pretty power-ful." Molly sighed. "I hope it works on Will, too."

Cleo squeezed her hand.

"Sorry. I didn't mean to make your situation about me. I'm glad you and your mom are talking again. But I'm even gladder that she's listening. Gladder – is that a word? More glad. I dunno, you're the wordsmith, not me. I'm happy she's being less dickish, how's that?"

Cleo smiled. "Me too. It hasn't been easy. Papa tried to mediate for a while, but she dug her heels in and refused to even meet me halfway. But she's slowly coming around to the idea that I can still be a straight-A student, have a jock boyfriend at the same time, and be successful even if it's not her idea of success." She rolled her eyes like she'd heard the lectures a thousand times.

"I'm so glad you're standing up for yourself and not taking any more shit from her."

"I'm so glad you're finally opening your heart up to the possibility of L—"

Molly slapped her hand over Cleo's face. "Nope. Don't you fucking dare, ChoCho. And just for that near-miss with The Feels." She shuddered theatrically. "You're going to buy me nachos."

CHAPTER 20

Finnegan

They'd won the game, they were Final Four champs. The roof had been lifted off the arena with the cheers of their fans, but none of it mattered. Not really. He was on his way to see his girl and he was going to celebrate in style – buried to the hilt inside her perfect pink pussy.

Molly stood at the end of the tunnel, chatting to the away team's goaltender about their loss. Somehow she managed to talk to the losing players without upsetting them even more than they already were. She had a capacity to write their pain on the page, while not rubbing in the fact they'd lost. *ESPN* were fucking crazy not to take her on for the summer internship. He was still pissed about it.

She lived and breathed the game almost as much as any player on the team – she always had. She was smart as a whip, sharp, and she had a way with people. One thing about Molly Morrison was she never half-assed anything. She always gave her entire ass to everything she put her mind to doing.

And with any luck, that ass would be doing him sometime soon. He already had a semi. Fuck.

She leaned against the wall, somehow cradling a Dictaphone between her last two fingers, and a notepad between her thumb and forefinger in the same hand. She was recording, but taking extra notes too, as the goalie spoke, and Finn couldn't help but smile at her thoroughness. Her features were soft, even in the harsh lighting. She had fur-lined brown ankle boots, jeans that looked like she'd been poured into them, and a Snow Pirates jersey that fell to her mid-thigh.

Something poked at his chest. She'd only ever worn her own name and her favorite number, #7, on her shoulders, but perhaps that was something he could change in the future. There was nothing hotter than the woman you loved wearing your name on her body.

Love. The word should probably have made him twitchy, but the more he thought about it, the more he realized he'd always loved her. His love for her simply was. Like the sky was blue and the grass was green. She also turned him into a soppy ass freakin' poet.

She tucked her pen into her back pocket and rubbed a soothing hand up and down the guy's bicep. She was elated at their win, Finn had seen her from the ice – hell, he could have sworn he'd *heard* her from the ice and given the fact it was a full arena with thousands of screaming fans that was no small feat. But as she stood comforting their opponent, the genuine empathy radiating from her was touching.

Finn shivered, he'd been on the receiving end of her empathy more times than he cared to count. She'd been there for him so many times over the years, but never let anyone be there for her. Would that ever change? Would he ever be able to be there for her like she'd been there for him?

When the player finally turned away from her, Molly said something into her Dictaphone and glanced around the hallway. When her eyes found his, she smiled and he could have sworn her breath hitched.

She tossed him a wiggle of her fingers and he jerked his chin at her, taking a step in her direction. "Wanna talk to a winner?" He winked.

She dragged her eyes down the still-open notebook in her hand like she was looking down a list of names, before checking her nails. "Thanks, but I already spoke to Seb."

"Ouch, Doll." He covered his heart. "You wound me."

Her smile grew into a savage grin. She reached between her and the wall, grabbed something, spun toward him and unleashed the biggest confetti cannon he'd ever seen right at his face.

A couple of heads poked out into the corridor from the locker room, but Finn just gawped at her while she giggled maniacally. She tossed him a nonchalant shrug.

"Oh. It's like that, is it?" He spluttered a piece of colored paper from between his lips and dusted a few off his shoulders and hair.

"Oh. It's definitely like that." She arched an eyebrow.

He waggled a finger at her. "This isn't over." If he wasn't mistaken, a shudder passed through her body at his words. Good. Let the anticipation drive her every bit as crazy as it was driving him.

"I figured we'd... talk... later." The pink flush blooming in her cheeks was fucking adorable. This softer side of Molly was one he rarely saw, but knowing he had an effect on her did things to him.

Finn leaned forward, brushing the curve of her ear with his lips. "I mean we can if you want, but I wasn't really planning on doing much talking later. Unless you count pleading with me to let you come."

She gasped, covering it with a cough.

"Still here?" Will clapped Finn on his back with one hand and handed him a brush to clean up the confetti with the other. Every muscle up his spine tensed. Had he heard what

Finn had said? Not likely, considering his fist wasn't embedded in Finn's face. He needed to be more careful. He couldn't let his overwhelming desire to make Molly blush ruin any chance they had at being together.

Will didn't wait for a response. "Good game, brother."

Finn turned to accept the awkward hug from Will. His captain, his best friend, his brother. Brother. Fuck. A lead weight sank deeper into his stomach. He wanted to come clean, to lay his heart on the line and tell Will his intentions with his sister. Maybe if they were upfront about it, it wouldn't be so bad.

But Molly didn't want it. He knew she was reluctant to expedite their deaths, she probably wasn't even convinced she and Finn would amount to anything, so there was no point in telling Will anything if it wasn't for real.

Except it *was* for real. Finn had opened the door to their future and Molly's toes were across the threshold. He loved her, with every ounce of his being, and while she might never openly say it back to him, she loved him too. Everything else was window dressing. They'd overcome it all.

He'd do it her way – for the time being – keeping their secret from the world. But that didn't mean guilt wasn't going to gnaw his insides like mice through wiring.

Will stepped back and turned to Molly while Finn swept up the pieces of brightly colored paper. "Need a quote?"

Another eye roll. "I mean, I suppose." She shrugged. "If I can't have the best player on the team to talk to now that Johnny's gone for an X-ray, I can probably make do with you idiots." She winked and nudged him with her elbow.

"I'm kidding. Get in here." She threw her arms around Will. "You fucking did it. Great game, Willy."

"Don't call me that." His muffled voice betrayed his good humor, and his emotions. Will had waited a long time to win, he deserved it. He was a good leader with a big heart and Finn was proud to skate with him.

Molly moved back and hit the button on her recorder. "Mr. Morrison, to what do you attribute tonight's win?"

Will stuck his elbow on the concrete wall and leaned his head on his hand like he was some kind of model. "Excellent leadership – obviously. I am clearly The Shit and they couldn't have done shit without me. I basically won all by myself."

Molly flicked his forehead. "Asshat. This is why I never interview you."

Will laughed. "I know it's trite to say that teamwork makes the dream work, but it's true. Any good sports team is built on a solid foundation. Our team is more than just a team, it's a family. We each have a role to play and when we do, we function like a well-oiled machine. We ended up three men down out there tonight, and while we felt their absence on the bench, the rest of the guys stepped up and picked up the slack."

Molly nodded and chewed on the end of her pen. She knew better than to interrupt Mr. Orator once he'd started his soliloquy. The guy loved to talk. But more than that, people loved to listen to what he had to say.

"I think something we had out there tonight that our opponent didn't, was trust. No matter who was on the ice, they trusted whoever they needed was where they were supposed to be. We practiced drill after drill, practice after practice." He laughed and ran a hand through his hair. "I wouldn't be surprised if the guys had voodoo dolls of me for all the extra practices I called."

Finn raised his hand. "Oh. We definitely made voodoo dolls – I gave mine a mullet." He grinned at Molly while he leaned the brush against the wall. "Manifesting that shit." He scrubbed Will's hair.

Will retaliated by grabbing Finn in a headlock and rubbing

his knuckles across Finn's skull sending shudders down his spine. "I couldn't have led the team to greatness without this guy. He's the best thing to ever happen to me." Will batted dreamy eyelids at Finn, licked his lips, and burst out laughing – but Finn didn't miss the deflation of Molly's shoulders and how her smile lost its spark.

"Betchurass that win was all my doing." Finn dusted his shoulder.

"Is there anything you think you can work on to improve your game going forward?"

Finn patted Will's chest. "I'll take this one, bro. I mean, we kinda won, Molly, so where else is there to go from here?" He stroked his chin. "Oh! I have it. Cheerleaders. Half nekkid cheerleaders would definitely make our game better." He nodded slow and sage like he was Yoda or some shit, enjoying the crinkles appearing in Molly's forehead at the mention of scantily clad dancers celebrating the team.

"This too – it's perfect. What about..." He waved his hand like he was showing her what he was talking about. "An arena full of people all wearing my name on their back." He wiggled his eyebrows at her.

The corner of her lips twitched. Was she considering it? Was it an opportunity? He made a mental note to pick her up a jersey with #15 O'Brien on the back. He'd ask her to wear it one night – just for him. He'd sink between her plush thighs, pry her legs apart, and eat her till she coated his face with—

"Finn?" Her eyebrows were raised, and her lips pursed. "Did you have something else to add to the Finn-worship list?"

"A really good blo—"

Will shoulder checked him. "Nope. You're not going to unleash that dirty mouth of yours anywhere near my sister."

Molly snorted then her eyes went wide like she realized she'd made the sound out loud. Finn needed to get Will the hell gone so Finn could put his dirty mouth *on* Will's freakin' sister. Maybe that's where her mind went as well.

Molly popped her hip and jammed her hand on it. "Are you two done fucking with me?"

"Never." Finn gave her the finger-guns. He knew she loved those. Not. True to form she flipped him off.

"You coming to the bar, Mol?" Will dusted off his suit jacket and smoothed out his dress pants.

Molly shook her head, a faint blush creeping back into her pale skin. "I need to write this up." She waved her recorder and notebook. "Gotta get it done and submitted before midnight." She glanced at Finn, uncertainty swirling with heat in those endless eyes of hers.

"That's a shame. Finn's buying." He threw his arm around Finn's neck but Finn shirked it off.

"Sorry man, I'm out too."

Will's jaw dropped. They could count on one hand the times Finn hadn't gone to the bar after a game. Never mind a championship win. Their *first* championship win. It was suspicious as hell. He'd have to pull out all the stops to make it believable – thankfully he'd laid the foundation during the period breaks.

He scrubbed at the back of his neck, as a flush crept over his entire body. Hopefully she'd understand this was a ruse, subterfuge, designed solely to throw her brother off their scent and was not at all based in fact.

Dear God, please don't let her believe this is fact.

"Man..." Finn dropped his voice and tossed a cursory glance at Molly. She leaned forward, she was invested in his explanation. Of course she was.

"You know I spent most of the period breaks on the shitter." He ground the words out around clenched teeth.

"That's where you were?"

Finn nodded. "Raging case of the shits, man."

Will jumped away from him like he was toxic. "You too? How the hell did you play? Adult diapers?"

Finn smirked and folded his arms. "I'll never tell."

"Where the hell did you guys eat? I'm never going wherever it is. Dang. Kudos for playing with the scoots though, that takes guts." He burst out laughing like he'd told the funniest joke in the universe. Molly rolled her eyes. Finn shrugged.

"Want me to walk you home before I hit the bar, Molly?"

Molly's eyes widened.

"I got her. You can't be late for your own celly, man. You earned it – go drink from the keg of glory. I heard someone mention they were doing body shots."

Will smirked. Finn winced and rubbed his stomach, like the idea of consuming alcohol was enough to trigger his bowels into motion. "I need to go."

Will shook his head. "I can't believe you're missing this, man."

"We'll have a do-over. Ain't no way we can contain a title celebration to just one night. We aren't amateurs."

Will looked sufficiently satisfied by that explanation and backed away with a shrug. "Guess I'll have to take one for the team." He raised an eyebrow. "Or a couple."

Molly scrunched up her face as she collected all the multi-colored pieces of paper and tossed them in the trash just inside the locker room. "You're all disgusting pigs."

Finn grabbed her elbow and guided her toward the side exit of the building. "This disgusting pig is taking you home."

She flashed him a small smile. "You can go out partying if you want, you know. I'm not going to stop you. Who am I to come between a man and some body shots?"

He walked her toward the wall, not stopping when her shoulder collided with a bump. "I need you to listen to me, and listen well so there's no room for misunderstanding. The only body I want to lick in any way, shape, or form – from here forward – is yours. Are we clear?"

Her jaw dropped open, she checked over both shoulders, and shoved him away from her with a hiss. "You can't say things like that to me here, Finnegan."

Something flickered across her face, something wanton and wicked. He advanced again. "Why not?"

She pushed him back. "You know why, asshole." She started toward the exit. "Let's get out of here before you get us both arrested for indecent exposure. Or worse – killed by my brother when he finds you with your dick in me."

CHAPTER 21
Molly

Molly's hands trembled as she slid the key into the lock of her apartment. It was really happening. She swallowed, pausing to settle the sparring snakes in her stomach. Finn stood so close his breath tickled the hair on the back of her neck, and if she rocked back just a little, her ass would brush against his crotch.

There was no taking things back once they'd slept together. The toothpaste would be well and truly out of the tube once his dick crossed her threshold. She cringed. Too far, even for her.

"Are we just standing out here staring at your door all night?" He brushed his lips along the curve of her neck, sending pulses straight to her core. "I mean, I don't mind banging you against the door, MoMo, but I'm still getting you naked."

His dirty murmurs against her skin sent shivers through her body and out her fingers and toes, making her drop her key. She leaned her head back onto his shoulder and he ran his hands from her hips all the way up her torso, squeezing her tits, and nipping on her earlobe. Fuck. Finn O'Brien's hands were on her body and she felt like a goddess.

"Open the door, Doll."

She nodded, her chest rising and falling with tormented intakes of breath. How could she be so turned on? Her nerves so lit up with aching need when he had barely touched her?

Her hands shook as she bent, picked up the key, and opened the door. "Cl-Cleo? Are you here?"

Behind her, the sound of a heavy coat landing on the chair next to the door had her clenching her pussy. He carefully placed his suit jacket on top of it before turning to face her.

The serpents in her stomach slithered around her organs and squeezed, hard. She closed her eyes for a moment, trying to stop the world from spinning so fast, but his scent invaded her nose, and the warmth from his close proximity tugged her toward him.

When she opened her eyes, he was there, right in front of her, concern pinching between his eyes as they searched her face. She reached out a palm, his playoff scruff tickling her hand. "I'm scared." Her confession escaped on a breathy exhale.

He reached behind her and tugged her hair tie, letting her mane flow freely around her shoulders. "Tell me your fears." He kissed her forehead. Then the tip of her nose... the hollow of her throat. "Out loud, Molly. Tell me your fears so we can face them together." She nodded and closed her eyes as he swept the hem of her jersey over her head, discarding it on top of his clothes on the chair.

She bit her lip as he dragged his nose down her sternum, over her stomach, and bumped against the top of the zipper on her jeans.

"Fears, Molly."

"Mhmm. Fears. Right." She sighed. Finnegan O'Brien was on his knees in front of her, cupping her ass cheeks like she was some kind of treasure, and she was all his. His. Fears. Right.

"I'm afraid..." Her voice cracked and she cleared her throat. "I'm afraid we might not have any chemistry."

Lies. Every time he touched her, her body reacted. They could probably see her thermal radiation on satellite pictures from outer space. He squeezed her ass cheeks, sending lightning bolts to her crotch.

"Liar." He smirked up at her from the floor. "But I'll prove that fear completely wrong once we get through the others." He tried to pull her zipper down with his teeth, but he couldn't get it to budge.

She laughed, some of the tension leaving her muscles.

He nuzzled his head against her stomach. "So mean, Miss Molly. Laughing at me when I'm on my knees."

She bit her lip as he opened her fly with his hands and shucked her jeans down her legs, gliding his palms over her hips and down the outsides of her thighs. Goosebumps sprung all over her skin under his hands as they moved.

Stepping out of her jeans, she swallowed. "I'm afraid we'll break what we have between us." Her heart picked up its pace. For all her bluster and fears, that was the biggest. Was she afraid of losing Will? Absolutely. Did she think he'd come round eventually? Probably. But losing Finn... her chest tightened.

His finger traced along the edges of her hot pink lace thong, before he buried his nose against it and... sniffed. The bastard was sniffing her pussy. Mother of God she was going to die.

"That once we take this step..."

He dragged his tongue along the scalloped edge of the scrap of fabric.

"We... we..."

A finger slipped behind the string in her asscrack and

traveled toward the hot mess at the apex of her thighs, tugging the thong from her body as his finger brushed against her skin.

"Fuck."

"It's true... Once we take this step, we fuck... yes, ma'am." He held the panties while she stepped out of them, swaying a little as she did.

Apparently it was hard to keep her balance while he was on his knees and at tongue-level with her bare pussy. "We can't go back. What if we ruin everything by—?"

He ran his flat tongue over the outside of her lips, drawing a feral moan from her chest.

"You waxed for me, MoMo?"

She slipped her fingers through his fire-red hair and clenched her fist so his head tilted and his eyes met hers. "I wax for *me*, Finny. You just have the honor of enjoying it."

A low hum vibrated through him as he jerked his head out of her grip. "And what a fucking honor it is... Do you know how long I've waited to taste this pussy?" He slipped a finger through her folds, but not touching her throbbing clit, which only served to make her hips lean forward of their own volition.

"N-no..." She hated how breathless she sounded, how breathless she was. Need pooled between her legs and only Finn could save her.

He sucked her arousal off the tip of his finger and she shuffled her legs apart. Maybe if she made her base wider, she wouldn't feel like a house of cards ready to collapse at any given moment. Maybe if she gave him more access he'd stop fucking teasing her and give her what she needed.

Another glide of his finger through her folds, and another lick of his finger, pulling it from his mouth with a satisfied pop. "You're so fucking delicious."

This had to be what madness felt like. With every touch,

another nerve ending sparked, and she sailed that much closer to O-Town.

He dragged his finger back through her pussy, using a finger from his other hand to circle her tight little hole in back. She might have purred. An honest to God purr like a fucking cat. He grinned, pressing against her ass, but not so hard as to gain entry. Finn O'Brien was a mother fucking tease and she was going to kill him.

Assuming she survived whatever dirty deeds he planned on bestowing on her anyway. Prying apart her slick lips with both thumbs, he teased her clit with the very tip of his tongue. "You were saying Doll? Something about fearing that we wouldn't have any chemistry..."

"I-I-I... you're making this really hard, Finn."

"No, Doll. I'm the one that's hard. I'm always fucking hard for you."

He circled her opening once, twice, a third time, but despite squatting to meet his finger, he didn't slip it inside her.

"You're a fucking tease, Finnegan O'Brien." She inched lower, thigh muscles holding steady from years of burlesque dancing. She could squat all day if she had to – she just didn't want to.

"We're not done talking about your fears, MoMo."

"I'm scared of losing you."

The earnestness in his eyes as he looked up at her, melted the bars of the ice prison that had held her heart captive for years.

"Never going to happen. Ride or die, boo. Ride or fucking die."

She sank lower, a futile attempt to line his face up with her pussy. "I'd like to ride you before I fucking die." She hated the desperation coating her words, but there was no escaping it, she wanted him, needed him... her body was a five-alarm fire and only one man was qualified enough to put it out.

With a wolfish grin he lapped at her clit like a starved man. Slipping his finger inside her, he groaned. A gasp escaped her as sensations crashed into her in waves.

He stopped. She sank lower onto his finger, clenching her muscles around him in a bid to trap him in her pussy. "Don't stop."

He chuckled. "Two things. One…" He rammed his finger deeper into her, curving it just enough to brush against her G-spot, sending tremors through her limbs. "You're not the boss of me, Miss Morrison. And two…" He withdrew his hand enough for a second finger to join the first. "Now that I've tasted this delectable pussy of yours, I'm never walking away."

She tangled her fingers into his mane and jerked his head toward her crotch. "Never's a really long time, Finny."

He lapped at her clit sending shivers through her spine and something that sounded like "Not long enough" made its way to her ears, but she was already halfway to the Promised Land. She ground against his face with abandon, his grunts and moans feeding into her building orgasm.

Her arousal grew with each sweep of his tongue. He was probably drowning, but gripped her ass with the intensity of a man possessed. She'd have butt bruises in the morning – if she didn't, she'd make him do it again until she did. The bite of pain in her ass was just enough to tether her to the ground as he ate her like a four course meal at a fancy restaurant.

The gentle caressing of her G-spot built to something closer to what she ached for, but still not the pounding she needed – like he was deliberately holding back. He wanted her to want him. He wanted her to ache for him. He was toying with her like a cat playing with a mouse.

Rolling her head back, she moaned and leaned into his hand as a third finger joined the first two, stretching her just a little. How big was Finn's dick? Did he have a delicious dick that curved in the perfect direction?

A blast of cold air and a wet nip at her inner thigh made her squeal. "What the fuck?"

"Come back to me. Your mind was wandering."

"How the fuck could you possibly know that?"

He grinned and pressed all three fingers against her inner wall. She melted against him.

"What were you thinking about?"

"How big your dick is."

"Well." He rolled his thumb over her clit making her gasp. "If you don't pay attention and let me have my fun right now. You'll never find out."

"You wouldn't."

"I've waited a long time for this, Molly. I have patience and I can assure you that you don't want to test me. Don't you like my tongue?" He trailed it through her pussy.

"I-I d-d-do." Fuck. She'd never been with someone who took so much time to get her off before. The anticipation was going to kill her before she came.

"Then stay in the moment with me, okay? No thoughts. No wandering mind. No grocery lists in your head. Just you, me, and whatever the fuck we want to do to each other, okay?"

She closed her eyes as he pumped his fingers in and out of her.

"I'm gonna need an answer, Doll." He withdrew his hand altogether, her wetness suddenly cold against the air from his absence.

"Noooooo don't stop. Put it back. Put it baaaaaack!"

"Are you begging me, Miss Molly?"

Yes. "Fuck no."

"Give it time."

She frowned. Her entire body hummed. Despite being naked from the waist down, her skin was hot and prickling with sweat. The man would be her undoing.

"Fine, I learned my lesson. I'll be a good little girl and pay attention to my darling Finny Winny, okay?"

She heard it before she felt it. The crack of skin against skin right before the spread of heat through her ass cheek. She couldn't even pretend to be outraged. In fact, her whole body swooned. Finn grabbed her hips, supporting her weight.

"I love your sassy mouth."

"Just wait till it's wrapped around your cock." She blew him a kiss. Her mind spun, her nipples tingled, and her clit ached with a deep and unsatisfied need. "Please, Finn..."

"Please what? Tell me what you need, Doll."

She grinned. She'd never had a problem with telling someone what she wanted or needed from them. "I want you to put your tongue back on my pussy and eat me like I'm your last meal on earth."

Her words seemed to pour gasoline on his already blazing fire. He jerked her hips to him, hooked one of her legs over his shoulder, and buried his face between her thighs like it was his life's mission.

"You're so fucking wet, Mol." He slurped and swallowed like he was eating a juicy goddamn pineapple. "I love how wet you are for me."

Two fingers hit her g-spot as his tongue wove circles around her clit. Her body tensed, trembling with the need to release. She'd never needed to come more in her entire life. She'd never before felt like if she didn't come, she might die. She needed to come, she needed him to know what he did to her, what he'd always done to her.

The sounds that escaped her were almost inhuman. Untamed wails and moans rose from her as she rubbed against his hungry tongue with a desperate eagerness, chasing her release.

The hand gripping her hip shifted, but the fingers inside her curled further, like he was gripping her so she didn't move.

His free hand trailed up the outside of her leg and around the curve of her ass cheek. Her pussy twitched and clenched around his fingers as she charged toward her orgasm, and Finn's unrelenting tongue was pushing her soul further from her body with each lick.

His fingers brushed across her tight hole before one pressed against it, gaining entrance. She dropped against his hand, needing him deeper, needing more in both her pussy and her ass. Her undecipherable screams piercing the air, as the release she'd been chasing hit her like a freight train. Her body exploded into an array of colors and sensations. Her head lolled back, her muscles unclenched, but her hands stayed wrapped around his head and tangled in his hair.

When he didn't stop after she'd come, she tightened his grip on her hair. "St-St-St... too sensitive." She hissed out a woosh of air and slid her leg off his shoulder.

As it turned out, she no longer had control of her legs. She sagged, but he was there, strong hands, firm grip, picking her up like she weighed nothing and carrying her through the room. Her thighs were damp and her pussy soaked and still convulsing.

He kissed her as he walked, his mouth still wet and glistening with her arousal. She cupped his face, biting his lip and demanding access to his swollen tongue. "Mmmmm."

"Sated?" He squeezed her nipple through her shirt and lace bra before placing her onto the bed.

"Just getting started."

"Good." He yanked off his belt and opened the bottom three buttons on his shirt. She leaned up on her elbows not wanting to miss a second of the Finn O'Brien gun show. "I need your pussy to clench me as hard as it clenched my fingers when you came."

Another three buttons opened. She'd seen him shirtless countless times before: pool parties, lazing around her parents' house, in the locker room after games, but she'd never been allowed to ogle.

"Why are you staring at me like I'm opening your favorite Christmas present?"

"Don't stop. Please. I know what's under the shirt. I love what's under the shirt. I just... I've never been able to stare at it without being afraid of being caught."

He started humming Joe Cocker's *You can leave your hat on.*

"Are you giving me a strip tease?"

"You've danced for me. It's only fair."

"That night was equal parts the best and worst of my life."

He raked a hand through his hair. "Tell me about it. I almost jizzed my pants in front of hundreds of people."

He started humming again, and when all the buttons were undone, he let the fabric slip from one of his shoulder, keeping the front of the shirt pulled closed.

Letting him enjoy the moment Molly fanned herself. "Oh my."

The shirt dropped a little more on one side. "What nice pecs you have."

He spun around and shook his ass at her. She couldn't stop the giggle-snort that erupted from her. She bolted up onto her knees, scooted forward, and pinched his ass cheeks with both hands.

Finn leaned forward, sending his ass even closer to her. "Do it again."

She smacked his cheek with an open palm. "Dance for me, damnit."

"What my lady wants, my lady gets."

His lady. Her body jerked to attention like someone hit the go switch on a carnival ride.

Finn's humming escalated to obnoxious singing as he dropped his dark blue dress shirt to the floor and swung his hips like he was an extra in a J'Lo music video. He tucked his thumbs into the band of his pants and jiggled them up and down, each movement slid his underwear down just a tad, revealing the V Molly's wet dreams were made of.

"Fuck." She licked her lips.

"Damn straight."

She laughed at how comfortable he was. "I can't say I've ever been so excited to see someone's dick."

"Enjoy the feeling babydoll, because this dick is the last dick you're ever going to need." He quirked an eyebrow. "Though if you want to sample a few others..." He shrugged. "I'm down."

His confidence was intoxicating, her nipples stiffened even more. His rock-hard cock springing free crowned out the screaming about forever in the back of her mind. "You're not...?"

He shook his head. "I'm not."

"But I thought all boys born in the US got circumcised?"

"My granny was from Ireland, my mother, too. I'm told the nurses kept trying, but Mom was insistent they weren't butchering my penis just because everyone else does it."

Molly leaned forward and curled her hand around it, enjoying the whoosh of air from Finn.

"Did you know...?"

She pumped her hand slowly from base to tip and back again. "Did I know...?"

"The US is basically the only country in the world where dudes get circumcised for non-religious reasons?"

"I didn't know that. Am I supposed to...? I mean... is there anything I should... do differently?"

He chuckled. "Thanks for caring, but it doesn't require any special treatment."

She dropped her voice and stroked the top of his head.

"What's he saying about you? You're a very special big boy, aren't you?"

The dick twitched in her hand. She slid the foreskin back and looped her tongue around the tip of his dick. Finn hissed. Fingers tangled in her hair and tugged her head back so her eyes were on his. "As much as I appreciate – and can't wait to fuck that sassy little mouth of yours. I need to fuck your pretty pink pussy first."

Her core pulsed. She needed that too. She unhooked her bra as he shuffled out of his briefs, hopping a few times when his foot got stuck.

She giggled. "The things you don't see in the movies, eh?"

He shook his head. "Just be glad I'm a graceful athlete, or I'd have gone down like a sack of spuds as my granny would have said."

She laughed again as he stepped out of them. "Too much chit-chat about your granny when you're getting ass-naked, Finny."

He smirked. Kneeling on the bed, his eyes roamed her from head to toe.

She could almost feel fizzles dancing across her skin as his eyes moved lower. He made his way over her, lowering his mouth to the space between her tits. His hard cock pressed against her leg, making her wiggle her hips.

"Patience, Molly."

She wriggled again. "I don't want to be patient. I want it now."

He kissed the sensitive skin between her breasts, lifted up one of her boobs and kissed underneath it.

"What are you doing?"

"Kissing the red marks your bra left."

Something about that was weirdly sweet.

"I vote you never wear a bra again." He brushed his scruff-covered chin over her nipple drawing a squeak from her.

Pinching her other nipple, he swept his nose against hers and captured her mouth before she could answer.

"I'm clean." She managed between almost violent, demanding kisses. "I get tested regularly, and I have an IUD."

"I haven't been with anyone in months."

She tried to jump back, but the mattress didn't give and instead, she cracked her head against his. "Wait, what? You haven't?"

Finn shook his head. "I couldn't do it anymore, MoMo. I couldn't stick my dick in another woman and wish it was you the whole time."

His face softened, his brow creased, and the pain reflected in his eyes broke something inside of her. Unable to put a voice to the surge of emotions bubbling inside her at his confession, she grabbed his face and yanked him to her, kissing him like he was her life force.

"You're it for me, Molly."

Lightheadedness overwhelmed her as his whispered words against her neck did more to turn her on than anything dirty he'd said.

Trailing light strokes of his fingers along the side of her ribs and over her nipples, while his lips feathered over her skin, his hard length still pressed into her leg.

"Stop teasing me and get the fuck inside me."

He leaned up on his elbow and dragged his cock through her wetness. She moaned. "You're trying to kill me, aren't you?"

"Is death by coital bliss such a bad way to go?"

She shook her head, tracing her fingertips across his forehead and down the side of his face. "No. But I'd really rather live long enough to do it again... and again..."

He smiled and something she couldn't place passed across his face.

"What is it?"

"That's what I needed to hear." He brushed a kiss across her lips, sending flickers to every hotspot.

He dragged his tongue along the column of her neck. "That this isn't a one-and-done for you. That I'm not some booty call, some one night stand, that you're really going into this with a future in mind, even if we don't know what that looks like right now."

Blood rushed in her veins, coursing through her like a tidal wave in a storm. A sharp pinch to her nipple sent another jolt of need to her molten core.

"I swear to every God that's known, if you don't hurry up and fuck me, I'm reaching into that drawer and I'm going to fuck myself with a dildo right here in front of you."

He nipped at the corner of her lips. "I can't say threats of you getting off in front of me will work, MoMo. I kinda like this needy..." His cock brushed against her pussy. "Demanding..." Another sweep. "Whiny... Molly..."

She opened her mouth to protest, but he was ready. He covered her lips with his and slipped inside her in one thrust. She cried out into his mouth and her body wilted against the mattress.

At last. Finn O'Brien's dick was inside her – and it didn't feel at all weird. In fact, the total opposite. His eyes searched her face as he held steady for a beat, then two. Was he waiting for her to change her mind?

She rocked her hips, chasing friction, and he grinned, tipping his in response so he inched just a little deeper. Picking up the pace, his skin slapped against hers as it seemed any trace of uncertainty was replaced by an undulating, all consuming need to fuck her.

"Yes... yes..." Her heavy breaths punctuated her cries of bliss as he drove into her with deep, precise thrusts.

She tightened around him, clawing at his scalp as she pressed his face against hers. Her muscles twitched and that familiar tingle was growing in her core. She wouldn't last much longer. He must have felt her reaction because he grabbed her thighs and angled her hips to get a deeper angle.

Her eyes rolled back as he pounded her g-spot. She slipped her hand between them to glide her fingers over her clit, coming undone with his name on a scream.

"Don't stop." His feral growl in her ear spurred her on. He was close, grunting with each thrust.

She clenched around his cock, locked her legs around him, and with a huff of breath, rolled him onto his back. "That was easier than I thought it would be." She moved her hips, building back up to the pace he'd set.

He clutched her hips as she rode him, her tits bouncing with every thrust. The pad of his thumb found her swollen, overly sensitive clit, and her body went into overdrive.

"So... close..." He held her gaze as she fucked him, but when his eyes rolled back and his thighs tightened between her legs, she brought him home.

Hearing her name fall from his lips on a roar as he came in a tangle of cuss words and deities made her heart soar.

"Yes!" He held both palms out to her and she met them both for a loud, hi-ten smack. Collapsing onto him with a grin, she sighed and snuggled her face into the crook of his neck.

"Not bad for a first time."

He grabbed her by her biceps and pushed her up to look at her face. "Not... bad... she says. That wasn't even a high-five-able fuck, that was a hi-ten fuck, Molly Morrison."

She couldn't help but giggle at the incredulous look plastered on his face. "Okay, fine. Above average." She leaned forward to grab a wad of tissues from the bedside cabinet.

"What do you think you're doing?"

Easing off his dick, she shoved the tissues between her legs.

"I don't want your ooey gooey cum running down my legs

thank you. And I'm going to pee. I don't want a UTI either." She stood up and grabbed a bottle of water from the mini fridge she kept next to her bed.

Sure it was mostly filled with her favorite Yeungling beer. But there was always a bottle of water in there for emergencies - and rehydration after excessive sweating post-sexercise. "Here." She tossed the bottle onto his stomach, giggling as he writhed like a cobra as the cold plastic hit his hot skin. "Hydrate before you die-drate."

She'd barely graced the toilet seat with her ass when he called from the bedroom. "Hurry up, I'm ready for round two!"

There was no trace of regret in his voice, no awkwardness or hesitation. It felt like they'd simply always been together. Was that what they'd been missing for years? Like the comfort of an old pair of slippers that blow your fucking mind every time you sink into them. Was this how it could have been the whole time they'd known each other?

Her heart spasmed as she flushed, leaning forward to brace herself on the cool porcelain for a beat to steady her breathing. The bigger question was, would it last?

CHAPTER 22
Finnegan

Whoops and cheers greeted Finn as he arrived home the next morning. As soon as he opened the door, Meghan Trainor's *Walk of Shame* blasted throughout the building and echoed down the street.

"About fucking time, Finnegan!" Slow claps tapped out the beat of his steps as he walked.

"Finally broke your dry spell, eh, Obi?" Will slung an arm around his shoulders and guided him into the kitchen. "Who's the lucky girl?"

If Finn had been thinking with his brain and not his dick, he'd have thought the aftermath through and come up with a better plan. In hindsight, staying over at Molly's probably wasn't his smartest move either.

To Will's left, Linc cringed and covered his face, Russell shook his head and flared his nostrils. It was probably a bad time to tell Will that Finn had in fact broken his dry spell with the long-term object of his affections: Will's younger sister. Finn shuddered.

Would there ever be a good time to tell him? Probably not. But he was going to want to know who the lucky woman was, and Finn had brushed off every potential alibi for weeks on end. Shit. He was really, *really* bad at this.

Will let go of Finn and strode ahead into the kitchen, where a pancake production line had been established.

Linc leaned close to Finn's ear. "You're really fucking bad at this, man." He shook his head. "For someone who'd wanted this for years, you could have done a better job at planning ahead."

Russ chuckled behind him. They weren't wrong. Austin sat at the table, reading a book about Buddhism or some Zen-shit, he lifted his head and quirked an eyebrow. Finn shook his head.

"At least tell me you got laid, man." Russ tugged on the tie hanging around Finn's shoulders. He had made his way home in his crinkled game night suit. "You definitely have that just-fucked glow in those pasty Irish cheeks of yours." Russ patted Finn's chops with open palms.

"I hate you both right now."

"Us?" Russ jerked a thumb between him and Lincoln. "You love us."

Finn dropped his head into his hand. "I'm so fucking bad at this. I should just tell him, right?" He stepped forward, but Linc and Russ each grabbed an arm and frog-marched him back a few paces.

"Wrong. Absolutely not. Bad plan."

"Fucking suicide. Don't be a dumb shit."

Finn shook his head. "The guilt is real." He rubbed at his chest in a bid to erase the tightness.

Will had claimed a tall stack of pancakes in the kitchen and sat next to Austin drizzling maple syrup and dumping fruit and crispy bacon onto his plate. "Celebratory breakfast of champions!" He toasted no one in particular with his fork.

Finn's heart pinched. He pressed down the guilt in his chest. The guys were right, he'd need Molly on board before he even considered taking it to Will. He couldn't do it behind her back. Never mind Will killing him, Molly would get there first.

Finn patted both his friends on their shoulders. "Moment's passed. I'm good." He walked into the kitchen and grabbed a plate as Seb flipped another pancake. "Austin, you having pancakes?"

"Y sont sans œufs," Seb called over his shoulder as he slid a pancake onto a plate.

"D'accord. Merci."

"What did you use instead of eggs?" Will was barely swallowing his pancakes as he shoveled them into his mouth.

"Oil because we had it. I'd have used apple sauce if we didn't." Seb gave a nonchalant shrug as though it was no big deal, but Austin always appreciated people going out of their way to ensure he didn't die.

"Awkward fucker. How do you survive? I don't think I'd last a day if I was allergic to eggs." Linc kicked the end of Austin's foot.

"There are lots of things you can use instead of eggs." Austin closed his book and placed it on the table in front of him. "And this is how I survive." He slid his epi pen out of his pocket.

"I wasn't really asking." Linc rolled his eyes and accepted a plate of pancakes from Russell.

Austin shrugged.

"I'm going to shower – I bet poor Seb will still be flippin' pancakes by the time I'm done." Finn turned to head upstairs when the doorbell rang. "I'll get it."

The team were fighting over each pancake as they cooked. Sébastien had pans on all four rings of the stove and was pouring batter and flipping like it was his job. Finn shook his head and opened the door.

Bang.

He flinched before realization hit that it was a confetti cannon. Colored paper rained over his head onto the floor. She'd gotten him again. Minx. She waited for him to meet her gaze before she flipped the hollow tube, letting it drop to his feet with a clunk.

With a grin on her face she bent to pick up a large package at her feet and pushed her way past him. "Walk of shame, eh?" She tossed him a wicked wink. "Still in last night's clothes. I hope she was worth it."

She didn't wait for an answer before making her way into the foyer. "I have caaaaaake!"

There was complete silence for a beat before a couple of the team trickled from one feeding station to another. Molly pulled a sheet cake from the bag in her hand.

"Did you say you had cake?" Russell and Linc walked toward her, forks in hand, scooping piles of pancake into their mouths.

"I did. But you might wanna keep it till you're done with first breakfast." She beamed and continued into the kitchen. "I hope no one's naked in here!"

"Fuck no!" Will's snarl made Finn cringe and Russ and Linc glance over their shoulders to offer matching sympathetic stares.

"Finn, come see this cake!" The last place Finn wanted to be was in a confined space with both Molly and Will, but his feet moved him forward to Will's voice nonetheless.

Molly brandished a long two-layer cake with the Snow Pirate's logo in the middle and everyone's name and numbers printed around it. A model version of Will, on skates, holding his stick stood above their logo, with a C on his chest and it said "Congratulations" in blue cursive writing around the skater.

"Did you make this?" Linc reached out to touch the frosting but Russ slapped his hand away.

Molly snorted. "I didn't. I got Quinn to make it. Sabrina's bestie? She's wicked talented in the kitchen."

Russ nodded. "Can confirm." He patted his stomach. "I've had to up my gym time to compensate for the deliciousness."

Molly slid the cake onto the table. "It's eggless too." She gave a pointed stare to Austin who smiled.

"Does no one actually remember that Austin doesn't even like sweets?" Will shook his head. "Poor fucker's forcing down pancakes and now he has to pretend to like cake?" He draped his arm around Austin's shoulders. "It's okay man, I'll save you from the cake."

Austin patted Will's arm. "Such a selfless man, Cap."

"I do what I can." Will dropped his empty breakfast plate into the sink, but kept his fork. He swept it through the corner of the cake, swooped up a huge mouthful, and crammed it in his mouth. He moaned. "I think I've died and gone to heaven."

"Do you need a minute, Willy?" Her laugh was like a breath of air to Finn's tight lungs. "Anyways, I just wanted to stop by to drop it off and say congratulations. We're all very proud of you guys." She made her way back toward the door, brushing her fingertips against Finn's as she passed, sending a jolt to his crotch.

Will followed her out, closing the door behind her after she left. When he turned back, he paused. "Weren't you having a shower before pancakes?"

"Not hungry." His stomach churned. "Still not right after last night."

Will nodded grabbing his arm. "Hey, did you talk to your mom? About the kidney thing?" Finn's personal life was public knowledge in the hockey house, so Will didn't need to keep it quiet.

"I did. She's still interested in having a relationship with me... in rebuilding. Or trying to rebuild, I guess."

Will scrubbed his chin. "I need to shave this shit off, it's driving me insane."

Finn laughed. "Right? Itchy as fuck, man."

"So." Will shrugged. "You gonna see her again? Your mom, I mean. Not your mysterious lady friend from last night."

The invisible cords around Finn's chest tightened again while he nodded. "I think so, yeah. We're going to take it slow. No family dinners with her new husband and son or anything. But I'd like to reconnect with her, get to know who she is now that she's on the mend. She's on antidepressants and anti-anxiety meds, she's in therapy... She's doing much better."

After a moment of heavy silence, Finn turned to climb the stairs. "Oh." He paused. "She said she'd like to meet some of my friends sometime. I know it's a lot to ask, but if we ever get to that point, I was kinda hoping..."

"Ride or die, brother. You know you don't even need to ask."

Finn's voice caught in his throat and continued to swell as he ascended the stairs to his room. Would it always feel so bad? So dirty? Like the ultimate betrayal of his friendship with Will? He swallowed, but the bitterness coating his mouth didn't budge.

At the top of the stairs, his phone vibrated in his pocket. He waited until he was in the privacy of his bedroom before he tugged the phone from his pants and read the message.

> Molly: Wanna come to an open house with me?

> Molly: It's not weird, right? To text the morning after?

> Molly: Too needy?

Molly: It's too needy, right?

Molly: Never mind. Forget I asked.

Molly: In fact, forget I ever texted.

He could almost see the cogs in her head spinning with each message that appeared on his screen. Flummoxed Molly was kinda cute, he enjoyed seeing her soft, vulnerable underbelly.

Finn: Stand down, Commander. It's all good. An open house? Like for a house sale?

Molly: Yeah, I thought it'd be fun to pretend we're buying a house. Pick one, pretend we're rich, schmooze with the realtor – and get free food.

Finn: You wanna pretend buy a house with me?

Maybe someday she'd really want to buy a house with him.

Molly: Too dumb, isn't it? I thought it'd be fun.

Finn: Get out of your beautifully busy head and send me the address and time. You knew you'd have me at free food.

Two hours later, showered, shaved, and dressed in another fly-as-fuck suit, Finn rounded his car to open the door for Molly.

"You know I can open doors myself, right?"

Finn grinned. "I know if you really had an issue with me opening the door, you'd have beaten me to it – and then beaten me with the door."

"Hashtag facts. Mmm. You smell good." She leaned toward him, closed her eyes, and inhaled.

"Thanks. It's eau de finally being able to change my socks."

She smacked his chest. "There's no way they let you wear the same pair of unclean socks for the entire duration of the playoffs."

When he didn't answer, her jaw dropped. "You wouldn't. That's too disgusting, even for you."

He shrugged. "Hockey players are incredibly superstitious beings, Molly. You know this. You've seen the movies, you've lived with one, you've watched them up close and personal." He ran his fingers up her forearm as it hung by her side.

She folded her arms. "I'd have smelled it. Or noticed your skanky socks last night."

"Maybe I changed after the game."

"Maybe I'm going to ask the team if that's fact or fiction." Her eyes narrowed.

He leaned over and brushed his lips against her cheek. "I love how invested you are in my hygiene, MoMo."

They were on the outskirts of town, suburbia, with little chance of being seen, so he slipped his warm palm against hers and clutched her hand as they walked up the path that split the front yard.

A for sale sign stood outside, with brightly colored balloons tied to it, and a "By appointment only" sign hanging below it.

While he'd gone with wearing dress pants and a dark, button-down shirt, Molly had gone with brown knee high boots, skinny dark wash jeans, and an oversized, plum cable knit sweater that hung off one shoulder to reveal the strap of a tank top underneath.

Her hair had been set in loose curls, her make-up looked like she was ready for a night on the town, and she had aviators propped on top of her head. She looked like a movie star.

She squeezed his hand. "You wanna talk about our back story? Or do you wanna come up with something on the fly?"

The front door swung open. "Oh my God. Finn O'Brien?"

His stomach dropped and Molly's hand shot out of his grasp faster than he could blink.

"Hiiiiiiiiiiiiii. I'm Mandy. I'm the realtor for this property. I had no idea you'd be coming here today to take a look." She put a hand next to her mouth to speak behind it and widened her eyes. "I'm a huge fan!" Her stage whisper skills needed work, and he didn't miss Molly's Olympic level eye roll next to him.

"Come in, come in. Let me show you around."

"Actually Mandy. Would you mind if we took a look by ourselves?"

Irritation flashed across her face but she quickly covered it with a fake and beaming smile. "Of course, absolutely. And if this house isn't suitable for your forever home, please do give me a chance to talk through a few other options on the market right now. Am I to assume you're going to be playing...?"

She paused and checked over her shoulders. "Locally next season?" The stage whisper was back. "And you're clearly looking for a..." She dragged her eyes over Molly from head to toe and back up again. "Family home."

Finn draped his arm around Molly's shoulder, ready to out their fake-relationship to *Mandy* the nosy realtor as they'd talked about. But before he could open his mouth, Molly was already stepping forward out of his grasp with a hollow laugh.

"Oh, we're just friends." She patted his chest. "I'm here to make sure he doesn't just buy the first shiny thing he sees. You know how they can be."

"Men?"

"Rich hockey players." Another eye roll from Molly.

Mandy chewed on the end of her pen, and her eyes danced like all she saw when she looked at Finn was dollar signs. And while there was talk of him staying in Minnesota to play pro after graduation, they hadn't yet made an offer.

"Well, let me know if there's anything..." Mandy puffed out her chest. "Anything at all I can help you with."

"We will, thanks." Molly mirrored Mandy's smile with a fake one of her own.

When Mandy left, Molly jerked a thumb over her shoulder. "She's nice."

Finn groaned.

"What a catch."

It was his turn to roll his eyes.

"A real keeper. I feel like she's already spent your first NHL paycheck." She shuddered.

Sliding his arm around her waist, he tugged her to him, burying his lips into her hair. "Well, if you'd stuck with the plan, Miss Thing, she wouldn't have turned on her... eh... charm."

"What if she tells someone she saw us together and it somehow gets back to Will?"

"We could have just told him you were protecting me from the predatory blonde who saw dollar signs when we walked in the door."

"And how, exactly, would we explain to him why we were even here in the first place."

He stopped at the bottom of the stairs. "Okay, fine. Good point. Up you go." He ushered her forward with a smack on her ass as she passed. "Let's see if this place is our forever home."

At the top of the stairs was a huge den area. While there was no furniture in the space, it was easy to picture. "That's where the widescreen would go."

"For NHL on the PlayStation?"

He nodded. "And game night – y'know, when we aren't on the ice. And over here, we'd put an air hockey table."

She laughed. "You're off to the races with the décor on this place, Finny."

"Little known secret, MoMo." He swallowed, knowing it would probably put the fear of God into her, but also needing to be fair to himself, to both of them, and tell her upfront. "Despite my rep as a player, I can't wait to settle down."

To her credit, she didn't faint, stumble, or visibly react, she just walked the perimeter of the room. Was it something she'd thought about? If not settling with him, with someone, anyone else? Or would her flighty soul never let her tether herself to another person?

He ached to press the topic, to ask her whether it was something she saw herself doing in the future. But it was too much, too fast. He had to let her come to terms with the fact they'd opened the door between them, and had slept together before suggesting something quite so long term.

If he pushed, she'd spook and he'd lose her. She'd either want to settle down, or she wouldn't, all he could do was own his truth and tell her what he wanted. It was out there now, hanging between them as they walked through the bedrooms, and into the master bathroom, and unless he was sorely mistaken, it hadn't gotten weird.

"Holy crap! That bath is huge."

He closed the space between them, pressing himself against her ass. "All the better to fuck you in, my dear."

She giggled, but tipped her head to the side, granting him access to her neck. "Yes, please."

Dragging his splayed palms up her ribcage, he nipped at

the skin where her neck met her shoulder, drawing a moan from her. "We need to leave before I fuck you on someone's bathroom counter."

She wiggled her ass against his growing erection. "If I didn't think Mandy was standing outside ready to pounce the moment you dropped trou, I'd be game."

He groaned and dropped his forehead to the back of her head. "You'll be the death of me."

"At least you'll die happy, isn't that what you said last night?" She reached behind her and cupped his balls, giving them a gentle squeeze through his dress pants. "Another reason why you can't BS me about wearing dirty undies."

His eyelids flickered closed. "Why's that?"

She squeezed tighter, leaning back so she spoke close to his ear. "I know you don't wear any."

She stepped away from him and moved toward the bathroom door. But he snapped out his hand to stop her, cupping her at the apex of her thighs. She sank against his hand, rubbing as he held her.

She dug her nails into his bicep as he slid his hand up to the band of her jeans, popped the top button, and ran his fingers along the inside of the band.

Her chest lifted and fell with effort, her pulse hammered at the base of her neck, and when she closed her eyes on an inhale, his fingers moved lower.

"Seems I'm not the only one who likes going commando, Miss Morrison." When his fingers found their target, she sagged against him. "Even in jeans... I like it."

She fisted his dress shirt as his fingers strummed her clit. His dick yearned to be where his fingers were.

"You two doing okay up there?" Mandy's voice broke the spell and Molly's lolled-forward head snapped up with a hiss.

"We're fine, thanks, Mandy. Just admiring the size of the tub. It would be great for ice baths after games."

"Oh, absolutely!"

He withdrew his hand from Molly's pants and sucked his fingers clean without breaking eye contact. "It would also be spacious enough for two people, don't you think, Doll?"

A shiver rattled up her spine, making her stand upright. She cleared her throat before making her way back through the master bedroom.

"Finny?"

"Yeah, MoMo?"

"Were you serious about fucking me while I fucked someone else?"

Like he needed more fuel to his already stiff-as-a-rod fire in his pants. He blew out a huff of air. "Are you trying to kill me?"

She shook her head, gesturing to the empty bedroom. "Genuinely curious. You said you wanted to settle down. And while I'm not in the lifestyle... I like..." She glanced at the door.

Sweeping her dark waves from her face he nodded. "I'm more than cool with you being sexually adventurous, Molly. Kinks or otherwise. You want to seriously talk about a threesome, then we'll talk about a threesome."

"What about you?"

"What about me?"

She ran a finger along the collar of his shirt. "Do you have any fantasies?" The look she shot him from under her fluttering eyelashes stoked his need to be inside her.

"As a matter of fact, I do." He stepped toward her. She took a step back.

"Tell me." Her voice was barely a whisper.

He took another step. She walked back again, her back meeting the wall next to the door of the bedroom. He boxed her in, palms flat on the wall on either side of her head.

"I saw you making out with someone in the bar not too long ago."

She nodded, rolling her lips between her teeth.

"I wanted to fuck you from behind while you did."

She gasped. "You did?"

"I did. For days all I could think about – day and night – was burying my dick in you while you fucked her, or ate her out…" He pressed his crotch against her, in case she didn't believe him. "Don't dare talk to me about your deepest darkest fantasies, Molly Morrison. Not unless you want me to make them come true. Because I will."

Another gasp and her eyes went wide as she reached for him. A low rumble rolled through his chest as he pressed her against the wall for a hungry kiss.

"You'd do that for me?"

He moved the strap of her tank top and dragged his teeth along the bare curve of her shoulder. "I'd do anything for you."

CHAPTER 23

Molly

"He... s-s-aid that?" Cleo's mouth hung wide open under her bugged out eyes. She tugged at the collar of her sweater. "Ay, Dios Mío, Molly!" She fanned herself. "That's so fucking hot."

"I know, right?" Molly slurped at her large iced coffee, and dragged her finger through the cinnamon sugar at the bottom of the box of donuts between them on the sofa in their living room.

"What did you say back?" Cleo leaned over the box, like she hung on Molly's every word.

Molly groaned. Days later, her clit still shriveled at the memory. "Nothing. That ho-bag-ass-face-Mandy burst into the room to tell us there was food downstairs."

Cleo laughed. "Tell me how you really feel, Mol."

"She stormed in like she fucking owned the place."

"Or was trying to sell the place..."

"You think you're sooooo funny. But that bitch knew exactly what she was doing. She timed it so my lady balls were all-the-way blue. They're still blue. I haven't been able to see him since."

Cleo snorted. "Your lady balls are always all-the-way blue. You're in a perpetual state of horn dog."

"No lies detected."

Cleo picked up a Dulce de leche filled donut and took a bite. "Almost as good as sex."

"Almost. But not quite." Molly tore a bite from her second donut of the morning, then licked the caramel from her lip.

"Wanna talk about it?"

"Nope." Molly hard popped the 'p'.

"You sure?" Cleo crammed another bite of donut into her mouth, the caramel oozing from the end as she chomped down on it.

"Talk about what, ChoCho? How I didn't get any of the summer gigs I applied for? How I leapt off the edge of the cliff with the boy I've wanted forever and now we're – gag – dating, or – puke – worse, *in a relationship*? Or how I'm keeping it under wraps from my brother so we don't both die?"

"Yes." Cleo gave a firm nod. "All those things."

Molly guzzled her coffee. There wasn't enough caffeine in all the world to ready her for a serious conversation about feels with her helplessly romantic bestie.

"Don't make it something weird, ChoCho."

Cleo tipped her coffee at Molly. "Dude fingered you in the bathroom of a house you were looking at to fake buy together. Pretty sure it's already weird."

She wasn't wrong.

"You aren't in Kansas anymore, MoMo."

Molly rolled her eyes.

"What are you going to do about it?"

"Do about what?"

"Any of it. What's your plan? The boys are graduating next month – are you going to tell Will why you're trying to fuck Finn through his gown? Or why you're fussing over his... cap?" She snorted.

"No. I'm never going to tell him. Never ever. I'm just going to keep banging Finn behind his back until we're all old and gray. He probably won't notice, right?" She gasped. Old and gray? Was she really in it for the long haul?

Cleo arched an eyebrow. The question wasn't whether or not Will would notice. The question was how he hadn't noticed yet.

"You have a month to graduation. Once the boys are done with school things will be easier to hide. But I gotta ask, Mol. Do you really want to hide it from him?"

Molly's insides clenched. "What's the alternative?" She swallowed. "*Tell* him Finn and I are doing the nasty?"

"Ah." Cleo held up her hand. "But that's not all you're doing, is it? The two of you have been fighting feels for so long – now you're not ignoring them anymore, you've basically jumped ahead in your dating life. Yes, you've only been together a short time and already did the deed."

Molly snorted.

"But you're further ahead in your relationship than most start-ups. You've known each other and been friends for years. You're skipping the awkward: *does he suck his teeth?* phase, and the *does he have demons in his closet?* phase."

"I already know all of Finn's demons." Molly drank again. Her huge plastic cup was getting too close to empty for her liking.

"Exactly my point. You know each other. If you were a trope in a romance novel you'd be friends to lovers." She slurped on her drink. "And brother's best friend, but that goes without saying."

"And how do brother's best friend relationships play out in books when the brother finds out the best friend has been screwing his little sister?"

Cleo's face fell, and Molly gestured her cup at her. "My point exactly. It never ends well."

Cleo wasn't giving up so easily. "I still maintain things would be better for everyone in a brother's best friend romance if they all just came clean right off the bat." She leaned back against the couch.

"What if things don't work out between Finn and me?"

"I get why you're scared, I do. Big feelings can be pretty overwhelming. And it's a huge deal that you both stepped across the line you've been toeing for years. But if you keep thinking shit is going to go wrong with Finn, shit *will* go wrong with Finn."

Molly groaned. She'd woken up to a text from him saying 'Good morning, beautiful,' but hadn't yet replied.

Pulling her phone out, her screen lit up. He'd texted her again.

> Finn: Not to go full needy puppy on you, but I already miss your…

> Finn: That wasn't a typo. I was giving you time to make sure no one else can see your screen before I said what I'm about to say.

> Finn: I miss your pussy. And other things about you, obvs. Can I see you soon?

Fifteen minutes later, he'd sent another one.

> Finn: Too much, too fast? Or you don't like me texting about your pussy?

The body part in question tingled. She missed him too. Sleeping curled against Finn's rising and falling chest had been everything she'd dreamt it would be. She'd been scared when she woke up things would be awkward, but Finn had kissed her good morning, flipped her onto her stomach and taken her in the ass.

Three screaming orgasms and a mug of coffee later, there was still no trace of regret between them, and she dared to hope that it might never come.

"Your face is doing the thing." Cleo's voice dripped with smugness.

Molly looked up from her phone. "What thing?"

"The dreamy thing heroines do in those chick flicks. I'm amazed there aren't glitter filled hearts popping out of your head right now."

"Take it back."

Cleo shrugged. "No, ma'am. You gotta get used to it. It's here to stay. You're all loved up. I'm going to poke fun at your adorable, puke-worthy reactions to Mr. O'Brien. Firstly, it's what any good best friend worth their salt would do. And secondly it might help you come to terms with the fact that your relationship with him isn't going anywhere. The more you talk about it, the easier it'll get."

Every muscle in Molly's body was tense. "You know this is my idea of hell, right? Feels. Commitment. Lying to Will…" She sighed and tucked her cup between her thighs so she could rake her hands through her hair.

"I know. But this thing with Finn… it's the real deal. Once you open your heart up to the fact that it's not a one-and-done kinda thing, I think you'll find things get easier."

"You know I can't talk to you when you bring the logic, ChoCho."

Cleo smirked. "Answer your boy, Molly. Before he appears at the door and wants to do nasty things to you right there in front of me." She cringed. "Exhibitionism isn't my kink."

Molly's lips twitched.

"I know." Cleo held up a hand. "I know. You don't need to say it's yours. I've been to enough parties with you to know you like doing shit in front of people and you like watching. I'm all too aware of your kinks, Molly Morrison. The walls in this apartment are paper thin."

Molly snorted and picked up her phone.

Molly: My pussy misses you, too.

She swallowed hard. She was going to have to find her brave at some point. Would he laugh at her? Maybe. But at least she couldn't see his face over text message.

Molly: The rest of me kind of misses you as well.

Molly: I liked the snuggling.

Finn: You can't see me right now, but there's dancing.

Molly: I do like it when you shake your thang.

Finn: I had typed out a soppy text this morning about how much I loved sleeping with you in my arms, but I deleted it because I was afraid you'd think I was coming on too strong and I'd spook you.

Molly: I also like your arms.

Finn: Waking up with you is one of my very favorite things.

Molly: Even with the birds nest hair? The bad morning breath? No make-up and boobs stuck at 10 O'Clock and 2 O'Clock?

Finn: As much as I love your kick-ass red lipstick, au natural is my favorite.

> Molly: So if I stopped waxing my beaver?

Finn: I just snorted milk. 0/10 do not recommend.

Finn: You do you, boo. I love you regardless.

Molly sighed.

"What?"

Molly shook her head. "He just typed the L-word again. I don't get how he can just throw that down and not expect my brain to short-circuit."

Cleo glided her thumb up the screen of her phone. "I know it's new information to you, but that boy has loved you for a while. I doubt it feels weird to him to say it at last."

Finn: L-word freaked you, didn't it?

> Molly: How can you just toss it around like a throw pillow?

Finn: Fucking LOVE a good throw pillow.

The laugh that rattled through her body melted some of the ice building in her veins. She loved throw pillows too – but that was beside the point.

> Molly: We've been dating for a hot minute, Finn. How can you just... say that?

Finn: I told you, I've loved you for an age. It's been sitting in a corner of my heart, growing – despite my attempts to ignore it and pretend it wasn't there.

Finn: It hurt to keep it trapped inside like some dirty, ugly secret.

> Finn: I know it's scary for you, and freaks
> you all the way out, but for me... finally
> being able to say it out loud... finally
> running toward it, instead of away from it –
> it's like I can breathe for the first time in a
> long time.

Her heart raced.

"Do you feel the same way?" Cleo's voice was so close to her ear Molly shrieked and dropped her phone. "Sorry not sorry. I needed to make sure you were okay. Your face did this weird thing, and it looked like you might cry. And you ignored me when I said your name three times."

"You're reading over my shoulder?"

"Best friend privilege. It's my duty to help you lean into the big scary feels, rather than tuck tail and run the fuck away. So again, I ask: Do you feel the same as Finn? Do you feel freer now that you've given into his roguish charms?"

Molly gulped down the last of her coffee with a loud slurp. "Never... *ever* let him hear you refer to him as roguish, or charming."

"Noted. Stop avoiding my question."

"I don't think I've given in to anything but his dick yet. I'm so scared it's all going to go tits-up and I'm going to be left with a brother who hates us both, and a friendship that's in tatters."

Cleo tucked her leg under her and frowned.

"What? What's with the frown? Is this another romance novel thing? You know my life isn't a friggin' romance novel, right? I'd make a terrible heroine."

"Stop fighting it. It's another thing that messes shit up in my books."

"You read too much smut. Can't you read something productive, like Gray's Anatomy? Encyclopedia Britannica?"

Molly eyed a third donut. Was she feeding her feelings? Absolutely. But she gave zero fucks.

Cleo held her hands up in surrender. "I'm just sayin'. Fighting it, keeping yourself at a distance while Finn goes all-in? It's not fair to either of you. Open yourself up to him, Molly." She paused, paled, then gagged. "Ew. Ew. Double ew. That's not what I meant."

"We both know I've already opened up to him just fine."

Cleo leaned forward as Molly lifted the donut to her face. Cleo's hand smacked across Molly's mouth, squishing the donut against her lips.

"What the hell?"

"TMI, MoMo. T-M-fucking-I." She retracted her hand and dusted the sugar off on her thigh.

Molly laughed as her phone chimed.

> Finn: You're really not good for a man's confidence you know.

Her heart twinged.

> Molly: Sorry. Talking through my feels with ChoCho and trying not to give in to the desire to flee.

> Finn: You can run, you can hide, but – spoiler alert – my dick planted a homing beacon inside you.

She laughed out loud.

> Molly: Damn. Seems I really can't escape.

> Finn: Do you really want to?

> Molly: No.

> Molly: In fact, I kinda want more cuddle time.

> Finn: And sexy time.

> Molly: That too.

> Molly: You know I'm not good at this, right?

She pinched the bridge of her nose. Understatement of the year. Not good? Considering the only relationship she'd ever had ended badly – she pretty much sucked at relationships.

> Finn: Can you breathe please? You're good at being you. Great at it in fact. You don't need to change, or do anything different. This isn't going to get weird unless you want it too.

> Finn: I mean, part of me is kinda sorta hoping we get weird – but not awkward weird. Like freaky weird.

She laughed. Maybe she could do it. Maybe she could let go of her fear enough to let Finn into her heart. Maybe he could be the warmth she needed to breathe life back into it. Maybe if she gave him her heart, he could even be trusted enough not to break it.

CHAPTER 24

Molly

"I'm so fucking proud of you." Molly smoothed the shoulders of Finn's dress shirt in her parents' living room. Tears welled in her eyes as she traced the line of his jaw with her fingertips. "You're going to do great things, Finnegan O'Brien."

"I already have." He pecked her on the forehead and her heart exploded.

It had been almost a month since they'd first gotten together, and so far, so good. Lying to damn near everyone she knew about her relationship with her brother's best friend got a little easier each day. She had no words to say back to his sweet statement, but she held his gaze, hoping he could see her swirling emotions instead of her making a mess of trying to voice them.

Dad cleared his throat behind her as he came into the room, and she jumped back from Finn. "You kids ready to go?"

"Can someone help me with this damned tie?" Will appeared through the doorway Dad had just walked through.

By clearing his throat, Dad had unknowingly saved her ass from being busted by her brother.

The muscles in her shoulders and neck tightened. Both Finn and Will had made their dreams come true by getting drafted by the Wild, Minnesota's local NHL team; they'd start in the fall. And while they talked about sharing a house together, they'd ultimately decided on getting apartments in the same building instead – thank fuck.

"C'mere, Willy. Let me help." She couldn't meet his eyes as she fixed his tie and straightened it. Would he see the guilt that suffocated her every day? Did he sense the near miss?

Hands clapped together behind her. "Oh, my! Look at you three."

"Three? Mom, you know I'm not graduating yet, right?" Molly gestured at her knee-length blue dress and four inch sunshine yellow sandals.

"I do." Mom sniffed. "But you're all grown up. The three of you look so... so..." She waved the tissue clutched in her hand.

"I think your mom's trying to say you're not fifteen years old anymore, Bug." Dad gave her a pointed look. "You're all grown up and heading out into the big bad world, making all kinds of decisions for yourselves."

Dad flicked his gaze to Finn before shifting it back to Molly. Did he know? Her chest constricted. Surely not. They'd been so careful. Molly nodded, still not breathing.

"Everything's going to be okay, Molly." Dad stroked her upper arm, and the taut cords inside her almost snapped.

"I need to pee." She hurried past Mom toward the bathroom.

"Didn't you just go?"

"Must be nerves." Dad's voice carried something she couldn't identify.

"It's not even her graduation." Will's irritation prickled under her skin.

"Maybe she's scared you're going to trip on your gown and fall on the stage."

She smirked at Finn's comeback.

"Why? Why would you even put that out into the universe, man?"

She shook her head, staring at herself in the bathroom mirror. It had to be guilt feeding her paranoia, there was no way Dad could know that Finn was her boyfriend. Right?

She couldn't splash cold water on her already made-up face, but she ran the faucet, letting the cool water pass over her wrists as it loosened the tight knots in her chest.

"We're heading out to the car." Mom's keys jingled together as she picked them up from the bowl next to the door. "Lock the door behind you, Molly."

"Yes ma'am."

Awkward wasn't a severe enough word to describe the drive to the graduation ceremony. Sandwiched between Will and Finn in the back seat of her parents' SUV, with her thigh pressed against Finn's, Molly held her breath for almost the entire ride.

When Dad helped her out of the back of the car, she heaved a full breath. His soft eyes radiating warmth. "You okay, Mol?"

She nodded. If she opened her mouth she'd squeal like a sinner in a confessional box. It wasn't the time or the place to unburden her shoulders.

Mom hugged Will and Finn, tears in her eyes. "I'm so very proud of you both."

Will rolled his eyes, but Finn's welled with unshed tears. "Thanks Mrs. M. My mom should be here to meet you any minute."

Finn had snagged a last minute ticket for his mom to

attend the ceremony. He'd met her once a week over the past month, and while things weren't magically fixed between them, they were both making a concerted effort to get to know each other and move forward.

She's missed out on enough, he'd told Molly while he paced Cleo and Molly's kitchen, trying to make a decision. *She should be able to come if she wants to come, right? If she wants to watch me graduate... I can't take that away from her. It's an once-in-a-lifetime experience.*

Molly bit down on her lip. Dad hugged both boys, and said he was proud, too. Molly threw her arms around Will, gripping him like it was the last time she was ever going to see him.

"I can't say I'm surprised you've done so well, Willy. But I will say I'm proud, and more than a little envious of just how well you do. At everything."

Mom handed him his gown from a hanger in the trunk. "Don't forget this."

Finn rocked back on his heels, searching Molly's face. Was he seeking permission to hug her? Steadying her breath, she stepped toward him, straining against the urge to launch herself at him. Pulling him into a hug, she breathed him in. "I love you, Finnegan."

His arms tightened around her at her whispered confession.

"I'm so proud of you, Finny." She stepped back, speaking at a normal volume so everyone else could hear and shoved his shoulder playfully. "Try not to fall on your faces out there, mmkay?"

Mom gave Finn his gown and the two men turned to leave.

Dad's knowing smirk smacked the panic button in Molly's chest. He had to know. He didn't seem mad about it. Just amused. She'd have to talk to him at some point, but if – by some miracle – she was wrong and he didn't know, she didn't want to tip him off either.

Ugh. Why was everything so complicated? Molly was many things, but a global woman of mystery she was not. She would never make it as a spy. Only a month in and she was already flagging from all the deception and sneaking around.

Mom shrugged. "Or a woman. I'm not picky. I just want grandbabies."

"I can get pregnant from a one night stand, you know."

"Meabh! It's so nice to see you."

Molly cringed. While she didn't care whether Finn's mom liked her or not, she could have done without the woman hearing how she could get knocked up from a one night stand.

"Hi." Meabh wrung the front of her shirt as Mom pulled her into a hug. "I'm so proud of him."

The woman collapsed against Mom's shoulder in a wave of tears and Molly struggled not to break.

While the two mothers hadn't been friends before, they'd bonded since Finn opened the door for Meabh to come back into his life.

Mom said they talked on the phone a couple times a week, and they had coffee together sometimes too. Mom would pull out old photo albums of Finn's late teen years and his college life and tell Meabh about the time she had missed. Mom said she couldn't get enough.

"You could definitely do worse for a mother in law." Dad's voice was so low Molly wasn't sure she'd heard him until he winked at her. She could only assume he winked and it wasn't her own eyes twitching at the information her brain frantically struggled to process.

"You know." Her voice was a croaked whisper.

"The bigger shock is how no one else does. If ever I needed proof that the human race sees only what they want to see, I got it when you and Finn started your not-so-secret dating. I thought Mom knew, but after she mentioned finding you a suitor just now... I guess not."

Molly smashed her lips closed and shook her head.

"It's about time."

Molly's brows shot up.

"But I think you need to tell Will, Molly. Not because you owe him an explanation or anything. But because Finn is his best friend, and I don't think any of you would want him to find out from someone else."

Her stomach lurched and all she could do was nod.

"I get why you're holding off. Will can be... hot headed sometimes. And we know he's protective of both you, and Finn. But he's going to be hurt more because he didn't know."

"You're not mad?"

Dad chuckled, glancing at the two still-hugging mothers. "What do I have to be mad about? Finn is everything we could ever hope for in a partner for you. I knew that from the minute he gave your high school boyfriend a beat down for breaking your heart."

Molly's jaw threatened to unhinge with how quickly it snapped open. "Wh-what?"

A confused frown pinched Dad's forehead and he tipped his head. "Who did you think gave that jerk an ass-whoopin'?"

She didn't reply, too busy combing through her memories in a frantic bid to figure out whether Finn had lied to her or not. "I thought... I thought Will..."

Dad chuckled again, before pulling her into a hug. "Will couldn't punch his way out of a wet paper bag, Molly. For all his huffing and puffing about kicking butt if anyone came near you. He's a lover, not a fighter."

He squeezed her hand. "Don't get me wrong, he has it in him if someone were to hurt you. But Finn... he took one look at your tears that night in Chilis and clenched his fist so hard I thought he might break a bone. Can't say I was surprised when the boy's parents showed up at the door."

How had she not known? How had she missed something so huge?

Dad's laughter wasn't mocking, but it still crawled under her skin. "I'm not sure how you thought Will beat up that enforcer. He was twice as big as your brother. I guess you always did think of him as a superhero." His smile was soft, and he sighed, like a wave of nostalgia had hit him square in the chest.

She'd never come right out and told Will she wouldn't date his teammates. But after he'd run off and beaten up her cheating hockey player ex, she had never wanted to put Will in the position where he could get hurt because of her.

Dad was right, Will wasn't a fighter, and something deep inside of Molly had shriveled when she'd learned he'd fought because of her. In that moment, she'd vowed to protect him from her, from himself, and stay away from the guys on his team.

Except Will had never thrown a single punch because of her. She'd spent all that time ignoring his teammates and fighting her attraction to Finn to spare her brother. And while Will had been a douche canoe and threatened every hockey player she knew. In front of other people. And while she had every reason to believe he'd fuck someone up if they laid a hand on her, he hadn't already. Finn had.

"You fought your feelings for Finn for way longer than you should have done, Molly. I thought about intervening, thought about giving you the permission you seemed to need. But then I'd catch a glimpse of something and I'd think, okay, this is it, they'll stop fighting it and take a chance. But you never did."

Words jammed in her throat and her surroundings spun. "But Will..."

"But Will nothing, Molly. What gives any man – even your own brother – the right to tell a woman who she can and can't be with? Or what she can and can't do with her own body? Didn't your mother and I raise you to know better than that?"

White noise assaulted her ears as she struggled to process his words. She hadn't ever wanted to so much as sleep with anyone else on the team but Finn, and she'd never imagined having a chance with him.

But at the same time she'd been running from her feelings for Finn, she'd also enabled her brother to publically control who she could and couldn't date.

"We need to move inside," Mom called from behind Dad.

"You two go ahead, we'll follow behind."

When Mom's brows pinched, Molly smiled. "I have to grab something from the trunk."

The two moms walked toward the entrance of the stadium, and Molly pulled her oversized purse from the trunk of the car, checking her weapon of choice hadn't escaped during the drive.

"Life is too short to worry about what your brother thinks, Molly Morrison. Sure, he'll be pissed for a while, but he has no damn right to be. He should be happy for you, for both of you. His best friend and his sister have both found happiness with each other – that's something pretty special."

He swung the trunk closed and offered her his arm. She slung her bag over her shoulder, linked her elbow with his, and they made their way to the main entrance.

"You know you can always talk to me, Bug. About anything. Any time. Sure, I imagine depending on the subject matter it has the potential to get awkward, but when have us Morrisons' ever backed down from something difficult?"

She giggled, his words churning through her mind with each step. She needed to tell Will. She needed to square her shoulders, straighten her spine, and tell him she'd been in love with his best friend from the minute they'd met in their backyard.

She squeezed Dad's arm. "Thank you."

"Don't let fear control your life, Molly. Figure out what you want in this world and pursue it relentlessly."

As soon as Finn stepped off that stage, diploma in hand, she was going to talk to him about telling Will. They needed to come clean, to step into the light and own their love once and for all.

Her stomach sloshed as she walked to her seat, her heart raced as she sat through speeches, and her soul about left her body when Finn found her in the masses and threw her a wink from the stage as he accepted his diploma.

Her throat was hoarse from screaming for them both, and her face ached from smiling. She waited with her parents and Meabh for the boys, bouncing on the balls of her feet as she gnawed on a stubborn cuticle.

"You seem nervous Molly, is everything okay?" Mom's concerned eyes pinned her while they waited.

"Yeah, I'm fine. Just about to prank Finn, so I'm a little nervous."

Before Mom could answer, Finn and Will rounded the corner and made a beeline for their small group. As they approached, Molly slipped her hand into her bag, curled her fingers around the oversized confetti cannon, and deployed it right in Finn's face with a gleeful shriek.

A few bystanders gasped and squealed at the sound, pointing and laughing.

"Check. Mate." Molly flipped the empty tube with a flourish, not taking her eyes off his as the cardboard crashed to the floor with a clunk.

Finn shook his head. "Far from checkmate, Mini Mo. I'll find a way to get you back."

Will scrunched up his nose and gestured at the multicolored ticker tape scattered at their feet. "Someone want to tell the rest of us where this battle came from?"

"Tiktok." Molly and Finn answered together. Heat prickled up her neck as the parent's in front of her went from wide-eyed and open-mouthed, to frowns and pursed lips.

"There's this couple on Tiktok and they spend their free time trying to one-up each other with a confetti cannon war." The more Molly spoke, the more her skin caught fire. It really was a dumb idea, but it was fun and she loved it. "It looked like fun." She shrugged.

Finn nodded. "They hide in different parts of the house, lying in wait for their spouse to find them – cupboards under the sink, under their car, anywhere you can fit a human being really."

He bent down to pick up the empty tube and waved it. "They have confetti cannons hidden all over the house, and they refill their tubes from oversized bags of shredded colored paper. Their kids even get involved, hiding the confetti cannons for their parents, and giving them a heads-up when they're coming."

She crouched down to sweep up the pieces of paper with her palms. "They can get pretty creative."

"The husband leveled up to colored foam filled balloons."

Molly jabbed a finger at him. "I would kill you dead, Finnegan O'Brien."

He held his hands up. "I believe you. Which is why I'll stick to colored tissue paper."

Meabh bent down and helped Molly collect the shards of paper. "How did this little battle start between you both?"

Molly shrugged. She didn't want to out Finn's February-Funk to his mom, even if it was probably common knowledge, or easy to assume.

"Molly started it."

"Doesn't she always?" Will had pulled out his phone and was frowning at his screen.

Molly took a breath to reply, but both their parents spoke at once. "Don't start, Will."

Molly smirked. Just like when they were kids.

"Molly correctly assumed I needed cheering up around Liam's anniversary. She showed up at my door, blasted a confetti cannon in my face, threw down the tube like a declaration of war and laughed at me."

"Sounds about right." Mom chuckled.

Molly held out the plastic bag from her purse for Meabh and Finn to put the piece of paper and the three of them stood up.

"I like it, it's fun." Molly tucked the bag, and the empty tube back into her purse.

"And competitive." Meabh patted Finn's shoulder with a knowing smile. "You were never one to turn down a challenge."

"Exactly. I'll get you back for that one, MoMo. But..." He rubbed the back of his neck. "Even I have to give you props for it. Not bad."

She huffed out a grunt and threw him an eye roll. "Not bad my ass."

"We should get going." Mom clapped her hands together. "We have a graduation feast to prepare."

As a family, they'd decided on a low-key afternoon bbq at home with only a few additional guests. The hockey team had plans to celebrate together, and there'd be a fancier wider-family to-do in the near future, but Finn had begged Dad to make his state-fair-award-winning brisket on the day of his graduation.

It took days of preparation and cooking, so it wasn't something he did often, but he was only too happy to make it for their special day. A garden bbq to celebrate was definitely Finn's kind of vibe.

Will would have happily stepped off the stage, added his diploma to the pile of accolades on his shelf, and forgotten about it in favor of working on the next thing, but Molly always made him celebrate every milestone. Always. Even if it was just a cupcake, or a movie together.

What was life without celebration? She shuddered.

They were all hanging out in her parent's kitchen. Meabh washed vegetables in the sink while Mom flitted about with a notepad and pen, a kitchen towel draped over her shoulder and an apron tied around her waist.

Will sighed, like he'd given the information a dozen times already. "I already told you, Mom. She's bringing her roommate Sabrina."

"Are any of the team stopping by?"

Like she didn't already know. The first time Dad made his brisket for the Fourth of July weekend, word had spread through the locker room like a wildfire. Every player on the team turned up hungry and ate them out of house and home.

Will frowned. "You said it was okay, right? Dad made enough brisket to feed the neighborhood."

"And if anyone catches a whiff of it they'll be lining up at the door with empty plates in hand." Finn rubbed his stomach.

"Of course it's okay, I'm just checking. I don't want to make a ton of food and have it all go to waste." Mom scribbled something on her notebook and everyone chortled or guffawed.

"Right. Like we'd let any of your cooking go to waste, Mrs. M." Finn pulled out his phone. "But since you're afraid our little family soiree will become something more, I'll double check who planned to gatecrash."

Mom nodded, her cheeks already pink. "Thanks, Finn."

Will lifted his head from his phone. "Linc and Russ will both be here."

Finn checked his screen. "I think that's it."

"ChoCho is coming!" Molly grabbed a glass and filled it from the water dispenser on the front of the fridge.

After a beat, Will waved his phone. "Austin's in."

Mom's lips twitched. "I like that we're keeping it small." Her eyes met Molly's and Molly giggled.

"I'm pretty sure you knew this was going to happen. It's why Dad is making so much brisket." Molly shrugged.

"Hashtag facts, Mrs. M." Finn crossed the kitchen to kiss her on the cheek. "Just imagine, next year it'll be a yard full of NHL players."

Mom paled, Meabh squeaked, and Dad cracked open a beer and handed it to Finn who arched an eyebrow. "You're a graduate now, day drinking isn't as frowned upon."

Mom tutted. "What he means is, this is a celebration, don't make a habit of it."

"Yes ma'am." Finn raised his bottle to her and took a long pull.

Dad cracked another beer, and clinked it against Finn's. "Congratulations, son. You did yourself proud. You did all of us proud."

Molly's heart squeezed. Knowing how much Finn would appreciate the fatherly pat on the back. She studied Meabh's profile as she peeled potatoes at the sink, her eyes were filled with unshed tears and her shoulders curled forward.

Finn wasn't ready to play happy families with her new family, and Meabh had said she understood, but it still must have been hard. Watching Finn be familial with another clan must have bubbled under her skin and buried itself in her chest.

Molly stepped up beside Meabh at the sink, put her arm around her shoulders, and squeezed. Teary eyes met hers, and Meabh gave a trembling, thin smile. "His father wasn't always an asshole, you know." She kept her voice low.

Molly nodded.

"I'm just glad Finn let me back into his life in some capacity. Today meant a lot to me."

"He's grown into a good man."

Finn laughed at something Dad had said as they sipped on their beers, Will had finally taken his head out of his phone and joined them.

"You mean a lot to him." Meabh swept her hair from her face with her forearm, still keeping her voice low.

"He means a lot to me, too."

When she didn't reply, Molly met her stare. She had that knowing parental look on her face, like she was privy to a secret, and Molly swallowed. Did everyone but Will know? Was she really so transparent?

Molly's breath caught. It wouldn't matter for much longer. She was determined to tell Will after the graduation BBQ, then everyone in the world could know for all she cared.

CHAPTER 25

Finnegan

Molly was being weird as hell. She was smiling, laughing, and hanging out with her friends as they arrived at her parents' place, but something was afoot. She kept tugging on an invisible thread on the hem of her dress – at least when she wasn't otherwise occupying her hand by chewing her nails to shit. What the hell was going on?

"Molly? Can you nip out to the garage and see if we have more Solo cups and paper plates please?"

Mom's dreams of having an intimate BBQ lunch served on her best china were quickly stomped out when she'd learned that it wouldn't just be the six of them for lunch. She not-so-secretly loved it though. She was never happier than when her house was full of laughter and bustling with noise.

It was also no secret that Molly had inherited her mom's love of peopling and parties. Any excuse for a shindig and the Morrisons were there – the female half at any rate.

Molly brushed past him as she made her way to the side door of the house and out to the garage. Mr. M turned to Finn and took the root beer from his hand. "You should go help her out there, Finn. I'm pretty sure those Solo cups are too high for her to reach and we both know she's too stubborn to ask for help."

Finn chuckled. "You're right, she definitely doesn't need any more medical bills, or busted limbs. Be right back."

Finn followed Molly's path through the house, pulling the door closed tight behind him. He hadn't had a chance to see her alone since before the ceremony, and he couldn't remember if he'd told her how beautiful she looked in her pretty blue dress and sunflower yellow heels.

He also hadn't had a chance to check underneath said dress to see if she was wearing panties.

"Molly? You in here?"

He peeked his head through the garage door. Molly stood on one leg on top of a stack of precariously balanced paint cans. She reached for a packet of red Solo cups on top of some shelves.

"You have got to be kidding me!"

"I'm fine. It's fine. I've got it."

"I don't think that word means what you think it means. Finn rushed to her feet and wrapped his arm around her lower legs. "You'll have a broken limb if you're not careful. Do you really want to wear another freakin' boot so soon after the last one?"

She laughed as he slid her down his body and plopped her onto her feet in front of him. Rolling her lips between her teeth, she hugged the plastic cups to her chest.

He cupped her chin. "What is it?"

Her eyes darted back and forth between his, like she was looking for an answer to a question she hadn't asked. "True or false."

His muscles stiffened. *Uh oh.*

"You beat up my ex-boyfriend after that night in Chilis."

Double uh oh.

He sighed. "True."

"Finnegan."

His name on her whispered sigh was both a question and an answer.

"Why didn't you tell me?"

"Because I wasn't going to disabuse anyone of the notion that Will was ready to throw down, Molly. It made him look good, and it kept douchebags like Johnny fucking White away from you."

She placed her palm over his jaw and trailed it down his neck and chest, landing over his heart.

"It served my cause, MoMo." He swept her waves back from her face and cupped her chin. "The more afraid of Will everyone was, the less likely it was that I'd have to watch you fall in love with one of my teammates."

A smile tugged at the edges of her lips. "That's quite the monumental cock-block, Finny."

He dropped his forehead to hers. "I'm pretty sure watching you love someone I played with would have resulted in murder, or hard time in prison. If I needed to play the role of another over protective big brother, or have Will's back when it came to keeping jocks and assholes away from you..." He shrugged.

"I should be mad at you." She chewed the inside of her cheek.

"I figured if you ever found out, you'd tear me limb from limb."

She nodded. "The feminists would demand the sacrifice."

He smirked. "But...?"

"I've only ever wanted you, Finn. If I couldn't have you, no other Snow Pirate would do."

His heart swelled as he claimed her mouth with his, fingers threading into her hair. Dragging kisses along her jaw, he tugged her head to the side creating space to enjoy her neck.

Trailing his tongue down the curve of her shoulder, a shiver passed through her. "I want to tell him, Finn. After the party. I want to come clean to Will."

Cradling her face with both his hands, he pulled back. "You do?" He frowned. "That's not going to go well."

"I don't care. I can't carry this weight anymore, Finn. I can't..." She heaved a breath. "I can't pretend I'm not happier than I've ever been." She winced like the sentence physically hurt her to say. "Or that I'm not in love with you. I can't keep it inside anymore."

Finn grinned. "That pained you to admit, didn't it?"

She wiggled her tongue like the words left a bad taste in her mouth. "Tell anyone you've driven me to romantic, flowery bullshit and I'll kill you dead."

"You're hot when you're mad." He dropped his hands to her hips and placed a kiss on her lips. "But if you want to tell Will you're my girl." Another kiss. "Then we tell Will."

She blew out another breath and smiled, a soft, warm, vulnerable smile that undid him at the core. "Are you ready for the world to know that I love you?"

"We've kept it to ourselves for too long." He brushed his lips over hers, as she walked her fingers up his biceps and threaded her hands together behind his neck, tingles spreading under his skin with each movement.

"We should probably go back inside."

He nipped at the sensitive skin along her neck and nodded. "We should."

"I'm..."

He nipped at her again and her breath hitched.

"...Not wearing any panties under this dress."

"Fuck." He rolled his head back. "You're a vixen, Miss Morrison."

With a wicked grin, she pushed his hands down from her hips and slipped them under her dress. She covered one of his hands with hers and pushed it from the outside of her thigh to between her legs, rocking her hips so her bare pussy dragged along his palm.

Finn hissed. "Fuck. This is a bad, bad idea." He turned his head to make sure they were still alone.

She widened her eyes and fluttered her eyelashes. "Be bad with me, Finny." She licked her bright red lips and quirked her eyebrow, taunting him. She had him and she knew it. He'd give her the world if it was his to give.

He squeezed her pussy and she ground her smooth skin against the heel of his hand.

"I'll be quiet."

He snorted. "You don't know the meaning of the word."

She turned around, leaned forward, jerked her skirt up to reveal her perfect ass, and planted her hands on the table littered with old paint tins.

His dick throbbed against his pants. Torn by indecision, and driven by the unrelenting need to be inside her, he checked over his shoulder one last time before freeing his cock from his pants and gliding the head through her wetness.

What was life without a little thrill, right?

She moaned and shuffled her feet further apart as he sank into her and clasped his hands over her hips.

"Stay quiet." He growled. "And it's gotta be quick."

She grinned at him over her shoulder. "Are you gonna keep talking about fucking me, or are you gonna get to it and fuck me?" Slipping a hand between her legs, she leaned forward as she played with her clit, rocking back against him.

"Did you guys find the Solo cups?"

Finn froze at the sound of Will's voice and Molly bolted upright with a shriek, tightening around Finn's bare cock.

"Finn?"

Finn's whole body seized, he dropped his forehead against the back of Molly's head. "Yeah."

"Is there a chance...?" He sucked in a breath. "I..." A popping sound permeated the air like he'd cracked a knuckle. "Finn... are you balls deep in my sister?" Will's hard voice sent shards of ice into Finn's back.

Despite Will's tone, Finn fought a chuckle. Of course he'd be the one to find them. They'd made the decision to tell him later that day so of course the universe conspired to fuck Finn up. Fuck. He was going to die.

"Tell me I'm wrong here, Finn." The tightness in his voice pushed any trace of humor from Finn's body. "Tell me I'm not seeing what I think I'm seeing."

Molly shifted her weight, easing Finn out of her. Finn hissed.

"Will, I can explain." She turned toward Will, her face instantly paling at whatever she saw. Finn slipped his hand into hers, squeezing. She met his gaze. "He's gone."

The door slammed. Tears trickled down her alabaster cheeks and her lip trembled. Finn tucked his dick away and zipped up his pants. Clasping her hand, he brought it to his lips and kissed it. "Whatever happens, I'm here."

She nodded, pulled her hand from his, and took off into the house at speed. "Will! Will, wait."

Finn followed close behind her. If Will was going to lash out at anyone, it needed to be Finn. Will stood in the kitchen, hand clasped around a Solo cup, gripping it so hard it wrinkled in the middle.

"Sweetheart, did you find the—?" Mom gasped and dropped the fork she was holding when her eyes found Molly. "What happened?"

Bodies stilled around the room. Finn didn't dare look behind him to see who else was watching, but they definitely weren't alone. Sweat beaded across his forehead and prickled on the back of his neck.

Molly shook her head at her mom, reaching for Will's arm.

"Don't." He yanked away from her grasp.

"W-Will... p-p-please." Heavy tears dripped from her chin, and Finn's chest caved, he ached to take her in his arms and hold her till they stopped.

The smells of mac and cheese, and potato salad permeating the kitchen, which usually made him salivate, turned Finn's stomach.

Will spun to face them both, a snarl pinned to his face, while he gulped the contents of his cup, his hand trembling against the plastic. So, this was happening, and it was happening in front of their friends and family. He shook his head and slammed the plastic cup into the sink.

"Will?" Mrs. M's brows pinched, deep creases crinkling her forehead. "What's going on?"

"Ask them." He snorted, gripping the counter behind him, his knuckles turning white.

"Will..." Molly's pleading voice was barely a whisper. "Not here."

"Ha! You probably should have thought about that shouldn't you?" His nostrils flared and a muscle in his jaw ticked. His cheeks darkened with heat and his gaze flitted everywhere around the room but at Finn. Will shook his head like he couldn't believe what he'd seen.

He jabbed a finger at Molly. "You... I should have expected this from you. But, you..." The anger so visible on his face morphed to pain. His eyes softened and his jaw slackened. "How could you?"

"Will, please." Finn's voice didn't sound like his own. "Let's step outside and talk about this."

"Like you stepped outside to fuck my sister?"

"Will!" Mrs. Mo gasped his name as she covered her chest with her hand.

Someone moved closer to Finn. Irritation spread under his

heating skin, and he forced air into his lungs. "We were going to tell you."

More gasps rolled around the room behind him as though confirmation of Will's accusation was more surprising than the accusation itself.

"Tell me what? That you fucked my sister at our graduation BBQ? How does that come up in conversation, Finn? Hey Will, I banged your sister in the garage? Lacks a certain... something... don't you think?"

Finn shook his head. "Take a breath, and let us explain."

Will straightened his spine, his eyes darkened. "There's nothing you can say to me right now that will erase the image of your dick buried in my fucking sister from my mind." His voice shook.

Molly grabbed his hand, her face blotchy from crying, but fire flickering in her eyes. "Would you shut up for a goddamn minute so we can talk about this like adults?"

Will's eyes narrowed. "Is there anyone you won't drop your pants for?"

Finn's arm moved before his brain caught up. The crack of Finn's fist against Will's jaw spurred the room into action. Strong arms closed around Finn's biceps, pulling him back from Will.

Will surged forward, Molly stepped in between them, pressing a hand on Will's chest, but he kept advancing. Linc moved to place himself in front of Molly who withdrew to stand next to the fridge, wrapping her arms across her body.

"We've been here before, man." Linc grabbed Will by his shoulders.

Finn seethed, straining against the arms holding him back. He jabbed a finger at Will. "I don't care what the fuck you say about me." He shook his head, flecks of spittle spraying from his mouth as he spat every word at his best friend. "But you need to watch your goddamn mouth when it comes to her. I don't give a flying fuck who's watching. I will fuck you up. Are we clear?"

He couldn't see past Linc to see Will's face, but Linc's back foot slid on the tiles like he struggled to contain Will.

"Will. This isn't the time or place." Linc straightened his spine, resetting his stance. "I get that you're surprised."

Will snorted.

"But the last time we were in this situation, at the party, remember? I warned you, you don't talk to her like that ever again." Linc's voice was level and quiet, but there wasn't another sound to be heard around the room save for Finn's heavy breathing. Everyone hung on every word.

"He fucked Molly." Will swung his hand seemingly at no one in particular.

Finn stood straighter, shirking the arms off his own with a dismissive wave. He was fine. He wasn't going to launch himself at Will again. But he'd be damned if Will was going to reduce what he felt for Molly to a sleazy fuck. A hand clutched around Finn's bicep and a voice spoke low to his ear. "Focus on your breathing." Austin and his fucking breathing. Fuck him. Finn wanted to rip Will in two for the look of despair painted on Molly's face.

Linc nodded. "Right, he did. But we talked about this, too. Molly's body, Molly's choice."

Will's eyes narrowed as understanding flickered across his face. "You knew."

Linc's body tensed. "Will. You need to go walk this off."

Will surged forward, shunting Linc toward Finn. "You knew he was... that they were..." He raked his hands through his hair, his chest heaving with each breath. Linc didn't back down, but Will peered around his towering frame. "So this wasn't a one off? I don't know if that makes it better or worse. Was my whole team keeping your dirty secret?"

Finn lurched forward, arm outstretched to seize Will.

Austin grabbed at him, but his hand was already wrapped around Will's throat. Linc braced his arm across Will's chest, holding him back against the counter.

"Finnegan... please?" Mrs. Mo's voice cut through the haze enough for Finn to loosen his grip around Will's throat, but he didn't move his hand.

"This isn't some sordid one-night-stand." Finn sucked in a breath. "I've loved her from the minute I saw her in your back-yard." Another breath. "But I fought it. I fought her. Because of you. *For* you." Another breath. Despair curled like fog under his skin. "For our friendship." His voice cracked.

"I was afraid of losing you." He turned to Molly, black mascara tracks led down her cheeks and her pale skin stood out even more against her red lips. He swallowed. It might be the only time he got to say anything to Will, so he'd better say it all. "Afraid I'd lose your family. *My* family. The people who saved me, who held me together after Liam..."

Someone gasped at his brother's name, probably Meabh.

"But my fear of losing her... leaving college and playing pro hockey... Not being here to have her back... watching her fall in love with someone else..." He dropped his hand from Will's neck, blinking back tears. He pressed his fist against his racing heart. "I can't do it anymore, man. I needed to tell her how I felt before it consumed me from the inside."

Will's cheek flexed as he clenched his teeth together. Linc's body had softened, but he hadn't moved, still caging Will to the counter.

"I tried not to love her. And I was wrong. I wasted years being apart from her because you didn't want her with someone on your team and I respected that, respected you. But I was wrong."

Will turned to Molly, whose jaw still trembled. Her eyes flitted back and forth like she was trying to find something on Will's impassive face.

"You could have had anyone, Molly. Anyone in the whole world and you had to have him? He might not be smart enough to know you'll move on to the next one when you get bored, but you... doesn't he mean more to you than that?"

She opened her mouth to speak but Will rushed on.

"Or has it been a forbidden romance from the get-go for you as well?" His mocking tone crawled under Finn's skin.

"Easy. Don't let him rattle you. He's lashing out." Austin's quiet, calm voice spoke close to Finn's ear. "Steady."

Finn was anything but fucking steady. His whole body vibrated. Sure, he'd expected Will to be surprised and upset, but he was just being a dick.

Molly chewed her lip but nodded at Will.

"How long?" he demanded.

She cast her eyes over the spectators. Finn still had no clue who had stayed or who had gone, but if he knew his teammates, they'd all stayed to make sure there was no bloodshed, and their girlfriends had stayed to ensure their boyfriends didn't get hurt.

Molly heaved out a sigh, as though she was too exhausted to form words. "Since I met him."

Will slammed his hand on the kitchen counter with a thud, and Molly jumped. "What the fuck?" He moved toward her, but Linc pivoted, blocking his path. Will growled. "Why didn't you say anything?"

"Because, Will." Molly's control wavered as her volume inched higher. "Because you were always so adamant I couldn't go near your precious teammates. Because I thought you'd beaten the shit out of my boyfriend for cheating on me."

Will's eyebrows shot up. "I never did that." He glanced back at Finn.

"Well I know that *now*, don't I?" Molly flapped her hands against her thighs.

A heavy tension filled the air, suffocating. The presence of

Finn's friends and family around him brought the walls even closer.

"I thought if anyone ever broke my heart again you could end up really hurting someone... Getting arrested... I thought it could impact your future." Her voice dropped. "You're the Golden Boy, Willy. You can do whatever you'd like, and if you decide to go work for the CIA or go to MIT or some shit, having something like that on your record could be pretty damaging. So I got my jollies off elsewhere."

Will raked his hand through his hair. "I..." He sucked in a breath. "I can't." He stepped forward, but Linc boxed him in.

"Don't leave angry, man."

Will met Linc's pleading stare. "Did everyone know?"

Linc shook his head.

"I guess that's something." If looks could kill, Finn would already be dead. Will's eye-dagger game was strong as he passed Finn toward the back door. He paused, turned back, pointed at Finn, then back to himself. "We're done."

We're done. Molly's heart had torn in two at her brother's pained declaration. He'd picked up his keys and left without another word. Austin stood next to Finn, speaking quietly in his ear, but Finn's face was flushed, his jaw hard set, and unshed tears glistened in his eyes when the light caught him.

Cleo said goodbye to Linc and Russ, who were probably leaving to find Will. Sabrina was nowhere to be seen, and Mom and Meabh made coffee, while Dad stood quietly next to the back door.

Molly's entire body shook. Cleo rubbed Molly's biceps, standing in front of her, brows drawn together in a deep frown. "It's going to be okay."

Molly tried to smile, but her lips didn't offer up much more than a grimace.

"It will, you'll see."

"This isn't a Disney movie, ChoCho." She swallowed, but the bad taste didn't shift. "Will's stubborn. He clearly feels betrayed... Ironically we were going to tell him when you all went home. I just had to tempt fate, didn't I? Couldn't keep it in my pants." A bitter laugh trickled from her mouth.

Neither of the mothers looked her way, were they angry with her, too? Dad's soft smile only made Molly feel worse. "I'm so sorry, Daddy." Though she whispered, the noise still carried. "I messed it all up."

He walked to her and folded her into his arms. "That's enough, Bug. Cleo's right, it'll all be okay in the end."

Molly shook her head. "I ruined Finn and Will's friendship. I messed up my interview and didn't get an internship. I don't even know what I want to do with my life." With each thing she listed, she buried her head deeper into her dad's shoulder.

"Will will come around." He rubbed her back. "And you do know what you want to do with your life, you always have. It's just tempting to give up because it's not going your way right now. But nothing worth doing is ever easy, Molly."

Molly sniffed, a fresh wave of hot tears coursing down her cheeks. "Will thinks I'm a whore, Daddy. He thinks I'm stealing his best friend. He thinks I'm going to hurt Finn. He thinks... He..." Her shoulders shook.

"Shhhh. Take a breath. Will doesn't know what he thinks right now. And even if he did, what he thinks doesn't matter. You and Finn are together, and Will just has to accept it. He saw what he saw and he needs to process. I think when he takes a minute to think about things, he'll find that he feels guilty that he's the reason you've been apart from Finn all this time."

"I feel like I'm to blame." Mom stepped forward, joining the conversation, cradling a cup of hot coffee. She offered it to Molly. "I told him... I..." She shook her head. "I asked him to take care of you. To make sure no other shitty hockey players broke your heart like that other jerk in high school."

She rubbed Molly's hair like she often did when Molly was

little. "You were so broken, so sad, and it spurred you to become this..." She stroked Molly's cheek. "Beautiful, strong, gladiator of a woman and I was afraid some other jock would dim your shine. I didn't mean for him to put a blanket ban on his teammates. Or..."

She kissed Molly's forehead. "Get in the way of true love."

Molly's cheeks heated and a snort lodged in the back of her throat, making her cough. Placing her mug on the counter, she covered her mouth as she spluttered. She didn't do fairy tales or happy ever after. And if she'd ever needed a reminder of why she'd just gotten it.

Love shouldn't be so difficult. Would it have been easier if she'd come right out and said it way back in the beginning? Perhaps. But there were no guarantees it would have gone any better. Looking backwards didn't do anyone any favors. She had to figure out a way forward.

"I appreciate you looking out for me, Mom. But I think we're all at fault in some way. Me for not being braver and telling Finn sooner. Will for being so damn overbearing when he had no real need to be. Finn for not telling me he was the one to hand out the beat-down to my piece of shit ex... There's enough blame to go around."

A throat clearing pulled her eyes back to Finn and Austin. She wanted to reach out and yank Finn's anguish from his body and throw it in the garbage disposal. He looked inches shorter and years older. Head lowered, face pale, eyes sad. Her vibrant Finn, nowhere to be seen. Her heart pinched.

"I'm going to take him for a walk." Austin's damn near irritating calmness was oddly contagious. Like if she took a deep enough inhale, his soothing tone could curl itself around her insides, bringing some kind of peace.

She almost grabbed him by the shoulders and breathed him in like a goddamn Dementor from Harry Potter. But instead, she simply nodded.

"Finn?" Suddenly she didn't care that her parents could see, that his mom could see, that Will had left in a blaze of 'fuck you,' she just wanted to make sure he was okay.

His red-rimmed eyes met hers. Did he blame her? Or worse, did he blame himself?

Without hesitation he closed the space between them, side-stepping Cleo and Dad, and pulling Molly to his chest. "I'm so sorry, Doll. I'll fix this. Whatever it takes." His mumbles into her hair made her tighten her arms around his body as he squeezed her against him.

"Not whatever it takes." She pulled back enough to look into his eyes. "I'm not prepared to lose you."

He smiled but the sparkle in his eyes was gone. "You sure? I figured you'd feel like being with me is too much trouble." He brushed his lips against her forehead like their parents weren't standing watching the entire exchange.

"I'll admit, I'm freaking out."

He nodded, his head against hers.

"Do you want me to stay?"

She shook her head. "I know you need to work this off." She peered around Finn's head to Austin. "Just... be careful if you're going to the cages with him, okay?"

He gasped. "You don't think I can take Austin? I'm wounded."

"I think Austin could break you with his death stare alone."

Austin chuckled. "I've got him. Just my home gym, not the cages. I'll make sure he doesn't do anything too crazy."

Molly cocked an eyebrow. "Too crazy?"

Austin shrugged. "If he wants to get an 'I love Molly' tattoo across his ass that's his business."

Despite everything, Molly giggled. "Let's not, mmkay?"

"No promises. You gonna be okay here?" Finn squeezed her arm.

"I'll be okay. I'll Irish-up this coffee, slip on some denial, and stay out of his way." She nodded, but her insides shriveled. "You too, okay?"

He left without as much as a glance at his mom, or her parents. Austin gave her a firm nod before following Finn out the door, taking with him any ounce of chill she had left.

"What if Will never talks to me again?"

"It'll make for some awkward holiday meals to be sure." Mom tossed her a wink. "He'll calm down. And like dad said, if he doesn't, screw him. Everyone deserves a shot at their happy ever after, Molly. Just don't let your father convince you to let them do what he and Uncle Jack did."

"Wait..." Molly turned her head between her parents. "Whaaaaaaaaaaat?"

Cleo recoiled at Molly's screech and covered her ears. "Dial down the drama, llama."

Molly pointed at her dad. "You... you and Uncle Jack were..." She jabbed her finger at her mom. "And you... with Uncle Jack's best friend?"

Mom shrugged. "He was big mad at first. Zero chill."

Molly threw an eyeroll. "No one says that anymore, Mom." She narrowed her eyes. "What happened?"

Dad chuckled, Mom smacked his arm playfully, Meabh moved closer, like she needed to hear the answer as well.

"They kicked the crap out of each other." Mom shook her head. "It was in high school. We didn't fight it like you and Finn did. We waited a couple of months, stolen glances, brushes of shoulders, notes in our lockers – y'know, all that romance movie stuff."

Molly grabbed her lukewarm mug and sipped. "You didn't. How do I not know this story?"

"After a while, I couldn't do it anymore. I couldn't not be her man. I couldn't hide my feelings. So I walked right up to him after school one day and told him straight." Dad chuckled.

"How did he react?"

"With a mean left hook."

Meabh gasped, Cleo's jaw dropped.

"He didn't!" Molly's eyes widened.

"He did." Mom pulled the coffee pot off the counter and topped off everyone's mugs. "The two of them threw down right there on the sidewalk."

"So you see, Molly. It probably wouldn't have made much of a difference if you'd told him then. There's a weird bond between a brother and his sister. Doesn't matter if she's older or younger. By ten years, or ten months." Dad rubbed his jaw like talking about the past made it ache.

He chuckled and shook his head. "It's all very caveman-like and wholly undignified. But once he got it out of his system and realized it didn't scare me away from your mom... he accepted it and we went back to being friends."

"Back... to being friends?" Was that a possibility? Molly pinched the bridge of her nose. "You had this huge, ugly fight in front of everyone, then everything went back to normal? You stayed with Mom and Uncle Jack and you stayed friends? What in the fucked-up-witchcraft?"

Mom stroked Molly's arm. "It's going to be okay. Will was way out of line to say those things to you, he has a lot of ground to make up before things can go back to anywhere near normal. But it'll happen. I have faith."

Dad nodded. "Make him grovel for a while first." He winked.

Molly took another drink of coffee, letting their words filter into her blood with the caffeine. "Make *him* grovel? I'm the one who..." Her cheeks flared again. "Who is with his best friend."

"You followed your heart, Bug. Will was ugly. Even in the

heat of the moment his reaction wasn't cool. He knows as much as anyone how you can't take back what you say once you say it. He's the one who's at fault here, not you." Dad paused and covered his face with his hand. "Though maybe next time you could do us all a favor and hold back on the sex in our garage part."

Finn: You awake?

Molly: Yeah. You okay?

Finn: Let me in?

Molly hopped out of bed, tugging a shirt over her head as she made her way out of her bedroom and to the front door.

Blood dripped from a cut over Finn's eye, and bruises darkened his cheekbone and jaw. Her stomach dropped. "You weren't supposed to go to the cages."

She led him inside, closing the door behind him. "Sit." She pointed at the couch and took off to find the first aid kit in the bathroom.

Linc poked out of Cleo's bedroom. "Everything okay?" His hair was mussed and mercifully he wasn't completely naked.

Molly nodded. "Just Finn."

Linc arched an eyebrow and opened the door wider. Molly put a hand on his bare shoulder. "I got him. Thanks, though."

She hurried into the bathroom and grabbed the first aid bag from the cupboard above the sink. On her way back to the living room, she stopped in the kitchen to get a bowl of warm water and a washcloth. "What happened to Austin taking good care of you?" She sighed. "This might need stitches, Finny."

He shook his head. "It doesn't. You've cleaned up worse."

He was right, she had.

"I saw Will." Finn sat upright, blood still trickling down the side of his face.

A chill passed through her. "What? But we agreed to let him cool off. We said..." She took a shaky breath. "What happened?"

"I know I'm supposed to fly the 'we don't need him as long as we've got each other we're fine' flag, but it's hard. I've been scared of his reaction to this since before I ever thought about taking it beyond friendship. Him finding out isn't *a* big deal, it's the biggest deal."

Molly nodded. "I know."

"I couldn't let it drop. I couldn't let him think this wasn't end game for me."

Her heart fluttered as she dabbed at the blood trickling down his face.

"I couldn't let him think I'd even think about throwing our friendship away over a one-and-done thing."

"What did he say?"

The corner of Finn's lips tugged into a humorless smile. "He hit me." He ran his fingers along a bruise on the right side of his jaw.

"He didn't!" She dipped the edge of the washcloth into the warm water and squeezed off the excess.

"He did. Not bad for a lover not a fighter." He shook his head. "It didn't escalate far, the guys made sure of that. I don't think he's ready to talk, or listen just yet though. I hope he'll come around."

Molly swept the blood from Finn's face and placed the wash cloth on his wound. "Apply pressure while I cut the Band-Aids."

"Yes, ma'am."

She smirked.

"I kinda like it when you're bossy."

She picked up the scissors from the first aid kit and started cutting the Band-Aids into butterfly stitches. "I'm always bossy."

"Exactly." He winked at her, then winced. "Just like old times, eh?"

She took the cloth from his hand and put it on her leg before moving his hands to hold the two edges of his wound together. She swiped some petroleum jelly over the seam before taping the first butterfly-Band-Aid over the cut. Pressing down the edges she sighed.

"This is one part of our past I could do without reliving. I hated what your dad did to you."

Finn nodded. "I know. But knowing you would be there for me on the other side, even just to sit in silence while I strummed my guitar, or have a shake at the diner... it meant the world to me."

She stuck the second stitch across his cut. "As awful as it was, it meant a lot to me that you let me see that side of you. I know it wasn't easy. And if I'm honest, there was a piece of me that loved being the only one to know that part of you."

He cupped her face. "It was easier to show you than you might think."

She ignored the swooping and flipping in her stomach. "You can't charm your way out of me being cranky that you fought."

He grinned. "Can too. I'm sorry. Austin was there the whole time and he made sure I didn't fight anyone I shouldn't have."

Rolling her eyes, she giggled. "Uh huh. I get it. I want to hit things too. I'd just die if I went to that skeevy warehouse you boys play in."

"Austin plays. I usually only watch, honest. I just needed something more tonight."

"I'm pissed at you."

"I deserve it."

"I can't stand your face right now."

"Maybe you should sit on it so you don't have to look at it."

She snorted. "If you hadn't busted it all up, I'd consider it."

"My tongue works just fine."

She frowned, not quite ready to let it go and placed the third and final stitch. "Did you win at least?"

His shoulder shook with silent laughter. "Got my ass handed to me in my first fight, decided I was done for the night, and came here for you to patch me up."

"I'll always patch you up."

Finn rubbed at his chest with a closed fist. "I just can't shake this feeling. I don't regret things happening between us, but..."

"You're scared he won't come around."

He heaved out a sigh. "Yeah."

Molly zipped up the first aid kit and smacked her thigh. "Know what you need?"

He wiggled his eyebrows.

"Not that." She paused. "Well, that too. But first, you need a wallowing board."

"What the fuck is a wallowing board?"

Taking his hand, she stood and led him into the kitchen. "I'm so very glad you asked. Sit." She tossed the bag on the counter before linking her fingers, flexing them, and rolling her neck. "Prepared to be amazed."

She grabbed two ice packs and kitchen towels and handed them to him. "Ice yourself while you wait. That bruise on your cheekbone looks kinda gnarly." Before closing the freezer she took out three pints of ice cream.

She picked up the oversized wooden chopping board from next to the microwave and laid it flat on the counter. Taking a small bowl, she broke up some chocolate, placed it in the microwave and hit the start button. "This is only to be used in wallowing emergencies, okay?"

He pressed his lips flat like he was holding back a smile and nodded.

Pulling open the fridge, she grabbed strawberries, cherries, raspberries and dropped them on the counter. She paused to stir the melting chocolate and hit the start button again before digging out graham crackers, chocolate chip cookies, and marshmallows. She washed and sliced the fruit, before cutting up an apple and arranging it all on the cutting board.

"I'm overdue one of these. ChoCho and I were supposed to have one after I heard back from the last internship I applied for. They're only to be used in severe wallowing situations." She pointed at him. "And not to be misused."

Finn nodded solemnly and crossed his heart. He watched her work in silence as she lined the ice cream tubs down the middle of the board, then placed the chopped fruit around it. She gave the chocolate another stir before placing it in the center of the board, grabbing toothpicks and spoons, and setting it between them on the dining room table.

His eyes widened. "This is a thing of beauty." He picked up a spoon and jabbed at the cookie dough ice cream.

She pointed her toothpick at him. "Wallowing emergencies only."

He nodded. "New rule."

She quirked an eyebrow before popping her dunked marshmallow in her mouth, savoring the silky melted chocolate on her tongue.

"From now on, we wallow together."

CHAPTER 27
Finnegan

Finn closed his eyes and felt the strings under his fingers as they moved, strumming the chords of his favorite Beatles song, *Let it Be*. The doorbell to the hockey house rang, but he was comfy on his beanbag. It was early, but everyone was already up for the day. Whoever was at the front door could be someone else's problem for a change.

"I used to love listening to you play when you were younger." Meabh stood six feet away in the den, holding a foil wrapped pan of something in her hands. "I figured you might be interested in an early lunch."

He stopped playing, and, tucking the guitar on its stand, he stood. "You know I'm never one to say no to food. You're lucky you didn't get mauled on your way in."

She smiled. "I knew what I was walking into. I brought enough for everyone."

He followed her out of the den and into the kitchen. Johnny stood by the sink, talking in hushed tones on the phone, but otherwise it was just him and Meabh. Finn wasn't quite sure if that was comforting, or unsettling.

"What is it?"

"Spinach, potato, and cheese. And I have some chicken in my bag. I just need to warm it all in the oven." She crossed the space, and, as though she'd been in his home before, she placed the food into the oven, and turned it on.

Johnny made a quick exit, scowling as he listened to someone chatting loud and fast into his ear.

"I brought root beer and ice cream. Feel like a float?"

"Breaking out the big guns." Finn reached into the cupboard and pulled out two glasses.

"It worked when you were a kid, I guessed it might still do the trick."

Something warm wrapped around his insides as he sat at the dining table.

"Spoken to Will yet?" She busied herself putting together root beer floats, gesturing at his face with the ice cream scoop. "Looks like he did his talking with his fists."

"This wasn't him. Austin fights at the cages sometimes. I usually watch, but last night... I was a bit too pent up to just watch. Will wants nothing to do with me. I hope he comes around, but I'm not sure I'll know how to move forward if he doesn't."

She nodded. "I get it. Friendships can be tough." She handed him a glass before taking hers and sitting across from him. "And I know I'm not in a position to swoop into your life and offer you motherly advice, but I'm here if you want to talk about it. Things are changing in your life right now and that can be overwhelming and scary. You're not alone." She squeezed his hand, and somehow his heart as well.

Swallowing the lump in his throat, he nodded. "I appreciate it." He took a sip of his drink, relishing the foamy bubbles that tickled his nose. "Are the Morrisons pissed at me for defiling their daughter?" His neck heated. "I didn't stick around to talk to them to find out."

"Too embarrassed?"

He shook his head, dragging his finger up the side of the glass to catch some melted ice cream that trickled down the side. "I'm not sure I could handle Will never speaking to me again. But if Mr. and Mrs. Mo turn their back on me..."

He couldn't even bring himself to say it out loud. They were as much his family as anyone he was related to by blood. They'd taken him in when he had no one, and when he'd needed someone most. They'd made sure he didn't turn to a life of drugs and alcohol, they'd made sure he stayed in school, got therapy, kept playing hockey.

His life would likely look a lot different if it hadn't been for their intervention after Liam died, and he had no idea how he'd ever repay them.

Meabh's eyes softened. "They speak very highly of you, Finnegan. I don't think you have anything to worry about when it comes to them. They're good people."

"The best," he croaked, taking another drink to try to clear his throat.

"If you want my advice, go talk to them. They know Will, they know Molly, and as much as it hurts my heart to admit, they know you better than I do. I'm sure they'll be only too happy to talk things through with you."

They sat in silence for a few moments, sipping on their floats. "I'm glad you came to graduation... Mom." The word tasted foreign in his mouth. It had been so long since he'd called her it, and he wasn't sure he was ready to use it, but it didn't hurt to use as much as he'd expected.

"I'm very grateful you invited me, Finnegan. Even though I've been gone for a while, I'm still terribly proud of you and everything you've accomplished."

The stubborn lump rose in his throat again. He couldn't look at her, so he focused on the half-empty glass in front of him.

"I know we'll never recover from Liam's death, but you

didn't let it break you like it broke me and..." She sniffed, taking a huge breath. "You've always been resilient, but I hope you recognize how truly strong you have been to have endured such pain, yet done so well. It's not an easy feat."

His breath came in short bursts and his fingers trembled around the glass. "I should have gone for help."

"No." She shook her head and clasped her hand over his. "The adult who ran him over with his car should have gotten help. I know you were always mature for your age, Finn. But you were still just eleven years old."

She took another sip. He wasn't sure he was ready for the gravity of the conversation he was suddenly faced with, and the ice cream weighed heavy in his stomach.

"I know I checked out pretty quickly after it happened. Aunt Lacey filled me in on bits and pieces. I know I spent my days in a med-induced haze and left you to fend for yourself."

"He kept it together for a few years." Why he was compelled to speak up for his father, he had no idea. "I guess he had no real choice."

She nodded. "He was always the strong one. But everyone has a breaking point. I'm so sorry I let you down, Finn."

He shook his head. "You didn't beat me, Mom. He did."

Tears trickled down her cheeks. "When did it start?"

Other than Molly, Finn hadn't ever voiced out loud to anyone what his father had done to him. "Just before I turned sixteen."

"And you met Will and the Morrisons when you turned seventeen?"

He nodded.

"So for a whole year he... he..."

Finn picked up his near empty glass and swirled the mixture around the bottom. "Just a smack here or there, nothing major at first. He'd been cold since Liam died, so it wasn't a huge personality shift. Looking back I wasn't overly surprised. The more he drank though... the worse it got."

Her body shook with sobs. "I'm so sorry, Finn."

He swallowed, unable to meet her gaze. "The Morrisons saved me. They gave me somewhere safe to go to escape, to hide, to heal."

She clutched his hands as though he might flee.

"I'm angry at you – for checking out and leaving me, for waiting so long to get treatment, for not coming back when you got out, for making a new family... replacing me... replacing Liam." His throat was raw and tears slid down his own face. "But if we keep looking back, we can't ever move forward."

She stared at her glass, tears plopping on the table under her chin. He might never understand how a mother could leave her child, not even after a traumatic event, but he knew once she was back, he didn't want her leaving again.

"I'm not sure I know how to move forward, Finn." Her sad eyes almost broke him.

"Every journey starts with the first step, right? So what about I call my therapist and schedule an appointment for both of us together."

"I think that would be helpful. I need to earn my way onto your wedding guest list." She winked at him before brushing tears from her cheek.

"As much as I'm in it for the long haul with Molly, she's not a wedding kinda girl, and I have no intentions of trying to convince her otherwise. I don't need a piece of paper to prove she loves me."

"Well, maybe not." She turned to pull her purse from her chair. "And if you decide never to get married, then maybe you can just give this to her for her birthday or something." She dug around in her bag, producing a small, dark blue velvet ring box.

"This ring was given to your great grandfather by his mother. It has been passed down over the years and your father gave it to me when he proposed. I figured you might want it for Molly."

He snapped open the blue box. "Wow."

A vintage ring sat tucked into the padded box. An emerald lay nestled in a circle of diamonds.

"It's a cushion-cut emerald, surrounded by round-brilliant cut and pear-shaped modified-brilliant-cut diamonds. And when it was given to me..." She sniffed. "It was one of the happiest days of my life. But I have Bob now, and this was always destined to go to you. Seeing you with her yesterday... it was a no brainer. This belongs to Molly now."

His chest tightened. She was right. Molly was end game for him. Which meant only one thing. He had to go talk to her dad.

Weary legs carried Finn up the path leading to the Morrisons' house. Still raw from his conversation with his mom that morning, he wasn't sure he had it in him to have another emotional conversation, but he needed to face his bonus parents and at minimum tell them his intentions with their daughter.

He lifted his hand to knock, hesitating for just a moment before the door swung open.

"Forget your key, son?" Mr. Mo tilted his head.

"No, sir. I just... I wasn't sure... I didn't want to assume..."

Mr. Mo sighed. "Get in here, kid. You look like you could use a beer."

Finn pulled the door closed behind him and made his way into the dining room. He dropped onto a chair at the table and cradled his head in his hands. "I'm so sorry Da—Mr. Mo—"

"Finn." Mr. Mo popped the cap off a bottle of Blue Moon and handed it to Finn. "I understand your fear, but you've been like a third child to us since you first walked into our yard five years ago. That's not going to change because Will and you had a fight."

The knot sitting on Finn's chest began to unravel. "It's not?"

"No, son. It's not. You're family. Whatever that means to you, however it looks, nothing has changed for us. Sure, we've loved Will and Molly longer, but we love you every bit as much."

A fresh wave of tears spilled down Finn's face, as the tightness in his body loosened.

Mr. Mo popped the top off a second bottle and took a drink. "We love you in your own right. Not because you're a friend of our kids. If you never speak to Will again... if you and Molly break up... none of that impacts our relationship with you."

He clasped his hand over Finn's shoulder and squeezed. "And if you ever knock the front door again when you have a key in your pocket, we're going to have words."

Finn gave a watery smile. "Yes, sir."

Mr. Mo tugged him to his feet and wrapped his arms around him. "You're never alone. You hear me?"

Never alone. For the past five years of his life he'd been terrified of winding up alone again. To have confirmation that not only would that not have happened if he'd acted sooner, but it would also never happen, shifted something inside of him.

"Doesn't matter how old you get. Doesn't matter how far you go. If you need us, for anything, we're there for you."

Finn pulled back and sat down again, sipping on his beer to delay having to speak.

"Y'know, as her dad it's my duty to warn you to take care of her. But I've watched you over the years, Finn. I don't need to say anything to you about Molly. You know her better than anyone, and I see how you love her – even from a distance."

Finn's jaw dropped open.

"For the record – you won't ever need to ask me for my blessing. For one, she'd kill you stone dead if she ever found out you did something so inherently patriarchal. And for two, you've had it for a long time."

Finn picked at the label on his bottle. "I've been afraid to admit to having feelings for her, in case... in case I ruined everything."

Mr. Mo shook his head and raised his bottle. "Never going to happen."

CHAPTER 28

Molly

"I need my own fucking caution tape, ChoCho." Molly held her hands up in front of her, about a foot apart. "Caution: extra salty. Or 'approach with caution, salty bitch ahead.'"

Cleo laughed. "Just sit there and decorate your cookies."

Molly narrowed her eyes, but picked up the piping bag full of hot pink frosting. "You're not the boss of me."

"I don't wanna hear your complaints. You're staying here where I can see you so you don't go out and sabotage your relationship."

"What makes you think I'd sabotage my relationship?"

Picking up the black frosting, Cleo arched an eyebrow.

"Okay, fine. I admit, I did scroll through the one-night-stands in my phone. It did cross my mind to go find someone who didn't come with a side of sibling drama to make me feel better for an afternoon."

"But?"

Molly shrugged, taking the bag of black from Cleo. "The idea of hurting him, or leaving him made my teeth hurt."

"Why do you need black? Let me see your cookies!"

Molly spun her tray of cookies around. She'd iced her cock-cookies off-white, with a little cum spraying from the tip. She'd drawn a hand wrapped around it, with hot pink nails and underneath the hand – across the balls – she'd written *Lick the Dick*.

Cleo laughed. "Who are those even for?"

Molly picked one up, still wet, and took an oversized bite from the tip. "Can't I eat my own cock-ies? Mmmmm. Great cock."

"I'm very proud of you." Cleo had opted for a tray of inclusive cookies. She had peach-colored dicks, various shades of brown and black, arranged in a circle on her pan.

"I might still fuck up." In fact, it was her greatest fear.

Cleo added a smiley face to the head of one of her cookies before shaking sprinkles over the balls. "We all do sometimes. A smart woman once told me that fear makes us do some crazy shit."

Molly's phone rang on the table in front of her. "Unknown. No thanks."

"Answer it – what if it's someone at ESPN and someone bailed on their internship."

Molly's stomach flipped, but she swiped the screen to answer. "Hello?"

A cookie slipped off the edge of the table, hit her thigh – frosting side down – and splatted on the floor. "Damnit. There's a cock-ie on the floor. Don't step on it."

Cleo smothered her giggles and shook her head, pointing to the phone.

Shit. Not a good impression to make if it was ESPN on the other end. "Hello?"

"Uh... hello? Is that Molly Morrison?"

"Yes, ma'am."

"It seems I've caught you at a bad time." The woman on the other end of the phone giggled. "But my name is Tracie, I'm calling from the Minnesota Wild's office."

Molly's stomach clenched, and her ears rang. "Huh?"

The woman made another polite laughing sound. "Finn gave me a call. O'Brien. He asked if we had any positions open for internships here at the Wild."

All moisture in Molly's mouth disappeared. "Is this a joke?"

"It's not a joke. I really do work for the Wild, and I really am calling you."

"Oh my God. I'm going to kill him."

Cleo had paused her cock-ie decorating and was listening with interest.

"As a representative of the Wild, I'd like to formally request you don't kill one of our soon-to-be rookies."

Molly snorted. "No promises. I can't believe he called you."

"He called me and sent me a sample of your work. I took your number and told him I'd be in touch if anything came up."

"When did he call you?"

"A couple of months back. He said, and I quote: 'You're going to want to get her before ESPN snatch her up, T.'"

Molly laughed. "Sounds like him alright."

"We currently have two internships we are trying to fill. One is a HD radio internship, and the other is in marketing and public relations."

"He called you before we were together." Her voice was barely a whisper, and Cleo grinned as she picked up another bag of frosting.

"I'm sorry?"

"Hm? Oh. Nothing. I just can't believe you're calling."

"You still have to submit an application form, and go through the same process as everyone else."

"So if I get it…"

"Yup, all by yourself."

Molly could tell Tracie was smiling as she spoke. "That's important to me."

"He said as much when we chatted."

"What?" Molly pretended to be offended. "The jerk never even *asked* for special treatment?"

Tracie laughed. "Men, eh? Well, if you send me your email address I can shoot the application form across and get everything started."

"All joking aside, Tracie, I truly appreciate your call." Her heart raced and her palms were clammy as she recited her email address and hung up. So she hadn't bagged a spot with any of the places she'd applied to, that didn't mean she couldn't convince the Wild she was worth a shot.

The doorbell rang, and Cleo sprung off her chair. "I'll get it, Linc said he was going to call around for a while."

After a couple of minutes, Finn and Cleo walked back into the dining room. He picked up a cock-ie from in front of Molly, and read the message. "I wholly endorse this message." He took a giant bite from one of the balls. "Hey…" He waved the cookie at her. "These aren't bad."

"Finnegan?"

"Uh oh." He stepped back from her, taking another bite.

"What do you mean, uh oh?"

"I know that tone. That's an in trouble tone. I didn't do it." He frowned, then hissed. "Stupid cut." His face was blooming into a kaleidoscope of colors, his jaw was already yellow-green, but his cheekbone was dark purples with splodges of red.

"Tracie at the Wild called me." She narrowed her gaze, pointing a bag of frosting at him.

His shoulders relaxed and he approached her again, sitting on the seat next to her. "Oh. Is that all? I didn't do anything but place a phone call to someone who'd said – and I quote – if you ever need anything, please feel free to call. So I did." Smugness dripped from his every word.

"You called her before we were together."

He took another bite. "Surely that only makes it better. I didn't run to my new team once I'd won you over in the sack."

Cleo choked on her drink, coughing, and spraying soda over herself.

"I was trying to say thank you."

"You're welcome." He leaned forward and swept a kiss across her lips before stealing another cook-ie. "These are moreish."

"I've been saying that for years and they call me a ho."

"I don't think you're a ho." The sudden addition of Will's voice to the conversation made Molly shriek, and drop her bag of frosting onto her still-wet cookie. "Shit." She bounded to her feet. "What are you doing here?"

"I figured we should talk." Dark circles underlined his eyes, and he wouldn't look at her, but he held up a plastic bag.

"What's this?" She peered inside the bag. Graham crackers, caramel Ghirardelli, and marshmallows.

"A peace offering."

She chewed on the inside of her cheek. "Yeah?"

"I figured we could light a fire, Finn could play his guitar, and we could have s'mores."

"But it's the middle of the day."

His lips curved into a small smile. "When has that ever stopped you before?"

"Fair point."

He jabbed his hands into his back pockets, and peered around Molly to the table behind her. "Can we talk first?"

She nodded and dropped the bag on her chair before

leading him to her room. While part of her wanted to launch herself at him and squeeze him, a currently larger part wanted to claw his face off for suggesting she was a whore.

"I'm sorry." He started speaking before he'd even closed the door behind him. "I don't know what the hell came over me yesterday when I said those things to you. I was way out of line."

She folded her arms. Damn right he was out of line. The slice in her heart where his words had cut throbbed. It wasn't as though he'd only made one pointed comment about her. He'd repeatedly made reference to her being slutty, and it sure as shit wasn't okay. She couldn't meet his eyes, and wrapped her arms around herself in case he happened to throw anything else her way.

"I know I don't deserve forgiveness, but I have the gall to ask for it. I really am sorry. I don't think you're a ho. I was mad... I'm not even sure what I was mad about, but I was mad, and I said shit I didn't mean."

She stayed silent. He'd been a mondo dick, she wasn't letting him off with an 'I'm sorry.' Toeing at the floor she still didn't look at him. How could she? Her big brother judged her very nature.

"I feel like this whole situation has become this huge thing, over something so small." He chuckled. "You thought I'd go to prison for killing Finn if you went near him. Finn thought he'd lose our whole family if he went near you. I was trying to keep your heart safe from unworthy jackasses. It's like some fucked up game of telephone."

He plopped down onto the chair next to her vanity. "And the worst of it all is we all trust each other implicitly, so we have no real reason to be afraid." He shook his head. "I've loved you since the day you were born."

She snorted. "Lies. You hated me for our formative years."

"Okay, fine, almost your entire life."

She lowered herself to the edge of the bed, arms still folded, spine rigid. "You really fucking hurt me, William."

He winced. When she finally met his eyes, her resolve wavered. Such sadness, such genuine pain. But he'd hurt her too.

"I really would do anything for you though. Anything. And I'm sorry it hasn't seemed that way lately." He rubbed his hand over the back of his neck, meeting her eyes in the mirror. "I guess I've been kind of jealous."

Her stomach dropped. Straight-A student, captain of the hockey team… what the hell could he be jealous of her for?

"I don't have a lot of friends. Even the guys on the team don't really know what to do with me. I'm geeky, awkward, I don't watch what they watch, and I don't read what they read… for the most part some of them tolerate me because I'm their captain."

Sadness wrapped itself around her. "That's not—"

"It is, and I'm okay with it for the most part. I have my boyband." He winked at her. She'd called him, Finn, Linc, and Russell a boyband once and it became a running joke between them. "But every now and then I see you living the life you want to lead. Outgoing, funny, confident, comfortable in your own skin, and it tugs on something inside me that I don't know how to do."

She opened her mouth but he held up a hand. "I'm not saying any of this to try to defend my words or actions yesterday. I was a complete douche bag and I am truly sorry. I just wanted to explain where some of my feelings came from."

He picked up a bottle of red nail polish from the counter. "You're my sister, I love you, and I know I come off as an overprotective oaf sometimes, but I do trust your judgement."

A hysterical giggle bubbled up inside her. "You've literally never been okay with me being with anyone, William."

"For the most part. And you're right, if someone hurt you,

even Finn, I'd absolutely get my ass kicked defending your honor."

She snorted. "You don't think I have any honor."

He winced. "I really am sorry." He raked his hand through his hair. "What an epic asshole."

She smiled. He wasn't wrong.

"I think the idea that the two of you would be together, and that it might result in less time for me in either of your lives, hit me pretty hard. I know. Selfish brute, right? Immature douche." He pinched the bridge of his nose. "I can't believe I'm admitting this out loud, but it's true. I don't want to lose either of you, even to each other."

His sigh condensed on the mirror and he drew a heart in it with an F+M. "But the more I think about it, the more I realize you two are pretty freakin' perfect for one another. And the fact I in any way came between you, or stopped you from having something amazing?" He rubbed his chest. "That's not okay with me."

She raised her eyebrows.

"I could do with never, ever, seeing his dick in you. Like, never again."

She held up her hands. "Consider it done."

"And I know you don't need my blessing to date him, but you have it. I think you'd have had it back then too, though it might have taken a bit longer for me to come around."

She stood and ruffled his hair. "You're all mature and grown up now, Willy."

"I dunno about that." He examined the back of his hand. "I clocked my best friend in the face, and lost my shit at two consenting adults having a relationship. None of that screams either mature, or grown up."

She couldn't help but laugh. "When you put it like that..."

"I really am sorry for what I said."

"I know. I forgive you. But only because you brought s'mores."

Finnegan

Will had convinced them all to head over to the hockey house. Molly and Cleo were inside preparing snacks, and Lincoln was on his way. Finn strummed his guitar, while Will lit the fire pit. Despite riding from the girl's apartment together, they still hadn't spoken a single word to each other.

"I'm sorry I hit you." Will rolled his hand looking at his knuckles. "Though I feel like I did more damage to myself than I did to your face. Guess it serves me right for choosing violence."

Finn jerked his chin at him. "You didn't do too badly at all for your first time. I'm sorry I didn't tell you."

"I understand why you didn't." Will plucked two beers from the small cooler at his feet and opened them before handing one to Finn.

"I'm sorry I fucked your sister in your parent's garage."

"Bullshit. You're sorry you got caught."

"True story. I really do love her though."

"I can tell. I dunno how I missed it this whole time. Now it's been pointed out to me, it's all I see." Will nodded before taking a sip of his beer. "If you hurt her though..."

"I know, I know, you'll kill me."

"Weeeeeeell... I'd probably get Austin to do it. Hitting you hurt like hell and I'm pretty sure you could take me, so I'd need to get someone else to do it."

"Austin's already volunteered for the job." Finn placed his beer at his feet and strummed a few chords.

"What is it about you men folk?" Molly thumped her chest as she crossed the yard. "Must protect women folk by beating other men. The cavemen called, they want their crazy back."

Molly dragged a collapsible stadium chair next to Finn and sat down. Cleo followed behind her with a tray of ready-to-make s'mores ingredients.

"I don't actually know." Will took another drink and sat on the other side of Finn. "I think you could probably hit Finn better than I could."

"She definitely could." Cleo pierced two marshmallows with a wooden skewer.

The backdoor opened and Linc appeared, six-pack in hand. "Rumor has it we're doing some day drinking."

Finn raised his bottle. "You're already behind."

Linc paused. "Do I need to sit between you boys, or are we going to keep our hands to ourselves?"

Will shook his head. "We're cool. Well, we're not magically cool, but my hand still smarts from my one punch and I have no desire to do it again."

"They're using their big-boy words to work through it." Molly walked to the s'mores table and jabbed a marshmallow with her skewer before putting it into the fire.

"Ah." Linc nodded. "Hurt her and I'll kill you?"

"How'd you guess?" Molly rotated the marshmallow in the flames.

"I speak brother."

When Molly's marshmallows were sufficiently toasted, she

sandwiched them between graham crackers with a square of caramel filled chocolate. Mallow oozed from around the edge of her s'more, and Finn's breath caught in his chest as her tongue darted out to swipe the fluffy melted marshmallow.

Fuck.

She opened her mouth to take a bite. Molly Morrison didn't do dainty little bites either, she took a mouthful. Graham cracker crumbs stuck to her lips, strings of caramel and melted mallow trailed down her chin, and he fought every base urge to drag his tongue over her mouth to help clean her up.

"Here." Will threw a packet of napkins at his head.

"What's this for?"

"If you're going to actively ogle my sister, you're at least going to have to mop up your drool."

Molly

"I can't believe he came around so fast." Molly tugged off her shirt. She smelled of smoke from the fire pit, but she was too tired to shower. Cleo and Linc were still over at the hockey house, so they not-so-subtly snuck back to their apartment for some alone time.

Finn's body pressed against her bare back as she stood next to her bed. "I'm glad he did, but I'm done talking about other family members while you're not wearing any clothes." He swept her hair aside and kissed from her left shoulder, across the back of her neck, to her right shoulder, sending tiny shivers down her spine.

He dragged her leggings to the floor and she stepped out of them before he trailed his fingers along the inside of her leg on his way back up. He circled her tight hole, making her arch forward, pressing her ass against his finger.

He left her wanting, dragging his fingers through her arousal instead, and brushing his thumb ever so gently over her clit. Goosebumps spread across her skin. "Get naked."

"I'm already shirtless." His hand dropped from her pussy

and fabric rustled behind her. "And now I'm all the way naked."

"Hurry up." She clenched her thighs, anticipation zapping at her skin.

"I fucking love it when you get bossy." He inched his dick into her, breathing out a hiss when he was buried all the way. "Fuck. How did I resist this for so long?"

She flexed around him. "I dunno. What the fuck were we thinking?" She shuffled her feet apart and circled her slick clit with her fingertips.

Finn readjusted his grip on her hips, angling her so that he hit even deeper inside. "You know I can do that for you." He reached around to cover her hand.

"I got this, just fuck me." Her legs already trembled as she leaned forward. Something about him brought her to fever-pitch in an embarrassingly short time.

He stilled before tightening his grip on her with one hand, building up a rhythm with his hips against her ass as she played with herself. His breathy pants turned to growly grunts as he slammed into her.

"Harder."

"So." He thrust. "Fucking." Another thrust. "Bossy." On the third thrust he slid his thumb into her ass making her moan.

"Harder, Finnegan." She didn't care who heard her demands.

On a low rumble he banded his arm around her waist, strapping her to him as he drilled into her at speed from behind.

"Yes. Yes. Harder." Her orgasm didn't build slowly, it didn't creep up on her, it crashed into her, everywhere, at once, tingles exploding all over her body and an intense wave of heat rushing to her core.

"Fuck, Molly." Finn gritted her name out, but didn't stop

thrusting into her. His breathing quickened, and he came on a roar.

She dropped onto the bed, face first, her skin clammy and hot.

"Don't get too comfy. I'm far from done with you."

"Promises, promises, Finny." She rolled onto her back and flashed him a grin.

He licked his lips and she almost came apart again. "Promises I intend to keep, Miss Morrison." He hooked his arms under her knees and tugged her toward him. Pressing her knees toward her chest, he climbed onto the bed. Her heart quickened and every muscle thrummed.

His dick was already hard again and the head nudged against her ass. "Please, Finn."

"Please Finn, what?"

She hooked her arms around her thighs, hugging them close to her, splaying her ass wider for him. "Fuck me."

"Where, Doll?"

"Here." She dropped an arm from her thigh and dipped her finger into her ass, sending a shudder through her whole body.

"You mean, here?" He slipped the tip of his cock into her ass, drawing a feral moan from her.

"Y-yes. More, Finn. Please. I want it all."

He eased in, and slipped all the way back out. She wriggled her hips, her ass jiggling as he smirked. "Lube?" He canted his head.

"You know I don't fucking need lube. Stop teasing me and fuck me already."

"Hold on tight, Doll. I'm not stopping till I blow my load in your pretty little ass."

Epilogue
MOLLY

<u>6 months later</u>

"Name one thing that's always been on your bucket list." Finn traced his fingers around Molly's bare nipple as she lay on his chest in his bed.

"Cats."

"Cats?" He frowned. "Owning one? Pretending to be one? Giant cats? Like are we talking Tiger King? Gimme a lil something to go on, MoMo." He pinched her nipple, sending a sharp jolt through her body.

"I've always wanted a bunch of cats. But Mom's allergic and dad hates them."

"Why didn't you and Cleo get one?"

She shrugged. "I didn't want to have to kill my best friend to gain custody of our cat when we graduate and go our separate ways."

"I'm allowed pets." His fingers drifted over the curve of her breast and down her stomach, circling as they moved.

"Are you asking me to get a furbaby with you, Finny?"

"I like cats. I'm not allergic. There's no rules against

having them here, and if it'd make one of your lifelong dreams come true, then abso-fucking-lutely. Let's go." He pushed her off his chest and leaped off the bed.

"You can't be serious." She yawned and stretched. "There's a whole adoption process. You have to go pick out your animal, there's home visits, there's a fee..."

"I think my NHL salary can cover it, Doll. Quit stalling." He tossed a pillow at her. "Get up and let's go get a cat."

She scrunched up her face and repeated his sentence. "You're so humble, Finny. But not even a pro-hockey player can show up to the animal shelter and just..." She swept her arm at him. "Take home a cat."

"That may be so." He pointed finger guns at her. "But we can start the process at least. And you might be surprised by how quickly we can make it happen. Oh hey, one thing before we go, though..."

She lifted herself onto her elbows. "What's that?"

He reached down the side of the bedside cabinet and produced a confetti cannon, popping it over her ass-naked body. "Gotcha."

"Is your mom coming to the game this weekend?" Molly cradled the cat carrier in her arms as Finn opened the door to his apartment.

"Yeah, I told her I'd leave three tickets for them. She said Henry about shit his pants when she told him his big brother plays for the Wild." He sucked in a breath, but Molly didn't have any free hands to reach out and touch him.

"Still feels weird calling him that. You think I'll ever get used to it?"

She wasn't sure how to answer. Things between Finn and Meabh had improved. They attended mother-son therapy sessions on-the-regular, and Finn's half-brother had taken a shine to his superstar big brother – understandably. But there was still so much work to do between them. The only real answer to his question came with time.

"Yeah, me neither. It feels like I'm somehow cheating on Liam."

"You're not cheating on him, Finnegan. Not at all. I know it feels weird, but it's going to take time."

He scratched the back of his neck. "Well, they're sitting next to Cleo and her mom."

"That's another relationship we weren't sure would work out. And look how that's healing. Don't give up hope, Finny. I know it's not easy." She shifted the carrier onto the coffee table in the living room. "It'll get easier though. And calling him your little brother doesn't take anything away from Liam."

He nodded, placing the matching carrier in his arms onto the table. "I can't believe you talked me into getting two."

"Lies. Everyone expected it."

"I feel like I need to get better at saying 'no' to you, MoMo, or we'll be overrun with cats in no time."

"Would that really be such a bad thing? Cats are much cooler than humans."

He opened the door and pulled out the tiny ginger kitten. "What are we going to call them?"

"Mallow and Hershey?"

"Ben and Jerry?"

"Jack and Daniel?" She opened the second carrier and reached in to grab the second kitten but he curled in the corner and clawed at her hand when she got close to him. "Little fucker's evil." She giggled. "Fine, evil cat. The carrier's open, come out when you're ready."

"I've got it." Finn grinned as he leaned back on his plush navy sofa. "I figured out what we should call them."

"You really think you can beat Ben and Jerry? Those are two pretty on-point names for this family."

"Taco Cat and Evil Olive."

She tapped her bottom lip. "Tacos. Dirty martinis. Evil cat. It definitely tracks."

He pointed a finger at her. "And palindromes."

She thought it over for a moment. "Geeky Uncle Will's gonna love that."

"Hi, is that Molly?"

"Tracie?" Molly squeezed her thighs together and prayed her bladder would hold out for the duration of the call. She spun to Finn and covered the microphone on her cell phone. She jabbed a finger at Evil Olive and Taco Cat. "Keep your eye on those two, I gotta take this."

Molly and Tracie had become friends during Molly's internship at the Wild, they'd even kept in touch after it ended. Molly slipped out of the bedroom and into the bathroom. Scrunching up a wad of tissue paper she tossed it into the toilet and plopped her naked ass on the seat. "Hey girl. How are you?"

Wincing at the echo in the bathroom she scrunched her eyes shut. Should she wait to pee when she was speaking? Or should she take a risk and pee when Tracie spoke? What were the odds Tracie would even hear it?

Peeing straight after sex was a rule above all others for Molly, add in the fact she'd had three cups of coffee already that morning and bam: inopportune bladder emergency.

"We have an opening on the communications team."

"Mmhmm." Molly relaxed her muscles, praying she'd put

enough tissue in the toilet to dull the tinkling of her pee against the bowl. "Tell me more." She breathed out in relief as she peed without detection.

Tracie laughed. "I'll wait until you've washed your hands."

Molly's jaw dropped and her phone slipped. "Damnit, I thought I was being stealthy."

Tracie laughed again. "I've both made and received enough drunk, bathroom stall calls to know when I'm talking to someone in a bathroom."

"Talk about the height of professionalism." Molly groaned and covered her face.

"You set the tone when I caught you and Finn doing the nasty in the cleaning supply closet at the rink."

Molly stared at herself in the mirror, her cheeks were flushed and her just-fucked hair was more akin to a birds nest than those hot, post-coitus mussed looks people got in the movies. "Yeaaaaaah. That too."

"I mean, I don't lean that way, but you have a really nice butt."

It was Molly's turn to laugh. "No shame in my horny game."

"Nor should there be, girl. If I was dating someone as hot as Obi... well. I'd climb him wherever I could, too." She made a whooshing noise, like she was blowing air, or fanning herself.

"Still no luck with Mr. Hottie?"

"Shhhhh!" Muffled sounds preceded a drop in Tracie's voice. "We don't talk about that. I regret telling you anything."

"You didn't." Molly started the faucet, clasping the phone between her chin and shoulder as she washed her hands. "I saw how you looked at him." She sighed. "I know he's the enemy, being a dirty Raccoon at heart and all..."

"But?"

"But I gotta give it to you, T. Dude definitely earned his Hottie nickname."

"It's complicated."

"Isn't it always?"

After a beat of silence Tracie cleared her throat. "This isn't about me." She said hi to someone on the other side of the line. "Look, I gotta get back to work. There's an application form in your email, fill it out and send it back. Or don't. I'm happy to never see you again for as long as I live."

Molly patted her hands dry. "Lies. You love me."

Tracie heaved a sigh. "Tacos on Friday?"

"Like I'd miss it."

Molly hung up and flushed the toilet. When she returned to the bedroom, Finn was snoring, and Evil Olive was chewing on something on the bedside cabinet next to his head. "Finnegan!" Molly grabbed his dirty t-shirt from the floor at her feet and flung it at his head causing Evil Olive to scarper.

Finn bolted upright. "I'm up. I'm up!"

"What was she chewing?" Molly gestured at the cabinet.

"Uh..." He rubbed his face, then picked up the purple silicone she'd been chewing on.

"Shit! Where's the other piece?"

"What other piece?"

"Finnegan. So help me." Molly pinched the bridge of her nose. "I will end you if I have to take that cat to the vet because she swallowed part of a cock ring while you napped when I specifically told you to watch the demon spawn kitten."

Finn burst out laughing.

"What?" She planted her hands on her hips.

"I hereby proclaim, every argument we ever had must be done while ass naked."

She wagged a finger at him. "I'm not letting you distract me from your carelessness with my nudity."

"Your titties jiggle when you're mad."

She stormed across the room, pulling up the quilt so she

could look under the bed. "If I don't find the other piece of that fucking toy, I'm going to murder you."

Finn laughed again. "It's here." He gasped a breath before bursting into laughter again. "It's next to me in bed. Fuck, I can't breathe."

"Finnegan Aiden O'Brien." She stood up and smacked the mattress. "You're a dead man."

"I'll make it up to you." He shifted across the bed and placed a hand on her hip.

"Oh, you'll definitely do that. You're checking her poop until tomorrow."

"What kind of cat dad would I be if I wasn't prepared to check poop for pieces of our dirty exploits?" He winked at her and a smile tugged at the corner of her mouth.

Cat dad. Her ovaries tangled themselves in knots as her heart swelled. Cat. Dad. She shook her head.

He trailed his hand down the outside of her thigh and hooked the back of her knee, lifting her leg over his head. He cupping her ass as she settled over his face. "For the record," he mumbled, shifting her weight. "If we ever get married, arguing naked is going in the vows."

Her eyes rolled back in her head as he dragged his tongue through her folds and circled her clit. She slid her fingers into his hair and tugged. "Less talking, more licking."

If you're not yet finished with Finnegan and Molly, click here to grab their bonus epilogue.

Keep reading to get a sneak peek of book 5, Mackenzie and Austin's story, Two for Boarding, now!

CHAPTER 29

Mackenzie

For those of you who aren't interested in reading a BDSM story, I'd recommend you skip book 4 (**Two for Boarding**) and go straight to book 5 Two for Tripping for Molly's brother, Will's story.

Author note 1: These books are not in timeline order. This book happens before Finn and Molly's story. I know, I know. Don't blame me, it's the characters who are the arseholes, I'm just their minion.

Author note 2: For those of you expecting a more sensationalized, or Hollywood Dominant/submissive story, this might not be the book for you. For many couples in the lifestyle, the kink is everything. There is no turning it off, there is no leaving it at the front door, everything they live and breathe together is their BDSM lifestyle. Once they step into their accepted roles, every experience they have is seen and felt through that lens.

This book is heavy on the D/s dynamic, light on hockey, and light on appearances by characters from previous books. You will, however, be meeting a bunch of new people who will be part of a spin-off series and there will still be some old favorites who drop in from time to time.

In this book, Austin, our hero, is a 'softer' Dominant. He is a pleasure Dom who encourages, challenges, and absolutely adores his heroine Mackenzie. If you're looking for a pain Dom, sadomasochism, or degradation – this book doesn't have it.

"Heavens to Betsy, y'all, are we in a... a... sex club?" As it turned out, Mackenzie's whisper, hadn't been much of a whisper at all. Her blurted-out question drew narrow-eyed, suspicious looks from the two women leaning on the bar to her right. The taller, skinnier one with a striking inverted bob dressed in a skin-tight, PVC French maid's outfit, smirked at her corset-and-collar-wearing friend who rolled her eyes.

Kenzie's traitorous bestie, Addison, shook with laughter and grabbed Paige's arm as though she might collapse from the hilarity of it all.

"Uh... Surprise? Welcome to Protocol." Addison reminded her of her sister Bea; she was the light to Kenzie's dark, headstrong, beautiful, and lived for the smug satisfaction of being right.

"So this is why I'm dressed like I'm performing at a burlesque show." Kenzie tugged at the hem of her studded leather skirt. It barely covered her ass cheeks. And while she wasn't a prude, she also didn't think the whole world needed to see her booty.

"This is the last time I follow y'all blindly into the unknown. No more ride-or-die. I'm done with you bitches." She waved her hand at them. "When I get home I'm finding new best friends on Craigslist."

Her friends' giggles continued as she made her way to the bar. Her heart pounded in her ears and pulsed in her temples as she attempted to take in the bustling crowd clad from head to toe in leather and PVC, trying desperately not to stare too hard, or seem too out of place.

"Bitches."

The French Maid raised her eyebrows as a wave of heat flashed across Kenzie's cheeks.

"Not y'all. Y'all aren't bitches. They..." She pointed over her shoulder. "They are the bitches."

French Maid and Corset-and-Collar picked up their drinks and fled out of sight before Kenzie could suck in another breath to explain any further. She didn't blame them, she was acting a little odd and needed to calm the fuck down. While she wasn't generally someone to yuck someone's yum, as a former Sunday school attending, pageant girl from Pearland, Texas, she was most certainly in over her head.

Her body-hugging purple corset with black lace trim grew tighter as three men in dress pants and pressed shirts walked by her.

"How come they didn't have to wear pleather skirts that barely cover their butt crack?"

The giant, bartender with a blond man-bun to her right, laughed. "You didn't either. Can I get you anything?" He placed a black, square drink napkin with an emblem printed in silver and the word 'Protocol' above it, on the shiny black bar top in front of her. It looked like a yin yang symbol with three of the darker, yin shapes.

She traced her fingers over the three "arms" curving out from the center and merging with an encompassing circle. "Yes sir. New best friends?" She groaned, dropping her forehead to the back of her hands on the cool surface.

"We don't serve those here. At least not behind the bar. But I could provide you with a delicious beverage that might take the edge off. Who knows, maybe your new best friend is out there waiting." He jerked his stubble-encased chin at the space behind her. "Give it a chance. I get that it can be intimidating, but you passed the first hurdle of getting in the door and not peeing yourself or running away screaming."

She pointed her index finger at him as someone bumped her from behind with a muttered apology. "You don't know that I haven't peed myself. And maybe I haven't yet bolted because my legs don't work anymore 'cause I'm frozen in place. Have you considered that...? Thor?"

His broad shoulders shook as he laughed. "I get that a lot."

"Must be because you look like a Viking."

He winced and covered his heart. "I always thought it was because I look like a god."

She rolled her eyes. Another bartender, seemingly half the size of the blond giant and in every way his polar opposite appeared and patted Thor's expansive chest. "He likes to think that. Thor, Melissa called in sick. It's just you and me tonight, your god-ship." The second bartender's lip rings glinted in the light as he grinned and the much narrower man, with wild short red hair bowed at Thor and smiled at Kenzie.

He made his way past Thor to the far end of the bar where he took orders from the three men in dress pants without a notepad. She envied people who could keep everything in their head. There wasn't a day that went by when her to-do lists didn't sprout to-do lists just to keep her on the path to successful adulting.

She narrowed her eyes. "Is your nickname really Thor?"

The blond giant with almost inhuman blue eyes shrugged his shoulders. "Maybe I'm the real Thor of Asgard and I'm here to protect you from all the PVC and kinky fuckery that's afoot behind you with my massive hammer. Maybe I really am the God of Thunder." He waggled his eyebrows and pointed behind her. "Ask anyone, they'll corroborate my identity."

In her haste to get to the bar, and cover her behind with a high-backed barstool, she hadn't truly stopped to take in her surroundings. She'd glanced around and panicked at her instant overwhelm. She wasn't sure she was ready to look at what was behind her, no matter how curious she might have felt. She groaned and her head thudded against the bar. "Ugh."

"I'd ask if it was your first time, but you have this blinding neon sign right above your head. It's kinda distracting."

She sat up as he leaned on his forearms in front of her. "What can I get you, sugar?"

"Three margaritas. Espolon if you have it. Salt rims."

"She likes her rims good and salty." Paige snorted as she and Addison joined Kenzie at the bar.

The corner of his lips twitched.

"What?"

"Most clubs with play are dry spaces." He grabbed a glass from the rack overhead. "Sometimes they are BYOB. We have timekeepers and dungeon monitors to ensure that anyone in the play spaces is not under the influence. It becomes risky for consent as well as activities that require coordination. As a general rule, most believe that there is no space for alcohol or drugs in the kink community during play, or introductions, for safety reasons. A common mantra at the places that do have a serving option is 'kink then drink'. We are not one of those places."

"No tequila?"

He shook his head. "'fraid not."

"I hate you both." She flipped her friends the bird.

"If that were true, you'd have ordered only one margarita, not three." Adi slipped her arm across Kenzie's shoulders. "Admit it, you love us."

"Maybe I planned on drinking all three. Fine. Virgin margaritas then. I'll imagine the tequila."

"So... you want lime juice and sugar syrup?" Thor was doing a terrible job at hiding his amusement at the situation unfolding in front of him.

"Do you have a better suggestion?" She shivered as someone opened the door behind her, sending a blast of frigid November air through the bar area. She was already regretting her outfit choice even despite her heavy coat, which she was clinging to like a life raft.

"Pfft. Don't insult me." Thor flashed a grin. "I make the best virgin cocktails in the city."

"It's true." Paige nodded. "We'll take three citrus sippers please, Thor."

"What the fuck is a citrus sipper?" Kenzie folded her arms. The night was going downhill fast.

"Lime, cranberry juice, ginger ale, and white grapefruit juice." Thor answered, as he assembled the ingredients on the bar in front of them.

"Sounds distinctly lacking in tequila."

He was already making their drinks and shook his head. "Give it a chance, lady. If you hate it, you can always leave, no one's tying you up unless you want them to." He winked at Addison whose eyes bugged out of her head. "Plus, you can always grab a 'don't fucking talk to me' wristband if you want to."

"A wristband?"

Both Paige and Addison waved their arms in front of

Kenzie's face. She grabbed Adi's arm. "What does orange mean?"

Addison squared her shoulders, casting a furtive glance at the tall, blond, and totally-her-type bartender. "It means taken but exploring submissive. It means I'm not all the way in the 'don't fucking talk to me' camp. I mean, I'm single..." She batted her eyes at Thor who did little to hide his approving gaze as it traveled down Addison's face, landing on her ample cleavage. "But I want to play it safe for the night. If that means pretending I'm in a relationship to ward off the throngs of potential suitors..." She shrugged.

She also wore a corset, but hers was brown, steampunk in style, and had leather straps crisscrossing under her bust. Her cheeks pinked. "This way I have an out for not hurting anyone's feelings. I can just flash my band and say I'm taken. Just cause I'm single doesn't mean I'm open to just anyone. A girl's gotta have standards."

Thor handed her a tumbler of pinky orange liquid. "She does indeed, my lady. And if anyone gives you any hassle here tonight, you come find me. Thor of Asgard will take care of you."

"With his massive hammer." Kenzie tugged at the top of her corset and turned her head to avoid the come-fuck-me eyes her friend was giving the giant bartender they'd just met. One of the three dress-pant-clad guys at the end of the bar looked vaguely familiar from his profile, but she couldn't place him, and he and the two men he was with were gone before she had a chance to confirm.

"See?" Paige elbowed Kenzie in the ribs. "Thor here says it's all good. If you wanna play you can play, if you wanna watch you can watch, if you want to leave... we'll be very sad about it, won't we, Adi?"

Addison still made gooey heart eyes at Thor, but she nodded.

"Y'all made me dress up like this when I didn't have to. If I wasn't so dang self-conscious about what I'm wearing, it wouldn't be so bad."

Paige snorted. "Lies. If you were wearing jeans and a Brett Young tour T-shirt from five years ago you'd still feel out of place and even more self-conscious. This is better." She clutched her glass and gestured it up and down in front of Kenzie's corset. "This is hot as fuck. And you do have to. There's a dress code."

"She's not wrong." Thor handed Kenzie her glass and she ignored the straw in favor of chugging half of the cold, bitter-sweet mixture in one go. "Dress codes keep people from showing up who are not part of the community."

"What is the dress code?" The more he talked, the more her curiosity grew.

"A good rule of thumb is "no pink" should be visible on men or women. For men, a well-tailored suit is often all that is required. Black and red are often easier to pass. That is the easy entry. I have also worn chest harnesses with jeans and button down shirts, carried a rope, or worn other leather gear on the outside of my clothing. The biggest piece of importance is that the clothing fits. If it looks like you borrowed someone else's suit, you will likely not get in."

Kenzie tugged on her corset, thankful it was hers from the previous year's Halloween costume and that she hadn't gotten turned away at the door for her overwhelming ignorance at what she was about to walk into.

Thor mixed more of their mocktail and refilled their glasses. "Men and women have to meet the dress code alike. Even still there are often boys who enter the club with a thought process of getting the opportunity to beat on a woman and a guaranteed line up of vaginas in front of them."

Kenzie gasped, but Thor continued. "Often the DM's will

spot and remove these individuals quickly, but there are cases where people have been seriously injured."

"Dungeon masters." Paige correctly guessed that the abbreviation was lost on her.

"Are all clubs the same? Do they all have dress codes?"

He shook his head. "Entry to dungeon spaces typically requires a strict dress code. The more the location focuses on targeting swingers vs general kinksters, the more likely it will have a vanilla vs strict dress code. If you have stocks and gags, it is likely a dungeon and there is also likely a dress code in place." He sighed and threw his cloth onto the bar. "I feel like I need to adequately prepare you since your friends were idiots and didn't."

"Hey." Addison's protests were drowned out by Thor not pausing for breath.

"There's a staircase that takes you to the basement." He pointed over her left shoulder. "Most of the time play happens in private and there are a lot of rules around more public play and what is allowed. A good rule is also to ensure you ask prior to using any equipment."

Two men called out their drinks order, and Thor grabbed their alcohol-free beer without missing a beat. "There are a lot of signs around the club to remind you of the rules. Even sober, people have a tendency to forget it's generally not a free-for-all play space where you can let loose anywhere. Penetrative activities and those that would result in body fluid etc. are in more enclosed areas. For safety reasons. But you're still going to see things."

Her heart quickened. Watching people do... things... was one thing, but all out intercourse? Or rather all-in-tercourse? Shit. Her face burned. If her mama could see her now she'd have her hauled down to Pastor Mullholland's church for a conscience cleanse.

"A sex dungeon." Addison clapped her hands, her eyes

wide and sparkling and a grin that could light up the Houston power grid spread across her face.

He nodded, returning her grin. "We have 'house doms' resident in the club. They will be more front and center in a shared space to perform some acts for those interested. It's a way to introduce spanking, flogging, whipping, shibari, wax play..." His approving gaze swept over Addison, making Kenzie blush.

"Shibari is rope play," supplied Paige, sipping on her second drink.

"Consent, as always, remains important, even with our house doms who have a release you sign prior to engaging. When you leave the dungeon, you enter a lounge with traditional drinks. The lounge also has a separate entrance where you can choose to only attend there for drinks without passing the dungeon. No play is allowed in that space. I'd suggest you get a wristband like your friends – unless you're into being dominant rather than submissive, in which case you'll need a different color to both of them."

She sipped her drink in silence as her friends both turned to stare at her with round, hopeful eyes. Addison kicked the heel of Kenzie's over-the-knee black leather boots. "Come on K-K. Pleeeeease? You've been so busy since you started working with those fucking Snow Pirates that we hardly get to hang out anymore." She threw a pointed glare at Paige as if to encourage her to join in.

Thor quirked his brow. "You a student at the U?"

Kenzie snorted and rolled her eyes. "My college days are far behind me."

"She's right, Kenz." Paige slurped at the remaining liquid in the bottom of her glass. "I've wanted to check this place out for ages. If we'd waited for you to get on board, we'd have grown old and died."

They weren't wrong. As it turned out, working as a physiotherapist for the local college hockey team was sucking her of all her energy.

"All work and no play makes Mackenzie a dull girl. And by extension, her friends." Addison sipped her drink. "If you really wanna leave, we can. But Paige and I will go take a quick look around first."

Kenzie stared at the slow melting ice cubes in the bottom of her glass. She'd played by everyone else's rules for so long when she lived back in Texas – her estranged husband, her family, society – everyone and their grandma had their own opinions of how she should look, talk, act. But in Minnesota she could be anyone she wanted to be. She'd left that old life behind.

She'd changed her name, her hair, and her attitude. In Minnesota she could be the fun-loving Mackenzie Abbottt who went to the local sex club with her friends and wasn't embarrassed to admit to herself she was all-the-way curious, and more turned on than she expected to be.

"Fuck it." She drained the last of her drink. "I'm in."

Paige bounced on the balls of her feet and clapped her hands. "Whoop! If you get uncomfortable and want to leave, just holler. We should give her a safe word." She rolled her lips between her teeth. "If you need to escape the kinky sex dungeon just say... uh... starfish."

"Starfish?" Kenzie tipped her head.

Paige shrugged. "It's mine."

Thor wiped the bar with a washcloth. "And if you end up comfortable and want to have sex with a stranger, the dungeon has cleaning stations with safe sex supplies, spray, towels, wipes, etc. You are expected to clean a space before you leave so the next person can enjoy it safely. The monitor or timekeeper quality checks before allowing the next person in the space."

A shiver rattled through her from head to toe. Clean up team. Condoms. Kink. If the entire room wouldn't see them every time she moved in such a short skirt, she'd have hurried home to put on her Big Girl Panties. But for the moment, she, and the only black thong she owned, had to pray everyone else had better things to look at than her big butt.

Paige looked like all her Christmases had come at once. She slipped her red velvet jacket off her shoulders to reveal a black dress. A tulle panel across her chest exposed her breasts, and she had diamanté crystals covering her nipples under the sheer fabric.

Under her bust, a leather insert pulled her waist in with what looked to be a corset – held together with braided leather and golden hoops. There was more tulle at the bottom to create a pleated skirt.

Coupled with her boob-length, jet-black wavy hair and blood red lips the look had even Kenzie questioning her sexuality for a moment. "Wow. You came prepared. Wait. You're not wearing an orange band." She grabbed her friend's arm. "What does green mean?"

"Available switch." Paige's grin was hungry and wicked.

Addison's arched eyebrow suggested she was every bit as lost as Kenzie was. "What the fuck is a switch?" She handed her empty glass to Thor.

"A switch is someone who goes back and forth between dominating and being submissive depending on their mood, circumstances, and the vibe between partners." Thor smirked. "This isn't your friend's first rodeo."

Paige shrugged. "It was time for you guys to see my dark and twisty side." She jabbed a finger at Addison and Kenzie. "No judgment from you bitches, or I will cut you."

Addison held her palms up to Paige. "Girl, you didn't judge me for that abomination of a dye job I got last year. Or that guy who brought his mom to our first date. Let that freak flag fly. Maybe I'll find my kink tonight."

A jolt of excitement rippled through her. Maybe Kenzie would, too.

To continue reading Mackenzie and Austin's story, book 4, Two for Boarding click here.

To skip to book 5 and read Will and Quinn's story, Two for Tripping, click here.

Also by Lasairiona McMaster

Two for Interference - Minnesota Snow Pirates book 1

Freezing the Puck - Cedar Rapids Raccoons book 1

Two for Tacos - A Snow Pirates Novella

www.Lasairiona.com

This book almost killed me. Hot damn, y'all. I probably say this with each book, but this book was the hardest to date – by a country mile.

This book didn't come out anywhere near where I expected it would. I followed my regular process. I outlined, I spent time developing the characters, and about a third of the way into the book they told me to go fuck myself – and to take my outline with me. Assholes.

They abandoned all form of rational discussion and did their own thing. I've never written a book in pieces before, but this one came out in fits and starts. I wrote in one document. I wrote in a separate document, I married the two – it was a mess.

I tried to corral them back into line, but after a few days of screaming into the void I realized that they needed to tell their story their own way and everything came much easier when I stopped fighting them.

This is my longest book to date, it's my most anticipated book to date, and it's the one that's scared me the most to write. With Molly being such a free spirit and Finn being so vulnerable and broken, I wanted – so very badly – to do them justice. Have I done that? Jeez, I hope so.

I knew early on that I wanted to write a book about fear. Fear of doing the scary thing, of taking the chance, of putting yourself out there. I wanted to write about fear keeping you from doing the thing that might be 'The Thing' that changes your entire world for the better.

I wanted to write about the danger of assuming intent or potential reaction from someone to your actions. Molly assumed Will would beat seven shades of shite out of Finn if he touched her. Finn assumed he'd lose the Morrison family if he confessed his feels for Molly. Will assumed responsibility for keeping Molly safe from everyone on his team when in fact he became the obstacle.

Everyone assumed. No one opened their mouths to ask, and as a result, they all carried these unnecessary burdens through the book.

Brother's best friend tropes are always fun, the dynamic between the Heroine and the hero, the hero and the Heroine's brother. The push-and-pull before they finally give in to what they're feeling and just let it happen. There's something delicious there, and again, the characters had their own plans for this book.

Once Finn got Molly, he refused to let her go. There was no break up, no doubt, no questioning his choice. Finn had taken the step he'd wanted to take for years and once he did, there was no putting that back in the box.

For those of you who don't know, the character of Molly in this book is based on my dear friend Amy. She's my favorite Enneagram 7. Sevens are "Enthusiastic Visionaries" and have the motivational need to experience life to the fullest and avoid pain. Sevens value a sense of freedom and focus on optimism, being inspired and taking opportunities as they present themselves. Sevens approach life as an adventure and appreciate being playful and spontaneous.

When Amy read book 1 in the series, *Two for Interference*, she messaged to say she related to Molly – hard – I can't tell you how amazing that felt. She hates feels, loves fun, and broke her ankle one night while out getting tacos from a food truck.

Unfortunately, 2021 was a bitch of a year for Amy, she found a lump in her breast. She told me about her process, her treatment, scans, and how she nicknamed her boob her titanium titty. Even though I'd already outlined this book, I knew I had to add it into the story, as a little reminder to all the ladies reading to cop a feel of your jugs! Early detection, and self-checks are so important. Take care of those titties, y'all!

Finally, I wanted to normalize women who love and celebrate their bodies and who just love sex. Everything from Molly's burlesque classes, watching porn, and loving anal was an ode to women who unapologetically love pleasure. If you're reading this and feel like you're a freak for enjoying things that society says makes us 'dirty,' here's your spoiler alert: it's not dirty. Keep doin' you, boo.

Acknowledgments

I almost quit this book more times than I'd like to admit. I hate quitting, I really do. And under normal circumstances, I thrive under pressure. But this book – the shorter turnaround time between books, the longer length, among a slew of other issues I've had (who hasn't?) Y'all, it was h-a-r-d.

They say it takes a village to raise a child. I'm here to tell you that it takes a village to write and publish a book. Hold on to your knickers – these acknowledgments might end up as long as the friggin' book.

Robynne – My emotional support barnacle. This book wouldn't exist if it wasn't for you. That is a fact. I'd have given up when shit got hard, hit delete, cancelled my pre-order like a drama llama, and moved to book 4 like there was nothing to see here.

You made me stop. You made me breathe. You made me catch a grip of myself and stop panicking. You read my book for me when so many people were busy and you provided a sounding board for me to talk through plot issues.

You basically did this book all by yourself ;)

I can't thank you enough, for pushing me, for listening to me, and most of all for knowing when I just needed my hair stroked and my hand held and told it would all be okay. I love you more than you know and I can't wait to go with you for your first tattoo next year.

Savannah – Boy, am I ever glad you joined my ARC team, and then became a raging stalker – I mean friend. Your cheerleading has gotten me through the darkest of days, your feedback always makes me laugh, cry, and improve my words, and I love you MOST!

Melissa – Again, without your early feedback on what was lacking from the first part of this book, I'm not sure I'd have figured out where I was going wrong. Who knew writers didn't always get it right the first time, eh? Thank you – for your time, your friendship, and for checking in on me from time to time to make sure I hadn't set fire to my laptop.

LeeAnn – Two words: Day Drinking. Thank you for not only enabling me to have a festive Baileys hot chocolate to spur me across the line, but for long-distance-drinking with me to ensure I wasn't alone. This book has taken its toll on me and made me even more of a yappy wench than I usually am. Thank you for keeping my spirits up, for not smacking me across the head, and for encouraging me to just keep going. Thank Shannon for me too ;)

Tracie – My big sister from another mister, my 6am sprint partner, and my mentor. I didn't realize when you wrote a short story about a vibrator that you'd become such a huge part of my life, only that I needed to have you in it. Thank you. For your kindness, your patience, your knowledge, and for keeping me focused on the finish line (translation: dragging me across it kicking and screaming.)

Heather – I say it every book, because it's true for every book. Our Thursday mornings mean more to me than you'll ever know. You've been my pressure valve for the last two years, making sure I don't explode, and that's no small feat. Thank you for the blankets and hot water bottles, and for listening when I feel like I'm alone.

Kate and Josie – my accidental dinosaurs, my greatest champions, my confidants. A million thank-yous, for the knowledge, the support, the space when I need it, and the unrelenting belief in me that someday I'll be a household name and all the shit will someday be in the rearview. I love you both so fucking much.

CastleCon Bitchez – in November 2021 I was supposed to fly to Vegas to speak at a 20Books conference. While the US opened up again during the Coronapocalypse in time to make it happen, I couldn't afford to change my flight and make it work, so I couldn't go. Instead, myself and four other authors, got together in a castle lodge on the far side of Dublin for a week, and we watched the conference remotely, bonded, and wrote. I wrote about a third of my book during that week, and I had a lot of fun doing it, too. Marion, Susan, CeeCee, and Charlotte – thank you for the authentic French cheese, the authentic French wine, the recipes, the memories, and aaaaaaall the words.

My editor Cassie – who stepped up at the last minute to take on what was a dumpster fire when I lost my ever loving mind – you the real MVP girl. Thanks for saving my skin. Again.

My Betas – Marion-the-comma-queen, Susan, Micky, and Erika, thank you for still wanting to read my words even after weeks of hearing me grouse about them. I'm so grateful for your friendships, and your eagle eyes.

Kate Farlow at Y'all That Graphic – for another hot AF cover.

My ARC readers, my Facebook reader group *Margaritas, Men, and Mischief with Lasairiona*, and to each and every one of you readers who picked up this book: Thank you. I hope you loved it enough to pick up the next one, and to tell someone in your life how awesome I am. I'm trying to grow my flock. Get to it.

In all seriousness, though, I appreciate each and every one of your likes, comments, shares, reviews, and purchases. Without you, I wouldn't be able to write for a living – so thanks for that.

About the Author

Lasairiona McMaster writes sassy, classy and badassy women and strong, yet vulnerable men. She challenges reader's expectations by openly dealing with mental health issues, often exploring tough-to-handle topics and 'taboos' and books with a whole lotta heart.

She can either be found enjoying a gin and lemonade by the Irish sea, or baking sweet treats in her kitchen while singing at the top of her lungs. When she's 'home' in Texas, and isn't eating fresh-popped popcorn while buying things she has absolutely no need for in Target, she can be found at Chuys eating her body weight in chips and queso and washing it down with a margarita swirl. She loves to make friends out of strangers.